# ISLAND
## TO FOREVER

**SOPHIE PEMBROKE**

To Jessica,
for making this book twice as fun to write.

# CHAPTER ONE

ROSA GRAY TIED her dinghy up on the jetty and looked out across the water behind her, back towards the mainland. It would be so easy to just hop back in the boat and set sail again for mainland Spain. And, actually, it was entirely possible that no one would even miss her. Especially her sister, Anna.

Except that her mother had sounded panicked when she called. Sancia Garcia never panicked. Not when she decided to leave her husband when Rosa was sixteen, not when Rosa's grandfather died three years ago and left Sancia in sole charge of the luxury island resort of La Isla Marina. Not even when Rosa was eight and had tried a flying dive off the highest point of the island coastline, and almost brained herself on the rocks below.

No, Rosa's mama was the epitome of laid-back grace. Of letting things work themselves out in time, and trusting the universe to provide.

Until, it seemed, she was faced with the wedding of a New York socialite, and the realisation that the luxury island resort was no longer quite so luxurious.

Rosa stared up the wide, open path that led to the main villa at the centre of the island. Dotted on either side were a few of the low, white bungalows that made up the island's accommodation, all shining bright in the fading afternoon sun.

It still looked pretty good to her. But then, maybe she had a slightly skewed view of luxury, after a month spent deep in a South American jungle for a job. Or, more likely, St Anna had already fixed whatever she believed was wrong with La Isla Marina.

Anna always believed she could fix anything, if she just made enough lists, worked hard enough, or nagged often enough. But she hadn't been able to fix their family, had she? Rosa was almost hoping she'd given up trying by now. If she'd learned anything from her mother it was that, at a certain point, the only thing to do was to cut and run. No point flogging a dead horse and all that.

Or, in Rosa's case, no point dreaming that her family would ever be the sort of Christmas-advert perfect family where everyone was equally respected and listened to. So why hang around and wait for the impossible?

Which didn't explain why she was on the damn island in the first place. The only thing Rosa could put that down to was that thin thread, the one that started deep down inside her, connecting her to her mother, her sister, even her father. The one she'd never been able to sever, no matter how far or how fast she ran.

Maybe Anna felt the same. Why else would Rosa's big sister be here fixing everything for the mother who'd run off and left her in charge when she was only eighteen? Unless it was just to prove she could.

Either way, Rosa was about to find out.

Shouldering her rucksack, Rosa set off for the central villa at a steady pace. No point putting it off now she was here: it was time for the grand family reunion.

La Isla Marina was less than a mile across, so it didn't take her very long to reach the villa that housed the family and staff accommodation, as well as the administrative offices for the island. On the way, Rosa searched for changes that had taken place since she was last there, for her grandfather's funeral, three years ago. Surely there must be some? But she was hard pressed to find them.

Pausing on the path, Rosa drank in the view of the central villa, surrounded by lush greenery and bright flowers. The large white building, with its graceful arches and turrets, and tiled courtyards within, looked more like a Moorish palace than a Spanish villa, but to Rosa it had always felt like home in a way that nowhere else in the world did. Its twin turrets, housing two bedrooms—one for her and one for Anna—had seemed like the most magical places ever, when she was small. In some ways they still did.

How strange to be back again, without her grandparents there to welcome her home. Three years since her *abuelo* had died, and another year before that without her grandmother, and Rosa knew that she'd never grow used to it. It was almost as if the soul had left the island when theirs had.

Another reason she hadn't made it back for so long.

Her fingers itched for her camera, packed safely in her bag, to capture this perfect moment—the villa almost glowing in the sunshine, the azure sky behind it—before any people intruded on the picture and the calm was broken.

She wondered what sort of a welcome *would* be waiting for her. Sancia would be pleased to see her, as always. Rosa was her baby girl, and for ever would be. She might not be the academic success her sister was, or be the useful, sensible sort of daughter that parents wanted, but Rosa knew her mother would always adore her all the same. And, unlike her father, respect her life choices, which meant a lot.

Of course, it was probably easier for Sancia to let Rosa be Rosa from afar, wasn't it? When she only saw her for holidays and high days, even before she left to explore the world, as soon as she turned eighteen? That was what Anna would say, anyway. Anna who had taken over to deal with Rosa's 'difficult teenage years', as their father referred to them.

She needed to stop channelling Anna's thoughts, or she was going to drive herself mad. Except Sancia wasn't the only family member waiting on the island. She might have called Rosa for help, but Rosa knew she wasn't Sancia's first call. That had gone to Anna, the useful, sensible daughter. As always.

And St Anna wouldn't have made their mother wait two weeks, as Rosa had. Whatever their differences— and there were plenty—Anna would have dropped everything to help Sancia. In her defence, Rosa had been stuck in the middle of a South American rainforest at the time, and contractually bound to stay there until she had the full story and photos she needed for the magazine hiring her. But that didn't mean that Anna wouldn't have something to say about that delay. Or, knowing her sister, many somethings.

And nothing at all to say about Rosa's career successes. Anna probably didn't even know that Rosa was booked up months in advance, when she wanted to be, by publications looking for her particular style of photo journalism. Rosa was making quite a name for herself in her industry, not that it would mean anything to Anna and their father. Anything that happened outside the dreaming spires of Oxford's academic elite simply didn't matter to either of them.

Oh, well. La Isla Marina might not be huge, in island terms, but it had plenty of hidden corners and secret places—and Rosa had discovered all of them over the years. From secret coves for skinny-dipping to secluded bars and 'relaxation zones' dotted between the bungalows, Rosa could always disappear when she needed to. And if the worst came to the worst, she could pick up one of the island's boats and head across to the mainland and Cala del Mar for some truly excellent tapas and views.

And she didn't have to stay long. She never did. Her *modus operandi* was get in, get what she needed, and move on again. Always had been. It served her well in her work, and she had a feeling it would serve her just as well on La Isla Marina this week. She loved her mother dearly, but it was generally better for everyone if they didn't spend more than a couple of weeks in each other's company. They were just too alike—in the same way that she and Anna were just too different—to get along all the time.

It was all about identifying objectives. On assignments, she knew which shots she needed to tell the story that was playing out before her. Here, it was about reassuring her mother, making sure that everything was stable on the island again, then moving on guilt free.

Chances were, Anna would already have done all the hard work for her, and Rosa could be on her way again inside the week. There was a situation in Russia that she'd been keen to get closer to…

A pang of guilt twanged through her as she thought about her sister. How bad had things on the island really had to get for Sancia to call *her*? And how mad would Anna be that Rosa had left her to deal with it?

The thing was, it wouldn't have mattered if Rosa had taken the first flight out. Anna, based over in Oxford, would still have beaten her there by sheer virtue of time zones and air miles. Which meant that Anna would have already taken charge, and taken over the island.

Anna had always made it very clear that she expected to do everything herself, her way, and to feel martyred about it afterwards. So really, what point had there been in rushing?

Besides, it wasn't as if Sancia had dragged Anna away from anything important. Probably. Last time they'd spoken, Anna had been busy living up to their father's academic ideals, and giving up any semblance of fun or a social life to mother him excessively in Sancia's absence—despite the fact Professor Ernest Gray was an intelligent, grown man who could clearly take care of himself.

Rosa couldn't really imagine that that situation might have changed in the last three years.

Three years. Had it really been three years since she last spoke to Anna? Three years since their grandfather died? Three years since she'd yelled back a whole host of home truths at her sister, then left the country? Three years since she'd been back in England, or to La Isla Marina? Three years since...well. She wasn't thinking about that. About him.

She'd made a point of not thinking about Jude Alexander for a grand total of thirty-six months. She wasn't breaking that streak now.

It was just that it was all tied up together in her head. That awful argument with Anna, everything that happened with Jude, why she had to get out of the country... and now, knowing she was about to see Anna again had brought it all back.

Well, tough. She was going to rock up to the villa, deal with her sister, hug her mother, accept the inevitable offer of a glass of wine, check that everything was fine now, and make plans for leaving again.

Easy.

Hopefully.

With a sigh, Rosa shifted her bag higher on her shoulder and carried on walking. She'd already lingered on the side of the path longer than necessary. The last thing she wanted was one of the guests reporting some suspicious character with a bag loitering in the greenery.

She frowned. Actually, she hadn't seen any guests. At all.

It was late May; the island should be teeming with holidaymakers, enjoying all the luxuries the resort had to offer. So where was everyone?

Unless things were worse than she thought…

Rosa quickened her step and, in a brief few minutes, found herself standing in the cool, tiled reception area of the central villa. White arches soared overhead, leading to small, secluded balconies with wrought-iron bars and plenty of brightly coloured cushions on their chairs. Just beyond the main area, through wide open doors, was the central courtyard, with reflecting pool and more lush potted greenery, and plenty of places to sit and take in the view. In high season, it was used as the main restaurant area for breakfasts, and even now it should be buzzing with early evening cocktail seekers.

It was empty. As was the reception desk.

Refusing to ring a bell in her own home, Rosa dropped her bags by the desk, bypassed the winding staircase to the upper levels, and the hidden doorway that led to the private, family quarters. Instead, she moved through the courtyard, and out the other side of the villa onto the sheltered patio that overlooked the beaches and the wide expanse of turquoise sea on the more exposed side of the island.

There, at last, she found signs of life, and her family. If not exactly the ones she'd been expecting.

She froze, her chest tightening, as if she were preparing to run—or hide. Surely her eyes were playing tricks on her?

'Dad?' Rosa pulled her sunglasses off to be absolutely sure of what she was seeing. Nope, she hadn't imagined it. There, looking incongruous in a white shirt and stone-coloured jacket over chinos, and a panama-style hat, sat Professor Ernest Gray himself, a thousand miles and more away from where Rosa had expected him to be, locked up in the ivory towers at Oxford.

Of course, he was playing Scrabble with a dark-haired guy who had his back to her, so he was still finding some way to demonstrate his mental prowess. As usual. Rosa pitied his opponent.

Except now she'd drawn his attention, she'd given him a new target. It could only be a matter of time now before he turned his sharp mind and sharper words onto her—her choice of career, her lack of education, her inability to stay in one place, her unreliability… How could he possibly get through all her faults in one short visit?

'Rosa.' Her father inclined his head towards her, without smiling. 'Your mother told us you'd be joining us. Eventually.'

And that was about all the family love and welcome she could expect from him, Rosa supposed. What was he even doing here? As far as she knew, he'd had as little contact with Sancia as possible, after she left, and they'd been separated ten years or more now. In all that time he'd *certainly* never visited the island that she'd escaped to. Why would he? Following Sancia to La Isla Marina would have been tantamount to admitting that he'd made a mistake, given her reasons to leave him. And if Rosa understood one thing about her father it was that Professor Ernest Gray would *never* admit that he was wrong.

So what could have brought him here now? Were things worse than she thought? Maybe it wasn't the island that had Sancia panicked. Maybe it was something else. She should have got here sooner...

Her heart raced as all the worst-case scenarios flooded her mind. Rosa grabbed for the memory of meditation practice in India, two years ago, and focussed on her breath until she had it under control again.

No point getting worked up until she had some answers. Which meant asking questions. 'Where is Mama? And Anna? And the guests, come to that? I was expecting—'

She didn't get any further, because as she started talking her father's Scrabble companion turned around and Rosa got a good look at his face, pale and shadowed in the cool of the patio shade but still absurdly perfect, with cheekbones that emphasised the beautiful shape of his face, and the incredible blue of his eyes.

It was too late to run. Too late to hide. And Rosa didn't even know *how* to fight this sudden intrusion. Her whole body seemed fixed to the spot as a hundred perfect memories ran through her mind, racing over each other, all featuring the man in front of her.

Whatever she'd been expecting from her return to La Isla Marina faded away. Because there in front of her, on her Mama's back patio, sat the last person she'd ever expected to see again—and a perfect reason to join Sancia and start panicking.

Jude Alexander.

La Isla Marina, Jude had decided within a few hours of his arrival, was the perfect hideaway from the real world. It had sun, sand, sangria and—most importantly for him—solitude. In fact, he wasn't all that bothered about any of the first three items on the list, as long as he was left alone while he was there.

Fame, it turned out, was overrated. Especially the sort of fame that meant he couldn't go anywhere without being recognised, or do anything without the world having an opinion about his actions. It might have taken him a while to see the downsides of celebrity, but now that he had…well, Jude was experiencing them in spades.

So it was sort of ideal that his main companion on the island was an ageing Oxford professor who hadn't got the slightest idea who Jude was. Professor Gray was perfectly content to play Scrabble for hours, or talk about events of the last century, or the one before—without ever asking a question about Jude's own life. The man's self-absorption—or perhaps his preoccupation with the historical world—made Jude's quest to escape the person he'd become all the easier. The professor hadn't even explained why he was there himself, let alone asked Jude what had brought him to the remote Spanish island.

If Professor Gray didn't know or care who Jude was, his ex-wife, Sancia, and daughter Anna were too busy to even notice. Apparently there was some sort of event happening at the island later in the month—Sancia hadn't gone into details—and it was all hands on deck to prepare for it. All hands except his and Professor Gray's. Jude got the feeling he'd been cast in the role of companion, or perhaps nurse, to the professor since they'd arrived together. Whatever the reason, it was all working out fine for him.

Until a voice he'd never dreamed or hoped he'd hear again spoke.

'Dad?' He hadn't realised what he was hearing, at first. That one word wasn't enough to make the memories hit—which surprised him, given how many other things seemed to trigger them.

'Rosa.' That name, spoken in Professor Gray's cultured tones. That was his first clue. 'Your mother told us you'd be joining us. Eventually.'

But still, Rosa had to be a reasonably common Spanish name, right? There was no reason to imagine it was *his* Rosa. Or, rather, the Rosa who'd made it very clear that she'd rather leave the country than belong to him.

The Rosa he'd known, three years before, was probably still thousands of miles away on the other side of the world, chasing whatever dreams he couldn't be a part of. Dreams she'd never even told him about, even as he'd spilled every one of his to her.

That Rosa couldn't be here. That was insane. Maybe the latest events in New York had actually driven him mad after all. It would explain the midnight flight to Spain, anyway.

'Where is Mama? And Anna? And the guests, come to that?' But as she spoke Jude realised there was no point denying what he was hearing, not any more. Only one person, one voice, had ever made his heart shudder like that.

There was no point hiding. La Isla Marina was his best shot at a hiding place, and she was already here.

Time to face his demons.

Jude turned around.

'I was expecting—' Rosa cut herself off, staring. 'Oh.'

She looked just the same—same wild dark hair, same wide, chocolate eyes with endless lashes. Same sweet, soft mouth. Same curves under her jeans and T-shirt, same smooth skin showing on her bare arms. Same neat, small feet shoved into flip-flops.

Same woman he'd fallen in love with, last time they met.

'Hello, Rosa.' Jude tried for a smile—that same smile

that graced album covers and posters and photo shoots. The one that never felt quite real, any more. Not since Rosa left. And definitely not since Gareth.

There was no answering smile on Rosa's face though, only shock. Who could blame her? It wasn't as if he'd planned this, either.

He might have done, three years ago, if he'd known about this place—or rather, known that this was her home. Because now, too late, all the pieces were falling into place. She'd left him to go back to her mother's family home, for her grandfather's funeral—and never come back again. La Isla Marina must have been where she'd run to.

If he'd known that then, would he have followed?

Or would he have accepted that she'd not told him where she was going for a reason?

Oh, who was he kidding? Even if he'd known where she was, he'd have sat there waiting for her to come back because he'd had *faith* in her. Something that had turned out to be seriously misplaced. And the day he'd realised that was the terrible day that everything had happened with Gareth, and he wasn't going anywhere for a while. Except down, in a despair spiral he almost hadn't made it out of. And then, suddenly, up the charts, for all the wrong reasons.

After Gareth, how could he have let himself see her again, anyway? He'd broken every promise he'd ever made for this woman, and she'd walked out anyway, leaving his world destroyed and empty.

Of course he hadn't chased her across the globe. Even if he'd wanted to, and hated himself for that.

So many conflicting emotions tied up in the curvy, petite woman standing in front of him, all tangled and tight around his heart. Would he ever escape those bonds?

Rosa was still staring at him, stunned, and Jude hunted around for something to say. For some of the many, many words he'd wished he could say to her over the last few years. The accusations, the questions, the declarations, anything. But nothing came out.

'You two know each other?' Professor Gray was looking between them, confused.

Something about his voice seemed to snap Rosa out of her shock, as she gave them both a lopsided smile that never quite reached her eyes. 'Oh, Dad, everyone knows Jude Alexander. He has possibly the most recognisable face in the world, right now.'

Professor Gray turned his curious gaze onto Jude, as if searching for fame in his features.

'Your daughter photographed me for a publication a few years ago,' he explained, blandly. No hint of the true story between that four-week study when Rosa travelled with them on tour, capturing every moment of their rise to fame. Of Gareth's last tour. 'I'm in a band, you see.'

'*A* band?' Rosa scoffed. 'Jude is the frontman of The Swifts, Dad. Hottest band of the decade, some are saying.' She raised an eyebrow at him, and Jude tried not to squirm under it. Not just because of the inevitable uncomfortableness that always came when someone referred to *him* as the frontman, instead of Gareth. But because he had *so* been enjoying not being *that* Jude Alexander for a while.

'You know I don't follow popular culture, Rosa.' Professor Gray dismissed his daughter's words with a wave of his hand. 'But Jude here is an almost competent Scrabble player, at least.'

Jude watched as Rosa's gaze flicked over to him at her father's words, meeting his for just a second. Just long enough for him to feel the same connection he'd experienced the night they'd met. It hit him deep, inside those tangled threads around his heart, a piercing guilt tied up with want and need and lust.

Still. Nice to know he hadn't imagined it, that connection. Even if it clearly never had the same effect on Rosa as it had on him.

'I'm so glad you've found a playmate, Father,' Rosa said, her tone scathing. 'But Jude's Scrabble abilities don't answer any of my questions. Where are Mama and Anna? And what on earth are you doing here?' She glanced at Jude again as she asked the last question, leaving him uncertain as to whose presence she was most baffled by.

Jude didn't blame her.

Now the initial shock of her arrival had passed, he found himself watching her more closely, looking beyond the familiarity of the woman he'd known so intimately— if, apparently, incompletely—three years ago. There *were* changes, ones he hadn't initially spotted. She was leaner now, he realised, harder even. Her mass of long, dark curls had been tamed back into a braid that hung over her left shoulder, and her dark eyes were far more wary than he remembered. Even in her relaxed jeans and fitted T-shirt, her sunglasses dangling loosely from her fingers, she looked poised to run at any moment. As if this beautiful island resort was more of a trap than her home.

What had made her look that way? And why, after all this time, did he even care?

'Your mother is talking with the cook about dinner, I believe,' Professor Gray said. 'And as for your sister, I have no idea.'

'She went to Barcelona with Leo,' Jude put in, since apparently he was paying more attention to the professor's family than he was.

'Leo?' Rosa's nose crinkled up as she said the name. 'Who on earth is…? Never mind. Dad, why are you here?'

Professor Gray observed his daughter mildly. 'Why, is it such a crime for a man to wish to spend time with his family?'

From the look Rosa gave him in return, Jude rather thought her answer might be yes.

'Professor Gray?' Maria, the only non-family member of staff that Jude had actually met on the island, appeared in the villa doorway. 'There is a phone call for you at Reception? From Oxford?'

'Still no mobile phone, huh, Dad?' Rosa asked.

'I have one,' Professor Gray answered, loftily, as he got to his feet. 'I merely do not see the requirement for it to always be on my person. Or switched on.'

'Of course you don't.'

As Professor Gray made his way into the villa, Jude found himself staring at Rosa again. What was it about this woman that captivated him so, that he couldn't look away, even now, after everything that had happened because he'd fallen for her? He wished he knew. Maybe then he could break free of it. As it was…

'So.' Rosa moved to take her father's chair opposite him, and Jude knew exactly what was coming next.

She was going to ask him a question, and he was going to have to decide how much of the truth he wanted to tell her. Given that last time he'd told her everything—opened up every part of himself and shared it with her—and she'd left anyway, he had a feeling that this time discretion might really be the better part of valour.

Or, as Gareth would have said, if he were still alive to say it, *Screw me once, shame on you. Screw me twice…*

Jude wasn't going to let that happen. In any sense of the word.

Rosa sat down, and caught his eye across the table.
'What are you doing here, Jude?'
Jude opened his mouth, and prepared to lie.

# CHAPTER TWO

HE WAS GOING to lie to her.

Three years, and Rosa could still see the tell in the way Jude glanced to the side before speaking.

She supposed she couldn't blame him. She hadn't exactly done much to earn the truth from him.

But on the other hand, this was her home, her place—and she'd never told him about it. Had he been stalking her, searching for her, these last three years? Had he come here to find her? And if so, why on earth now, not three years ago?

No, that was ridiculous. She hadn't known she was coming herself until two weeks ago, and she had a hard time believing that Sancia and Anna had teamed up to come up with some outrageous story to get her there, just to help Jude out.

Unlikely as it seemed, this had to be some kind of crazy coincidence.

Rosa wasn't entirely sure if that made it better or worse.

'Believe it or not, I came here to work on some new music,' Jude said. Just the words conjured up memories of watching him composing, trying out new melodies on his guitar at the back of the tour bus, folded up to sit on the narrow bunk she lay in. Some of the most precious moments they'd spent together in that too-short month were times like that, when no one else was there or awake, when it was just them and the music.

But she couldn't think about that now. Memories weren't going to help her figure out what the hell was going on here.

'So you had no idea that this was my mother's family home?' Rosa asked, her eyes narrowing. It didn't hurt to double check these things, right?

'None at all.' That, at least, seemed to be the truth. So where was the lie? He was a musician, of course he'd come here to work on music. Except where was the rest of the band, in that case? Or what was left of it.

The memory hit her harder than she'd expected. An article online she'd caught by chance, that had left her crying in a foreign airport for a man she'd known and grown fond of. For another star gone too soon. And for Jude, left behind—the only time she'd let herself cry for him at all.

The band she'd known, when she'd toured with Jude that summer, wasn't the same band he was with now. Not without Gareth.

No wonder he hadn't come after her. He'd been dealing with his own tragedy, while she'd left to attend her *abuelo*'s funeral and had her whole world changed.

But that didn't change the truth of him being here, now. 'So you expect me to believe that this is just a bizarre and unfortunate coincidence?'

'If you like.' Jude gave a small, one-sided shrug, but the smile on his lips told her that wasn't entirely how he'd put it. 'To be honest, it doesn't much matter to me what you believe, any more.'

It had once, though. For one brief, shining month in time, what Rosa had believed had mattered to Jude Alexander. And what he'd believed about her had mattered to her, too.

Which had only made it harder to let him down when she'd walked away.

Of course, that was how she knew it was the right decision, too. But that didn't mean there hadn't been moments since, days when she'd been lost and alone and confused, when she'd wondered how different things would be if she'd gone back to him when she'd left La Isla Marina, instead of hightailing it for the Middle East, then Australia, then the Americas.

A whole life she'd thrown away and never lived. Of course she thought about it. She just didn't let herself imagine it too often, or in too much detail. She didn't want the regrets—not when she'd done the right thing, and found the life she'd always promised herself because of it.

She wondered if Jude would understand that, if she told him. Or maybe he'd been relieved when she hadn't come back. After all, he'd chased and caught his own dreams, too. But they'd come at a high price.

Rosa picked up a few of her father's Scrabble tiles, and began rearranging them on the rack, spelling out Spanish words he'd never use, for her own amusement, trying to find the words she needed to say.

In the end, she settled for blunt. It was her style, after all.

'I heard about Gareth. I'm sorry. You know how fond I was of him.' It had been hard not to adore Gareth. His optimism, his openness, the joy he'd found in the world… It was hard to imagine the band without him.

Hard to imagine Jude without his best friend.

Jude looked away. 'Yeah.' The curt word told Rosa her sympathies weren't enough. Of course they weren't.

Nothing could make up for Gareth's death. Certainly not anything *she* had to offer.

It wasn't her place to ask what happened, to tell Jude he could talk to her, if he needed to. Wasn't her place to comfort him for a three-year-old tragedy that obviously still cut him deep.

She'd given up that place when she left.

Time to move on. She was never good at the touchy-feely stuff, anyway.

'So, where are the others?' Always a good way of figuring out whether a person was lying to her—ask a question she already knew the answer to. 'Jimmy and Lee and Tanya?' The rest of The Swifts. After all, Jude hadn't got this famous all on his own, whatever the gossip magazines seemed to think.

And right now, the gossip sites didn't seem to know *what* to think. Rosa didn't make a point of following Jude's every career move, or anything—in fact, she made a point of not listening to his music any more than she had to, which was made more difficult by the fact it seemed to be playing *everywhere* at the moment. Even in the rainforest, someone had brought speakers and been playing The Swifts when they'd set up camp the other week.

But even she hadn't been able to avoid the news that Jude Alexander had dropped off the face of the earth. The rest of the band had been photographed out and about in New York City, but there had been no sign of their lead singer.

Not that Rosa had been concerned about that. Much.

'New York, I think.' Jude looked away again, down at his own tiles. He wasn't lying, so maybe just hiding something? Rosa couldn't tell, any more. 'I'm working on some...different stuff.'

'Solo stuff?' Because *that* she hadn't read anywhere online. 'You're planning on leaving The Swifts?'

'No,' Jude said, too quickly. 'I'm not. I couldn't. I just… I needed some time away, is all.'

'And you picked La Isla Marina?' Because, really, that was too much of a coincidence to not bear some investigation.

'I heard someone talk about this place once. I can't remember who, exactly. One of Sylvie's friends, maybe.'

Sylvie. That would be Sylvie Rockwell-Smythe, Rosa's ever-helpful brain for useless knowledge filled in. Jude's beautiful, red-headed, heiress and model girlfriend. Exactly the sort of woman a celebrity like Jude should be dating.

Except, if he was here in paradise, and she was still in New York… 'How is Sylvie?'

'We split up,' Jude said, shortly.

'Ah. Sorry.' There was that old talent for putting her foot in it, rearing up again. One day she'd learn not to just say the first thing that popped into her head. Maybe.

Jude shrugged. 'I wouldn't be.'

'Like that, huh?'

'Pretty much.'

Rosa sat back and surveyed him, taking in the changes the last three years had wrought on a face she'd known so well, once. He looked thinner. No, not thinner, exactly. Leaner. As if some stylist had decided to play up his pale and interesting aspect. But they couldn't style away Jude's broad shoulders, or the muscles in those arms.

But he looked tired. Worn down, maybe.

'So. How's fame going?'

'Overrated.' Jude met her eyes. 'Haven't you heard the latest? The entire of the continental US is talking about it.'

'I've been kind of out of touch,' Rosa admitted. 'I was working on a story down in South America…wait.' Hadn't she read something about a book, somewhere? A kiss-and-tell sort of a book, all about Jude? Maybe Sylvie had something to do with that… 'Is this about the book?'

*'Jude: The Naked Truth.'* Jude shook his head in disgust as he quoted the title. 'That's the one.'

Whoever had written it should have come and found Rosa. She could have told them plenty of secrets about Jude Alexander.

She wouldn't have, of course. That was just one of the many differences between her and Sylvie. That and the fact that the other woman was a supermodel. And at five feet three and with too many curves, Rosa would definitely never be that.

'I haven't read it.'

Jude didn't respond, and Rosa resigned herself to looking him up on the internet once she'd got her laptop hooked up to the island Wi-Fi. It wouldn't be the first time, anyway. And Jude didn't have many secrets from the media these days, it seemed to Rosa. She could probably download the eBook and know everything she wanted to about him in a couple of hours of reading.

Except she didn't want to. Those books never told the whole truth, anyway. And she knew more about him than any pages could contain.

Or she had. Once.

Before.

She turned back to her father's Scrabble tiles, and ignored the letters 's' 'e' and 'x' to find something else to think about.

'So. Been a while,' Jude said, and Rosa looked up from her Scrabble tiles to take in the sight of him in the sunshine again.

He was too pale, she decided. He couldn't have been on the island long or he'd have lost that grey pallor that came from too long spent inside with only his guitar for company.

But he was still every bit as gorgeous as she remembered. As she'd tried to forget.

Her fingers flexed, reaching for the camera that wasn't hanging around her neck for once. She wanted to capture him here, now, in the moment. A comparison piece to the famous, laughing photo of him she'd taken three years ago. One photo in thousands she'd taken that month, but the one everyone remembered most. The one that had made her name. Kick-started her career, when The Swifts had hit the big time.

She'd been assigned to the up-and-coming band by a magazine she'd done some work for before, asked to follow them on tour for an in-depth photo piece with some interviews. Someone high up at the magazine had a feeling about them, she'd been told, and they wanted to get in there first, before anyone else.

Whoever that person was, they'd been right. And they'd changed Rosa's world with that one commission, in too many ways to count.

If she hadn't taken the job, she'd never have taken the photo that started her rise to the top of her profession, that gave her the luxury of picking and choosing jobs wherever she wanted in the world.

If she hadn't taken the job, she'd never have met Jude. And if she hadn't met Jude, she wouldn't have spent three years taking any job that kept her away from England, Spain and New York.

'Three years.' As if he didn't already know.

'You look good.'

'You look pale.'

Jude laughed, the first true emotion she'd seen from him since she arrived. 'You never were very good for my ego, were you?'

'You never needed me for that.' He'd always had plenty of hangers-on and groupies, ready to tell him how wonderful he was, even back then, before The Swifts took over the music world. Gareth might have been the lead singer, but Jude was the mysterious lead guitarist, and that had its own appeal.

And he'd had Gareth to keep him optimistic. To keep him humble.

How had he coped without him?

She should have called. It was three years too late to be asking these questions. But back then...she couldn't.

Rosa shoved the last of the Scrabble tiles aside and got to her feet. 'I really should go and find my mother. Let her know I'm here.'

Jude inclined his head in a small nod. 'Of course.'

She waited, just a moment, in case he was going to say anything more, but he was already studying his letters again. If those groupies could see him now—wild-child rock-and-roll star plays Scrabble. Wouldn't they be disappointed?

Was *she*, though? Rosa wasn't even sure. Already this trip home was nothing like she'd expected.

But she couldn't be certain if that was a bad thing or not. Not yet.

She paused as she reached the archway leading into the villa.

'Jude?'

He looked up. 'Yeah?'

'Did you really not know I'd be here?'

'Honestly?' Jude gave her a sardonic smile. 'I would never have come if I did.'

Rosa looked away. Well. That told her.

And really, what else was she hoping for?

Shaking away the conversation with Jude, Rosa headed inside to find her mother. And some answers.

Jude watched Rosa go, then realised she'd stopped, just inside the archway to the villa.

Not that he cared.

He shouldn't care.

He absolutely shouldn't care enough to want to watch her every move.

Except…he did. Even after everything.

Trying not to be obvious about it, Jude tilted his chair just enough for him to see inside the villa, to where Rosa had found her mother. Both women seemed far too pre-occupied with each other to be worrying about him, so he took advantage of their distraction to shift his chair around a bit more, so he could watch them properly.

It wasn't his place to spy on a reunion, he knew. But since his own with Rosa had been so anticlimactic, he wanted to know what a real one would look like.

Inside, Sancia threw her arms around Rosa and held her tight, swaying her back and forth with her outpouring of affection.

Once, Jude had imagined that his and Rosa's reunion might be full of love, like that. Filled with passion, at least—the same kind of passion they'd shown each other during their brief time together.

Sometimes, late at night, he'd allowed himself to picture it. Rosa coming back, finding him backstage, just as he was finishing a gig. He'd be on a performance high, anyway, and when he saw her…everything would crystallise, fall into place. He'd sweep her up into his arms and never let her go again.

Except she'd never come back, had she?

And then Gareth had died, and he'd been so lost. So hopeless, without his best friend. He'd needed Rosa, then.

But she was long gone. And even if she hadn't been... how could he let himself love her again, knowing what that love had cost him?

From the moment they'd met, when Rosa had arrived on the tour bus and introduced herself as the person who'd be documenting their every move for the next month, her presence had filled his whole world, pushing everything else to the edges. The connection had been instantaneous, even if the physical side of their relationship had developed more slowly. Rosa had spoken to them all, of course, taking notes, filming them, her camera always to hand. But somehow, when it had been just the two of them, Jude had found himself giving up far more than she'd asked for—details about his life, his mind, his friendships, his heart. Details she'd never used in the article, because they were just for her.

Whenever the music was done, they'd gravitate towards each other, letting the others head out to party while they headed back to the bus or a hotel room. And soon, all those late-night talks had become midnight kisses, and more, as Jude had lost himself in the wonder of Rosa.

Unbidden, memories of their last night came back to him, filling his brain with the images of them together. The hotel room, the champagne, the post-gig euphoria that always came over him—and Rosa. Rosa's eyes, bright with excitement. Her hair, loose and soft and dark as it hung over her bare shoulders. Her olive skin, so smooth and welcoming under his hands.

The feel of her against him, both of them mindless

with the kind of passion Jude knew didn't come around all that often.

Or ever, for him, it seemed, unless it was with Rosa.

It was crazy. He'd been with supermodels, Hollywood actresses—some of the widely acknowledged most beautiful women in the world.

And they'd never made him feel an iota of what he felt in one night with Rosa.

He pushed the memories aside. It was that passion, that uncontrolled connection, that had made him forget the promise he'd made to Gareth after his first close call. Jude had sat beside that hospital bed looking at his best friend—too pale, too lost, so close to being utterly ruined by the drugs and the alcohol and the life it was so easy to live as a band on the road. And he'd made the most important promise of his life—he'd promised to keep Gareth safe from then on. To be the one Gareth could rely on to steer him away from temptation, to remind him how much he had to live for.

But then he'd met Rosa and let that promise slide, too distracted by passion and infatuation to notice his best friend slipping again.

Until it was too late.

Shaking his head, he looked away as he saw Sancia putting an arm around Rosa's shoulders as she led her further into the villa. He had to stop living in his memories.

He needed to focus on what this meant for his future.

He'd made a new promise, when Gareth died—an echo of the one he'd made him a year before, except *this* one he'd kept, would keep on keeping. He'd live life for the both of them. He'd have the success that should have been theirs, chase the fame Gareth had always wanted. Live the life Gareth should be there to enjoy.

The Swifts' success wasn't his. It wasn't even Jimmy's or Lee's or Tanya's. It was all for Gareth.

And that was why he could never walk away from it. He owed his friend, for the life he got to live, without him, and for the promise he should have kept.

But even then, he couldn't stay in New York for the publication of that book.

He'd come to La Isla Marina with a very firm objective in mind—to stay out of the public eye for a few weeks, long enough for all the fuss about *The Naked Truth* to fade away again, and to give him time to think about his next move, musically.

But Rosa being here…that could change everything. He mustn't forget that he'd actually met Rosa when she was photographing the band for some British music magazine. What were the chances she was still doing that sort of work? Just because he hadn't seen her at any of his gigs since didn't mean she wasn't still in the game.

And even if she wasn't, she was a freelance photojournalist. A few shots of Jude Alexander hiding out on a remote Spanish island, when no one else had been able to get a hint of where he was…that would pay big money. Enough for a struggling freelancer to not have to worry about bills for a while, anyway.

Would she sell him out?

Three years ago, Jude could have answered that question without hesitation: never. Rosa wasn't that sort of person. He might have only known her for four weeks, but he'd learned more about her in one month than he'd known about his own parents in a lifetime.

And maybe it still meant something. After all, she hadn't used his secrets in the eventual article that had been published about that month-long tour. And there was no mention of Rosa—or any of the secrets only she knew—in That Book. There were whole chapters on Gareth, his death, Jude's guilt over it, and everything that happened next, but no mention of the part Rosa had played in everything that happened.

Of course, probably the author just hadn't known to look for Rosa. If they had…

No, she still wouldn't have talked. She wasn't that sort of person, he was sure.

But that didn't mean it wasn't worth making sure she was on the right side of his hide-and-don't-seek game with the press, before she let something slip to the wrong person.

The last thing Jude wanted was to have his hiding place uncovered now, just when his last remaining secret had walked back into his life.

# CHAPTER THREE

'MAMA. MAMA!' Rosa interrupted her mother's non-stop flow of conversation with an impatient shout. It might be rude, but she knew from experience that if she didn't get in there quick before Sancia got lost in one of her conversational tangents, she could be stuck discussing anything but the matter in hand for hours before she got back to the point.

Sancia stopped talking, smiled, then hugged her again.

Rosa hugged her back. Maybe there were some parts of this homecoming that weren't completely awful. Hugs from her mama were definitely one of them. Whatever their family issues, Rosa knew she was lucky to still have her mother in her life. Ten years after she left, Rosa had long forgiven her for walking out on them—understood why she'd needed to, even. Rosa knew that, in her place, she'd have done the same.

If she couldn't fix a situation, couldn't get what she needed from it, she broke free. Just as her mother had done. Just ask Jude.

'I'm sorry, *querida*,' Sancia said, with a warm smile. 'I'm just so excited to have both my girls home with me again.'

Which led Rosa neatly into the first of her very many questions. 'Where *is* Anna, anyway? Jude said something

about her going to Barcelona with someone called Leo?'
Which seemed utterly unlike her sister, to be honest.

'Ah, you've already met Jude! Isn't he a delight?'
Sancia beamed. 'We were so lucky he decided to come
and stay here, you know. And he brought your father
over with him, for which we are all grateful.'

'He…brought Dad?' Rosa frowned. That made no
sense at all. But then, Sancia's ramblings often didn't.

'Well, they arrived together. They travelled over from
the mainland in the same boat.' Which was not at all the
same thing, Rosa realised.

Sancia didn't always operate on exactly the same
plane as everyone else. It wasn't worth explaining the
difference—or asking if Sancia had even realised who
Jude was. The Swifts wouldn't mean anything to her
mother. And she definitely didn't want to mention their
past acquaintance.

Which left her with her more immediate concerns.

'So, Mama. Anna. Where is she?'

'Why, Barcelona, like Jude said. With Leo.'

'And Leo is…?' Rosa pressed.

'Anna's…well, not boyfriend, exactly. At least I don't
think so. Lover, I suppose.' Sancia sounded far too happy
with that answer. Rosa tried to imagine Anna's face if she
heard their mother describing any man as her 'lover' and
bit back a laugh. 'And he's close to the bride, of course,'
Sancia went on, bringing Rosa quickly back to the matter at hand.

'Why don't you tell me more about this wedding,
Mama?' she suggested as she manoeuvred her mother
further into the villa, towards the small office that sat
behind the reception area.

'Of course! You'll need to know all about it,' Sancia

agreed, a little too readily for Rosa's liking. 'Anna has left you a list of all the things she needs you to take care of.'

'Has she?' Of course she had. St Anna always did need to be in perfect control of everything. She wouldn't let a little thing like, oh, not actually being there get in the way of that.

Sancia nodded enthusiastically. 'Oh, yes. She's thought of everything. Just look!' She rustled around on the desk until she pulled out a clipboard, with a neatly typed list that, Rosa was almost certain, would prove to contain no typos or grammatical errors.

Although it did seem to contain an awful lot of work to be done.

Rosa took the clipboard from her mother and flipped through the three pages of jobs. 'Seriously? What's *Anna* been doing since she got here?'

'Oh, everything!' Sancia clapped her hands together, pride shining from her eyes. 'She and Leo, they've re-painted all the bungalows, tamed the jungle growing out there on the island, fixed all the little things I've been meaning to get around to around here, sorted out the swimming pools for the season…everything!'

'And did she walk on water as well?' Rosa muttered as she looked through *her* list.

'Sorry?' Sancia asked, thankfully unable to make out the words.

'Did they do all that alone?' Rosa asked, instead of repeating her original question.

'Well, Anna's got a whole lot of extra staff coming in this week to help finish it off. But she's organised it all—and been out there with her paintbrush doing more than her fair share!'

Guilt gnawed at Rosa. 'I'm sorry I couldn't get here sooner, Mama.'

'It's fine.' Sancia patted her shoulder. 'You were busy. I understood. And so did your sister.'

That part, Rosa found harder to believe. Even harder than picturing pristine St Anna with a paintbrush in hand.

'Well, she's left me plenty to do to make up for it, anyway.' Rosa stared down at the list again. Then she turned it over so she didn't have to look at it any more. 'So, tell me all about this wedding.'

*And why on earth it's sending this whole island into general insanity.*

Twenty minutes later, Rosa had her answers. She just didn't like them very much.

'So, when you called and said that there was a wedding booking on the island, what you failed to mention was that it was a five-star, luxury, last-minute wedding for Internet sensation and supermodel Valentina, whose every move is documented online to millions of fans.' A wedding like this could make or break La Isla Marina for the foreseeable future. If they could live up to Valentina's expectations, the resort would be fully booked for years. But if they screwed it up...

That didn't bear thinking about.

Sancia smiled. 'Anna says it's a great opportunity. Apparently Valentina is very popular.'

Understatement. Even in the middle of a South American rainforest, Rosa hadn't been able to avoid Valentina's doings. 'She's about as famous as Jude is.'

Sancia's expression turned curious. 'Jude is famous?'

Oh, honestly. How was she supposed to work like this?

'Just take my word for it, Mama.' She thought about Jude, unrecognised and playing Scrabble with her father. He was hiding. Even if he hadn't fully admitted it yet. 'And maybe don't mention the fact that he's here to anyone, okay?'

'Of course. But Rosa…can you do all these things Anna has asked?' Sancia chewed on her lip, nervously. Because only St Anna could be useful and take care of the family business, right? Only Anna was reliable and dependable—never mind that Sancia had no time at all for those traits usually. Now that she was in trouble, of course it was *Anna* that she needed. Not Rosa.

'I think I can manage a little bit of organisation, for once,' she said, drily. 'Don't worry about it, Mama. I've got you covered.'

She resisted the impulse to look back down at the list and wince. How hard could it be, really? Arranging hotel rooms and putting up decorations was hardly the same as trekking miles through war zones or eluding border patrols, now, was it?

'Oh, good.' Sancia's face relaxed into its usual smiling countenance. 'Then how about I go and fetch you some wine? And some dinner—you must be starving after your journey!'

Rosa knew it wouldn't have mattered what time of day she'd arrived, Sancia would still assume she needed feeding. And a glass of wine. Today though, she wasn't wrong. However, there were a few other things she needed to get straight first.

'In a moment, Mama. You never explained what Dad is doing here.' Rosa remembered what life had been like with both her parents in the same house as a child, and she wasn't sure she wanted to experience it again. For years, Sancia had lived life her way—ignoring her husband's requests for more order in their lives. She'd picked up new creative hobbies that had covered the house in paint or pottery, and brought new friends home to open their lounge up for art classes or book groups. And through it all, Ernest's only comments would be to stay out of his study and clear up after themselves. Rosa wondered, sometimes, if some of the crazier ideas Sancia had come up with—like the midnight picnic in the garden, with fairy lights and music, or the time she'd repainted the whole house yellow, or the last-minute road trip across the country with no preparation or, as it turned out after the first fifty miles, petrol—had just been attempts to get her husband to pay attention to her, for once.

If they had been, they hadn't worked. Even when she'd left, Rosa's father had just increased the time he'd spent at his college, and let Anna take over.

So why was he here, now? And…was Sancia blushing? Really? Rosa was fairly sure her mother had never been embarrassed by anything ever—she just wasn't that sort of person.

Yeah, there was definitely something odd going on here.

'Is it something to do with the wedding?' Rosa pressed. 'Or the island? Is the resort in trouble?' If things were really bad, maybe Sancia had needed to call in the big guns—not just the responsible daughter, but also the ex-husband who'd tried to structure their family lives together to the point of insanity, while Sancia had fought to keep them spontaneous and freeform, until the day she'd left.

Of course, then Anna had taken over organising Rosa's life, so it wasn't as if it had made all that much difference.

But for Mama to call Dad now…

'That's not it at all,' Sancia replied, sounding affronted. Rosa had never been very good at treading carefully around other people's feelings. She suspected it might be a family trait.

'Then why is he here? I mean, now, after all this time?' It had been a full decade since Sancia had left the family home in Oxford. Of course, that was supposed to just be for a holiday—at least, that was what she had told them. And knowing Sancia as Rosa did, she'd probably believed it herself, at the time.

But a holiday had turned into an extended stay—to help her parents out with the resort, all perfectly understandable.

Except for the part where she'd never come home again.

Rosa wasn't even sure her parents had ever officially divorced. It would be just like her mother to leave things completely up in the air as far as officialdom was concerned. And just like her father to refuse to do anything to agree to a situation he hadn't planned for.

They were both as bad as each other, in some ways.

'Your father knew that Anna was here helping me, and he was worried about me,' Sancia said, in such a defensive way that Rosa knew it couldn't be the whole truth.

'And?' she pressed.

'And apparently his cardiologist might have suggested that it was a good idea, too,' Sancia admitted.

'His cardiologist?' That horrible, guilty feeling was back, clenching around her own heart, as she remembered that last argument with Anna. The one that had started out being about their father's health, and ended up being about *them*, and all the ways they were just too different to ever have that sisterly relationship Rosa had once believed just came from having the same parents.

Of course, since their parents were complete opposites, perhaps it stood to reason that their daughters would be, too.

'Apparently some sun, sea and relaxation are just what

he needs—and, of course, La Isla Marina is perfect for that!'

Sun and sea Rosa could agree with. Relaxation seemed an awful long way off right now.

'And you look like you could use some of the same.' Sancia frowned at her youngest daughter, before giving her a little shove towards the door. 'Go on. You go and be nice to our guests, and I'll bring out some food and wine for you all. It'll be a party!'

The headache forming behind Rosa's eyes told her that the last thing she needed was wine, or to spend any more time with the father who had never understood her, or the one man who maybe could have, if she hadn't walked out on him.

But Sancia in hospitality mode was a force to be reckoned with, so it appeared that Rosa didn't have any other choice.

Jude was instantly aware, the moment that Rosa appeared on the patio again. Once, he'd have believed that was a sign of their cosmic connection. Now, he knew it was merely a sign that Rosa was unhappy, and her stamping feet made her flip-flops slap against the tiled floor noisily.

Apparently, questioning her mother hadn't gone well.

'Mama's bringing out food and wine.' Rosa threw herself back into the chair opposite him, the one her father hadn't come back to claim, and tossed a clipboard on top of the Scrabble board between them. 'I couldn't stop her.'

Apparently they were ignoring the tension and difficulties their first conversation in three years had raised, forgetting all about their past connection, and moving on. Well, Rosa always did like to run away from things; maybe he shouldn't be surprised.

And really, it was probably for the best.

'Why would you want to?' Jude asked, following her lead and focussing on the present instead of the past. 'Sancia showing up with food and wine periodically is basically my favourite thing about the island.'

Rosa shrugged. 'Principle, mostly.' He gave her a confused look, and she laughed. 'Let's just call it my contrary nature. Someone tells me I have to go and sit down and make nice with *Melody Magazine*'s Most Gorgeous Man of the Year, while drinking good wine and eating delicious food, and I instantly want to do anything but that.''

'That must make life interesting,' Jude said, drily. But a part of him couldn't help wondering if that 'contrary nature' of hers explained a little of their history.

He'd always felt, right from the first, that Rosa was a bit like a wild animal—not one to be tamed, exactly, but one he needed to avoid spooking if he wanted to keep her near.

He just wasn't at all sure what he'd done that had scared her off so much that she'd run away without leaving a forwarding address—and stayed as far away as possible thereafter. His ex, Sylvie, had regularly told him that he was a disaster with women, and she didn't even know about Rosa. He just wished that someone would explain to him what he was supposed to be doing differently.

Except, maybe it wasn't him. Jude leant back in his chair and surveyed Rosa as her gaze flickered from the clipboard on the table, to the archway where Sancia would probably appear from, to him—ever so briefly— then back to the clipboard again. She chewed on the edge of a nail as she did so, and her knee didn't stop jiggling as she sat, sprawled across the chair.

Anyone not watching her carefully might think, from

her posture, that she was as laid-back as it was possible to be. But Jude, looking closer, saw more.

Rosa was coiled as tight as a spring, and he was pretty sure that wasn't his doing. Maybe her running away that night wasn't entirely his fault, either.

But right now, whatever was eating her up was making *him* tense just watching.

'So, what's got you wanting to flee in the opposite direction right now?' He regretted his turn of phrase the moment he said it, and he could tell from the way that Rosa's gaze flew to his that she had the same, instinctive memory at the words—of her, disappearing from his bed and running off into the night, without so much as a goodbye.

She didn't mention it, though. Jude couldn't quite decide if he was glad about that or not.

'This wedding Mama has agreed to hold on the island.' Rosa waved a hand towards the clipboard. 'Apparently Anna has run off with her new *lover*, and left me with all the grunt work.' She dragged out the word 'lover', as if she didn't really believe that was what Leo was.

Jude had seen Anna and Leo together—not intentionally, but they weren't exactly subtle—and he had absolutely no doubt that 'lover' was the right term.

'Who's the wedding for?' he asked, idly. Sancia had mentioned it in passing, when he'd checked in, and he knew Anna had been stressing about it. He'd assumed a family member, or something, but that clipboard had an awful lot of names on it. How big was this thing?

He looked a little closer, and froze as a familiar name caught his eye. *Sylvie Rockwell-Smythe.*

'Valentina.' Rosa sighed. 'Internet sensation, supermodel, millionaire and all-round beautiful person, by all accounts. God only knows why she wanted to hold her wedding *here*.'

Jude knew why. Because he suddenly remembered who told him about La Isla Marina in the first place. Who was responsible for his late-night Internet-searching and his decision to escape to the island.

He'd only met Valentina a handful of times, usually at the sort of event his label loved for him to attend and he tried everything in his power to get out of. But she was a friend of Sylvie's, so when they were in the same place they tended to spend time together. Valentina hadn't been anything like he'd expected her to be—of course, she was beautiful, but so were all the other women at these events. And of course, she was successful, but any suspicion that her fame had been acquired by chance or luck had been dispelled within a few minutes of talking to her.

Valentina was a shrewd businesswoman with a good eye for opportunity. She was curvier and shorter than supermodels were expected to be, but by building her brand online, and tapping into the hashtag, instant-photo-update world, she'd gathered a following that businesses would spend a fortune to access. And they did.

But what had surprised him most, he remembered now, was the night he'd ended up alone at some party with Valentina, late on, when most of the other partygoers had passed out or given up. And she'd spoken, for the first and only time—to him at least—about her childhood in Spain. Growing up as the illegitimate and unacknowledged daughter of a Spanish aristocrat, watching her mother trying to scrape together a life for them both, any way she could.

'My favourite time was when Mama worked as a cook on this fantastic island resort—La Isla Marina,' Valentina had said. 'I thought it was the most magical place in the world.' The name had stuck in his head, and when he'd been looking to escape for a while, he'd plugged it into a search engine and been on a plane less than twenty-four hours later.

Why hadn't he remembered that sooner? And if he had, would it even have made any difference?

He hadn't thought for a moment that Valentina would plan a trip here, too. Yes, she had fond memories of the place, but that wasn't the same as relocating her entire wedding there—especially since, last time he'd had an update on the wedding planning from Sylvie, when they were still together, Valentina and Todd were getting married in some top-notch, luxury villa somewhere. Between them, Todd and Valentina could afford any wedding venue in the world. So why were they coming *here*?

Maybe this was fate. Destiny's way of making him deal with all the things about his life, his future, his whole existence that he'd been putting off for too long. The breakup with Sylvie and the book's release had lit the fire under him, and now look where he was—stuck in the middle of nowhere with the one woman he'd thought he could love, and the one he knew he couldn't arriving imminently. That definitely felt as if the universe was sending him a message about dealing with his issues.

Except, just in case some more earthly powers were behind this unlikely coincidence, Jude decided it was worth asking at least one practical follow-up question. Especially since he knew La Isla Marina wasn't Valentina's first wedding venue choice—however nostalgic she was for the place.

'I thought Valentina was getting married out in some incredible luxury villa somewhere?' Somewhere very much else.

'Apparently it burnt down.' Rosa sighed. 'Which is

very sad, obviously, but she seems to have decided to move the whole shebang here, decorations and all, despite never even doing a site visit.'

Because she had it all in her memory, of course. But Jude wasn't going to spill Valentina's secrets for her.

'Well, I'm sure she'll love it here,' Jude said, trying not to look around him for evidence to the contrary. He knew what sort of luxury Valentina and her friends were used to and, despite all the hard work Anna and Leo seemed to be putting in to get the bungalows up to scratch, Jude had to admit that La Isla Marina wasn't quite the magical paradise that Valentina seemed to remember. Yet, anyway.

'Not right now, she wouldn't,' Rosa said bluntly. She'd worked around celebrities, of course. She knew the expectations, too. 'Mama says that Anna's arranged for an army of seasonal staff—including a plumber, joiner and builder—to arrive tomorrow and finish off the work of making the accommodation decent.'

'Well, that's good, isn't it?' The way Rosa said it, he suspected not.

'I suppose. Except it means that I'm left with all the wedding stuff. Allocating accommodation for the guests, decorating the pagoda, working out seating plans, dealing with what is sure to be their many, many issues when they arrive.'

'And you'd rather be painting?' Jude guessed.

'I'd rather be thousands of miles away with my camera, chasing a good story.' She gave him a half-smile, as if to indicate that she was joking—which Jude was pretty sure she wasn't. 'It's just that this sort of thing—admin and paperwork and people—it's not really playing to my strengths. I'm better with a paintbrush in hand.'

'So why has Anna given these jobs to you?'

'Punishment, I reckon. For showing up two weeks

after she did.' Rosa sighed, and pulled the clipboard towards her. 'I mean, look at some of these names. Tyrana Lichfield-Burrows. Ursula Pennington. Isadora-Marie Woodford-Williams, for heaven's sake. Do they sound like my sort of people?'

'Actually, Isadora-Marie is nice. And funny. But I can tell you now you're going to hate Ursula.' It was a flippant remark, but Jude realised his mistake almost instantly.

Rosa's gaze sharpened, fastened on his face as she leant across the table towards him. 'You know these people,' she said, in the sort of voice he'd never been able to lie to.

Wincing, Jude nodded, reluctantly. 'Yes.'

# CHAPTER FOUR

Rosa smiled. This guest list featured some of New York's most celebrated and fabulous citizens—*of course* Jude, rock-star celebrity, would know them. And probably know them well enough to be able to tell her who shouldn't be sat next to whom, and which of them were likely to cause the most trouble. She might not like doing the admin and organising side of things—she'd always been more of the 'make it up as you go along' type, like her mother—but if she *had* to do it, then some insider knowledge would most definitely prove helpful.

'You can help me, then,' she said, and saw Jude wince again. What was the problem? These were his friends—he should be looking forward to seeing them. Except… she flipped through the guest list. 'Hang on, why aren't you invited to this shindig?'

Jude sighed. 'Probably because one of the bridesmaids broke up with me six weeks ago.'

'Sylvie. Right.' That might explain all the wincing. 'So, was it her or the book that you ran all the way to Spain to escape from?'

'Bit of both,' Jude murmured, but didn't elaborate.

'I guess you won't be staying for the wedding, then?' At least his answer had proved her right about one thing—Jude *was* hiding. But how bad an ex-girlfriend were they talking about that he had to run away to a decrepit Spanish island to escape her?

Mind you, she'd run to the other end of the earth to escape him, and he'd been pretty much perfect.

Of course, that was why she'd run. Perfection was terrifying—especially in the face of all her faults.

'Depends, I guess,' Jude said. Then he shook his head. 'I honestly don't know. I came here to get away from everything, but now…maybe this is meant to be. Maybe it's time to face some demons from my past.'

His gaze caught hers as he said it, and suddenly Rosa felt the knowledge that they weren't just talking about his ex, or some book any more weighing heavy on her heart.

She'd tried not to think too much about Jude after she left—that way, she was pretty sure, madness lay. Or at best, running back to him, just when she'd escaped his thrall. Rosa wasn't the sort to dwell. She moved on, got over it and kept going. That was all she knew.

He talked about being here to face his demons as if it were a good thing. If Rosa had the choice, she'd be running as fast as she could in the opposite direction from everything and everyone on La Isla Marina.

'So…you're planning on staying?' Rosa asked, surprised. 'And I kind of have to stay.' At least, if she wanted her family to speak to her ever again. Although she'd gone three years without that from Anna and her father already… No. Rosa didn't have so much family that she could be *quite* that cavalier about losing them.

'So we're both here. On the island. For the duration.' Jude's gaze was heavy and meaningful, and Rosa had an awful feeling she knew exactly where he wanted this conversation to go: back to the night she left, and searching for explanations why.

Yeah, she really wasn't ready to have that talk yet. Let

him deal with his other demons—whatever they were—first, and come back to her last. Like when someone was taking for ever to make up their mind choosing from the menu in a restaurant, and asked the waiter to ask them again at the end.

But Jude wasn't a waiter. And if she couldn't avoid Jude any longer, she might as well take advantage of the fact he was there. Apart from anything else, giving him something else to focus on—like the impending arrival of his ex—might distract him from their own past. And honestly? She could use the help.

Pasting on a bright smile, she ignored the vibes and merrily changed the subject. 'Great! Well, in that case, you can definitely help me out with all these tasks Anna's left for me. I'm sure your insider knowledge will be invaluable.'

Jude didn't seem particularly excited at the prospect. In fact, he didn't look as if he wanted to change the subject at all.

'Rosa. Don't you think we need to talk—?'

'Not really,' she said, honestly. 'I think we were friends, three years ago, before anything else. Maybe we can be that again. I have too much to focus on here for this wedding to even think about anything else right now.'

He didn't agree with her; she could see it in his face. Jude was the talking sort, and she, well, wasn't. Not unless she had to be.

But then, just as Jude opened his mouth to argue, Sancia appeared in the doorway, holding a tray of tapas and flanked by Rosa's father, carrying wine.

She had, quite seriously, never been so pleased to see her parents in her whole life.

'Mama! Dad!' She jumped up from her chair and bounced across the courtyard to help them with the plates. Her father in particular looked surprised at the welcome. Understandably, she supposed. They'd never been affectionate, the two of them. Professor Gray kept even people he loved and liked, like Sancia or Anna, at arm's length, and he'd never known what to make of his younger, wilder daughter. It was as if blood was the only thing they'd ever had in common.

Until now. Now, they all had the future of La Isla Marina in common. And she and her father had the added connection of Jude's friendship.

Now, they were all going to have to try and get along for a while.

And they could start by getting her out of a very awkward conversation with Jude. 'Why don't you come and join us? Jude has lots of questions about the island.'

Once Sancia got talking about La Isla Marina, it would be impossible for anyone to get a word in edgeways. Especially if that word was the one question Rosa really didn't want to answer. *Why?*

Because, seeing Jude again, all of her reasons had already started to fade away. And she couldn't afford to let that happen. Not when she knew she was leaving again, as soon as this wedding was over.

Jude awoke the next morning to the sound of the sea lapping against the rocks outside his bungalow window, the sun already shining through the thin gauze curtains. He lay for a moment just enjoying the peace, the solitude and the beauty of La Isla Marina.

And then his brain caught up with his body.

Rosa was here. Sylvie was coming here. And he'd promised to spend his day helping Rosa prepare for the socialite wedding of the year.

Just perfect.

His head suddenly aching, Jude forced himself out of bed and into the shower. So much for his idyllic secret getaway. From the look of Rosa's clipboard, half of Manhattan was now following him there. And it wasn't even the half he really *liked*.

Letting the water sluice over his skin, Jude thought back over the strange events of the day before. Had he been imagining it, or had Rosa been trying to avoid talking about their history together? She certainly hadn't let on to her parents how close they'd been, once. Instead, she'd talked about him as just one more subject she'd photographed and written about.

Maybe that was all he was, to her.

Could he have imagined that connection between them? That instantaneous, shocking attraction?

Had she just been patiently listening three years ago, as he'd poured out his heart to her, in the hope that she'd find a good story?

No.

He shook water droplets from his hair as he stepped out of the shower, letting the warm Spanish air dry his skin.

He'd seen the same confusion and amazement in Rosa's eyes, that first night they'd been together. That overwhelmed, overtaken look that had echoed exactly how he'd felt.

She'd been as rocked by their connection as he had. She'd just reacted differently.

And maybe now the universe was giving him the chance to find out why—whether she wanted to tell him or not.

Rosa might have distracted him last night with Sancia's tales of the island, and the truly excellent wine and tapas she provided. But today was another day—and they'd already arranged to meet at the villa to go over the guest list and arrangements.

Jude smiled to himself as he pulled on his dark linen trousers and a crisp white linen shirt. If Rosa wanted his help, she'd better be prepared to pay in her secrets.

Especially since she already knew all of his.

The villa was deserted when he reached Reception, so Jude loitered in the cool shade of the tiled reception hall. The white painted arches overhead and the cool vistas reminded him more of a Middle Eastern palace than a Spanish villa, but he liked the feel of the place. It felt as if time had stopped, or at least slowed to a lazy, honey-slow meander. After the bustle of New York City, Jude was enjoying the change of pace.

Sancia had told him the romantic tale of how the island came to her in her family the night before: how Sancia's grandparents had built the villa as their retreat from the world when they married, and how Sancia's parents had built the resort around it when they inherited it. At one time, it was supposed to have been a jewel in the Med, *the* place for the movers and shakers of the time to be seen.

He supposed it would be again, soon. If they got all the necessary work done on time.

Jude was about to reach across the reception desk to pick up the phone and see if there was a direct line to the office, or someone—anyone—who might know where Rosa was, when she suddenly appeared before him.

He blinked. 'Where did you come from?'

'Mama didn't show you the secret door, then, when she gave you the tour?' Rosa grinned. 'Good. A girl has to have some secrets.'

'Secret door?' Jude honestly couldn't tell if she was teasing him or not. 'Are you kidding?'

Rosa shook her head. 'Nope! There's a secret door somewhere in this reception hall that leads to the family quarters. How else are we poor staff supposed to get some peace and quiet from all you demanding guests?'

'I'm going to spend my entire stay trying to figure out whether you're making this up or not,' Jude admitted, which made Rosa's grin grow even wider.

'I'm okay with that,' she answered.

'So, where do we start today?' Jude nodded at the clipboard in Rosa's hands. 'Want to go through and see how many names I recognise? Or how about you run me through the schedule for the week, see if I can highlight any potential danger zones.' If he was here to be useful, he might as well make an effort. And by pure osmosis—and listening to Sylvie gossip—he thought he could probably offer some pretty good insights. Who was likely to abuse the free bar and might need to be kept away from the sea afterwards. Who would find something to complain about regardless, so it was worth giving them a tiny flaw in their bungalow that was easily fixed, just so they'd feel happy. Hell, he even knew one of the bridesmaids was allergic to fresh-cut flowers!

How much of his brain had been taken over by this world—Sylvie's world? The world of celebrity that his label wanted him to be seen in.

What had happened to the music being the most important thing?

'All of those sound like great ideas,' Rosa said. 'But actually… I thought we might take a walk around the island, first. I kind of want to see what Anna's been doing here for the last two weeks, and get an idea of what shape we're in, before I get down to the nitty-gritty stuff.'

'Makes sense,' Jude said. 'Of course, it also sounds

like a total procrastination attempt to avoid doing the *actual* work Anna left you...'

Rosa hit him in the arm with her clipboard, not hard enough to hurt, but enough to make him shut up and grin at her.

This was interesting. Last time they'd met, they'd been on his home turf—as much as a band tour bus could be called anyone's home. They'd been in his world, before The Swifts had really hit the mainstream and started playing stadiums instead of pubs and tiny music venues. He'd known his place there, in a way he didn't quite, these days.

But this time, they were on Rosa's patch—her family home, even, for all that it was also an island resort. This was the place she ran to when they called—rather than running away.

And that meant he got to see a whole other side of Rosa, this time. Maybe he'd even see enough to understand why she left.

Rosa led them out of the villa, down the long, straight path that led back to the jetty and escape from the island. But before they reached the sea, she took a sharp right down a narrower path, through recently cut-back lush greenery. It was the opposite direction from Jude's own bungalow, but, still, things looked familiar.

The bungalows they passed were just like the one he was staying in—low and white, half hidden between the plants and brightly coloured flowers. The smell of fresh paint lingered as they got closer to one; Jude knew that even a few days ago many of them had been grey and dingy. One or two he'd seen on his rambles across the island had displayed broken roof tiles and wooden shutters that hung from their hinges.

Not now, though.

Now, every bungalow gleamed in the sunlight, the freshly painted shutters giving a splash of colour against the white walls. The jungle Jude had fought his way through on arrival had been tamed, so the island looked lush, fresh and green, rather than overtaken by plants. Even the patios outside the bungalows had been swept, scrubbed, and the iron patio furniture cleaned and looking ready for use.

It was quite the transformation. If Jude had been paying more attention to the island, rather than his own thoughts—and Scrabble games—he would have noticed sooner. As it was, suddenly he could see what had drawn Valentina to the island.

Rosa was surveying it with a more critical eye. 'How bad was it? Before the work started, I mean.'

Jude shrugged. 'It was already pretty far under way when I arrived.'

'But some parts weren't done yet, right? What did they look like?'

'They were…' He winced as he tried to find the words to describe how run-down and derelict parts of the island had looked, just a week or so ago.

'That bad, huh?'

'Worse,' he admitted. 'Anna and Leo—and their crew—have done an incredible job around here.'

Rosa let out a long sigh. 'Then she's going to be even more unbearable when she gets back.'

'What do you mean?' Jude dropped to sit on the cast-iron chair on the patio of the nearest bungalow. Motioning across the table, he indicated for Rosa to take the other seat.

'We should have brought coffee with us,' she grumbled as she sat.

Having tasted Sancia's coffee, Jude definitely agreed. But getting Rosa to talk about herself, that was good, too.

Part of him wondered why he still cared—why it still mattered to him at all. It had been three years since she'd left him, and it wasn't as if they'd had a lengthy relationship before that. It had been a short, hot fling—and if he had any sense at all, he'd just keep the memory of that and move on.

Why had he expected anything else, anything more? Because it had felt so real, while it was happening. And like a dream once it was over.

There'd been women since, of course—short-term and long-term. And his life had changed beyond all measure—the tour bus replaced with a private jet, and the grim pubs they'd played with hundred-thousand-seater stadiums. His music was recognised, loved, had gone double platinum—twice. The band had grown closer still, as they'd gone through all the changes together. Especially after they'd lost Gareth. They all knew they had to take care of each other, in a way they hadn't been able to take care of Gareth. In the way he *should* have taken care of Gareth.

But somehow, Jude had become the star—more recognisable than his bandmates, the one the papers and magazines wanted to interview, to photograph. The one who drew the rumours and the stories and the lies.

Still. He had so many people in his life now—from bandmates to friends to acquaintances to his agent to the people at the label to the *über*-fans—that Rosa should have faded from his consciousness completely. He shouldn't even have *recognised* her when she walked in last night.

But he'd known her voice in an instant.

Maybe it was just that he knew what had gone wrong

with every other relationship in his life—but Rosa's motives for leaving remained a mystery. But deep down, Jude knew it was more than that.

He'd opened his heart and his soul to this woman, let her see everything that he was. She was the only person he'd ever done anything close to that for—besides Gareth. But Gareth had been his best friend since they were three. He'd known Rosa less than a month. And still, she was the only person in the world that had seen every inch of the real him. The only one to know him at all, once Gareth died.

And she'd run away. What did that say about the real him?

No wonder he hadn't let anyone else so close since.

He wanted to know her as well as she'd known him, then. Wanted to understand her—find what was wrong with him, or with her, that she'd left and never looked back.

Starting with her obviously acrimonious relationship with her sister.

'So. What's the deal with you and your sister?'

Rosa stared mutinously at him. 'We're sisters. What do you expect?'

Jude thought about his cousins—three sisters who were so close they could practically read each other's mind. 'I guess all sibling relationships are different.'

'You're an only child,' she pointed out, and Jude felt a small jolt as he realised she'd remembered that small fact about him. 'What would you know?'

She was right, he supposed. He'd had Gareth, but that wasn't the same. They'd grown up together, sure, but they hadn't had the same parents, lived the same life in the same place, not until they were eighteen.

'So tell me,' he suggested.

Rosa sighed. 'Anna and I…there's only two years between us, but sometimes it feels more like decades.'

'You're not very alike?'

'Physically? Sure—we both look like Mama, in case you hadn't noticed.'

He tried to remember what Anna looked like; he'd only met her briefly a couple of times since he arrived. Obviously she couldn't look too like Rosa or he might have noticed sooner. 'I suppose…' he said, slowly. 'I mean, yes, you look like Sancia. And so does Anna. And yet, I never looked at Anna and thought she looked like you.' And he would have done. He'd spent three years looking for Rosa in strangers.

'Dad used to say that when you looked at the two of us in photos we could be twins,' Rosa said, sounding a little wistful. 'It was only when you saw us in motion that it became clear we were completely different people.'

Jude tilted his head to look at Rosa, taking in her slouched posture, one ankle resting on her knee. Her long, dark hair hung over one shoulder in some sort of complicated braid, and she was watching him from under long, dark lashes.

She was trying to look relaxed, he realised. And maybe to other people she'd look that way. But Jude could almost feel the tension coming off her in waves—the same as last night.

With another sigh, she sat upright again, leaning her elbows forward onto the patio table. 'The thing is, Anna was always Dad's favourite. She's just like him, really— all academic and serious and organised and stuff. And me, I'm more like Mama. A free spirit.'

'That's why you don't get on?' Jude asked. 'Too different?'

'Partly.' She bit her lip, bright white teeth sharp against

the lushness of her mouth. Jude felt a jolt of lust rush through him as he remembered the last time he'd seen her do that. She'd been sitting astride him at the time...

He swallowed. Hard. 'What else?' Focussing on the facts, that was what mattered now.

He was going to learn why Rosa left him. He was going to understand, finally, the terrible string of events that led to Gareth's death. And then he was going to turn around and leave her, and any influence she had on his life, behind. Move on himself, at last. That was the plan and he was sticking to it. Memories be damned.

'My mother left us. I must have told you that?' She looked at him, waited for him to nod a confirmation before she carried on. 'Before then life was...balanced, I guess. Dad would spend all his time at the university, or in his study, only appearing to complain about the state of the house, or to try and install some sort of order into our lives. And Mama...she just concentrated on us all being happy. She didn't care if we arrived at the beach without the picnic, or our swimming costumes. We'd have ice cream for lunch and swim in our knickers.'

'They were the ultimate in opposites attracting, then?' Jude guessed.

'Pretty much.' Rosa gave him a lopsided smile. 'But it worked, you know? At least, until it didn't.'

'What happened?'

Rosa sighed. 'Can we walk while I tell this story? I talk better when I'm moving.'

He remembered that, Jude realised. All those nights cramped on the tour bus, and it was always him whispering secrets and telling his soul. Rosa only started to talk when they escaped—when they ran down Southend pier at night together, or explored the streets of London, just the two of them. That was when he got to hear the inner workings of Rosa's heart.

'Where do you want to go?' he asked, getting to his feet.

Rosa had already jumped up, and was halfway down the track. 'To the sea, of course,' she said, the words tossed back over her shoulder.

Jude didn't mention that he'd had enough of the sea on his crossing from the mainland, or that his bungalow was right next to the shore. Why wasn't he surprised that Rosa—shiftless, always moving Rosa—was drawn to the ocean, with all its ebbs and flows and tides?

At least the sea was predictable, to a point. Except for tsunamis and stuff.

Even they seemed more predictable than Rosa.

Jude kept quiet and waited for her to start talking again as they walked. He caught up easily, and walked beside her on the narrow path that wound across the island, down to the shore.

Eventually, she spoke.

'When Mama left…she didn't exactly walk out. That's not Mama's style, really—a monumental decision and a fight and a definite end.'

'So what did she do?' Jude couldn't quite quash the hope that somewhere in the story of why Sancia left Ernest Gray would be the explanation for her daughter's hit-and-run attitude.

'She came here, to La Isla Marina, for a holiday.' Rosa's smile was too tight, too fixed. 'It was only supposed to be for a week or two. She left Anna and me with Dad.'

'How old were you?'

'Sixteen. Anna was eighteen. About to sit her A-levels.'

'And you must have had your GCSEs,' Jude pointed out.

'Yeah. But they didn't matter in the same way. Anna

was always the academic one.' Rosa shook her head. 'Anyway. Two weeks turned into a month. Mama said that our grandparents needed her help—that running the resort was too much for them now they were getting older. And it wasn't a lie—I mean, you saw this place when you arrived. But…somehow, she just never came home again.'

Jude's heart ached for this girl who'd lost the only family member who made her feel as if she belonged. 'I can't imagine how that must have hurt.'

Rosa shrugged. 'It wasn't so much Mama leaving, I don't think. I mean, I visited her out here every holiday and, to be honest, the weeks I spent here on the island were the happiest I remember. And *she* was so much happier here. It wasn't until she left that I saw the truth—how unhappy, how stifled she'd been in Oxford, surrounded by people who needed academic proofs and publications to back up their every feeling.'

'People like Anna and your dad.'

'Exactly! Mama was never like that. She was all impulse and fun and living life in colour. She needed to be free.'

'Like you.' Because that was always how he'd remembered Rosa. Full colour. Even when he felt stuck in black-and-white noir.

'Maybe.' She gave him a sidelong look. 'Anyway, with Mama gone, it was just Dad and Anna. And Dad retreated back into his office again, so Anna took over everything else. Running the household, organising Dad, and ordering me around.'

Jude winced. 'I'm guessing that didn't go down so well with you.'

'You guess right.' Rosa sighed. 'The worst thing is, now, with ten years of hindsight, I can't even blame her completely. We were both trying to cope with a monumental change in our lives, and I guess we each did it differently. But then… I just felt so hemmed in and frustrated. Before then, we'd always got on well. Yes, we were different, but we were sisters and we were close. It was us against the parents, you know? But when Mama left…'

'It was you against Anna.'

'And it has been ever since.' Rosa pushed a last, stray branch out of their path, then moved ahead of him, her long braid swaying in time to her hips. It was almost hypnotising. As if she could take over his mind just in the way she moved. Which, on past evidence, wasn't entirely untrue. 'We haven't spoken in three years, now.'

Then she stopped in front of him, so suddenly he almost crashed into her. Jude's hands came up, ready to grab her hips for balance, but at the last moment he realised the insanity of that plan and held onto the nearest tree, instead.

Rosa breathed in deeply, her shoulders moving with the motion. 'I miss the sea, when I'm away. Other oceans don't smell quite the same.'

'It must be strange to be home, with your whole family here.' Jude let Rosa step out onto the small beach in the cove they'd arrived at. It was secluded, idyllic and, under other circumstances, wildly romantic.

'Very,' Rosa admitted. 'There are so many memories tied up in this place…' She trailed off, then gave a low laugh.

'What?'

'Talking of memories, I just realised where we are,' she said. 'This is the beach where I lost my virginity.'

# CHAPTER FIVE

ROSA REGRETTED IT the moment she said it. *When* would she learn to think before she spoke? When she was little, her father had always told her she needed to learn that lesson more than any other, before she grew up. Now she was twenty-six, she was starting to think that it might be a permanent condition.

What else could explain her impulse to mention sex in front of the one man she was busy pretending she had never slept with?

She glanced quickly at Jude's face, looking away almost instantly to stare out over the sea. This was one of her favourite spots on the island—always had been. That was why she'd chosen it for what she'd imagined would be a memorable night—her first time.

It was memorable, she supposed, if not entirely for the right reasons. It had basically been a disaster.

Much like the conversation she felt coming.

Jude came to stand beside her, close enough that his arm brushed against hers. His skin was too pale, Rosa thought, looking at it next to her own. As if he'd been locked away somewhere, forced to make music and never see sunlight.

No wonder he'd felt he needed to run away to a sunny island in the middle of nowhere.

'Talking about sex,' Jude said, his voice soft, his gaze fixed on the horizon. 'Are we ever going to?'

'Have sex?' Rosa's voice came out squeaky, even as she realised that *of course* that wasn't what he meant.

'Talk about it. What happened between us.' He turned his head to look at her, and his bright blue gaze seemed to see right through her clothes, her skin, deep into the heart of her.

That was the problem with Jude. He always saw too deep.

'Why you left,' he added, and Rosa broke away from his gaze.

'Do we have to?' she asked, kicking at the sand with the front of her flip-flop.

Jude's cool fingers came under her chin, lifting her face so she had to look at him again. 'Rosa... I can't help but think that I'm here on this island for a reason. To find closure, on all kinds of things—starting with what happened between us, and everything that happened afterwards. And if you want us to work together on this wedding, I think we're going to have to, you know...'

'Have the talk.' Rosa sighed. Why couldn't she have fallen for one of the roadies, or even one of his bandmates like Jimmy, three years ago? Most men she met would run a thousand miles rather than talk about their feelings—which suited Rosa just fine, thanks.

But no, she had to go and fall for the sensitive artist. The one person who wanted to *understand* her.

Even if she didn't want to be understood. Even if she didn't understand herself, sometimes.

'I'll do you a deal,' Jude said, his voice more normal suddenly—as if they weren't talking about sex and love any more. 'You tell me what happened that night—why you left, and why you never came back. You help me understand that, and we never have to talk about it again, okay? We can just be acquaintances—friends, even—spending time together on a holiday island. Okay?'

'Okay,' Rosa said, slowly. It sounded good, she had to admit.

The only problem was, for all her brave words, she couldn't imagine ever being friends with Jude Alexander. Not after what they'd shared.

But she was willing to try if he was.

Taking a few steps forward towards the sea, she kicked off her flip-flops and sat on the edge of the sand, letting the waves lap over her toes.

Leaning back on her hands, Rosa shut her eyes. The warm sun on her skin felt like home. Like love.

'So,' she asked, her eyes still closed. 'What do you want to know?'

She felt rather than saw Jude settle beside her, and wondered if he'd taken off his shoes, too. Maybe even rolled up those dark linen trousers. He might have a slender, rock-star frame, but his shoulders were broader than you'd think, and there were muscles on that frame, too, she remembered. Could almost see through his thin white shirt if she didn't concentrate on not looking…

She opened her eyes. Jude had his bare feet in the water, just like her. Rosa smiled. Good. He needed to relax more.

'Was it something I did?' he asked, staring out at the sea. 'Or did you just not feel the same way I did?'

Rosa swallowed, tasting regret in her mouth. 'How did you feel?'

'Like magic had walked into my life, the moment I met you,' Jude said, simply. 'Like I'd been waiting for you for centuries.'

Guilt pierced through Rosa's heart. She knew exactly what he meant, and *of course* she'd felt it, too. But how could she tell him that was the whole problem? That sort of perfection wasn't meant for the mess that was her. She'd screw it up sooner or later, and sooner was better, in her experience.

'And that's why you're the songwriter of the two of us,' she joked, her heart breaking as she said it. 'You can take a tour-bus fling and make it into poetry.'

'Is that all we were?' Jude shifted on the sand so he could look at her, almost lying down on his side as he spoke. 'A tour-bus fling?'

God, but it was so tempting to curl up there with him, safe in his arms. But Rosa knew she might not have the strength to leave them twice.

'We knew each other for four weeks, Jude,' she reminded him, gently.

'I knew all I needed to in the first day.'

She remembered. Remembered the way their eyes had met and she'd just *known*. Known that this man was going to be important.

Rosa didn't believe in love at first sight, but if she had…

She shook her head. What difference did it make if it was love or not? That didn't change everything else that it was.

A burden. A chain. A prison.

She'd seen what happened when a woman fell in love—so deeply in love that she gave up all her own dreams and moved to Oxford to live his life, instead of hers. She'd seen her mother live it, so she didn't have to. Twenty years of frustration and bitterness, followed by her finally leaving for her island refuge.

Rosa had known, even then, that she wasn't willing to live that life. Wasn't willing to compromise her own dreams one bit to live someone else's.

She needed to end this now. She needed to tell Jude enough to get him to stop asking—to give him his closure. Then they could both move on, and she'd be as free of him as he was of her.

That was what she wanted. It was all she ever wanted: freedom.

'I told you why at the time,' she said. 'I had to come home for my *abuelo*—for my grandfather's—funeral.'

'Except you didn't tell me where home was,' Jude reminded her. 'Or that you weren't coming back.'

And there was the sticking point. She hadn't really known that, at the time. It was only once she was out of Jude's sphere, without his smile or his hands or his eyes influencing her decisions, that she realised the risk. When she knew that she had to stay away.

That, and a terrifying two weeks when her body told her she might have made a monumental, life-changing mistake, that first, impulsive night she'd spent with him.

As she'd waited, too scared to even buy a pregnancy test and know for sure, too distraught dealing with all the funeral stuff to even really think about it, one thing had been abundantly clear to her.

If she went back to Jude when she left La Isla Marina, that would be it. If four weeks in each other's company, in his bed, could have this kind of impact on her life, her heart, then going back would be a life sentence.

She'd fall irrevocably in love with him, and never be able to break away. She'd live her mother's life—following him around the world as he toured, always being his plus one, and never finding her own life, her own self. Her own happiness.

Or worse, she'd be Anna—managing Jude's personal life as Anna managed Dad's, giving up her own opportunities and possibilities to him.

She couldn't do that. Couldn't sacrifice all her dreams for his dream of stardom.

And she'd had no doubt that Jude would be a star—anyone who'd heard The Swifts play had known that it was only a matter of time before they made it big. And Jude and Gareth, they'd made a pact, when they were barely teenagers, that one day they'd be famous together. They'd escape all the people who told them they'd never make anything of themselves, the families and schools who told them it was impossible. They were going to conquer the world together—and they'd already been so close, when Rosa met them. She knew it wouldn't be long until the name Jude Alexander was on everyone's lips.

Would he even want her around, then? When beautiful women were throwing themselves at him, and every door was open to him?

By the time her cycle had returned—delayed by stress, rather than her carelessness in bed with Jude, it seemed—the funeral was long over and Rosa had made a decision.

She needed to find her own life, her own happiness. She wouldn't make her mother's mistakes all over again, falling for a man whose career would always come first, who would forget she existed for weeks at a time.

And so she'd run as far away as she could—and ended up back here with him three years later, anyway.

Looking at him, Rosa knew the risk was still there. If she let herself get too close to Jude, let herself hope, she could fall anyway, despite all the distance she'd put between them. And if she gave him a hint that she still felt that way…

So she had to lie. Or at least, not tell the whole truth.

'Honestly?' she said, knowing she was being anything but honest. 'I hadn't decided when I left what I was going to do next. But then an opportunity came up for a new commission out in the Middle East, and it sounded interesting so…' She shrugged. 'You know me. I like to keep moving, finding new experiences, seeking out the next big thing.'

Jude grabbed her hand suddenly, making her turn to face him, staring into her eyes as if he could see the truth behind them. Rosa held her nerve, ignoring her heart beating too fast in her chest, and let him look. Nothing she had said was *technically* untrue, after all.

'So, is that what I was?' Jude asked, after a moment. 'Just another new experience?'

No. He'd been *the* experience. The one she judged every other moment of her life against. And all too often found them lacking.

No other man had ever lived up to four weeks with Jude. And yes, she'd had regrets, had imagined what could have been.

And he couldn't know that. Because regrets didn't change anything. The only way she knew how to move was forward.

Rosa gave an apologetic shrug, and Jude dropped her hand.

'So, does every experience have to be new?' He'd gone back to staring at the sea again now, and Rosa's heart had started to settle back down to a normal rhythm. Maybe that was why she didn't think carefully enough about her response. As usual.

'Some are worth experiencing twice,' she admitted, her words coming out soft and husky.

Jude's gaze snapped back to hers, and she saw the lust there. The want. The *need*.

And the worst thing was she was almost sure her eyes were reflecting the same feelings right back at him.

Rosa leapt to her feet. 'Right! We should get back to work.'

'Work.' Jude shook his head. 'Sure.'

She'd given him the answers he wanted, and now he owed her his help with this damn wedding.

And if Rosa wished she could have told him the truth?
She'd get over it. She'd move on.

She always did.

Jude stared at the room full of boxes, all with comprehensive shipping labels stuck on them.

Somehow, the resolution he'd made to be all business with Rosa was coming back to bite him. He'd *almost* rather live through that soul-crushing conversation with Rosa on the beach all over again than sort through fifty boxes of wedding decorations and accessories.

But only almost. He wasn't sure he could take hearing Rosa tell him how he was just one more experience again.

It wasn't as if he hadn't known she was a free spirit back then—it was one of the things he liked most about her, the way she surged forward after her own life, not caring about schedules or plans or what other people thought.

She was the way he'd always thought *he* was, until he realised how much of his life was organised by other people.

Music—that was supposed to be the ultimate freedom, wasn't it? Creating something from nothing, something from inside the soul, something that touched millions of others. It was supposed to be his escape—from a town with no work, a father who told him he was a waste of space and a school that told him he had no future. He and Gareth had dreamed of the day they'd prove them all wrong—and they'd never doubted they could do it, together.

Music was *their* thing. The one thing in the world that no one could take away from them. But then the world, and addiction, had taken Gareth away from him. Maybe that was why he felt sometimes as if it wasn't his at all, any more.

That was why he'd come to La Isla Marina—to find his freedom again. The fact that he'd found the one person chaining him to his memories of the past was beside the point.

Jude knew it all came down to what happened with Gareth. It was all tangled together in his head—the promise he'd made, and broken. If Rosa hadn't been there, he'd have seen the signs sooner. He'd have been at whichever party it was when Gareth decided just one more hit wouldn't hurt. He'd have noticed one becoming two becoming every night again.

Gareth had overdosed less than a month after Rosa left, and Jude knew that if he hadn't been so focussed on his own pain during that month he would have noticed Gareth's. The events were all tied up together, running together like two melodies in his head, twisting together to make a new song. However much he told himself that Gareth's addiction wasn't his fault, wasn't Rosa's fault for leaving, he knew he was the only person in the world who could have stopped it.

He knew he'd always blame himself for his friend's death, more than the drugs that had caused it. Because when Gareth had needed him, Jude had been too caught up in Rosa to even notice. He'd broken the most important promise he'd ever made—the promise he'd made in that hospital room, a year before Gareth died, that he'd be there for him. That he'd keep his friend safe.

He shook his head, and tried to focus on the task in hand. Gareth was gone. All Jude could do now was live their dream for both of them. Enjoy the success Gareth had craved, and the high life he'd looked forward to so much. Show the world that had dismissed them that they could do anything—even if the price they had to pay seemed far, far too high.

And as for Rosa... He had the closure he'd asked for, at last. He knew why she left—however much he didn't like it.

Now he had to keep up his end of the bargain. Which apparently involved wedding decorations and accessories.

'Did you count them yet?' Rosa asked, clipboard in hand. 'Anna's notes say there should be fifty.'

'What could Valentina possibly need for her wedding that requires fifty boxes?' Jude asked as he started counting again. Just the sight of Rosa in her tight jeans, rolled up to show off slim ankles, and her close-fitting white T-shirt was enough to make him lose count.

'Everything, according to these lists.' Rosa stared at the clipboard with disgust. 'My sister and her bloody lists.'

'When is Anna getting back? And it's definitely fifty, by the way.' Jude pointed to the boxes when she looked confused.

'Of course it is. Just like on the list.' Rosa ticked something off, and scowled at it again. 'Mama says she and Leo should be back this afternoon. With a full report of the catering staff that Valentina's flying in from Barcelona.' Perhaps her sister's imminent return explained Rosa's bad mood.

'This is going to be quite the wedding, huh?'

Jude opened the first box to find string after string of fairy lights, all neatly wrapped around pieces of card. The next box revealed larger lanterns to house candles, and the one after that the candles themselves.

'Is Valentina expecting some sort of power cut?' he asked, motioning towards the boxes.

Rosa laughed. 'Sort of. She wants a very traditional

Spanish wedding, apparently—which means it doesn't start until the evening and it goes on all night long. And since it's all taking place outside…'

'Hence the candles.'

'Exactly.'

Rosa perched herself on the edge of the nearest box, sitting gingerly until she was certain it could take her weight. She'd pushed her sunglasses onto the top of her head, and her usual heavy plait hung over her shoulder. Jude couldn't help but watch her. What was it about her that drew his eye, even after everything? Even now he knew the risk of getting caught up in Rosa again?

She was beautiful, of course. Maybe even more beautiful than she'd been three years ago. She'd been fresher then, he supposed, but there was a new worldliness about her now that he liked.

The tension he'd noticed on the first day was still there, tight in the lines of her shoulders and her mouth, for all that she kicked her feet casually back and forth. She chewed a pencil as she stared down at her clipboard.

'Okay, so as far as I can tell, this is what's happening. The bridal party arrive on the Wednesday, for general wedding prep and whatever it is bridesmaids do before a wedding.'

'Drink, mostly, I think,' Jude said. 'Have you never been a bridesmaid?'

Rosa looked at him as if he were crazy. 'Aren't they supposed to organise things and commit to being in the country on the right day and stuff? Who on earth would ask me to do that?'

'Good point,' he allowed. Rosa wasn't the woman you went to for commitment. He had the heartbreak to prove it.

'Anyway, the groom and his family and groomsmen arrive on Friday night, then the wedding is on the Saturday evening, so that whole day will probably be pretty hellish with last-minute traumas. If you wanted to run, I'd suggest you do it then.'

She was watching him from under her lashes, Jude realised. Waiting to see what his reaction to the idea of leaving was.

Did that mean she wanted him to stay? What had she said last night? *Some are worth experiencing twice.* Well. If that wasn't a hint…

'I'm not going anywhere,' he said, cursing himself a little as he did so. What was he doing, promising to stay for the woman who'd been running from him for three years?

'Want to stay and see the ex-girlfriend, huh?' Rosa asked, and Jude realised he'd actually forgotten for a moment that staying would mean seeing Sylvie.

'Not really.' Especially since thinking about her still made his blood boil.

'You said it was a bad breakup?'

'She fabricated stories about me to sell for the stupid kiss-and-tell book about me.' Of course, the made-up ones were easier to laugh off than the true, private ones she'd also sold. The ones where she'd talked about Gareth, and his remorse and guilt over his death. The broken promise. Those were the ones that hurt the most.

Gareth was no one's business except his.

'*The Naked Truth* thing?' Rosa winced. 'Ouch.'

'Yeah. The book came out this week.'

'Which is why you decided to be on a remote Spanish island at the time.'

'Exactly.'

'Except now your fantastically twisted love life is following you here,' Rosa commented.

Jude shot her a look. 'In more ways than one.'

'Well, you said you wanted closure.' Jumping down from the box she was sitting on, Rosa busied herself with sorting through a box full of orders of service and menus and such, sending them flying into haphazard piles on the other boxes. Jude foresaw a lot of resorting them in his future.

A figure appeared across the courtyard: Anna. Rosa's sister picked her way carefully past the reflecting pool towards them.

'Looks like you have some closure coming your way, too,' Jude said, nodding towards her.

Rosa spun round, then froze as she spotted Anna. The tension that had been hidden under casual, forced relaxation was suddenly obvious to all—but only for a moment. As Jude watched he could see Rosa purposefully relaxing her shoulders, her arms, as Anna grew closer. She took a few lazy steps towards her sister, then hopped up to sit on the large wooden table Sancia used for breakfasts, leaning back on her hands and waiting, letting Anna come the rest of the way to her.

Jude busied himself with the boxes, hoping it wasn't too obvious that he was eavesdropping.

They didn't hug. That was the first thing he noticed as the sisters greeted each other. What had Rosa said? That it had been three years since they'd last spoken.

He wondered if it was a coincidence that her last conversation with Anna must have been around the same time as she left him. Or was there more to the story than she'd told him before?

'You made it back, then,' Rosa said. 'I thought you might decide to just stay in Barcelona with this Leo I've heard so much about from Mama.'

'Not really my style, abandoning the family when they

need me.' Anna's tone was mild, but Jude could hear a bite behind it.

'Right.' Rosa heard it, too, judging by the tightness of her reply. 'Mama gave me my chore list, by the way.'

'Good. Any problems?'

'Other than the fact I'd be much more use to Mama out on the island, dealing with stuff, than stuck going through lists of bungalow allocations and boxes of fairy lights.'

Anna looked past her and her gaze alighted on Jude, who looked away quickly. He did *not* want to get drawn into a sibling squabble. It was the only advantage he'd found to being an only child—and besides, bandmate squabbles were bad enough for him.

'Looks like you've found someone to palm some of the work off onto already, anyway,' Anna said, drily. 'Why am I not surprised?'

'Well, since you were off gallivanting with your Latin lover, I had to work with what I had.' Jude hadn't expected Rosa to go into the details of their complicated history, but hearing himself resigned to leftover help stung a little all the same.

'As long as it all gets done.' Anna turned away. 'Let me know if you can't manage any of it.' She tossed the words back over her shoulder as she walked away, and Jude saw Rosa's hands clench up into fists before they relaxed again.

'You okay?' he asked softly, once they were alone again.

Rosa spun round so fast he wondered if she'd forgotten he was there. Again.

'I'm fine.' Her clipped words said otherwise, but Jude didn't call her on it. Not yet, anyway. 'Come on. Leave this. We're going sailing.'

# CHAPTER SIX

ROSA DIDN'T WAIT for Jude as she stormed down to the jetty. He'd catch her up if he wanted to come with her, and if he didn't she'd go alone.

So, it seemed that regular sex with a man Sancia had described as a hunky pirate hadn't mellowed Anna out any—which probably meant nothing could. She was still the big sister who thought she could run her life, who would always highlight her perceived mistakes and ignore her successes. Rosa didn't know why she'd imagined for a moment that three years apart would have changed anything.

The hardest part was, even now Rosa could see that eighteen-year-old Anna had only been trying to hold the family together after Mama left, it seemed that twenty-eight-year-old Anna still thought Rosa was the sixteen-year-old little sister she'd got used to bossing about. She still didn't trust her to take care of anything herself, not really. She had to control and manage everything, because only *Anna* could get it right.

Of course, some of that might be more to do with their argument three years ago…

Rosa shook her head. She wasn't thinking about that now.

The small boats the resort kept for guests to borrow

to sail over to the mainland were all neatly tied up along the jetty, each looking freshly scrubbed and cleaned—which made Rosa scowl even more. Just extra evidence of all St Anna's hard work.

She squeezed her eyes tight and tried to get a grip on her temper. She was better than this. Older and if not wiser, at least more rational. She'd seen sights all over the world that others couldn't imagine, highlighted horrific situations to the public, and uncovered forgotten treasures with her work. She was *not* going to let herself get all riled up by her sister's martyr complex. That was just one of many things she'd decided to break free from when she'd left Britain, three years before.

The other main thing she'd broken free from caught her up pretty quickly, standing beside her as they stared at the boats.

'So, where are we going?' Jude asked, and Rosa realised that you couldn't leave everything behind, every time.

Sometimes you had to stand and face them.

But not Anna. Not today.

'The mainland,' she said, choosing a dinghy and starting to prep it to sail. 'There's a little seaside village, Cala del Mar, just across the way. It has the best tapas outside of Barcelona. Also, wine.'

'Then let's go,' Jude said, stepping aboard.

He let her get a little way away from the island before he started asking questions, which she appreciated.

'So, you and Anna. Any more you wanted to tell me about that?'

'Not really.' Mostly all she wanted to do was get away from the island for a while. Even a few days there had left her feeling claustrophobic, in a way living in a tent in a war zone or an unexplored rainforest never did.

'Because I realised something. If it's been three years since you last spoke to her, that must have been around the same time I last saw you.'

He was fishing. Suddenly Rosa regretted bringing Jude along. She'd hoped they were done talking about their past relationship, now she'd given him the closure he'd asked for, but apparently he wanted more.

'It was at my Grandfather's funeral, actually.' The mention of death usually shut people up.

Not Jude. 'A difficult, emotional time for you, then.'

Sighing, Rosa turned to face him. He lounged, pale and beautiful, against the back of the boat. His sharp cheekbones and brooding eyes that looked so perfect on album covers looked oddly out of place here on the water, as if he were a being from another world.

In a way, he was, she supposed. The world of celebrity, a million miles away from La Isla Marina, before this week. Now it looked as if it was going to be packed with them.

Hopefully none of the others would be so interested in her past.

'Look, why don't you just ask whatever it is you want to know?' Rip the plaster off and get it over with, that was her way of dealing with difficult things. Anna, as always, disagreed, most of the time.

'I just thought you might like to talk about it,' Jude said, mildly. 'I mean, whatever that last conversation was, it was clearly a corker.'

It had been. Fireworks and hateful words and dramatics all together. The culmination of seven years of frustration and lack of understanding. Of Anna never listening to Rosa's feelings, Anna always knowing best and Rosa always screwing up.

Rosa sank down to sit on the little bench at the front

of the boat, where she could keep steering, but slowed them to an almost stop so they just bobbed in the water. She needed her full attention for this conversation.

Maybe it would help to talk about it. If she could explain her side of the story, and have someone understand, maybe she'd stop feeling so damn guilty about it.

'Like I said, Anna and I had both come to the island for our *abuelo*'s funeral. Anna was fretting about leaving Dad home alone, which was ridiculous, because he's a grown, intelligent man who should be able to take care of himself.'

'But she thinks he can't?' Jude asked.

'Apparently. But it seems to me that if he can run his department, organise his research and make a career as a semi-famous Oxford academic, then he is perfectly capable of arranging his own meals and remembering to take his pills.'

'Pills?'

Rosa waved a hand. 'A preventative measure. He has a heart condition—has had it for years—so he has to take a few tablets to keep it under control.'

'And Anna makes sure he does?'

'Well, yes. Because she's St Anna and she wants to have everyone rely on her and say how wonderful she is.'

Jude tilted his head as he watched her, and Rosa looked away. She didn't like that knowing look in his eye. 'Do you really believe that?'

'No,' Rosa admitted, talking down to the bottom of the boat. 'I don't. But I think she's got so used to controlling everyone and everything she doesn't know how to stop. And I think Dad takes advantage of that. He likes having her to deal with all the boring things he doesn't want to have to think about—like how food gets in the cupboard, or how the house gets clean. He likes having his

pills waiting for him by his breakfast plate in the morning, so he can pretend they're just vitamins and that he's
fine. He likes Anna looking after him because it means
he doesn't have to look after himself. You know, his cardiologist told him four years ago that if he changed his
diet, exercised more and started cutting down his hours
at work, he might be able to reduce the amount of medi-
cation he's on. But he wouldn't do it. Anna managed to
sneak in some more healthy meals—although he still
eats nothing but red meat and red wine when he dines at
the college, I'm sure. And she bullies him into taking a
walk now and then. But he won't even *talk* about retiring.'

'I've only known your father a week or so, but from
playing Scrabble with him I can confirm that he is a
very stubborn man.' Jude shifted, leaning forward with
his elbows resting on his knees as he looked at her. 'So
you were mad with Anna for letting your dad take advantage of her?'

'Sort of.' Rosa looked out over the water, back towards La Isla Marina, and thought of the real reason
Anna hated her.

'Something else happened,' Jude guessed.

'Yeah.' Taking a deep breath, Rosa let herself remember that horrible night. 'She'd been offered a visiting pro-
fessorship at Harvard, just for the semester, starting the
term after the funeral. She wanted to take it, of course,
but she—' She cut herself off.

'She didn't want to leave your dad alone,' Jude said.
Rosa nodded. 'She asked you to stay with him?'

'She said that if I was there to take care of him, she'd
feel like she could go. And it just made me so mad—not
that she wanted me to stay home, but that she was putting her whole life on hold for a man who just saw her as
a combination of nursemaid, housekeeper, chef and oc-

casional replacement for the wife who'd left him at college functions. He always said how proud he was of her career, but he was holding her back—by not taking responsibility for his own health and well-being.'

A niggling whisper in the back of her brain reminded Rosa that their father had been abandoned when Sancia left, too. That he'd been trying to cope, just as Anna had, just as she had. That he'd wanted to keep the family he had left close.

But that wasn't enough of an excuse for stifling Anna's whole life, was it?

'What did you say?'

'I told her that she should go anyway. That I couldn't stay with him—let's be honest, I wouldn't have been any good at doing all the stuff Anna did for him, anyhow.' Rosa knew her limitations. If she'd been forced to babysit her father for three months, one of them would have moved out within the first few days for sure. 'But that she shouldn't feel tied down by him. He's a grown man, not her responsibility any more.'

'She didn't go to Harvard, did she?'

Rosa shook her head, deflating from her righteous indignation. 'No. She stayed there and put her life on hold for him, like always. And I...'

'Ran to the other side of the world to get away from me.'

'Not just you,' Rosa admitted, meeting his gaze for the first time since the conversation started. To her amazement, she saw understanding there, rather than judgement. 'Like you said, it was an emotional time.'

'It sounds it.' Cautiously—he obviously wasn't used to being on the water—Jude crossed the boat towards her, crouching in front of her and taking her hand. 'I can understand why Anna would be mad and disappointed, but that doesn't mean you were wrong. If anything, it seems to me like you were trying to help her.'

'Not very well, it seems.' She blinked, hard, to try and stop the prickling behind her eyes. She was *not* going to cry about this. Especially in front of Jude.

'Oh, I don't know,' Jude said, giving her a small smile. 'I mean, it might have taken her a while, but she came here, didn't she? She left Oxford to come and help out your mum.'

'Dragging Dad after her for the good of his health,' Rosa pointed out. 'But maybe you're right. It's a start.'

And maybe Leo could be the next step for Anna. She should find out some more about him. Make sure he wasn't just going to take over Anna's life in their father's place.

But for now… Rosa looked down at Jude. He had the same look Anna had sometimes—the tightness around the eyes and the tenseness of the shoulders that told her he was trying too hard for the wrong things. He'd never looked like that three years ago. Then he'd been all enthusiasm and excitement—and loose-limbed, bone-deep satisfaction in bed afterwards.

No. She wasn't thinking about that. She was thinking as a friend, not an ex-lover.

And as a friend, she could see that Jude needed to cut loose a bit. Maybe she was the one who could help him lighten up.

'You know, you're far too pale for this place. Come on. Let's go get tapas and wine and sit in the sunshine for a while.'

Cala del Mar was a perfect, sleepy seaside fishing village. Jude strolled along the seafront with Rosa at his side and wondered if he'd be happier somewhere like this, than in

New York City. Rosa certainly seemed content enough—but he suspected that, like everything else in Rosa's life, would only last until she got bored.

And he had promises to keep. Music to make. And Gareth's memory to preserve, out there in the real world.

Fishing boats still bobbed out on the waves, under the slowly fading sunlight that sparkled and shone on the water. The air was warm around them and, for a moment, Jude could almost let himself believe that he was here with Rosa, celebrating their three-year anniversary or something—instead of as wary acquaintances working together on a celebrity wedding.

'The place I wanted to show you is up here,' Rosa said, leading him to a narrow flight of steep stone steps that wound up between the tiny painted cottages and shops into the heart of the village. The walls either side of the stairs were cold and damp, their location meaning they were permanently in shadow. Jude kept his gaze firmly on Rosa's swaying plait as they climbed, refusing to look lower, or let him think about all the things this evening wasn't.

It wasn't a date, however it felt. It wasn't even an opportunity. He'd learned that lesson too well the first time.

The tapas place Rosa led him to barely even qualified as a restaurant. It had two tables inside by the bar, and another three out on the balcony, looking out over the seafront. Rosa chatted happily in Spanish to the elderly man behind the bar, who welcomed her warmly, and moments later they were seated out at the best balcony table, olives, breads, oil, vinegar and a carafe of red wine between them.

Rosa filled up their glasses. 'Doesn't this feel better already?'

'Much.' It wasn't a lie, not exactly. It *did* feel wonderful to be relaxing in the sunshine with a beautiful woman, with good food and better wine. He just wished he could shake the feeling that it wasn't enough, just being with Rosa this way, unable to take her in his arms and kiss her whenever he wanted.

But then…the story she'd told him about her argument with Anna still pulsed around his head. And he couldn't help wondering, if she hadn't argued with her sister, might Rosa have come back to him? Had she felt that returning to him, to the tour, to his life, would be the same as Anna sticking with their father's life even though she wanted more?

It wouldn't have made any difference, in the long run, he supposed. Rosa there was as distracting as Rosa gone; he still might have missed the signs with Gareth. It was *his* obsession that was to blame there, not Rosa.

But if the argument with Anna *was* why she had left… maybe he could convince her that things were different, now.

Jude leant back in his chair and watched Rosa watch the sea. He didn't dream of for ever with her, not the way his younger self had. He knew she wasn't a for ever kind of girl. Rosa would never stay in one place long enough to be tied down by love—she was too full of life, a free spirit. He wouldn't *want* to contain her that way and make her unhappy.

And like it or not, his real life was waiting for him back in New York, once the furore over the book had died down. He'd go back to the band, to making music he loved, and doing all the things the label expected him to do to keep The Swifts in the public eye and their music selling.

But right now, while they were both here together… could there be a chance for something more between them? An island fling, perhaps, with none of the expectations and hopes he'd placed on them before.

If he could convince Rosa that all he wanted was right now, maybe he could have her in his arms again.

And maybe that would be worth the potential pain of watching her walk away once more. At least this time, he knew it was coming, and could prepare himself for it.

He wasn't angry at her for leaving him, not any more. He understood, even if he didn't like it. But Jude was starting to think that the closure he needed to *truly* move on didn't come in words. It wasn't explanations he needed.

It was touch.

'It's hard to stay mad too long in a place like this, isn't it?' Rosa said, looking back from the sea.

'Yeah,' Jude agreed. 'It is.' Only he wasn't talking about her argument with Anna.

He was imagining how the next two weeks might cure him of that anger and resentment for good.

Rosa had been staring at the guest list so long it had given her a headache. Over the handful of days she and Jude had made good progress with all things organisational for the wedding, but the bungalow allocations were still causing her trouble. Every time she thought she had it sorted, she found another name, or another couple who couldn't be near someone else, or who needed something specific that the bungalow she'd assigned them didn't have. When she added in the constant phone calls from guests to add extra requirements to their bookings, she wanted to throw the stupid clipboard into the sea and head for the airport.

It was, quite frankly, an impossible task. One even

Jude had given up on and disappeared off with his guitar after taking a call from his agent.

Rosa would be ready to admit defeat if doing so didn't mean telling Anna she wasn't up to the job.

And speaking of Anna…after her talk with Jude on the boat, Rosa had been doing a lot of thinking about her sister. And more specifically, about Anna and her new beau. Rosa had done some research, and what she'd learned hadn't made her any more comfortable with Anna's relationship. Leo di Marquez had *quite* the reputation—and it wasn't the good sort. International playboy, gambler and general debauched human being by all accounts, he was most definitely not Anna's usual type. In fact, she could only remember Anna dating anyone vaguely like that once before—and given how that had ended, Rosa didn't look forward to a repeat of the experience.

In the end, she realised she was going to have to talk to her sister. About Leo, and about the room bookings.

What the hell. She needed a walk anyway.

As it turned out, though, she didn't have to go far to find her sister—she was already in the villa reception area. Leaning against the office doorway, Rosa watched Anna staring out towards the courtyard, a soft smile on her face, and wished that she could just let Anna enjoy the fun and relaxation of no-strings sex with a gorgeous man. Except Anna didn't do casual, and the way things were going Rosa was pretty sure her sister was going to end up with a broken heart. Again.

'You're looking all doe-eyed. Does Señor Tall, Dark and Handsome have anything to do with that?' As an opening gambit, it wasn't great, but it got Anna's attention at least. She spun round and glared at Rosa.

Then she replaced the glare with an overly sweet smile. 'None of your business.'

Right. Of course.

'How's the paperwork?' Anna asked. 'Sorted out the wedding guests into rooms yet?'

Rosa's jaw clenched at the reminder. 'I don't understand why you're being so stubborn. You love spreadsheets and solving problems. I love being outside and fixing things. We should just swap…'

'If you'd hadn't arrived over two weeks late then you could have had your pick of jobs. As it was I had to get on and do what needed doing most. You keep going with the wedding planning and helping Mama with the office. It'll do you good to stretch yourself.'

*Still trying to control things for my own good, huh, St Anna?*

Rosa's good intentions faded away as her ire rose at the condemnation in Anna's voice. 'Of course you dropped everything and rushed straight here.'

'It's a good thing I did, look at what your *"stand back and let them make their own mistakes"* plan has achieved. This place was chaos…'

'Chaos until St Anna turned up and fixed it all?' Like always. She had to be the saviour, didn't she?

'Yes. Actually.'

'Dragging Dad with you? Couldn't trust him on his own for a month?' God forbid that anyone be allowed to take control of their own lives for a change.

'Dad turned up on his own.' Anna folded her arms over her T-shirt. 'You do know he nearly died?' she said almost conversationally.

'What?' Rosa's chest tightened. Then she realised Anna had to be exaggerating. 'Nonsense, he looks fine.'

'He looks fine now. He looks fine because he has no stress outside work, his meals are prepared, he takes his pills, he gets reminded to take regular walks. Not because I'm a saint, not because I'm a martyr, but because someone has to do it—and no.' Anna raised her hand as Rosa tried to interrupt. 'Don't tell me he's an adult. I know that. I also know that when he wants to be he's the most organised man alive. But his health isn't a priority, work is. And he would forget, just like Mama forgot to take care of the basics here. So what do I do, Rosa? Swan off to Harvard and let him get ill and Mama sink? Is that your answer?'

Yes. Yes, it was. Because it might not be the perfect answer, but what else was there? How could Anna mortgage her life to their father when he couldn't be bothered to even look after himself?

'I don't understand.' She never had. It didn't make any *sense*. But Anna's words—*nearly died*—echoed through her head again and again. 'I was ten before I realised other families didn't get given their own individual holiday itineraries and checklists two weeks before they went on holiday, and most families didn't stock check their cupboards monthly. How can he not remember to take his pills?' He could, if he wanted to. It was just easier to let Anna do it. That was all. And until she left him to take care of himself, it always would be.

'Things changed after Mama left.' Anna blew a frustrated breath. 'You were still at home then, Rosa. I know how self-centred you are, but surely even you noticed?'

She just couldn't resist getting another jibe in there, could she? Another complaint about how Rosa wasn't as perfect as Anna, and never would be. Really, when you knew you could never live up to expectations, why even try?

'I know you got bossier and more self-righteous than ever. I know you refused to move into halls during term time, staying at home to prove what a good daughter you are. At least until you started seeing that guy, then suddenly we saw another side of Anna…until he dumped you, that is. Then you got even more boring than before.' Rosa ignored the pang of guilt in her chest. This wasn't how she'd meant this conversation to go. But somehow, whenever she was faced with Anna and her perfection, she just lost any cool rationality she'd ever possessed. Why did the people closest to you sometimes bring out your worst side?

'It's always lovely catching up with you, Rosa, but I have a lot to do. Good luck with those spreadsheets.' Anna turned away, and Rosa realised she'd missed her chance. She'd screwed it up again, just as she always did with her sister.

No. This time, she was going to give it one more try.

'I'm just worried about you, Anna,' she said, and her voice stopped Anna in her tracks. 'Leo di Marquez isn't the kind of man you're used to…'

'I'm more than capable of handling Leo, thank you,' Anna said, dismissively.

'I just don't want a repeat of the Sebastian situation. I mean, he was an utter idiot, and Leo doesn't appear to be quite so arrogant, or as sleazy, but he broke you, Anna. I don't want that to happen again.'

Was Anna crying? No. Rosa couldn't remember the last time she'd seen her sister do that. 'Sebastian didn't break me, Rosa. I did that all by myself.' And with that, Anna walked away, leaving Rosa alone with her clipboard, and the feeling she might have just made things worse between her and her sister.

'I didn't even know that was possible,' she muttered.

# CHAPTER SEVEN

WITH ONE MORE day to go until Valentina and her bridal party arrived, it seemed that La Isla Marina was almost ready for its sudden brush with celebrity. Jude had to admit, the place was looking a lot better than when he'd arrived. And last time he'd checked, Rosa had *almost* finished the room allocations, which were proving more of a nightmare than either of them had predicted.

He was almost glad of his agent's call as an excuse to get away from helping for a while. Almost.

'What's up, Robyn?' he said, sauntering towards his bungalow and his guitar as he answered.

'When are you coming back?' Robyn asked, bluntly. 'With all the publicity about the book, we need you here, capitalising on that.'

'I think people are perfectly capable of talking about me without me actually being there to hear it.' God knew, they managed it often enough normally.

'Look, Jude, I know you're not happy about some of the things they say in the book—'

'I'm not happy that the book exists at all.'

'But it does. You can't unprint it now, or stop people from reading it.'

'I could sue for defamation,' Jude suggested, although he knew he wouldn't.

'Do you really want to have to go to court and prove which of those stories are lies?' Robyn asked, gently.

Jude sighed. 'No.' Because in doing so, he'd only be confirming that all the others were true. And all the worst ones were, unfortunately. 'I just wish they hadn't written so much about Gareth.' And how Jude had let him down.

His mind flashed back to that day in the hospital, almost a year to the day before Gareth died.

He could still hear Gareth's raspy, exhausted voice saying, *'I know. I know I have to stop. But I need help.'*

And his own reply. *'I'll help. I'll be there every day, reminding you of everything you have to live for. Keeping you out of trouble just like I've always done. I promise.'*

It wasn't the idea of the whole world knowing how he'd betrayed his best friend's trust that upset him. It was seeing that betrayal in black-and-white and knowing that there was nothing he could do about it. No way to change the past, however much he wished he could.

Somehow, the book made it all real, all over again. Just like seeing Rosa again transported him back three years to a time when the only place he could be happy was in her arms.

'I never met him, but from what you've told me about him? Gareth would have loved being the centre of attention in a bestselling book.' Robyn had only become their agent after The Swifts hit the big time. But Gareth was part of the band's legacy, its history, and it had been important to Jude that she know all about him.

Apparently she'd got a pretty good handle on him, after all. 'He'd have been mad the book wasn't all about him.'

'Do you wish it was?'

'If it meant he was still here with us? Definitely. As it is...no.' Bad enough to have his memory raked over the coals in a few early chapters of this book. But a whole book trashing Gareth's memory? Jude couldn't have lived with that.

'Jude…these books don't mean anything. Not really. You know that.'

'I know. I just… Sylvie gave them a lot of those stories, you know?'

'I suspected.' Jude was pretty sure Robyn was wincing on the other end of the line. 'She knows how to play the game, that one.'

'Yeah.' Rosa didn't. Rosa had no idea of the rules of any game but her own. 'Look, Robyn, I've got to go. But if you get lucky, you might get some photos of me online sooner rather than later.'

'Really?' Robyn perked up at the idea. 'Why? Where are you? And who are you with, more to the point? Because if it's a woman, a nice, juicy, romantic scandal would definitely distract from the book…'

Jude laughed, and thought of Rosa. 'I'll see what I can do.'

But not for the publicity. For himself.

To celebrate actually managing to get ready on time, beating all the odds, Sancia had insisted on a family dinner that night—a proper, five-course banquet with matching wines, by all accounts. Jude wasn't exactly sure what he'd done to make Sancia think he was family and issue an invite, but he wasn't about to turn down the spectacular catering at the villa, either. Besides, Rosa would be there, and that was enough for him.

Things had been so busy since their trip to the mainland that the time simply hadn't been right for him to propose any sort of rekindling of their relationship to her. But now, with everything almost sorted, perhaps tonight could be the night. And just because they hadn't been physically intimate, that didn't mean they hadn't grown closer. Working together, seeing each other every day, talking about their lives and families—sometimes, Jude felt closer to Rosa now than when they'd been in the midst of their passionate affair three years ago.

He'd been at a bit of a loss for a hostess gift for the dinner, since Sancia technically already owned everything on the island, but he had brought his guitar, in case he could offer some background entertainment later. He'd been listening to a lot of classical Spanish guitar music since he arrived, playing around with some ideas on the theme, coming up with new threads and melodies that might one day become actual songs. It was kind of exciting, to be working on new music again—just him, messing around with tunes that appealed to him, rather than arguing with the rest of the band about what direction The Swifts should be moving in, musically, and what fitted best with their brand.

Jude didn't want to be a brand. He wanted to be a musician. And here, on La Isla Marina, he almost felt as if he could be, again.

So, anyway, he was looking forward to dinner that evening. At least, until he sat down at the table.

Professor Gray sat at the head of the table on one end, with Sancia at the other. Jude found himself sitting opposite Rosa, either side of her father, with Anna on his left, and Leo opposite her. Straight away, he could feel the tension strung out across the table like the fairy lights hanging overhead.

Rosa didn't look at her dad, he realised. In fact, he wasn't sure he'd seen her talk to him at all since the day she first arrived on the island. He'd been so focussed on her relationship with her sister, he hadn't noticed the fissure between her and her father. But from everything she'd said about him, Jude wasn't really surprised. It was hard to imagine the buttoned-up and structured Professor Gray appreciating the wildness of his younger daughter.

Unfortunately, the situation with Anna didn't look much brighter, given the way she and Rosa were both avoiding each other's gaze.

Anna and Leo spoke quietly across the table, intimate and happy, as they worked their way through the first course. Jude tried to strike up a conversation with Rosa, of the sort they'd been having more often of late, but she was distracted, and he couldn't seem to connect with her. Eventually, he gave up and chatted amiably with Professor Gray about his latest research. As ever, the professor was happy enough to carry on a monologue for most of the meal, so it wasn't as if Jude needed to contribute a lot.

'So, Leo,' Rosa said suddenly, cutting across the other chatter at the table. 'Why *are* you helping out so much for Valentina's wedding?'

The hint was there, Jude realised, behind the question— the idea that Leo must have a prior relationship with the star, or something. What was Rosa trying to do? Drive a wedge between Anna and Leo? He knew she was concerned about Leo's reputation, but watching them together Jude couldn't help but think that Rosa had judged this one wrong. He'd never seen a man so obviously in love as Leo di Marquez.

'Valentina is Leo's half-sister,' Anna said, after a quick glance across the table to confirm it was okay to do so.

Rosa's eyebrows rose up towards her hairline. 'I didn't know she had a brother.'

'Not many people do.' Leo sounded obviously uncomfortable with the situation. 'We didn't grow up together.'

'Do you think she'll be pleased with the island?' Jude asked, trying to get back onto safer topics.

Leo's expression warmed. 'I think she'll love it,' he said, smiling across at Anna as he spoke.

'Oh, it's so lovely to have all my family here once more,' Sancia said, beaming around the table. 'And to see both my girls so happy with their men.'

Jude's gaze flew to Rosa, who stared back, wide-eyed and panicked.

'Oh, we're not—' she started.

As Jude said, 'Actually, we're just friends.'

Sancia didn't reply, just smiled knowingly at them both.

Rosa was silent for the rest of the meal. Jude tried to concentrate on his conversation with Professor Gray, but by the time they finished dessert he wasn't sure he could have said for certain what they'd even been talking about. His attention kept being drawn across the table, to where Rosa sat quiet and subdued, sneaking glances at her sister from time to time.

When Sancia motioned for the coffee and liqueurs to be brought out, Rosa pushed her chair back from the table, mumbling some sort of excuse. Jude watched her go, wondering if he should follow, or if he'd only make things worse. But when he glanced up the table, he saw Sancia staring at him, eyebrows raised, and realised that Rosa's mother, at least, had a clear idea of what was best for her.

'Take these,' she murmured as he passed, and Jude accepted the two wine glasses and the rest of the bottle of red gratefully. He'd take whatever help he could get in trying to understand Rosa.

He found her out on the back veranda, looking out over the far side of the island towards the sea.

'Thinking about escaping?' he asked, handing her a full glass of wine, and placing the bottle on the nearest table.

'Always,' Rosa replied, and Jude thought it might have been the most honest thing she'd ever said to him.

'I'd like it if you'd stay, for a while at least.' He perched on the edge of the table, looking up at her in the shadows of the night. Overhead, the moon was almost full, and he could make out every contour of her face, every uncertainty in her eyes, even in the darkness.

'You know they all think we're sleeping together,' Rosa said, bluntly. 'Mama is probably planning some sort of huge double wedding for me and Anna, even though we're not a couple and Leo is going to walk out and break Anna's heart any day now.'

'You don't know that for sure,' Jude said. Although, given what he'd heard about Leo's reputation, he could see Rosa's point.

'Ah, but you see, I do.' Rosa's smile was sad. 'Leo and me, we're cut from the same cloth, I reckon. Not made to stay. We have to keep moving to keep living.'

'Like sharks,' Jude said, absently remembering a nature documentary he'd watched on some flight to a gig, somewhere or another.

'I bite, too,' Rosa joked.

'I remember.' The words were out before he could even think about them, and instantly the image they conjured up heated his blood.

No wonder her family thought they were together. If his gaze was half as heated as the one she had trained on him, then they must look as if they'd been lovers for years.

Rosa licked her lips, and Jude felt the pressure building inside him. He had to say something. Do something.

He had to have her again—even if she left him to-morrow.

Just one more night with her, that was all he needed.

God, he sounded like Gareth, at the end.

*'Just one more hit. I'll quit tomorrow, Jude, I promise. Just one more. One more for the road...'*

Was he every bit an addict as his friend had been? And while his addiction might not be so deadly, could Jude really say it wouldn't destroy him, all the same?

But then Rosa said, 'Let's go for a swim,' and he stopped thinking altogether.

If he was an addict, maybe he didn't care any more. He needed one more night with Rosa Gray.

She didn't have to ask Jude twice. Whether he'd read her mind, or their mutual lust had just taken over his brain as it seemed to have taken over hers, he abandoned the wine and followed her down to the beach without question.

Rosa didn't think too much about what she was doing. Overthinking wasn't her style—she was more of an impulse person. She went with what her instincts told her were right and, if it went wrong, well, at least she'd been true to herself.

Tonight, she felt as if she was being true to an impulse she'd been denying for three long years. And the relief of it was almost overwhelming.

'There's a cove, just around here,' she said, picking her way over the rocks and out of sight of the villa. She really didn't want any of her family members coming looking for them tonight.

Tonight was about her and Jude. Not them.

She could feel him behind her, feel the heat of him jumping the inch or two of space between them.

Maybe this was inevitable. Maybe, from the moment

she'd first seen him sitting there in the courtyard, as if he'd been waiting for her, they'd been leading to this.

Maybe this was the *real* closure Jude had been looking for.

One more night together. Maybe that was what they both needed to be able to move on.

All Rosa knew was she couldn't have sat at that dinner table any longer, with everyone playing perfect happy families, when she knew what a lie it was. They were all pretending that they were settled, stable, that this was how things would be for ever. But none of that was true. Her parents hadn't been together in ten years—and if she knew them at all, she doubted they'd even talked about why Sancia had left, all those years ago. Nothing had been resolved. Anna and Leo weren't going to live happily ever after, whatever fairy tales Anna was telling herself. Things would get hard and Leo would run, and so would Sancia.

And as for Rosa and Jude…they weren't even ever a couple. Not really.

And they weren't about to start now.

But there was something between them, that much was true. And if she had to stay here on the island and witness all this hypocrisy, at least she could get to explore the fun side of it, too.

Jude knew who she was now. He wouldn't be fooled into thinking she'd stay, this time.

This time, it was all about transient fun. About freedom and enjoyment and letting the wildness inside loose again.

And what was more wild and free than swimming naked in the ocean?

The cove was just as she remembered: tucked away at the back of the island, protected by rocks and cliffs on either side, but with a small crescent-shaped beach in the centre. Rosa hopped down onto the sand, the sea already calling her. Even in the dark, it glistened in the moonlight, open and wide and free.

Without pausing in her stride, Rosa pulled off her top, and heard a sharp intake of breath behind her.

She spun to face Jude, still walking backwards as she fumbled with the clasp of her bra, letting it fall to the sand at her feet.

'Is this safe?' Jude asked, his eyes nowhere near her face.

'Do you care?' she asked, grinning.

'No.'

Rosa pushed her skirt and her underwear down her legs at the same time, stepped out of them and ran for the water, knowing that Jude wouldn't be far behind her.

The sea flowed cool and fresh against her hot skin, the salt stinging and sharp. Rosa welcomed every sensation—the rocks and sand under her feet, the water lapping against her, the breeze that blew loose strands of hair around her face. She stayed, treading water, just far enough out to be out of her depth—just where she liked to be—and watched Jude as he stripped off on the shoreline.

His skin was pale in the moonlight, his hair so dark it was almost lost in the night. But his body...oh, there were those lean, strong muscles she remembered. Those powerful legs, those well-defined arms and abs. That trail of hair that led down his body...

She remembered every inch of him. And she wanted him again.

He didn't flinch as he stepped into the cool water; she admired that. Throwing him a reckless grin, she flipped in the waves, diving underneath and kicking hard until she was further out. Let him chase her, the way he never had when she left.

That thought tugged at something in her mind, but she pushed it away to worry about another day.

Right now, all she wanted to do was enjoy the water on her skin, and Jude—when he caught her.

It didn't take him long.

She surfaced, a short way from where she'd watched him enter the water, and already she could see his powerful arms scything through the waves, propelling him towards her. He was barely even out of breath when he reached her side, treading water next to her as his arms reached out to slide around her waist.

His hands glided over her skin, under the water, pulling her close against him. Her whole body vibrated with the surety that this was right. This was meant to be. Here, now, like this. Wild and free and passionate—just the way they'd been together three years before.

She knew he was going to kiss her before his lips even lowered to hers, knew the surge of need that would pulse through her at the feel of his mouth, his tongue.

'Rosa.' He murmured her name like a wish.

'Let's take this to the shallows,' she whispered, pushing away from him and swimming for the shore.

Soon, Jude Alexander would make love to her again. And then maybe the island would feel like where she belonged.

# CHAPTER EIGHT

LATER—MUCH LATER—they lay in each other's arms on the beach and watched the stars overhead.

'Planning on running away yet?' Jude asked, pressing a kiss to Rosa's bare shoulder. Her olive skin felt smooth and soft under his lips, the clothes they'd abandoned on the beach protecting them both from the sand.

'Not *just* yet.' Rosa stretched out against him, her body pressing closer to his. 'I might need to do that a few more times first.'

A few more times. At least he had some idea of a time-table now, then.

So much for one more night. He should have known—having Rosa again only made him want her more. For as long as they had together, anyway.

'You don't need to, this time,' he said, trying to keep his tone light. He wasn't usually one for serious relationship talk straight after sex, but if he'd learned one thing about Rosa it was that if he didn't get in there fast she'd be gone before he ever got the chance to say anything. 'Run, I mean.'

'Oh?' Propping herself up on one elbow, Rosa looked down at him, her damp hair curling around her face where it had escaped her braid. 'Why's that?'

'Because I know the deal, this time.' Jude swept his

hands up her back, under her heavy plait, enjoying the opportunity to explore all that beautiful skin. 'No strings, no expectations, right? Just you and me, enjoying the time we have together on the island.'

'A fling,' Rosa said, her mouth twitching up into a lopsided smile. 'An island romance.'

'Exactly.'

'Sounds perfect.'

She kissed him again, then, and Jude forgot for a moment how much it had hurt when she left, before.

Not this time, though. This time, he was prepared, he knew what he was getting into. He could steel his heart against falling for Rosa Gray all over again. Right?

'Besides,' Rosa said, sliding down to nestle in the crook of his arm again, her head resting against his shoulder, 'you'll be running back to New York again yourself any time soon, right?'

'Yeah.' New York. The city for dreamers. The place he'd wanted to get to his whole life. Except now, it felt like the last place he belonged. Especially without Gareth there to share it.

'There's a considerable lack of enthusiasm in that "yeah",' Rosa pointed out. 'Want to talk about it?'

Jude sighed. Did he? Maybe it would help. And Rosa… Rosa was one of the few people, other than his bandmates, who knew him well enough to understand. She knew what he'd been looking for in his music, in his career. What he'd hoped for from fame.

She might understand why he was disappointed with what he'd found instead.

'I am aware that this could be considered as being ungrateful,' he said, as an opening disclaimer.

Rosa laughed. 'Remember who you're talking to here. Just ask Anna how well I know ungrateful.'

Jude hugged her a little closer to him. Whatever had been bothering her at dinner still rankled, it seemed. He'd hoped that the last hour or so of being naked in his arms might have cured it. Maybe he'd have to try again…

'You've stopped talking,' Rosa pointed out as he started kissing along her hairline again.

Talking. Right.

Jude sighed, and dropped his head back down to his shirt on the sand. 'Do you remember, on the tour bus, how we talked about music and fame and everything that went with it?'

'Yes.' He hadn't expected her to sound so definite. It was three years ago, after all. 'I remember it all, Jude.'

His heart contracted at that. He'd always assumed she'd cared less than him, to be able to leave so easily. But there was something in her voice, a weight he hadn't expected. Maybe he'd misjudged her.

Except that she'd still left. Nothing she said now could change that simple fact.

'I thought that making music and getting paid for it would be enough. Gareth always wanted more, of course—he was the one who wanted the stardom, really. Wanted to show them all. He needed the riches and the success and his face in every magazine… I just wanted… I wanted to create something new and share it with the world. It was as simple—and as naive—as that.' He almost pitied the younger man he'd been. The Jude who'd thought that music was enough and that Rosa would stay. That Gareth's star, burning so bright, wouldn't consume him in the end. That he could hold the world together the way he wanted it through sheer force of will.

Thank goodness he grew up.

'And now?'

'Now I know it doesn't work like that.'

Rosa pressed a kiss to his bare chest, right above his heart. 'Maybe it should.'

He huffed a laugh. 'Maybe. But instead… I shouldn't complain. I get to do a job others would do for free and I get paid obscene amounts of money for it. And normally I'm fine with what that means.'

'What *does* it mean?'

'It means…' Jude sighed as he trailed off. 'It means being Jude Alexander the brand, rather than the man. It means deciding if the songs I write fit the band's direction, rather than if I like them. It means considering the label, the fans, the advertisers before the music.' It meant being the person Gareth had always been, the one who thought about how to be a success first.

'Putting them all before yourself,' Rosa added.

'Sometimes.' The truth was, he'd got so used to being led to the decisions others wanted him to make, to automatically defaulting to the best business decision, he wasn't sure if he even knew what *he* wanted any more.

Except for one thing: he knew he wanted to live Gareth's dreams for him, now he was no longer there to live them himself.

That was what mattered. Gareth's memory, and the music.

He owed Gareth that much, at least, if that was all there was left to give.

'And then there was the book…' Rosa lifted her head to look him in the eye. 'I guess that didn't go down well with the label?'

Jude laughed. 'The opposite, actually. They loved it. It made me sound like a real rock star—affairs and parties and wild behaviour. Add in Gareth's addiction and everything that came after and it was exactly what people imagine rock-star life to be.'

'Was it true, though?'

'Some of it,' Jude admitted. 'Some of it was exaggerated, and some just plain fantasy. But it didn't seem to matter. The publicity around it, even before it came out, was enough to bump our latest album a bit further up the charts.'

'All publicity is good publicity, huh?'

'It seems so.'

'Not for you, though.'

Jude closed his eyes, shutting out the stars above. 'No.'

'Tell me?' He felt Rosa inch closer, her leg over his, her arm around his waist. She was wrapping herself around him like a protective blanket, as if she could ward off the dark or the bad memories or both. He smiled, involuntarily. For someone who never stayed, while she was there, Rosa could make a man feel as if he were the whole world.

Fame had done that for a while, too. He'd felt important, the big man in the city, just as he and Gareth had dreamed when they were poor schoolboys with no future. And yes, he'd taken advantage of it. He'd done things he looked back on and winced. He'd treated people badly, tossed his fame around like confetti.

But that wasn't who he really was. He knew that, now, even if the readers of *Jude: The Naked Truth* never would.

'Imagine someone printed a book that detailed every screw-up you'd ever made, every bad choice, every awful day, every time you were an idiot or just plain rude. And now imagine that anyone who ever thought anything of you is going to read that.'

Rosa squeezed him a little tighter around the middle. 'I don't think there's a book long enough for all my screw-ups.'

'Mine appears to be pretty lengthy, too.' He sighed. 'The worst part was realising all the people I'd trusted

who must have contributed to it. There are stories in there
that only a few people knew. The author—who has never
actually met me, by the way—couldn't have got them
from anyone else.'

Suddenly the warmth of Rosa's body next to him was
gone, and when he opened his eyes she was sitting up
over him, her arm across her bare breasts. 'I'm not in
there, right? Because, Jude—you know I didn't talk to
anyone, don't you? I wouldn't—'

'You're not in the book,' Jude told her, grabbing her
hands and pulling her back down to him. 'You...that's one
screw-up I know you'd never make.' She'd break his heart,
leave without a backward glance, but Rosa would never
sell him out. He'd doubted, for a time, but now he was sure.

'Okay. Good.'

'My ex-girlfriend, however, had no such restraint.'
And that still hurt. Yes, maybe he and Sylvie were never
going to make it long-term, but still.

Rosa winced on his behalf. 'You said she sold her story
after you broke up?'

'Worse. She sold it when we were still dating. I only
found out *after* we broke up.'

'Ouch.'

'Yeah.'

'So...not really looking forward to seeing her tomorrow, then?' Rosa asked.

Jude hauled her further up his body so he could kiss
her thoroughly. 'I'm really not thinking about my ex-
girlfriend right now.'

'Mmm, good.' Rosa returned the kiss. Then she pulled
a little way away, her gaze uncertain. As if she didn't
want to know the answer to the question she was about
to ask. 'Jude. What happened with Gareth?'

In a way, he was surprised she'd waited so long to ask.

Gareth had adored Rosa, and she'd returned the feeling. Jude had loved that—seeing the two people who knew him best getting along so well. Of course she needed to know the full, awful story.

But her question still hit him in the gut. Was he afraid of his own guilt, or passing some of it on to her by association? He wasn't sure any more.

'You read the newspaper reports, I'm sure,' Jude said, no emotion in his voice. 'They were very…comprehensive.'

Every single detail, spelled out in black-and-white print. They'd only just started making a noise on the scene, but Gareth was a big part of that noise. He was the one people had heard of, the one they wanted to see perform, back then. Jude had just been the guitarist, the accompanying vocals, not the frontman.

Not while Gareth was there to sing for both of them.

And when he had gone…of course, he'd blazed out in the most sensational way he could. Gareth wouldn't have known any other way.

'I read…it was at the awards show, wasn't it?'

Their first awards show. Their first award—best up-and-coming band, as voted for by *Melody Magazine*. The first sign that they were getting where they needed to go.

'He wanted to celebrate, of course.' Jude swallowed around the lump in his throat.

'Gareth always did.' Rosa's smile was soft, and he knew she was remembering. 'He celebrated everything, didn't he? A birthday, a gig, a sunrise. Hell, he threw a party the night we first slept together.'

'He said me getting laid was a rare enough occurrence that it deserved marking,' Jude said, drily.

'So. He went to the after-party to celebrate?' Rosa asked.

Jude's laugh felt so sharp it hurt his throat. 'Oh, Gareth

couldn't wait that long. He went straight to the gents and shot up there. With a little celebratory extra, of course.' And he should have gone with him, been with him to stop him, to keep an eye on him. Should have stopped it before it even got that far. As he'd promised. 'It was that extra that killed him.'

But he'd been at the bar, drinking away the knowledge that Rosa wasn't coming back to him.

'They found him an hour or so later, when someone got suspicious about why the stall was still locked.' That was the worst part. It hadn't even been Jude who realised he was missing. He'd just assumed he was off chatting up some woman, or partying with his other friends. He hadn't even realised Gareth was using again, he'd been so self-absorbed. 'He was already gone, but they called the ambulance anyway. The paramedics stormed through just as they were announcing the winner of Artist of the Year.'

And so, of course, it made all the papers. Every gossip rag and website had the story—and the photos. Jude, pale and gaunt beside the stretcher, holding onto the closest thing to a brother he'd ever had.

'I made him a promise, you know,' he said, squeezing his eyes tight shut. 'A year before he died, he had a close call. Ended up in hospital after an accidental overdose, and it was touch-and-go for a while. When he woke up, I swore to him that I wouldn't let it happen again. I would keep him clean and straight and away from temptation. I'd be the angel on his shoulder. I promised I'd keep him alive. He had so much to live for…'

'Jude.' Rosa's cool hand pressed against his face, followed by her kiss. 'That wasn't a promise you could keep. No one could keep that promise. Gareth's addiction…you couldn't beat it with words.'

'Why not?' Jude cried out, into the night. 'Everything

else in my life, it's all been words and music. That's what I have. I've fought everything else in the world with those two things. Why weren't they enough to save Gareth?'

'I don't know,' Rosa said, her voice small.

But Jude knew. He knew exactly why. 'It *was* working. Until I met you. It was like you took over my whole world, in that instant. And I stopped keeping my promise because I needed to be with you.' Rosa started to speak, but he cut across her. 'Oh, I know you weren't there when he died. But I was so caught up in my own misery about you leaving that I *still* didn't see what was right in front of my face.'

Rosa pulled away. 'So, you blame me for Gareth's death?'

Jude looked up at her, beautiful in the moonlight, and knew how unfair he was being. Reaching up, he pulled her back down to him. 'No. No, I don't blame you. I blame myself.' And he always would, whenever he remembered that image of Gareth being wheeled out of the awards ceremony in a body bag.

The next day, the calls had started, asking about what happened next for the band, and the others had nominated him as the new frontman without his even being there.

'I wanted to stop,' he said, softly. 'Afterwards. I wanted to walk away from it all. The band, music, everything.'

'What changed your mind?' Rosa's voice was still quiet, as if she didn't fully believe him about where the blame lay.

'The rest of the band. They told me…' He swallowed. 'They told me that I had to carry on. For Gareth. To achieve all the dreams he never would, now. It took me a while to believe them. But then one morning, about four months afterwards, I just woke up and knew they were right. Gareth and I had talked about making our band a success our whole lives, it seemed. I couldn't give up on that now. He'd never forgive me. I'd let him down so badly… I had to do anything I could to keep his memory and his dreams alive.'

Rosa's eyes were sad, and she kissed him so sweetly he knew that it had to be pity.

'Gareth loved you,' she said, and he believed her. 'He'd want you to be happy, more than anything else.'

'I know that.'

'Then why are you going back to New York?'

It shouldn't be so hard to think of an answer to that question that she'd accept. 'Because it's my home, now. The band are there. I couldn't leave them—or the music—now. I have an obligation—to them, and to Gareth's memory. And there are the contracts with the label, of course. I owe them all.'

'You sound like Anna,' Rosa said, softly.

Jude shook his head. 'This is different. This is my dream.' His and Gareth's dream. And he would live it for both of them.

'Then why do you look like you've been caged?'

There wasn't an answer at all for that one. 'Go on, then. What do *you* think I should do?'

'I don't know.' Rosa gave a one-shouldered shrug. 'I've spent pretty much my whole adult life avoiding getting trapped that way.'

And she'd keep avoiding it, he knew. Once the wedding was over she'd leave him again.

But this time, he knew that ahead of time. Which meant he wasn't going to waste a moment of the time they had together.

'I don't want to talk about New York any more,' he said. 'Or the past.'

Rosa raised an eyebrow. 'Oh? What do you want to talk about?'

'Honestly?' Jude ran his hands up the side of her naked body. 'I don't want to talk at all.'

'Works for me,' Rosa said, and kissed him.

The bridal party were due to arrive after lunch, so Rosa and Jude spent the following morning putting the finishing touches to the bridal bungalow, and hanging the more delicate decorations for the main function areas that had been left until the last moment, just in case. Basically making sure everything was hashtag perfect for Valentina's arrival.

Anna had already stopped by three times to check on their work, but even that couldn't dim Rosa's mood today. Every action, every moment seemed to remind her of the night before—of being wild and free, first in the sea, and then in Jude's arms. Even the darker turn the conversation had taken…as upsetting as it was to hear about Gareth's death from Jude's own lips, to hear how he blamed himself, she was glad that she knew, now. And if anything, it had only made her feel closer to him again. As if they were finding their way back to how they'd been three years ago, before she walked away.

He said he didn't blame her for distracting him from Gareth's slide into addiction again, and she wanted to believe him. And for now, that would have to be enough. It wasn't as if they had for ever for him to throw blame back at her. They had another week or two at most, and Rosa had very firm ideas about how they should spend that time.

She stretched up to secure a string of tiny lights, and felt a muscle ache, a physical reminder of her actions the night before, and smiled.

'You're doing it again,' Jude said, from across the way.

'Doing what?'

'Distracting me.'

Rosa laughed, just a little uneasily, given her earlier thoughts. 'I can't help that, I'm afraid.'

But Jude grinned back, and she knew he wasn't thinking about Gareth at all. That was good. As much as he'd loved his friend, he couldn't spend the rest of his life in mortgage to his memory.

It all felt so different this time, she realised, for all that it was the same. This time she was older and, yes, maybe even wiser. She didn't have to be afraid of getting drawn in and tied down to Jude. They both knew what this was—an island fling. When it was over they'd go their own ways, still friends, she hoped. It was a better ending than she'd ever hoped for, after she'd left him in London three years before.

And in the meantime…she intended to enjoy every moment they had together. The time limit made everything more intense, in her experience. That was why she kept reliving the night before over and over in her head. Why she couldn't wait for night to fall again so she could take him to bed…

'Right. Is that it?' Jude jumped down from the chair he was standing on and Rosa bit her lip as his loose shirt rode up displaying those tight abs again. Tonight… 'Are we done?' Jude asked, dragging her back to the present.

Rosa checked her clipboard for the list Anna had given her, and scanned the area they'd been working on. 'Believe it or not, I think we are.'

'In that case, I'm off to take a shower.' Jude tossed her a smile as he started unbuttoning his shirt halfway to the path. 'I'd invite you to join me, but there's no way you'd ever be ready to meet the bridal party then.'

'Mmm, probably not,' Rosa agreed, her eyes still fixed on his chest. 'Tonight, though?'

'Definitely tonight,' Jude agreed. 'I'm hoping you might even show me where that secret door that leads to your bedroom is...'

'Ha! You should be so lucky.'

In two swift strides, Jude headed back into the courtyard and kissed her. Thoroughly. 'Oh, I am.'

Rosa smiled after him as he finally left. Then she ran into the villa, through the secret door, and up the twisting wooden stairs to her childhood bedroom in the turret to get ready herself.

'It looks good down here,' Anna said as Rosa appeared. 'And you look nice, too, actually.'

'Thanks,' Rosa said, surprised by the unexpected compliment. She'd dressed in a hot-pink sundress she had a feeling that Jude might enjoy stripping off her later. Her wet hair was piled up in a messy bun, and her make-up was minimal, but she felt beautiful all the same. As if she was glowing.

And she knew that was all down to Jude.

'Their boat arrived a few minutes ago,' Anna said, all business again. 'I've got four staff members down there taking their stuff to the bungalows, and another one bringing them straight here for welcome drinks.' She indicated the table set up with pink champagne in flutes, just inside the courtyard.

Rosa heard a noise further down the path from the villa and stepped forward to the open doorway. 'Here they come.'

'Okay.' Anna took an audible breath.

'Are you *nervous*?' Rosa asked. She wasn't sure she'd ever seen that emotion in her sister before.

'Of course not.'

And then it was too late to press the issue, because the bride—instantly recognised from a million online photos—and her bridesmaids were there, all giggling and talking over each other.

Anna stepped forward and introduced herself to Valentina, who took her hand and pulled her into a hug. 'The island looks so beautiful! Thank you so much for managing to fit us in here for the wedding. It means so much to me and Todd!'

'It's our pleasure,' Anna said, sidestepping the weeks and weeks of work it had taken to be ready for the wedding.

Mind you, given how much Valentina was paying for the privilege, Rosa supposed that was only fair.

'This is my sister, Rosa,' Anna said, and Rosa braced herself for the over-enthusiastic welcome hug from the Internet sensation. 'Now, if you'd like to come through to the courtyard we have welcome drinks for you all, before we take you down to get settled into your accommodation before tonight's dinner.'

'It seems to be going okay,' Rosa murmured to her sister half an hour later, as waiters topped up the glasses of the bridal party—all except Valentina, who was far too busy opening last-minute wedding-week presents from her friends to hold a glass. So far she'd opened monogrammed slippers, robe, nightdress and underwear. Rosa was almost afraid to see what was in the last packages.

'It does.' Anna sounded relieved. 'And here come our men,' she added, nodding in the direction of the arch from the villa.

Rosa didn't correct her. Just the sight of Jude standing beside Leo on the edge of the courtyard, pale where the other man was tan, but both tall and broad and gorgeous.

Except neither of them were looking at her or Anna.

Leo, understandably, headed straight for his sister, embracing her warmly. Seeing them together actually made Rosa feel a little brighter about the possibilities for her own sister's relationship. Maybe there was more to Leo than the gossip websites would have her believe.

But when she watched Jude, her optimism for their own fling took a little knock.

How had she forgotten, even in her happy haze of lust, that his ex-girlfriend would be here? She scanned the gaggle of bridesmaids and picked out the only redhead. Sylvie Rockwell-Smythe, even more beautiful in real life than she was in her photos.

Why hadn't she prepared herself better for this? Because she didn't want to imagine it, Rosa admitted to herself. And because her time together with Jude here felt like such an escape from the real world, she didn't want any of it to intrude on it.

But when the tall, willowy redhead squealed with delight and ran across to embrace Jude, Rosa was pretty sure reality had come to find them.

'Jude!' Valentina broke off from opening presents to welcome him, too, the redhead still hanging off his arm. 'Sylvie didn't tell me you were coming! How wonderful!'

'I didn't know!' Sylvie gushed. She batted Jude on the arm. 'He must have flown out here to surprise me.'

Rosa winced, thankful that Anna had headed inside to deal with the catering staff and wasn't there to see this.

'Not exactly,' Jude said, his voice cool.

'Sorry?' Sylvie's brows knitted together without wrinkling her forehead at all.

Suddenly Rosa looked up to find Jude's gaze on her, his eyes beckoning her over as he disentangled himself from Sylvie's hands. 'Sylvie, Valentina, have you met Rosa Gray?'

# CHAPTER NINE

THE FIRST THING that struck Jude as he reached the courtyard was the noise—the high, excited voices of Valentina and her bridesmaids, so different from Rosa's warm, low, laughing tones. And then he saw her—Sylvie—her bright red hair and perfect body shining in the Spanish sunlight.

He'd thought he might love her, once, he remembered, but somehow it no longer felt real. Nothing from that world did—not when compared to swimming naked in the ocean with Rosa, with holding Rosa in his arms.

*That* was real. *Rosa* was real.

But it was Sylvie throwing herself into his arms, believing he'd arrived on the island just to surprise her.

Well, that was a misunderstanding he could clear up right away.

'Sylvie, Valentina, have you met Rosa Gray?' He gazed at Rosa, loving how she knew what he wanted, was almost halfway across the courtyard before he said her name.

He just hoped she'd play along a little longer.

'We have,' Valentina said, smiling happily, as a bride-to-be should. 'So, is she what brought you to this beautiful island—if you're not here for my wedding?'

'Jude and I are old friends,' Rosa said, returning an equally warm smile as she took his arm, pressing close in a way that showed everyone exactly what sort of *friends* they were. Jude's heart seemed to settle back into a rhythm he hadn't known it had lost as she touched him.

'I thought I'd come spend a few weeks here visiting with Rosa this summer,' Jude said, lightly. 'It seemed like a good time to be out of New York.'

Sylvie's cheeks flushed a little at that, and Valentina gave them both a knowing look.

'I heard about the book,' she said. 'I didn't read it, of course. But it does seem to be everywhere at the moment.'

Strange to think that Valentina had built an entire career out of letting people see into her life—every moment, photographed and filtered and shared.

'How do you cope with it?' he asked, suddenly. 'Everyone knowing every single thing that happens in your life, I mean?'

Valentina laughed. 'Oh, Jude. They know what I *want* them to know. That's the joy of controlling your own brand, the way I do. They never see more than I'm willing to show them.'

'You show them a lot, though,' Rosa pointed out.

Valentina shrugged her slim shoulders. 'I owe them a lot. It's only fair that I share plenty in return. But that doesn't mean I don't get to keep a few of my own secrets.'

Jude was glad, he realised. He'd hate for Valentina to feel the way he did—as if every inch of his personal space had been invaded, every precious memory passed from person to person to examine.

Rosa squeezed his arm, and he found himself grateful again that the author of *The Naked Truth* had never found out about her. Maybe he still had a few secrets left, too.

'Now, I hope you'll join us for the wedding anyway, since you're here?' Valentina asked.

'I'd hate to intrude,' Jude started, but Valentina laughed.

'Don't be silly! The more the merrier. And of course, if you'd like to bring a plus-one, I'm sure that would be fine…'

'Then thank you,' Jude said, already calculating in his mind how happy Robyn would be about this one.

Being seen at the wedding of the year could never be a bad thing. And having a beautiful woman like Rosa on his arm had to look good, too.

The fact it would rub Sylvie's nose in it a bit felt pretty great, too, if he was brutally honest.

Leaving Valentina and her bridesmaids to the presents, Jude led Rosa off to the shadows of the villa.

'So, that's the ex, huh?' she asked, glancing back out at them. 'She's beautiful. Like, absurdly so. Even more than the photos.'

'She's nothing compared to you,' Jude said, making her laugh, although he couldn't figure out why.

'She's a model, Jude. A six-foot-tall, beautiful, willowy redhead with perfect hair and a dozen modelling contracts. I am under no illusions about my own charms, but they're not a patch on hers. You don't need to lie to me to make me feel good.'

'I'm not lying,' Jude said, holding her close so she had to look into his eyes and see the truth of it. 'Yes, Sylvie looks beautiful. She's stunning.'

'Not helping with the not lying part.'

'But you…' He stared down into her wide, dark eyes, her long lashes sooty against her skin, trying to find the words. 'You're *alive*. You have so much life, so much vibrancy… She could never match that. She *looks* beautiful. You live it.'

He must have said something right, from the way she kissed him.

'You're such a *poet*,' she said, fondly.

'So you'll come to the wedding with me? It won't be any fun without you.'

Rosa pulled a face. 'I'll need to check with Anna. I'm supposed to be working that day, of course.'

'But she'll be going with Leo, surely?'

'That's true. I'll ask her, I promise.'

'Tonight?'

The smile Rosa gave him reminded him they had other plans for tonight. 'Maybe tomorrow.'

'Tomorrow works for me.'

'Anna, have you got a minute?' Rosa had been looking all over the island for her sister after another day of work. Anna had been strangely absent for most of it, until Rosa finally spotted her heading down the path to the jetty.

'Not now.' Anna didn't even look back at her. Wasn't that always the way with her? She wanted to organise her life for her, but only when it suited her.

Rosa took a breath and reminded herself she was asking Anna for a favour. She needed to keep her cool. 'It's about Jude. Valentina has asked him to the wedding and he wants me to be his plus-one. Will that be a problem? I can still oversee the seating charts and things, and you'll be there with Leo anyway…'

Anna finally glanced back, pushing her hair out of her eyes. 'Leo hasn't mentioned me accompanying him to the wedding,' she said slowly. 'We're not, I mean, it's not serious.'

If Leo and Anna weren't serious, then what on earth did that make her and Jude? 'Oh, come on, I've seen the way he looks at you.'

'It's not serious,' Anna repeated, and Rosa decided to worry later about whatever games her sister was playing now.

'If you say so. So you don't mind? It turns out Jude knows Valentina quite well, he used to go out with one of the bridesmaids—the redhead who complained that the bed is too hard and that we haven't provided the right range of herbal teas—and it ended, well, horrifically. Long story short, she was involved with the book, so it's a pride thing to accept the invite and bring a date, I guess. But what with the way we left things, I think…'

Anna held up her hand to silence her, and Rosa got the feeling she was mentally counting to ten, as she used to when they were small. 'Rosa, fill me in later. I have to go over to the mainland and I hate sailing over in the dark. Yes, go to the wedding. It's fine.'

The mainland? What on earth could she be going there for? Everything for the wedding had already been delivered. Unless this wasn't to do with the wedding…

'What's so urgent?' Rosa's voice sharpened, as she took in her sister's appearance for the first time. 'Are you okay? You're very pale. Do you feel ill?'

'Rosa, don't fuss. I just have to do something.' Yeah, that wasn't very reassuring—especially if Anna didn't want to tell her what she needed to do.

'I really think you should wait till morning.' Then, as Anna shook her head, 'In that case I'm coming with you. I'll drive the boat. The way you look you won't be able to get it out of the harbour!'

Anna wanted to refuse, Rosa could tell. But she wasn't going to let her.

Not waiting for an answer, Rosa took the boat key out of Anna's hand and led her the rest of the way down to the jetty. It was pretty clear that Anna didn't want to talk about whatever was going on, so Rosa didn't press her for details, concentrating instead on steering the dinghy over the short distance as speedily as possible. She pulled up alongside the jetty on the mainland with a smooth flourish. 'Right, where next? Anna, I'm coming with you. Don't argue.'

Anna opened her mouth to protest and then shut it again. Rosa smiled. For once, she was in charge.

Sancia always kept a car in the car park near the jetty, for whenever they needed to run errands on the mainland, and Rosa was relieved to see it there waiting for them. Anna pulled the key to Sancia's ancient rusty small car from her pocket and handed it to her, not responding as Rosa's hand closed over hers with what she hoped was a reassuring squeeze.

'The town,' she said, her voice husky. 'The pharmacy. There's one on the retail park this side of town, it's not far.'

The pharmacy. Oh, that didn't sound good at all.

Now Rosa was really worried.

The roads were deserted and it didn't take long to clear the small village and head towards the town. Rosa drove at her normal speed—ten kilometres above the speed limit—more concerned by the fact that Anna wasn't issuing her usual warnings to drive carefully than by the sharp turns and corners.

Something was definitely wrong here.

Spotting the retail park, and the pharmacy, Rosa swung the car into a free space and killed the engine. 'Do you want me to come in with you?'

'No. Thanks.' Anna made no move to get out of the car, though.

'Anna, let me go.' Rosa had a feeling she knew exactly what this was. And it was bigger than any argument that had ever been between them. 'Do you need me to buy you a pregnancy test? Is that what's happening here?' What else could it be? Rosa knew that panicked, lost look on her sister's face. She'd seen it on her own, once.

Anna froze. 'Leo doesn't want a family.' Rosa had a feeling that wasn't what Anna had intended to say. 'He'll think I've betrayed him.'

'Anna, honey, it takes two to make a baby. Leo's a grown man. If you are pregnant, he'll understand.' And if he didn't, then Rosa would beat understanding into him. Not that she was going to mention that part to Anna yet.

'No, he won't. He told me from the start, no promises, no commitment. It's bad enough I've fallen in love with him. How can I be so stupid as to get pregnant, too? It's like Sebastian all over again, only much, much worse. I only *thought* I loved Sebastian.'

Okay, *that* was a surprise. But actually, it explained a lot. 'You were pregnant back then? Why didn't you tell me? Why do you never let anyone help, Anna?' The old frustrations rose up in her. If she'd known, she could have helped. She could have done *something*. 'You don't have to do it all alone. You don't have to be perfect. You can ask for help…'

'Last time I needed your help you walked away.' It was always going to come down to that between them, wasn't it?

Rosa bit her lip. Anna was never going to understand why she couldn't stay. And now really wasn't the time to confess all the other reasons—the ones that had nothing to do with Anna or their father. 'Things were complicated then. I'm sorry. But I'm here now and, I promise you, you're not alone. Now let me go and get the test for you and then, if you are, we'll figure out what to do. And if you're not then you and I need to have a long-overdue talk. Deal?'

'Deal.' Anna squeezed her hand tightly.

Rosa got out of the car and jogged over to the pharmacy. She might have let her sister down before, but Anna wouldn't have to worry about that this time.

And nor would her child, with Rosa as their auntie.

Something was up with Rosa.

Jude surveyed her over the rack of Scrabble tiles, ignoring the letters and potential words to consider the woman sitting across from him instead. On either side of him, Sancia and Ernest Gray were debating whether whatever obscure word the professor had come up with existed in the *Oxford English Dictionary*. Jude was fairly sure it didn't—the professor was a terrible Scrabble cheat.

The bigger mystery to him was what Rosa was thinking about.

Whatever it was, it had distracted her completely, all evening. She'd barely responded to his hand on her hip as they walked to the table, she'd had nothing to say over dinner, and now she'd barely managed more than a three-letter word all game.

Scrabble, Jude had discovered to his surprise, was the one area of the world where Professor Gray and his youngest daughter actually seemed to connect. He and Sancia usually just muddled through trying to keep up. They both fought for every tile, every triple word score, every definition.

But not tonight.

Suddenly Rosa looked up, her attention drawn by something by the darkened arch leading out of the courtyard. Jude twisted in his seat to try and see what had distracted her.

Anna. Of course. And Leo, leading her away.

Jude turned back to Rosa to see an unfamiliar look on her face. Part hope, part fear, and all uncertainty.

'I'm going to go and fetch my dictionary,' Sancia said, rising from her seat. The professor followed her, arguing that since it probably wasn't the *Oxford English Dictionary* it wouldn't count, anyway.

Jude waited until the others were safely inside the villa before he slid over to Sancia's chair and reached for Rosa's hand.

'What's up?'

'Hmm?' Rosa turned to him, blinking. 'Nothing.'

'Liar.' She'd never lied to him before, that he knew of. Let him believe things that wouldn't happen, sure, but that was his false hope, not her fault. Now he was really worried.

But Rosa looked down at the table and said, 'Sorry. You're right. It's just… I'm not sure it's my secret to tell.'

Something relaxed inside him. That he, of all people, could understand. 'That's fine. But if it'll help to talk about it…you know I'm not one to share other people's stories.'

'I do know.' Rosa gave him a warm smile, then glanced back towards the villa. 'Come on, let's go. Take a walk or something.'

'You always talk better when we're walking.'

Rosa shrugged, getting to her feet. 'You know me. I work better in action.'

'I do,' Jude said, and realised it was true.

He *knew* Rosa, in a way he wasn't sure he'd ever known anyone else. He'd thought it was just because she lived life out loud, her every action proclaiming exactly who she was. But others—her own family—still didn't seem to understand her, even with a lifetime of observing her.

So maybe it was just something about their connection.

Maybe it was just him, and just her.

She led him along the winding path that trailed around the island, through lush foliage and flowers, past the bright white bungalows and their freshly painted shutters, skirting the beaches and waterfronts. When they came too close to the bridal bungalow, Rosa tugged his hand to take a different trail, one that led them away from the laughter and the chatter.

Rosa still wasn't talking, Jude realised. The romantic walk in the moonlight was nice and all, but it wasn't getting him any closer to figuring out what was on Rosa's mind.

'Is it Sylvie?' he asked, figuring he had to start somewhere. 'Has she said anything?'

'Who?' Rosa looked up, surprised. 'Oh, no. Not her.'

Of course. Because that would mean her actually being affected by his ex-girlfriend being on the island, and they'd both been very clear that this wasn't that kind of relationship.

Then he remembered the way she'd watched Anna and Leo leaving the courtyard. 'Your sister, then?'

Rosa didn't answer that time, which was how Jude knew he'd got it right.

'What did she do?' He could feel his irritation with Rosa's sister rising. Whatever their differences, Rosa had busted a gut helping her get the island ready for the wedding, and Anna had still managed to find fault at every turn.

'She got pregnant,' Rosa said, her voice soft, and all of Jude's anger faded away in an instant.

'Are you sure?'

Rosa shook her head. 'I took her to buy the test last night. She didn't tell me the outcome but…you saw her with Leo this evening. I could tell from her face, she was going to tell him. So I guess it must have been positive.'

'Wow.' Suddenly, a terrible thought occurred to him, and he tugged her to face him. 'Wait, do we need to—?'

Rosa interrupted him with a shake of her head. 'It's fine.'

'No, but I mean, I know we've been careful since, but that first time. In the sea…'

'Jude. It's covered. Trust me. With travelling the world and all the different time zones, my body got so confused the doctor put me on a contraceptive injection anyway. There's no chance, this time.'

'Right. Okay, then.' Jude was almost certain that the feeling coursing through him was relief. Just relief. Because disappointment would have been crazy.

If Rosa got pregnant, would she stay? Or, more importantly, would she ever forgive him?

He couldn't think about those impossibilities now.

'How do you think Leo will react?' he asked, instead.

'Anna seemed pretty sure the answer to that is "badly".' She sighed, dropping down to sit on one of the brightly painted benches that studded the island path at points where the view was even more spectacular than the average La Isla Marina vista. 'But he's an idiot if he doesn't just marry her and live happily ever after.'

'I never thought I'd hear you advocating settling down and living the traditional life,' Jude observed. He sat beside her, and she took his hand in hers, absently playing with his fingers.

'Well, not for me,' Rosa admitted. 'But you've seen the two of them together. How they look at each other.

To start, I thought Leo was just playing her, but now… I think he genuinely loves her. I just hope he realises that, too.'

'So do I,' Jude said, although he wasn't fully thinking of Anna and Leo.

He was thinking about Rosa. How fiercely he'd fallen for her, three years ago. How the love that had turned to shock and anger had become an aching loss, until he found her again. How, even now, even when he was protecting his heart the best he knew how, he knew it was going to hurt, when she left again.

This time, he realised, he would have to leave first. *He* needed to make that decision, take that control. It was the only way he'd ever be able to live with it.

'I have to admit, though,' Rosa said, staring out at the calm sea before them, 'I am kind of looking forward to being an auntie.'

'You'll be the cool auntie who sends them awesome gifts from all over the world, from places they couldn't even imagine from their boring house in Oxford.'

'Exactly!' Rosa flashed him a grin. 'And maybe… maybe they'll come here on holiday, and I can join them. Like we used to when we were kids.'

'You think you'll come back to the island more often, now?' Jude asked, surprised.

'Maybe.' Because there was never any certainty with Rosa, was there? 'I mean, it's the only place that's ever really felt like home.'

And suddenly, sitting in the moonlight, talking about someone else's child, Jude realised he knew exactly how she felt.

Only, for him, home wasn't a place.

It was a person.

# CHAPTER TEN

*ALMOST THERE.*

Just over twenty-four hours now until the wedding, and Rosa had ticked off the last of the day's jobs on her accursed clipboard. The groom and his family had arrived, and the Spanish-style lunch they'd arranged for the whole wedding party had been a huge success. Four courses over several hours followed by much-needed siestas had made the perfect introduction to the island, and Anna and Rosa had planned for beach games and a much more informal supper to be served at the beach later that evening. The informal evening would not only be fun, but crucially it gave the island staff plenty of time to prepare for the next day, when another hundred guests were due to arrive, and for the wedding ceremony itself, which would begin at seven o'clock tomorrow night.

Rosa had to admit, Anna had pulled off a near miracle. The island looked perfect. Every bungalow was ready and—thanks to her and Jude—every tree had fairy lights threaded through it, and the pagoda and central area were set up for the ceremony and party. Anna had confirmed that Valentina's dress had arrived that day, escorted by a dressmaker who would stay until Valentina was dressed, and last time Rosa had checked in on the kitchens Sancia had been harassing the chefs from Barcelona who were setting up. Fortunately her mother was easily distracted, and the chefs seemed to be working remarkably amicably with the island's own cooks.

Valentina glowed with happiness, her groom's wealthy parents were happy, and the bridesmaids—except for Sylvie—full of nothing but praise.

In summary, they were ready. Which meant Rosa was officially free to pursue her own interests for the rest of the evening—namely, Jude.

At least, she was once she'd reported in to her lord and master, Anna.

Rosa smiled to herself as she made her way up the path to the main villa. Actually, things between her and her sister were better than they had been in years—since before their mother left, even. Rosa had managed to get Anna alone the day before and get the full story from her. Yes, she was pregnant. No, she wasn't marrying Leo and living happily ever after. But she seemed content, all the same. As if the life within her had settled her—given her a focus that mattered to *her*, rather than keeping other people satisfied, as she seemed to with her work, or looking after their father.

Part of Rosa worried that Anna was just getting tied down in a new way, but the more reasonable part of her knew that this was different. A *baby* was different, especially for Anna.

But she couldn't stop remembering those terrifying weeks when she'd believed she might be pregnant with Jude's child. Then, at twenty-three, it had felt like the end of the world—a shackle on her life before she'd even figured out how she wanted to live it.

Now, three years and an awful lot of experience on, she wondered if it might feel different.

Not that she intended to find out. She had plans, still. Life still to live, adventures still to have.

When she'd left him, and La Isla Marina, and everything else behind last time it had been to find *her* life. The one no one else in the world could live but her. The person she was meant to be, even. And, over the last three years, she'd found it. She had a career she loved, that fulfilled her—and allowed her to keep moving, to experience new places and cultures and lives. She met more people from more different walks of life in a month than many people met in their whole existence. She never had to slow down to wait for someone else to catch up, never had to modulate her expectations or her impulses to satisfy someone else. She could be exactly who she was, without judgement. Or at least, without hanging around long enough to hear or care about any judgement anyone passed on her choices.

She had exactly what she'd wanted. Yes, it could be lonely, occasionally. But the benefits outweighed the negatives, right? And if, sometimes, she wondered if it was enough, well, as long as she kept moving she could push those thoughts aside. She didn't want what Anna seemed to—to settle down in one place and live one life with one man. And even then, Leo didn't seem as if he was going to give Anna her happy ever after. If St Anna couldn't make love work, what hope was there for her screw-up little sister?

And besides, even if Rosa and Jude had that sort of relationship—the for ever kind—she couldn't live his life. She couldn't smile politely at self-important celebrities and people trying to tell her what to do. She wasn't that person.

Jude, surprisingly, seemed to be. She'd thought he'd be raging against the requirements and constraints, but it seemed that he liked the fame more than he liked the freedom. Or maybe he just stuck with it for the sake of Gareth's memory. Out of guilt for the promise he broke.

Whatever his reasons, Rosa was never going to be that way. She couldn't be that woman he needed by his side, always.

Even if she wanted to be.

The villa was lit up with tiny lanterns, bright spots in the darkness illuminating the happiness and love that filled the island for Valentina's wedding. Rosa wished some of it could spread to Anna and Leo, but she knew that if it didn't, Anna would be okay. She was strong, and she could organise her way out of any situation.

Anna would be fine.

Rosa stepped through into the courtyard, and saw her sister bending to kiss her parents, one at a time. Which was unusual on many levels. Firstly, Anna wasn't a usually demonstrative person that way, and Rosa knew she didn't intend to tell their parents about the pregnancy until after the wedding, so it couldn't be that. Add in the ongoing weirdness of their estranged parents apparently spending all their time together again, after ten years apart, and Rosa was just baffled. What had happened to her dysfunctional, tension-inducing family? At least she knew what to expect from them. The new dynamics just confused her. Where was she supposed to fit in? Or maybe she wasn't. After all, she'd be gone again soon, and they could all carry on without her, in Oxford and Spain. Rosa knew when she wasn't needed.

She raised an eyebrow at Anna. 'It all looks very cosy in here—everything all right?'

'Everything's good,' Anna said. 'I was just discussing the possibility of staying on the island. After all, it's never been one person's job to run it before.'

Rosa's eyes widened, a hundred questions jostling for

attention in her mind while she tried—and failed—to choose one. 'But… Oxford…? Book…? Dad…? Here?'

'Quite,' Anna said enigmatically. 'Did you put the volleyball net up, Rosa? Don't worry, I'll go. I could do with some fresh air.'

And then she was gone, before Rosa could confirm that, yes, actually, she had put the net up. And also, what the hell?

Anna, staying on La Isla Marina, with their mother—and possibly their father, given how things were going—and her baby.

Anna, who for the last decade had focussed on exactly the same sort of academic success that had driven their father for so long—and driven their parents apart.

Maybe this was proof that people could change, after all. And for some reason, it made Rosa incredibly uncomfortable.

If Anna could change, did that mean *she* could? More to the point, that she *should*?

No. Rosa had fought too hard to be exactly who she was to give it up now.

'I'm going to go and help her,' Rosa said, but her parents weren't even listening. They were lost in their own conversation.

Rosa walked back out onto the island proper and sucked in a deep breath. Anna didn't need her help, because there was nothing to help with. Everything was done and ready, and the staff they had in place would be running the events perfectly. If Anna was there, she didn't need Rosa's help.

So she turned away from the public areas and all the fun wedding events, and headed down the path towards Jude's bungalow by the sea, hoping she could lose herself in his arms for a while, and forget all the questions buzzing in her head.

\* \* \*

Jude was sitting at the patio table when she arrived, his guitar resting on his knee as he noted something down in the brown leather notebook on the table.

Rosa leant against the wall of the bungalow and watched him as he picked out a melody on the strings, before stopping to write down something else. He was so handsome. Beautiful, even, in a way she'd never imagined a man could be. If she had her camera with her, she'd frame him against the night sky, the fairy lights behind him, highlighting the planes and shadows of that beautiful face.

It seemed strange now, to remember that he hadn't always been the star. The frontman of The Swifts, taking all the praise and glory. When he'd been in Gareth's shadow, others had barely even seemed to notice him.

But to Rosa, Jude had always been that bright, shining star in the darkness.

'Working?' she asked, softly, so as not to startle him.

Jude looked up and smiled. 'Playing, really.'

He strummed the melody again, carrying on for longer this time, the music almost familiar somehow.

'Do I know that one?' she asked, slipping into the seat opposite him.

'Parts of it, probably,' Jude admitted. 'It's a variation on a theme—I'm playing around with some of the local music here.'

'For the new album?'

Jude shook his head, looking down at the strings so his dark hair fell across his forehead. 'Just for me, really. I doubt the rest of the band would think this fitted with our brand.'

'Brand?' Rosa pulled a face. It always came back to that for him, it seemed. Trying to fit into a mould that he'd outgrown, even if he didn't realise it. 'Can't you just play the music you like?'

'Apparently not. At least, not back in New York. Here, however…' He strummed the strings again, making Rosa smile.

'Play me a song. One just for me.'

'Sure.' As he started to play Rosa stood up and made her way through the open patio doors into the bungalow bedroom, stripping her dress from her body as she went. The music stuttered for a second, then continued, Jude lifting his voice to join it, singing of beauty and life and water and sun.

Naked, Rosa stretched out on Jude's bed and gazed back at him, watching as he created something entirely new, something just for her. After a few lines, he looked up and met her gaze, and suddenly it wasn't her lack of clothes that made her feel exposed.

It was his eyes. The way he looked deep into the heart of her, the way no one else ever managed. She kept moving, kept talking, kept living, and no one ever kept up with her well enough to see the truth in her. But with Jude, she was frozen. Motionless. Naked—physically and emotionally.

He saw everything. And he sang it back to her.

Rosa wasn't sure if that was terrifying or wonderful. Maybe it was both.

The song came to an end, but Jude's gaze didn't leave hers. 'That what you wanted?'

'Yes,' she said, even though she wasn't sure she should have asked for it. 'At least, the first part of what I wanted.'

'Oh? What's the second part?' Jude asked, but she could tell from his smile that he already knew.

Still, she opened her arms to him to make it clear. 'You. Here. Now.'

Jude put his guitar back in its case, closing it hurriedly. 'I can do that.'

* * *

'You know, we're really, really good at that,' Jude said, running his hands over the smooth expanses of Rosa's skin, just because he could. For now, she was all his, here in his bed, in his arms. Like a song he never wanted to end.

'We really are.' Rosa twisted in his arms so she faced him, pressing a kiss against his chest.

He wanted to say it. Wanted to tell her that it didn't have to end, that she didn't have to run. That they could try a life together, for real, this time.

But he'd already said it all in his song. He'd poured his every emotion, every thought into that melody and those lyrics, sung his heart to her. She knew it all already. And if it didn't change her mind, he still needed to be able to walk away with his heart intact.

So he said nothing.

'Anna's decided to stay on the island,' Rosa said, suddenly, bringing Jude back to the here and now.

'Really? Because of the baby?'

'I guess.'

'You sound confused.' Was it just the idea of voluntarily staying on one sleepy island for ever that confused her? Or was there something more to this?

'No… I get it. I think.' Rosa sighed, and pulled away, sitting up and tugging the sheet up over her body, which Jude thought was a crying shame. 'No, I don't. As long as I can remember, Anna wanted to be an academic like Dad, living in Oxford, researching, writing her books and teaching her students. And now…she's changing her whole life.'

'Love makes us do strange things.' Jude's throat felt tight as he said it.

Rosa gave him a strange look. 'Leo's not staying with her.'

'I meant the love of her baby,' Jude explained. 'Although…she's heartbroken, remember. She probably imagined a whole future with Leo and now she's reassessing. She's finding a new future for a new her.'

'You sound like you know what she's going through,' Rosa said, curiously. 'Who did you love?'

'You.' He'd said it before he even realised he was going to. The horror in Rosa's eyes made it clear he had to take it back, though. And fast. 'Once, anyway. I mean, when you left last time. But that was a long time ago now.' He kept his voice as casual as he could, a careful eye on Rosa's face to watch the shock and fear subsiding.

'Yes. A long time ago.' Something flashed across her face though, something deeper than the horror.

'What?' Sitting up, he pulled her close again, needing her touch. 'What is it?'

'When I left… I did it badly, I know that.'

'It was a long time ago, Rosa. It doesn't matter now.' Even if she'd stayed, what would it have changed, really? Gareth would still have died, that much he realised now, seeing her again. She'd given him some peace with that, at least. But if she'd come back, how long would it have lasted? Another month? A year, if he was lucky? The axe would have fallen sooner or later, and later would have only hurt more.

'But that's the thing—it does.' She looked up into his eyes. 'I need to explain.'

'You already have,' Jude pointed out. 'You told me exactly why you left.' And to be honest, he wasn't sure he could hear it again—listen to her say how little he'd meant to her that she moved on without a backward glance, just because she didn't like to stay in one place too long.

'I didn't tell you everything.'

Her quiet words stopped his brain in its tracks. Leaning back against the pillows, he pulled her down with him, holding her tight against his shoulder. 'Tell me now?' He wasn't sure he wanted to hear it, but he knew he needed to know it.

Rosa nodded, her hair brushing his skin. And Jude waited to hear the truth.

'When I left, for my *abuelo*'s funeral… I planned to come back. I was going to come back to you.'

It was as if the world starting falling into place. As a discordant tune became a melody as the right notes were played instead.

He'd known it wasn't right. Known there was something wrong about her leaving like that. Their connection had been too strong for her to sever it so thoughtlessly.

Yes, he'd known that Rosa wouldn't stay for ever. She wasn't the sort of woman to settle down, and he'd accepted that. But he'd expected more from her than for her to just drop out of his life—that was the part that had haunted him for the past three years.

And now, it seemed, he was about to learn the truth about why.

'Why didn't you?' he asked, dreading and needing the answer in equal measure.

'Because I was scared,' Rosa admitted. 'What I felt for you…it was all-encompassing, and it scared me. When I was with you, I couldn't think about anything else. Couldn't remember who I was, what *I* wanted out of life. I was afraid that if I came back to you I wouldn't be able to leave again, and I knew I needed to, if I wanted to follow my dreams. And then—' She broke off.

'What?' He needed it all. Every detail. Even as his body buzzed with the knowledge that it wasn't just him. She'd felt it, too.

Whether she admitted it or not, Rosa had loved him, too. And it still hadn't been enough for her to stay.

'I was late. My body…all the stress of the funeral, and the fight with Anna, I guess it got to it. I was two weeks late and I thought…'

'You thought you were pregnant.' For a moment, the image of a tiny little girl with Rosa's dark eyes and hair flashed through his head. *There's no chance, this time.* That was what she'd said, when he'd asked if they needed to be concerned. And this was what she'd meant.

How could he not have seen that?

'I wasn't,' Rosa said, quickly dispelling the image. 'But the thought that I could have been… I realised how careless we'd been. How when I was with you I set aside everything I wanted for myself, every dream I had, every promise I'd made to myself that I wouldn't get tied down to a life of someone else's choosing, like Mama and Anna did. I forgot everything that made me Rosa, and that terrified me. So I ran.'

The worst part was, it all made perfect sense, in a Rosa sort of way. Of course she had run.

'I wish you'd been able to tell me, back then.' Jude's head was still spinning, imagining a world in which she might have done.

How could things have been different? Was there any way this could have ended differently?

Knowing Rosa, and knowing himself, he suspected not.

He'd been chasing fame, and she'd been chasing freedom. They couldn't have done that together, not really. He could never have asked Rosa to chase his dreams with him instead of hers, and she could never have asked him to abandon his, either. Especially not after Gareth died, and he had two people's dreams to chase already.

The worst part was, nothing had changed. They were the same people they'd been three years ago.

There was still only one way this could all end.

'I wish I had, too,' Rosa said. 'I know it wouldn't have changed anything, but still… I wish I hadn't left things the way I did.'

Jude rolled over so she was lying underneath him. 'I think we've more than made up for it, the last couple of weeks. Don't you think?'

'Definitely.' Rosa smiled up at him, so sweetly that he had to kiss her. 'But we could probably stand to make up a few more times, before we leave. Don't you think?'

That, Jude decided, was a question better answered with action, than words.

# CHAPTER ELEVEN

THE WEDDING WAS PERFECT.

The sun shone down on the evening service, while Valentina and Todd took their vows with laughter and joy in between the serious moments. The actual, legal part of the ceremony, Rosa knew, had been completed in New York a week or so ago. So technically, Valentina and Todd were already tied to each other for life. But today was the day that mattered most to them—the day where they confirmed that commitment to everyone who mattered to them. When they stood proud and said, 'I've made my decision. It's this person for me. For ever.'

Rosa tried to imagine being that sure of anything, but the only thing that came to mind was Jude. And they both already knew that wasn't an option. So instead, she decided to just enjoy the day.

Valentina looked more beautiful than ever, Rosa thought, in her designer dress. The white bodice clung to her curves before flaring out into a full, knee-length skirt. But it was the sheer overdress with its embroidered flowers, bold and beautiful in a red that matched the bridesmaids' dresses, that really made it something special.

Rosa took a perverse pleasure in the fact that Sylvie's dress clashed horribly with her hair.

Her own lemon-yellow sundress was maybe a little casual for such a celebrity wedding, but she hadn't exactly packed for the occasion. She'd made an extra effort with her hair, though, braiding it carefully and threading tiny white flowers through it. If she was here as Jude's date, even just for the day, she wanted to look as if she belonged with him.

And Jude was, quite frankly, breathtaking. While the groom's party were all in pale linen suits, Jude wore a darker charcoal suit in the same light material. His white shirt was open at the collar and his skin, while darkened a little by his time on the island, was still pale enough to make his blue eyes blaze against it, and the darkness of his hair.

It was strange, being at the wedding as a guest instead of an employee of the island. Stranger still to see Anna in her uniform of dark skirt and white blouse, her dark hair pulled severely back. Rosa kept wanting to go and help—to fetch more ice, or fix a torn hem, or mop up a spill. But instead, her job for the day was to hang off Jude's arm, look pretty and annoy his ex.

She could do that. For one day, anyway. For one day, it was a novelty. Any more, though, and she knew she'd be bored rigid.

As the sky darkened, the party went on. Food was served, music was played, speeches made. Valentina and Todd had already performed their first dance—a very location-appropriate tango, with enough heat in it that Rosa had caught Jude's eye and made a mental promise for later.

'Jude!' Valentina approached them, her hand still tightly clutching Todd's. She was beaming, happiness glowing from every inch of her. 'Isn't everything going wonderfully?'

'It's been a beautiful day,' Jude agreed, his hand resting on Rosa's thigh.

'And it's not over yet! Speaking of which… Since you're here, do you think you might be able to treat us to a song or two? Since it *is* my wedding day…'

Jude laughed. 'How can I refuse a request from the bride? Especially since I gatecrashed your wedding in the first place.' He smiled at Rosa. 'As long as you're okay here alone?'

'Absolutely.' Rosa relaxed further back into her chair. 'I'm going to sit here and keep eating these dessert canapés. You can come roll me into bed when you're done.'

'It's a deal.' Jude pressed a kiss to her lips, and disappeared off to fetch his guitar.

'You realise that when he goes back to New York he'll forget all about you.' Rosa's spine stiffened as Sylvie slipped into Jude's abandoned chair. 'When he's deep in his music he forgets almost everything.'

Rosa shrugged. 'That's not a problem for us.'

'Because you're *so* different?' Sylvie's laughter was sharp and ugly. 'Trust me, every woman thinks that.'

'No,' Rosa said, patiently. 'Because when he goes back to New York I'll be heading off somewhere else, on my next assignment. Russia, I think, this time.'

That, at least, seemed to surprise her. 'You're not planning on coming to New York with him if he asks?'

'He won't ask,' Rosa said, with certainty. 'Mostly because he knows I won't go. I have my life and he has his. It just so happens that they both intersected here for a while. That's all.'

'Do you honestly believe that you'll walk away from here and forget all about him?'

'Maybe not forget,' Rosa admitted. After all, she'd never forgotten him in the three years they were apart.

There was no reason to imagine she would this time. 'But I have plenty of other things in my life to focus on. I can't see me having time to pine, if that's what you're worried about.'

Except for all those nights, alone in a hotel room or a tent, remembering. Those were always the hardest.

'Worried? No.' Sylvie gave her a shark-bright smile. 'Relieved. If you're out of the picture in New York that gives me an opening.'

'Even if he forgets you for his music?' Rosa ignored the burning feeling in her chest that started when she imagined Jude and Sylvie together in New York. He wouldn't go back to her, would he? Not after everything she'd done. 'Do you think he'll even want to see you, after all the stories you sold about him?'

Sylvie dismissed both concerns with a wave of her hand. 'Honestly, it's more about the picture than the truth. As long as he's seen with me enough to get our photo everywhere it's good for both of us. The rest is almost beside the point.'

Beside the point. All the wonderful things she'd shared with Jude were, to Sylvie, unimportant beside his fame.

How could she ever explain to someone like that how Jude's fame was the least attractive thing about him, to her? Because it was his celebrity, his success, that meant he was tied to a life that would mean she would always have to follow. To be Jude Alexander's partner, instead of her own person.

And she couldn't do that.

A cheer went up around the crowd as Jude stepped onto the small makeshift stage the traditional Spanish band had used earlier. Sylvie disappeared, off into the crowd, presumably to be seen with someone more deserving. And Rosa settled back down to listen to Jude play.

He started with a familiar song—one of The Swifts' most classic numbers, but played in an acoustic style that rendered it almost something different altogether. Rosa had listened to plenty of Jude's band's music—it was hard to avoid anywhere where music was played, like hotel bars and supermarkets, not to mention the car radio. Sometimes, when she really wanted to torture herself, she'd even look him up online and read interviews with him, looking for the man she'd once known. The photos she'd taken on tour with them, what seemed like a lifetime ago now, showed a different man altogether, she always thought. Before fame hit, and the Jude the public saw became more polished, more careful.

But she'd never heard the songs this way before—just Jude and his guitar. There was so much more emotion in the music, she thought. They felt raw, but real, without all the production and effects added to the finished pieces.

She preferred them this way, she decided. But maybe that wasn't surprising. She preferred the man playing them to the one Sylvie described as Jude in New York.

The next song he played, though, sounded different again. Mostly because the last time she'd heard it, Gareth had been the one singing it. Rosa caught Jude's eye and saw all the emotions there. Had he ever even played this song since Gareth's death? Probably not, knowing Jude.

But maybe it was time. He'd said he wanted to find closure on the island, to face his demons. Coming to terms with what had happened to Gareth had to be a big part of that.

Rosa hoped it was helping. She wanted Jude happy, even if she wouldn't be there to see it.

Suddenly, Leo pulled a chair up next to her. 'Where's Anna?'

'I thought you were leaving.' Rosa stared at her sister's ex with loathing. Hadn't he told Anna he'd be leaving the island the minute the speeches were over? If he had nothing more to offer, then as far as Rosa was concerned, the sooner he left, the better.

'I need to speak to Anna.'

'Maybe she doesn't want to speak to you.' And even if she did, maybe she shouldn't.

'Maybe,' Leo acknowledged. 'It's important, Rosa, please.'

Rosa sat staring at the stage, at Jude. She didn't want Anna to have to wait three years for closure, as they had. 'She'll be back at the villa. She's overseeing the cleanup and packing.'

'Packing?'

'She's heading back to Oxford tomorrow.' Leaving Rosa to manage the week of post-wedding festivities Valentina had requested. Yay. Except, right now, Rosa couldn't deny her sister anything. Not if it meant Anna finally finding the life she wanted.

'I thought she was staying here?' Leo sounded surprised.

'Mama wants her to go back and think about it. It's a huge change. Everyone just wants her to be sure. To make sure she's doing it for the right reasons.' She gave him a sidelong glance.

'Thanks.' Leo got to his feet.

Rosa tried to resist the urge to say anything more, and failed.

'Leo? She's actually doing really well. If you are going to make matters worse then stay away or I'll make you sorry you ever messed with my sister.' Threat made, she turned her attention back to the stage, clearly dismissing him.

'Warning understood,' Leo said and walked away.

'It better be,' Rosa muttered, under her breath. But then Jude, still up on stage, started speaking, and she forgot all about her sister's problems for a moment.

'This is my last song tonight,' Jude said, to a chorus of groans and calls for more. He held up a hand. 'No, really. But I just wanted to say, before I play it, that I wrote this one here, on La Isla Marina. I think this island has romance woven into its soil and stone and sand, because I've never felt as inspired as I do here. Although, that might be down to a certain muse re-entering my life, too.' He looked straight at Rosa as he said it, and her heart stuttered at everything she saw in his eyes. 'I'll be leaving the island soon, but I know my memories of this place will live on. And, Valentina, Todd…if your marriage is half as happy as I've been here on the island, you'll be very fortunate indeed. And I hope that it's twice as happy as that. So, this one is for the bride and groom.'

But it wasn't, Rosa realised as he started to pluck the strings, in the traditional Spanish style. It was *her* song. The one he'd written for her as she'd lain naked in his bed the night before.

She watched his face as he sang, saw all the emotion that was bursting to escape from her heart echoed there. And as his bright blue gaze met hers as he sang of water on skin and moonlight overhead, a bone-deep truth resounded through her.

She was in love with Jude Alexander.

And there was nothing she could do about it, because he was going to leave her, this time.

For good.

The week that followed the wedding had been planned as five days of non-stop entertainment for the wedding guests. Since Anna had left for Oxford (with Leo in tow, after what must have been a lot of grovelling on Leo's part, Jude imagined) Rosa was in charge, which meant she was rather busier than Jude would have liked. Given that it was their last week on the island together, he'd have preferred she had nothing to concentrate on but him, but apparently that wasn't how this worked.

'Sorry,' she'd murmur against his skin as she slipped out of his bed in the morning. 'There's cookery lessons at the villa today.' Or, 'I'm taking a group horse-riding over on the mainland.'

'Can't you skive off, just for one day?' he'd asked, on the second morning. 'Stay here with me. We can go skinny-dipping again. Or you could finally show me the secret door to your bedroom…'

'Sorry,' she'd said again, smiling sadly. 'Anna left me in charge. And for once, I'm actually trying to live up to my obligations.'

And how was he supposed to argue with that?

There were a few trips he joined in with, though— namely the tapas tour of Cala del Mar, and the wine tasting at a local vineyard on the mainland. Rosa was too busy to dedicate all her time to him on those trips, but just the shared smiles across the room or a moment enjoying a plate of *gambas* together was enough to keep him going until the evening.

And the evenings, once all the entertainment was over, were magical.

It was as if, with their limited time together shrinking by the hour, they'd both been possessed with a sense of urgency that outshone even their previous passion. Jude didn't know how Rosa was coping on so little sleep, but she never seemed tired when she arrived at his bungalow in the evening. They'd fall asleep in each other's arms hours later, and then, before he knew it, Rosa would be slipping away, murmuring her apologies.

The coldness she left behind only made him more intent on enjoying every last second they had together.

But if their nights brought them closer than ever, the days seemed to put a strange barrier between them. He was a guest, no longer helping Rosa with the arrangements, but dancing attendance on Valentina and the others instead. Just being surrounded by the sort of people he was used to partying with in New York made him feel hemmed in again, and he seemed to spend his time dodging conversations about life in the city, or his plans for after the week was up. Most of all, he seemed to be avoiding Sylvie, who never had been very good at reading when a person didn't want to spend time with her.

Rosa, of course, charmed everyone she spoke to. She swept through the events and the days with a smile and a ready hand, fixing whatever needed fixing, keeping everything running so smoothly even Anna would be proud of her, Jude thought. But he was sure the only reason her easy charm never failed was because she knew this was only temporary. Five days of making nice with celebrities and rich folk and she'd be back to her real life.

Except this *was* his real life, to a point. He would be going back to this soon enough.

Was it so wrong of him to want to spend his last few days on the island with Rosa?

But she had work to do, so he let her get on with it, smiling at her across rooms and waiting for night to fall so she could be just his again.

For their last night on the island, Rosa had arranged a moonlight picnic on the beach for everyone. Given how late the sun set, quite apart from his objections to spending his last evening with Rosa with a crowd of people,

Jude thought this was kind of stupid, but Valentina had assured him it was romantic.

'You should definitely come,' she'd said, with a sly smile. 'You need more romance in your life.'

'I have plenty of romance,' Jude had replied, thinking of Rosa naked in his arms.

Valentina, seemingly reading his mind, had slapped his arm. 'That's not romance, Jude. Come on, join us tonight. And bring your guitar.'

'Now the truth comes out. I knew you only wanted me for my music.'

Valentina had laughed. 'I think Rosa and Todd would object to me wanting anything more, don't you?'

So that was how he came to be playing all the usual songs in an unusual place, sitting on a piece of driftwood on the beach, watching the moon play on the water. They'd lit a bonfire a little way away, and the staff were providing marshmallows and sticks to toast them on. They also had a full barbecue set up a little further away, as well as the picnic buffet. By the look of the amount of food and alcohol laid on, they were expecting this thing to go on all night. In which case there'd be a lot of hungover guests staggering to the boats to catch their flights home tomorrow.

Maybe he and Rosa could escape early, though, once everyone was suitably sloshed.

At least it wasn't the same beach where he and Rosa had gone for their fateful swim. He wasn't sure he'd have been able to keep his mind on the music if his brain had been reliving that night over and over. As it was, it was hard not to remember Rosa emerging from the sea, naked and glistening like a water goddess.

A discordant twanging sound came from his guitar, and he realised he'd managed to break a string, just imagining

Rosa naked. Thankfully, everyone was so busy talking, eating and drinking no one was even paying all that much attention to his playing, so he retrieved a spare string from his case and set about restringing the instrument.

'You okay there?' Rosa sank to the sand in front of him, her legs folded under her, as he finished fixing his guitar. Her eyes shone in the firelight, her dark hair curling loose over her shoulders for once, just as it was in bed at night.

'Depends,' he said, tuning up. 'Do you think we can get out of here soon?'

Rosa gave him a cheeky grin. 'You're just never going to see the ocean the same way again, are you?'

'Apparently not.' No point denying what he'd been thinking about. Not with Rosa. Especially since he was almost certain she'd been thinking the same.

'Play me my song again,' she said, softly. 'One more time, and then I'll take you to bed.'

'Your wish is my command,' Jude said, and started to play.

They only had one more night together. He'd give her anything she asked.

# CHAPTER TWELVE

THE FAMILIAR NOTES rose up into the night, circling above the fire, the beach, the crowd, the sea. Rosa closed her eyes and let them wash over her. She couldn't look at Jude as he played, even less so when he sang. The words cut too close, piercing her chest and brushing up against her heart.

She'd spent so long keeping everything away from there, ensuring that no one could lasso her heart and use it to keep her tied down. But it seemed that Jude had snuck in there against her best defences, anyway.

She was in love with Jude Alexander. She'd hoped that sudden truth of feeling might pass, but the week since the wedding had only confirmed it for her. She'd spent her days running events for the wedding guests, her brain only half functioning—because the other half was still thinking about Jude. And her nights...nothing about her nights with him had gone any way at all to persuading her to fall *out* of love with him.

The worst part was, she was starting to think nothing would.

She was irrevocably in love with Jude Alexander, and it was entirely possible she had been for the last three years and was only now coming out of denial.

She'd tried to tell herself that it didn't matter. It didn't change anything. Their situations were still exactly as they had been, so what difference did her feelings make? She'd vowed to make the most of their last week together, and then she'd move on. Just as she had a hundred times before. Easy.

But now she was down to counting in hours, and he was singing her song, and nothing about it felt easy at all.

How had she let this happen? She'd been so careful, always, not to let anything trap her with obligations and expectations. She'd rebelled against her father's academic expectations, lived down to Anna's expectations for her family life, run away from Jude's hopes for love and a future for them…and she'd ended up here, anyway.

Maybe Jude was right. Maybe them both being on the island at the same time was fate, or destiny. A way of making them face up to their demons.

But when her demons were as good-looking as Jude, it was so damn hard not to be tempted by them.

'I'll always see you in the moonlight,' Jude sang, the song coming to a close with a few more notes, and when Rosa opened her eyes he was staring right down into them.

She could stay lost in those blue eyes for eternity. And that terrified her almost as much as it excited her.

'Let's go,' she whispered. 'Now.'

Jude's slow smile was all the agreement she needed.

Rosa's body thrummed with anticipation as they slipped away from the beach, treading the familiar path back to Jude's bungalow. But for once, it wasn't the expectation of his hands on her body that made her blood buzz. This was something entirely new.

This wasn't sex. This was love.

Because she had to tell him. She couldn't let him leave without knowing how she felt.

Maybe it would change nothing, but she knew she'd

never forgive herself if she didn't try. And as her family well knew, Rosa didn't know how to *not* say whatever was on her mind.

The moment the bungalow door closed behind them, Jude dropped his guitar case to the floor and his hands were at her waist, his mouth at her neck, and it took all her mental strength to say, 'Wait.'

If they started this, she wouldn't be able to stop it. And they needed to talk first.

Jude pulled back, just enough to look into her eyes. 'What's the matter?' The concern in his voice was a warm comfort around her heart.

He'd loved her once. Maybe he could again.

Maybe even enough to give her what she needed to be able to have this.

'I need to…can we talk? Just for a moment?'

If he said no, this wouldn't last any longer, anyway. And if he said yes…then there was no rush any more. They could take all the time in the world.

The expanse of for ever stretching out before them, together, for the first time didn't feel like a life sentence. Like a punishment.

It felt like the ultimate in opportunity.

As long as it could happen her way.

'Sure.' Frowning, Jude led her to the small seating area, pouring them each a glass of wine from the carafe on the counter. 'What is it?'

Rosa bit her lip. She wasn't good at subtle; she never had been. And she couldn't twist words and make a fancy argument as Anna could. She relied on her pictures, an image to tell a hundred stories, with just a few words where necessary to illuminate the subject.

She wasn't a poet, like Jude. She couldn't express her emotions in clever rhyme and melody.

All she had was her truths.

What she knew to be true. So she started there.

'You need to leave New York.' Okay, so it wasn't the most romantic opening, but it was true.

Jude looked taken aback. 'Okay…why, exactly?'

'Because it's dragging you down. Your guilt for Gareth, your promises…and that place. When I met you three years ago, you were full of music, of life. And now…now it's all about the brand and the label and negotiations with the rest of the band and…don't you want to be free of that?'

'Maybe.' Jude put his glass down on the counter. 'But I owe it to Gareth's memory—'

'No! No, you don't.' That was what was keeping him back. The memory of a friend who couldn't ever be satisfied when he was alive, let alone now he was dead.

'You don't understand,' Jude started, but Rosa interrupted him again.

'Yes, I do. I understand that you made Gareth a promise to keep him alive. But you couldn't save him. No one could. It wasn't me being there, or even me leaving that made you break that promise. Gareth was an addict. He was sick, and he needed more help than one best friend saying, "That's a bad idea." And he needed to want that help. He needed to seek it out and find a way to break that addiction and he didn't. If he'd been ready to be helped, it wouldn't matter what was going on in your life. And even then…you couldn't give up your life to save his. He wouldn't want that, and you know it.' She felt breathless, saying all the words she knew he needed to hear but wouldn't want to.

'Maybe,' he acknowledged. 'But even if you're right, I still owe him. I made another promise, when he died, remember?'

'And you've fulfilled it! You found the fame you swore you'd both fight for. You've lived his success for him.' When would he see that he'd done everything he could? It was time to live his own life, his own choices now.

But Jude looked away. 'It's not enough.'

'It'll never be enough.' Rosa grabbed his hand where he stood beside her, willing him to understand. 'Nothing ever was, for Gareth. Even now…when does it stop? When do you say, I've gone as far as I can go?'

'I don't know.'

'Because that point doesn't exist!' She'd seen it before. And he *had* to believe her. 'You'll keep living your life for someone else—someone who isn't even here to see it—for ever. And you'll never be happy. And he'll never be satisfied.'

Jude shook his head, and Rosa knew he wasn't hearing her. 'It's not just about Gareth's memory, anyway. I also want to keep having a career, you know. Music was my life long before you came into it.'

'You'll always have that,' Rosa replied. 'Your music is iconic now. You could write advertising jingles for the rest of your life and it wouldn't take away from what you'd already accomplished.'

'Thanks for that vote of confidence in my musical future,' Jude said, drily.

Rosa waved a hand vaguely. 'You know what I mean.'

'I really don't.' His eyes serious, Jude moved to sit opposite her. 'Rosa. What, exactly, are you asking me to do?'

This was it. This was her last chance to put everything out on the line, and have him take it or leave it.

Take her or leave her.

And Rosa had never been more scared in her life.

She took a deep breath.

'Run away with me.'

* * *

*Run away with me.*

How many times over the years had he dreamt of hearing that from her? Of knowing Rosa wanted him with her, as she explored this wide world? Of having her choose him, for once, over her freedom?

Except she wasn't, was she? That was what it came down to.

She wasn't ready to give up what they had, but she wouldn't give up anything else, either.

Rosa didn't just want to have her cake and eat it, too. She wanted the damn bakery to deliver.

'You want me to give up everything I have—my band, my career, my life in New York, my future—to travel around the world at your beck and call until you get bored of me again?' Anger rose up in him, hot and furious, as he realised the truth of this.

This wasn't love. This wasn't for ever—because they both knew Rosa couldn't offer that. She never had been able to.

This was convenience. It was using his unsettled feelings, his vulnerabilities after the book's release, after Gareth, to get what she wanted.

If she'd approached it differently—suggested he extend his sabbatical away from the city until the buzz about the book died down—maybe he'd have considered it. But it was always all or nothing with Rosa. No compromise, no middle path. She didn't know how, and she wasn't willing to learn.

He looked down into her wide, dark eyes, and realised the truth.

He loved her. Of course he did. But that simply wasn't going to be enough.

'That's not what I was saying,' Rosa started.

Jude shook his head. 'Yes. It is.'

'No! Jude... I—'

'Don't say it.' If she was even *thinking* what he thought she was about to say, he couldn't hear it. He couldn't risk it. If she told him she loved him, there was no way he could walk away again, not knowing that. He'd give up everything to trail her around the world, and he'd end up resenting her for it.

A shocked laugh bubbled up from somewhere inside him.

'What's so funny?' Rosa asked, scowling.

'I just realised,' Jude said. 'This must be exactly how you felt, three years ago.' How Sancia felt in Oxford with the professor. How Gareth felt sometimes when Jude kept him safe, back at the hotel instead of out at the party where he wanted to be, blazing bright.

Maybe Rosa was right. Maybe he never could have saved Gareth. But he could decide to save himself from any more heartbreak.

It wasn't much. But it was what he had left.

'So you're punishing me. Is that it?' Rosa jumped to her feet, her colour high and her eyes blazing. 'I left you three years ago, so you won't even consider staying now? I know I hurt you, but, Jude, this is just petty.'

'Petty! Rosa, you tore my heart out and stamped on it, then breezed back into my life and told me you'd just been ready for something new!'

'I explained—' Rosa started, but Jude was in no mood to hear it. All he'd wanted was one last night with Rosa, one perfect memory to say goodbye on.

Instead he got this. Everything he ever wanted on a plate, except he knew it was laced with poison.

'You explained. Right. But what it came down to was the same thing it will always come down to with you. You value your own freedom, your own choices, above every-one else's. And that might work for you with the rest of the world. But for the people who love you? It's horrible.'

The colour faded from Rosa's face as she stumbled back-wards, grabbing a chair for support. 'What do you mean? Is it so wrong for me to want to pursue my own dreams?'

'No,' Jude allowed. 'But is it wrong of me to want to stay and look for my own?' New York might not be ev-erything he'd ever dreamed of, but he knew the rules there. He knew he was as safe as it was possible to get, knew he could look himself in the mirror and know he was living out his promise. New York had always been their dream—and Rosa was asking him to give it up.

'But you're not!' Frustration leaked out of Rosa's voice. 'You're doing what the label says you should, or the rest of the band. You're not making new music, you're just remaking the old stuff! Living for a memory. Does fame really mean so much to you that you can't give it up to pursue the music that really makes you come alive again? Like the song you wrote here, for me?'

Did she really not see? Did she really not understand? One look at her face told Jude she didn't.

'That wasn't the music, Rosa. That was you.'

'What?'

Scrubbing a hand through his hair, Jude sighed. 'I wrote that song—found the passion and the music—because I found you again. For three years, it didn't much matter what I wrote or played because you weren't there to hear it.'

'Then why didn't you come after me?' From the way her eyes widened, and her hand went to her mouth, Rosa was as shocked by her words as he was.

'How could I? You didn't tell me where you were going.'

'And in this day and age, with the Internet and everything, there was absolutely no way you could find out?' She was right, Jude knew. He *could* have found her if he'd wanted to.

But he hadn't.

'Gareth had just died. Forgive me if—' But she could always tell when he was lying.

'That's not why, is it? Tell me the truth, Jude. We owe each other that much.'

'I didn't come after you because I knew I couldn't take it if you turned me away again. You knew me, Rosa. You knew every depth of me, more than any other person in the world. And you turned your back on it and walked away. No, I didn't come after you. Because I loved you, and I knew I could never, ever be enough for you.'

'But you are!' Rosa surged forward, grabbing his hands to her chest. 'You are. You're everything I need. That's why I'm here, asking you. Come with me! I don't see what the problem is. We can run together, keep having the same fun we've been having here on the island. It doesn't have to end yet.'

'Yet.' That was what it came down to, wasn't it? With Rosa, there was always a time limit—and only she knew what that might be. And Jude couldn't live like that.

He'd known, deep down, that Gareth had a time limit, too. That however hard he tried, Gareth lived too hard, too fast, to live for ever, or even to old age. He just hadn't expected it to be so soon. He'd thought he could buy more time—just as he'd tried to do again on the island with Rosa.

God, he was an idiot. Trying to control time, and other people. Both were equally impossible.

The only thing he could control was himself. He could keep *himself* safe, even if he couldn't ever have done the same for Gareth.

Rosa would leave, sooner or later. It was all there in that tiny three-letter word: *yet*.

Rosa stilled as she finally caught his meaning. 'Nothing lasts for ever, Jude. Can't we just enjoy this while it *does* last?'

Jude shook his head.

'Why not?' Rosa slammed her hand down on the counter. 'Jude, I love you. Whether you want to hear it or not. And right now, I can't imagine ever loving another person my whole life—I haven't before, and I can't see that changing.'

The words pierced him straight through his body. She loved him. This was what he had always wanted.

And he was going to send it away. His choice, this time.

'So you'd marry me? Promise me for ever? Go with me wherever life took me?'

He didn't need to hear her answer. He could see it in the fear on her face.

'Why couldn't you come wherever I went?' she asked.

'Because I won't give up everything I have when I know that one day—sooner or later—you'll walk out on me again,' he said, simply. 'It almost broke me last time, Rosa. I can't risk it twice.'

'You can't trust me.'

'Can you tell me I should?'

She looked away. 'No.'

'Then I don't think there's anything more to say. Do you?'

She didn't answer.

Grabbing his guitar, Jude walked out on the love of his life.

He didn't look back.

# CHAPTER THIRTEEN

TEARS BLINDED HER as Rosa raced up the path back to the villa. Thank goodness everyone was leaving tomorrow. She could be packed and on a boat with them first thing, and on a plane to Russia, or Australia—anywhere—before breakfast. She needed to get as far away from La Isla Marina, and Jude Alexander, as possible—and fast.

What had she been thinking? Of course he wouldn't give up all his successes and fame to run away with her. Who would? Rosa had always been the screw-up, the wild and free one who couldn't settle for anything. Now it seemed she couldn't live up to Jude's expectations any more than she'd lived up to her father's or her sister's. She couldn't live up to his life in New York, or the memory of the best friend he'd lost. Especially when she couldn't promise him for ever.

Except...she'd wanted to. For a heartbeat of a moment, when he'd asked if she'd marry him, she'd wanted to say yes. Wanted to fall into his arms and be his for ever.

Until he'd added 'go with me' and she'd known she couldn't promise that.

She wasn't a follower. And neither was Jude. Neither of them would ever be happy trailing around after the other.

It was an impossibility. *They* were an impossibility.

It had been fun while it lasted, but she should never have expected anything more. She wasn't good at compromise, or giving, or other people's feelings. Hadn't Anna made that clear enough?

Her sister could change her path, change her mind, her life. But Rosa never had been able to live up to Anna's example.

For one, sharp moment Rosa missed her sister so much that it ached. They might not have always—okay, often—got along, but Anna was still family. She'd turned to Rosa when she'd found out she was pregnant, eventually, and now Rosa wished that she could do the same.

But Anna was far away in Oxford with Leo, and all Rosa had left were her parents. The mother who'd taught her that the best way to deal with difficulties was to run away, and the father who'd always wanted her to be someone she wasn't.

Somehow, she couldn't see either of them fixing this mess.

Wiping her tears away, Rosa stepped into the main villa, the place she'd spent so many childhood holidays, that held so many memories.

Then she stopped.

And she stared.

'Mama?' she whispered. Sancia didn't hear her. '*Dad?*' Louder this time. 'What are you doing?'

Sancia and Ernest broke apart, and Rosa regretted her question. It was pretty obvious what they were doing.

Kissing.

Her parents.

After ten years apart. Estranged. Not speaking. Now suddenly they were…

Kissing. Passionately.

'Rosa!' Sancia patted her hair as she smiled at her daughter. 'Um, we have some news!'

'So I can see.' Rosa crossed her arms over her chest. Was *everyone* else finding their happy ever after on this island? Or, more likely, was this sudden reconciliation going to end in disaster—just as Jude and hers had?

Sancia's brow furrowed. 'Are you okay, *querida*? Did something happen?'

'I just caught my parents making out. Other than that...' She didn't want anyone to know about Jude. Not yet.

Not when his words still hurt so much.

Her father pulled a face. 'Making out? Really, Rosa. Is it so wrong for two people in love to express their affection for each other?'

'When they're *my* parents...' Rosa shook her head. 'Never mind. Just...what's going on? What's your news?' In love? Had she really heard those words from her buttoned-up father's mouth?

'Your father is moving here to the island!' Sancia practically vibrated with excitement.

Rosa blinked. And she'd thought Anna's decision to stay on La Isla Marina was the about-turn of the century.

'Here? You're staying here?' she asked her father.

Ernest put his arm around Sancia and nodded. 'I think it's about time. Don't you?'

Time? Was that all it took? If she waited another decade would she be able to make things work with Jude? Somehow, she doubted he'd be willing to wait that long.

'But...how can you just give up everything you've worked for in Oxford? All your old dreams?' His career at the university, his professional reputation—they'd been all that mattered to him, when she was growing up. Everything in their lives had been arranged around them.

And now he was just throwing them away? It didn't make any sense.

'Your mother needs support here on the island. And Anna will be here, too, so I'd be alone in Oxford.'

So that was it. Of course. 'You mean, your nursemaid is moving here so you better had, too?'

'No.' Ernest's voice was sharp. 'I'm moving here for many reasons. Not least, my health and well-being. Rosa, you've told me often enough over the years that I need to take responsibility for my health. I'd think you'd be glad I'm finally retiring to do that.'

'I am,' Rosa said, quickly. 'I just…'

Sancia pulled away to put an arm around Rosa's shoulders. 'What is it, *querida*?'

Rosa looked at her mother. 'Ten years ago you got fed up of living the life Dad wanted all the time, and you left to come here. To find your own dreams again. Right?'

'I suppose,' Sancia said. 'I was tired of always coming second to his work and not being able to follow my heart. But most of all, I just missed my home, and my parents needed me more than he did.' Her smile turned sad. 'Even more than you girls did, in some ways. Your father and I were arguing more and more, and it was making me so unhappy… I knew it had to be affecting you and Anna, too. I didn't want you to grow up in an unhappy home, and I didn't want to regret staying when I should have gone…but, Rosa, leaving you girls behind, only seeing you in the holidays, that was the hardest choice I ever had to make. You know that, don't you?'

'I do,' Rosa said as Sancia hugged her close. Her mother had always made it clear that her leaving was nothing to do with the girls—even if it had taken Rosa a while to believe it when she was younger.

Perhaps that was why she'd never asked her mother

outright for all the reasons she'd left. She'd listened to what Sancia said, tried to believe it, and always just assumed it was because she was tired of life in Oxford.

But now she needed firm answers. She needed to understand. 'Dad, what if the same thing happens to you?'

'What do you mean?' Ernest asked.

'What if, living here, you get, well, bored? You're giving up everything that has always mattered to you. I don't want you to end up resenting Mama for that in a few months, or years. When you realise you're tied to her dreams and obligated to stay.'

She'd never seen the smile on her father's face before, Rosa realised. It was softer, kinder, more indulgent than any smile he'd given her before.

Professor Gray held a hand out to Sancia, who took it with a smile of her own. Rosa watched, confused.

'You're forgetting my most important reason to stay here, Rosa,' her father said. 'I'm in love with your mother.'

Love. The word caught her in the throat. Did it always have to come down to that?

'What if that isn't enough?' she asked, and the concern on Sancia's face returned.

'Rosa, did something happen with Jude?' she asked.

'I just need to know,' Rosa said desperately, her arms wrapped tight around her middle. 'What if love isn't enough?'

'Then nothing is,' Sancia said, simply.

'When it's true love, staying isn't an obligation. It's a privilege.' Professor Gray pressed a kiss to his ex-wife's head. 'I'm giving up my old dreams for new ones. Better ones.'

'We got it wrong last time,' Sancia said. 'Both of us. We thought there were more important things than love.'

'Aren't there?' Rosa felt as if the bottom were falling out of her heart.

'There are things that matter as much,' Professor Gray allowed. 'And there are circumstances that can over-whelm it, if you're not careful.'

'So if it's love, you have to give up everything?' Because that didn't sound like love to her.

'No, *querida*.' Sancia moved forward, guiding Rosa with an arm around her shoulder to one of the low, cush-ioned benches that were scattered around the reception area. 'Love is about accepting the other person as they are, and loving them in spite of your differences.'

'Or because of them,' her father added, sitting down beside her. 'Your mother and I…we're very different peo-ple. But those differences don't lessen our love any.'

'And in some ways they even make us stronger,' San-cia added. 'As long as we accept them and respect them.'

'You mean he has to love me for who I am?' Because in that case, there really was no hope for Jude and her.

Sancia laughed, lightly. 'That's the easy part, *querieda*. Who could not love you?'

Rosa stared at her mother in amazement. 'You *have* to love me. You're my parents. But I know I'm not easy to love. I know it's in spite of all my flaws and not because of them. I'm no Anna.'

'We never wanted you to be Anna,' Sancia said, sur-prised. 'We just wanted you to be happy.'

Beside her, Rosa's father was nodding his agreement. Rosa looked at him in confusion. 'But… I never could follow the schedule or plan ahead. I couldn't settle to anything, especially not studying.'

'And none of that meant we loved you any less,' Er-nest said. 'Or that we were any the less proud of you than we are of Anna.'

Rosa blinked, tears burning behind her eyes again.

'Oh, Rosa.' Sancia hugged her tightly. 'How could you think you are difficult to love? You're so full of life and spirit.'

'Just like your mother. That's one of the many reasons I fell in love with her,' Ernest put in. 'And you've taken that spirit out into the world, forging your own, brilliant path. Your sister collects all your photos and articles and saves them for me, you know. I have them all catalogued in my office.' He said it so casually, as if it were obvious. An inevitability. But the knowledge lifted Rosa's heart, even in the middle of her misery.

'We're very proud of you, *querida*,' Sancia said. 'And we love you very much. And if Jude doesn't, then he's a fool.'

Rosa shook her head. 'He's not. Last time... I left him. I broke his heart.'

'I wonder where you learnt to do that,' Ernest murmured, but he was smiling fondly at Sancia as he said it.

'Then he's a coward, if he won't take the risk of loving you again.' Sancia looked outraged on Rosa's behalf.

'I don't blame him,' Rosa admitted. 'I'm not sure I would. I'm asking him to give up everything.'

'Love does take some compromise, Rosa,' her father said, gently. 'But the rewards should always be greater than whatever you have to give up.'

'In the end, love is the only thing that lasts,' Sancia said, smiling at her husband as she stood, holding her hand out to him. 'And it's worth ten times of everything else.'

'Which is why we won't make the same mistakes again.' Rosa's father got to his feet, too, taking Sancia's hand.

'I'm glad,' Rosa said, the words thick in her throat. 'I'm glad you found each other again.'

'So am I,' Sancia said, and then Ernest swept her into his arms again, and Rosa turned away.

She couldn't watch their happiness. Not tonight.

Tomorrow. Tomorrow she'd be happy for them. She'd smile and offer congratulations on her way off the island.

Tonight, she just needed to mourn her own broken heart, and think about all the compromises she hadn't been willing to make, until it was too late.

And then she'd move on.

Jude didn't trust her love. She hadn't left herself any other choices.

Jude hadn't exactly planned on heading back to the beach, but that was where he found himself, all the same.

The party was winding down, the fire burning down low. Couples were dotted around the sand in cosy embraces, talking low, and Valentina and Todd were dancing on the shoreline as if there were no one else in the world but them.

Jude looked away. He couldn't quite bear to watch that kind of happiness tonight.

Settling back onto his piece of driftwood, he pulled his guitar from its case again. Music had always been his friend, his comfort, and he needed it tonight more than ever, since the day he lost Gareth.

Rosa would be leaving as soon as she could, of course. And he'd be left behind again, with his heart in tatters. Meeting Rosa had torn his life apart the first time, but he'd honestly thought he could withstand it this time. How much worse could she do to him, after all?

It turned out, quite a lot.

She loved him. Or she thought she did. Just not enough to give up any iota of her freedom, or give him any hope that she wouldn't leave him again without a backward glance.

Rosa was right, of course. Nothing did last for ever, and there were no guarantees in this life. Gareth had taught him that.

But he needed more than she could give him. He needed…something. Some sign that she was in this as deeply as he was. That she wanted it to last as much as he did.

Was that too much to ask?

'I didn't expect to see you back here tonight.' Sylvie settled herself onto the sand in front of him, too close to where Rosa had sat for Jude to feel comfortable with it.

'You know me. Always the last at a party.'

'Yes,' Sylvie allowed. 'But that was usually because I didn't want to leave until everyone else who mattered had. You never cared for them for yourself.'

'I'll have to get used to them again, I suppose,' Jude said.

'You're definitely coming back to New York, then?' Sylvie sounded surprised. 'I know Rosa said you were, but I assumed she was just being careful. That she was hoping you'd go with her, but she didn't want to fall too deep in case you didn't feel the same. It's what I would do.'

Jude gave a low laugh. 'Trust me, Rosa is never careful. With anything.' Including his heart.

'That's why you love her, I suppose,' Sylvie said, her head tilted to her shoulder as she looked up at him. 'She's so free and open. Like you were, when you first came to the city.'

'Who said I loved her?'

Sylvie's smile was sad. 'Oh, Jude. Anyone who has seen you together this week knows that. You're not subtle, my dear.'

'I wasn't trying to be.' He hadn't been trying to be anything, here. Not a celebrity, not a star. Not a musician. Not Gareth's best friend. Not even Jude Alexander, brand.

He hadn't even tried to be enough for Rosa—he'd known there wasn't any point.

He'd been just Jude. Himself.

And Rosa had loved him. Not enough to stay, sure, but enough to tell him. For Rosa, that was a lot.

More than he'd have expected, before tonight.

'It's better this way.' Sylvie stretched her long legs out over the sand. 'I know you don't love me. I'm not sure if I love you either, to be honest. But I think love might be overrated. You don't need love—especially not if it makes you look as miserable as you do tonight.'

'What do I need, then?' Jude asked, honestly curious. Maybe there was another path. One that hurt less. That would be good.

'You need someone to look pretty next to you at awards ceremonies. Someone who doesn't object to you being away on tour for half the year, or mind when you lock yourself away to write for days on end. Someone to keep the groupies and whackos at bay, at least a little bit. Someone who gets as much from the association as you do. Someone who fits your level of stardom.'

'Someone like you?' he guessed.

'Why not?' Sylvie shrugged those elegant shoulders. 'We were good together, Jude, admit it. It might not be love, but it was enough. Satisfactory satisfaction, if you like.'

She was right, Jude realised. Sylvie had been the picture-perfect partner for him, supporting his brand, making sure he was seen at the right places, giving him—and the band—the right level of glamour. Gareth would have been jealous as all hell.

No, Gareth would have snagged Sylvie himself, and shown her off all over the world. Gareth would have lived the life Jude had now with style and flourish and excitement. He'd have loved it.

But the thought of going back to it made Jude feel as if the sea were closing in over his head and taking him down.

And Rosa was the only one that could save him, pull him out of the water he'd been treading for too long.

'I can't do it, Sylvie.' He shook his head, placing his guitar back in its case, as clarity flowed over him like the tide. 'I can't live like that again.'

Rosa was right. Well, no, she was still more wrong than right about a lot of things. But she was right about him.

He had to let Gareth's memories, the broken promises, and all the expectations go.

He needed to be free every bit as much as she did.

And the only time he ever felt free to be himself was when he was with Rosa.

Which only left him with one option.

She couldn't promise him anything, but then nobody could. Not really. He knew, better than anyone, that some promises just weren't possible to keep.

Maybe they didn't need any promises. Maybe all they needed was love.

And the willingness to risk everything for it. Because some people were worth the risk. One person, anyway.

Gareth would have. Gareth always believed a risk was worth it, if the prize was big enough. For Gareth, the prize was always fame.

For Jude, it was Rosa.

And suddenly, Jude knew he would risk it, too.

# CHAPTER FOURTEEN

ROSA'S TURRET BEDROOM had always been an escape, before. A place of refuge from her family, or the guests on the island, or whatever. But now it felt like a cell, one she couldn't wait to escape.

She folded the yellow dress she'd worn for the wedding and placed it in her case, followed by the skirt she'd stripped off on the beach the night she went swimming with Jude. Tears dripped onto the fabric, and she shoved it in fast. She couldn't think about Jude. Possibly ever again, but definitely not until she'd put some considerable air miles between them.

She needed to move on. She didn't have any other choice now.

Maybe her parents were right and love could overcome, but not for her and Jude. She'd already burned that bridge. He was probably halfway off the island by now, and she wouldn't chase him. She smiled, sadly, remembering the reasons he'd given for not chasing her three years ago. Suddenly, she understood, in a way she couldn't have before. Not until she'd lived the same moment.

But things were different now. She understood herself better, and her relationship with her family. She was a different person. Maybe, in time, her dreams would shift, too. Maybe she'd even meet someone else, one day. In the distant, distant future. But even as she thought it, she couldn't believe it. Who could live up to Jude Alexander?

So, it was just her. Just like before. That was okay. She'd go to Russia. The story there sounded interesting, important. She'd get her camera out and seek truths through its lens. She'd live the life she'd always promised herself she'd have.

And she might not be happy, but she could be content. She could be herself. And that wasn't nothing.

But then the door to her room flew open and she spun to see Jude standing there, too big in the narrow doorway, his bright blue eyes wild and his black hair crazy.

Swallowing down the last of her tears, Rosa fought to keep her chin level and her voice even. It seemed absurd that, after everything they'd shared over the last few weeks, this was the first time he'd ever even been in her room. 'You found the secret door at last, then?'

'Your mother showed me.' His voice was rough, as if he was as close to tears as she was.

Damn Sancia. Wasn't her mama supposed to be on her side?

'What do you want, Jude?' Hadn't they said enough terrible, hurtful things to each other already? Rosa wasn't sure she could stand to hear any more.

But Jude looked her straight in the eye and said, 'You.'

'I think you made it very clear that you don't,' Rosa said, looking away. 'If you've come here to rub it in some more—'

'I haven't.' Jude stepped closer, taking the dress she was holding from her hands. 'Rosa, just listen? Please?'

It was the please that undid her. She never could deny him when he asked her in that voice. Why else had she had to disappear without word, last time? If he'd asked her to stay…she still wasn't sure she could have said no.

'Okay.'

She couldn't imagine what he'd have to say that could possibly make anything between them any better, though. He'd made it very clear that it was up to her to change the conversation—to change her mind, her direction.

Sancia had called him a coward. But it wasn't him, was it? *She* was the one who needed to be brave.

She needed to find the courage to make big promises. The for ever kind. And she might have to give up everything she'd ever fought for before to do that. Could she?

Would he even let her try?

Rosa thought again of the future she imagined—living her truths, being herself, being content. But never happy.

But what was her other option?

She had to make a promise she would have to keep. She had to live up to expectations for once, whatever her parents said.

She knew, deep down in her soul, that this was it for her.

This was love, and it was all she was going to get.

Anna had changed her dreams. Her life.

So had her father, and that had seemed impossible even a week ago.

Maybe she could do it, too.

She had to at least try, or she knew she'd regret it for the rest of her life.

'I've been thinking,' Jude said. 'I can't leave things as we did, not again. When you left me last time, I spent three years wondering what I did wrong, wishing I could have one more chance to put it right.'

'Or for me to do it right,' Rosa put in, and he smiled.

'So this time, let's try, yeah?'

Hope bubbled up in her chest. 'You're giving me a second chance?' This was it. This time, she wouldn't screw it up. The third time was the charm, right? She just had to stamp down on all those impulses that told her to run. She could stay.

'I'm giving us as many chances as we need to get it right,' Jude said.

But Rosa wasn't listening. Her parents' words were echoing through her mind and finally, suddenly, it seemed possible. If she had Jude with her, she could do it all. Couldn't she?

'I've been thinking… I could come to New York. There's so many stories there, so many photos. I could work there. It could work.'

'Rosa.'

'I could stay in one place.'

'No, you couldn't.'

'I could come on tour with you, then.'

'And follow me round like a groupie?'

Why was he smiling? He kept shooting down every possibility she gave him, and he was doing it with a smile on his face.

'Jude…' She was begging. She was actually going to beg. What the hell had he done to her? 'Just tell me what you need me to do and I'll do it. I'll do whatever it takes to be with you.'

Rosa's words stuck in his chest, and he caught her hands in his in their place, holding them to him. 'You don't understand. Rosa, you don't need to do anything. Except be you.'

She blinked up at him, those dark eyes he loved still wet with tears. Jude wanted to kiss away every tear on her cheek, but first he had to explain himself.

'I went back to the beach after you left. I spoke to Sylvie about New York and the more I imagined going back there, back to that same old life again…the more I knew I couldn't do it. I can't be that Jude Alexander any more. The man they wrote about in that book is gone—if he ever existed at all. And so is the best friend Gareth knew. I'm not the same, now. I can't play that part.'

'Well, I knew that,' Rosa muttered, and he smiled down at her.

'Yeah, well, you were always the expert at being true to yourself.'

'Even when it hurts others.'

'I shouldn't have said that,' Jude said.

Rosa gave a half shrug. 'It's true. I just… I don't know how to be anything else. But I'll learn. I'll figure it out if it means I get to be with you.'

'Luckily for both of us, I love you exactly the way you are,' Jude said, gratified by the sharp intake of breath his words caused in Rosa.

'You love me? Still?'

'Rosa, I've always loved you. From the moment you walked into my life three years ago, I always knew that there was no one else for me. No one else could be so full of life—or could make me feel so alive.' Jude took a breath. 'You asked me a question earlier, remember?' Rosa nodded. 'Will you ask me again?'

'Will you run away with me?' The hope in her eyes was what helped him answer. To step over the edge and give up the life he'd worked for, the fame, the proof that he was worth something, the dreams he and Gareth had dreamt together. Everything.

He'd risk everything for her.

'I'll run anywhere with you,' he said, and kissed her.

For a moment, the world seemed to tilt and turn and snap into place. For the first time in too many years, everything felt right. He didn't have to prove anything, any more. He didn't need to be anything except the man Rosa loved.

All he needed to do was love her back. And it felt as if he'd already been doing that for ever, anyway.

Rosa broke the kiss. 'Wait. How is this going to work? What about the band?'

'I'll tell them I need a break. Or I'll take some time to write—and I can do that wherever you are.' He kissed her hands. 'I can't let you give up your dreams for me, but maybe neither of us needs to give up anything. Maybe we can both just chase them together.'

'Are you sure?'

'Surer than I've ever been about anything,' Jude said. 'Think about it. We can not settle down together. We can spend time in the city when I'm recording, perhaps, and maybe you'd like to come on tour sometimes, when you're not away working.'

'And the rest of the time?'

'I'll come with you. Wherever you want to go.'

'And we'll spend our summers on La Isla Marina with Anna and Leo and the baby, and Mama and Dad?'

'Of course,' Jude replied. 'One of these days I'm going to beat your father at Scrabble.'

'No,' Rosa said fondly. 'You're not. He cheats.'

'I knew it!'

'But you'll play him anyway?'

'I will. But only because it would be rude to refuse my wife's father a game.'

'Your wife?'

'You liked how I slipped that in there?' Jude asked, grinning.

'I know I'm unconventional about these things, but I

seem to remember something about having to be asked, first.'

Jude dropped to one knee, her hands still tight in his as he looked up at her. 'Rosa Gray, will you chase your dreams with me?'

'Yes.'

'Will you love me for ever?'

'Definitely.'

'Will you let me love you and walk by your side for the rest of your life?'

'Oh, yes.'

'Then I think we might as well get married, don't you?'

Laughing, Rosa pulled him to his feet and kissed him, soundly. 'For a poet, that was incredibly unromantic.'

'I'll work on it,' Jude promised.

'Well, we do have for ever,' Rosa said, wrapping her arms around him. 'After all, I'm not going anywhere. At least, not without you.'

'That's all the promise I'll ever need from you,' Jude replied, and kissed her.

# EPILOGUE

La Isla Marina was beautiful in the late-afternoon sunlight. The tiny lights strung through the trees were already lit, glowing in the fading daylight, and lanterns lit the way to the pagoda, through the rows of chairs filled with friends and family, from the island, the mainland, Britain, the States and beyond.

Rosa peered around the corner, down to the pagoda where Jude already stood, her father at his side. Then her niece squirmed in her arms, and she resumed swaying in the way the baby seemed to like best, hoping she wasn't drooling on her dress. Being an auntie seemed to involve a lot of cuddles, which she was just fine with. Uncle Jude was better for the lullabies, though.

'Are you ready?' Rosa asked Sancia, as Anna fiddled with their mother's veil.

Sancia laughed. 'Ready? *Querida*, I've been ready for more than ten years. I was just waiting for your father to come to his senses and come after me.'

The fact that Sancia and Ernest had never actually got around to divorcing should have been a clue, Rosa thought. But at least it made things easier now—a vow renewal on the island was much more special than having to go to the mainland for a formal remarriage.

Anna held out her arms for her daughter, and Rosa

handed her over, feeling a brief pang of emptiness as she did so.

It didn't last long, though. She pressed a hand to her stomach, and remembered that wherever she roamed now, she did it with company. First Jude, and, soon, their child.

Looking down at the path at her feet to hide her smile, Rosa thought how much this would have terrified her a few years ago. Not now, though.

Now, it all seemed like the biggest adventure she'd chased yet.

'Right, that's the first signal,' Anna said as the music changed. 'Everyone ready?'

They'd agreed that they'd walk their mother down the aisle together. It just felt right, since they were entrusting her to their father again. They both had their own lives to live now—Anna and Leo on the island, and Rosa and Jude wherever the mood took them.

Leo appeared to take the baby from Anna, and reclaim his seat at the front. Then Sancia linked arms with both her daughters, and they prepared to walk down the aisle, just as Anna had nine months earlier, still barely showing, to marry Leo. Jude and Rosa had managed to avoid the big showy wedding so far, and Rosa wasn't entirely looking forward to telling her mother that, technically, they were already married. She had a feeling that Sancia wouldn't feel the quick register office service when they were passing through London on tour would really count.

But it counted to Rosa.

Right until the moment she said yes, she'd been half afraid she'd run—and she knew Jude had, too. But when it came down to it, she knew that their love was far more binding than any piece of paper or jewellery.

Really, what more could she give Jude than her heart, anyway? And he'd had that all along.

'It's so wonderful to have both my girls together on the island again,' Sancia said, squeezing them close as they waited for that second change in the music, the one that told them it was time to start walking.

'It is nice to all be together,' Anna agreed. 'Rosa, will you come again for longer, later in the summer?'

'We'll try,' Rosa replied, as the music changed and Anna signalled for them to take their first steps. Rosa grinned as she saw Jude waiting with her father up ahead. 'But come winter we'll definitely be here for a few months,' she said, not thinking.

'Really?' Sancia stopped walking, a pace before the aisle started, and Rosa realised that the middle of her vow renewal service might not have been quite the right time to tell her mother this news.

Oh, well. Timing had never been her strong suit. Or not blurting things out the moment she thought of them.

'Why, Rosa?' Anna had a small line between her eyebrows.

Rosa shrugged. 'Well, I need you both to teach me everything you know about babies. And pretty fast.'

Sancia squealed, embracing her tightly, and Rosa saw her father rolling his eyes over her mother's shoulder.

'You made her smudge her make-up,' Anna said, with a sigh. But Rosa knew from the grin on her face that her sister was happy for her.

'Come on, Mama,' she said, disentangling herself. 'Dad's waiting.'

'Oh, he's waited this long,' Sancia said. 'A few more moments won't make a difference.'

'Besides,' Rosa agreed, smiling at Jude at the other end of the aisle, 'the best things in life are worth waiting for.'

\* \* \* \* \*

# FORTUNE'S FAMILY SECRETS

## KAREN ROSE SMITH

In memory of my dad, Angelo Jacob Cacciola,
who taught by example that creativity could be
expressed in painting, woodworking
and model train platforms.

# Chapter One

Nash Tremont came down the stairs from the second floor of the Bluebonnet Bed-and-Breakfast and followed the aroma of cinnamon and sugar and some kind of bread. His boots didn't make a sound on the steps. After all, he was a police detective and instincts died hard.

At the bottom of the staircase, he spotted a sight that suddenly made him hungry for more than cinnamon rolls. He'd hardly said two words to the proprietress of the bed-and-breakfast but now he couldn't stop himself. "Even a veteran cowgirl should know better than to climb a ladder that's too short."

Cassie Calloway squeaked as if he'd startled her. Her name was an easy one to remember, but he wasn't thinking about her name as she tilted on the ladder, almost losing her balance. He rushed to her side and wrapped his hands around her waist. It was a tiny waist but she was plenty curvy above and below it.

"Sorry," he said. "I didn't mean to startle you."

Gaining her footing once more, she peered down at him. Her tousled brown hair flowed forward and her dark brown eyes moved from his face to his hands at her waist. He quickly removed them, though they tingled because he'd felt her warmth underneath her blouse.

"What makes you think I'm a veteran cowgirl?" she asked, climbing down the ladder.

"Your boots," he answered quickly. He'd been trained to notice details.

She looked down at her boots as if she hadn't remembered what she was wearing. They were brown leather, well creased, with the shine long gone.

"They're comfortable and I like to cook in them." She sounded a bit defensive.

"I came down because something smelled wonderful. But if we keep up this conversation, I have a feeling you're not going to give me anything you made for breakfast."

She laughed and it was a pretty sound. When had he last noticed a woman's laughter?

On the ceramic tile of the kitchen floor now, Cassie Calloway looked up at him. She wasn't short, maybe about five-seven. But he was six-three so her chin had to come up for her to meet his eyes. "You didn't come down for breakfast yesterday. Didn't smell the bacon?"

Yesterday he'd still been trying to make sense out of what he was doing. Oh, he knew what his mission was here in Austin, Texas. Although he was the love child of an affair between his mother and Jerome Fortune, aka Gerald Robinson, he wasn't in Austin about that. He had no desire to see his biological father. He *was* after information—information that could land Gerald Robinson's wife, Charlotte, in jail. He hoped he didn't run into any of his half brothers or sisters, either. He didn't want anything to muddy his investigation or sway his judgment. He was undercover and intended to keep a low profile.

"Maybe I just like cinnamon more than bacon." Teasing Cassie and seeing her smile seemed to make his day. Maybe because everything about why he was here was so serious.

"I didn't know financial consultants were so picky," she joked back.

He almost winced. He'd needed a cover story. A financial consultant on vacation from Mississippi seemed the perfect one to hide his real identity: a detective from Mississippi investigating fraud.

When Cassie Calloway looked into his dark brown eyes with hers, he felt his conscience stab him. He wished he could tell her the truth. But that was ridiculous. He didn't even *know* this woman, let alone know if she was trustworthy. Hormones were the downfall of many a man and he'd do well to remember that.

He nodded to the ladder and the smoke alarm in the ceiling. "What's the problem?"

She opened her hand to reveal a new nine-volt battery. "I need to change the battery, but I couldn't quite reach it."

"And you shouldn't have tried. Don't you have a handyman's number you can call when you need one?"

She scoffed at that and shook her head. "Handyman? I don't think so. I have a mortgage and I need to fill rooms. That's why I opened them to extended stays. You're the first one to take advantage of that."

Nash looked around at the quirky colors of paint on the walls—lime green and sky blue—as well as a mural that had to have been hand-done. It depicted a scene of children sitting under a huge oak. A cowboy was seated on a stool with an open book in his lap as he read them a story. It was really good and he realized the bright wall colors complemented those in the painting.

"You have a nice place here. Have you done many renovations?"

She moved a few steps away from him as if the distance was necessary to talk to him. "I fell in love with it as soon as I saw it. It was in foreclosure. It mainly needed fresh coats of paint."

He nodded to the mural. "Who did your artwork?"

Her cheeks turned a little pink. "I did."

"You've got talent."

Her eyes were bright and her smile wide when she said, "Thank you. I love to paint. I mean *real* paintings. I was an art history major in college, and I took education courses so I could teach. But teaching positions are hard to find in these days of budget cuts, especially *art* teaching positions."

Glancing around again, taking in the whole bed-and-breakfast's first floor as if it was a piece of art, he decided, "You shouldn't let your talent go to waste."

"Oh, I don't. I teach private art lessons, and I help with the community art center." After a brief hesitation, she said, "Now that I told you about me, why don't you tell me about Mississippi?"

He knew she'd called his reference in Oklahoma, the state where he was born. Dave Preston was a close friend who could and would adhere to Nash's cover story.

Nash held his hand out for the battery. "Why don't you let me take care of this before you actually need the smoke alarm?"

"If you're sure you don't mind—"

Not minding a bit, he took the battery from her palm. The tips of his fingers touching her skin sent an electric jolt through him. No, no, no! He didn't have time for an attraction now. He had to save his energy for the job he was here to do and not be distracted by a pretty woman.

Climbing the ladder, he easily changed the battery. Then he was down the ladder once more.

She glanced down at his well-worn boots. "Your boots look comfortable, too."

He had to chuckle. "Yes, they are. Perfect for walking or driving."

"Not for meeting clients?"

Damn it. He was going to have to buy a new pair of boots so he could show her he dressed up for client meetings. Not that he had any of those planned.

He winked at her. "I prefer black boots for a more professional look."

She seemed to look him up and down, from his dark brown hair, over his squarish jaw, down his red T-shirt and his jeans. Her gaze on him made him feel hot.

"I clean up well, too."

She blushed. "Oh, I didn't think you didn't. How about that cinnamon roll?" she asked, obviously embarrassed.

"That sounds good. Join me?" The question came out of his mouth before he thought better of it. He really shouldn't have asked her that.

She hesitated and he thought that was wise of her. After all, even though she'd called his reference, he was practically a stranger. But then deciding it must be safe enough to have breakfast with him, she waved at the eat-at counter on the kitchen side of the room. The other side of the room was filled with tables and chairs, no doubt for the dinner he remembered she also served. He hadn't taken advantage of that yesterday simply because he didn't want to get tied up with her or any other guests. Anonymity was best cultivated if he spent most of his time alone. However, after a quick canvas of the comfortable-looking sitting area, he could see himself working on his laptop there.

"Coffee?" Cassie asked.

"If it's black and strong."

"It is," she said, but then smiled. "I dose mine with cream and sugar."

He rolled his eyes in mock horror. "None of those for me."

"At least I don't serve flavored coffees."

He laughed at her tone. "Your guests don't ask for a hazelnut latte or maybe a caramel macchiato?"

"How do you know about that, since you're a black-coffee drinker and all?"

Their gazes locked for a heartbeat. It was just one of those awareness moments that passed between a man and a woman when they felt chemistry. "I've been in a coffee shop or two."

She looked away first. "I've been known to make a flavored pot of coffee for my women guests. Most of the men are like you and just want theirs black."

Just like him? He doubted that.

More serious now, she asked, "Is there a reason you

didn't stop for breakfast yesterday? You just filled a travel mug with coffee and left."

He'd have to watch himself around her. She also seemed to pay attention to details. "I was in a hurry."

"And not today?"

"I have an appointment this morning but it's a little later." Another lie. Well, not exactly a lie. He did have an appointment to use a computer at the library. He had research to do, and it was going to take hours and hours if not days or weeks. But he'd find what he was looking for.

She motioned again to the stool at the eat-at counter. "Sit and I'll get your breakfast."

"I can put the ladder away for you first if you'd like."

She seemed to contemplate that for a few beats. "Okay. Let me show you where it goes."

He noticed that Cassie moved quickly and gracefully. He couldn't help but watch the gentle sway of her hips as she led him through the dining area. To the right, there was a screened-in porch. It might be nice to sit out there with his laptop, too. He wished he could just access the records he wanted on there, but he couldn't. He didn't want any research being traced back to him. He'd switch around from computer to computer at the library on different days. Once he found what he was looking for, he'd have to have it printed out. There again he didn't want to send emails to himself and have a record of it. His boss in Mississippi had been totally against this investigation because their original case there had been closed. But once Nash had found that Charlotte Robinson could have used the alias Charlene Pickett, he just couldn't let it go.

Following Cassie distracted him from the work he

intended to do. She was sexy in jeans and a boyfriend shirt. She'd rolled up the sleeves and left the collar open. All too well, he could imagine her in one of *his* shirts.

Putting the brakes on that image, he let her guide him down a hall.

She motioned to the left to a half-open door. "That's my suite."

Continuing down the hall, she opened another door on the left. He could see right away it was a utility room with a washer and dryer, a step stool and an open ironing board.

She pointed to the back of the room. "Can you just prop the ladder there for now?"

It was a tight fit sliding past the ironing board but he slanted the ladder against the wall. Cassie had slipped into the area with him, probably to make sure the ladder was securely propped. She acted like a woman who was used to being on her own and doing for herself.

Suddenly, though, they were face-to-face and boots to boots. His eyes locked to hers and he could again feel the thrum of chemistry between them. From the surprise in her eyes, he could see she felt it and recognized it, too. Attraction to Cassie Calloway was way too dangerous to even contemplate.

Again she broke eye contact first and retreated through the opening between the ironing board and the washer and dryer. "I really should close the ironing board," she said, her cheeks an attractive pink. "But I hate setting it back up every time I want to iron something."

"You iron things often?" He was amused by that thought, though he knew his mother was particular about her clothes, too. She'd even ironed pillowcases.

"I like to be presentable," she answered, a little defensively. "Besides, my guests often need to iron their clothes after traveling. They have sleeve boards in the closets in their rooms, but sometimes they're not adequate."

"I do have a couple of dress shirts I should iron," he decided.

"Do you have many clients in Austin?" she asked.

"Enough." He knew to keep personal answers short and concise.

Cassie waited, possibly to see if he'd tell her more, but he didn't. Her cheeks still pink, she said, "I'll get your breakfast ready. Would you like eggs with that cinnamon roll?"

She was already a good five feet ahead of him as she sped out of the utility room.

He called after her, "No eggs." Yet he might have *two* rolls...if they were good.


Cassie didn't know what it was about Nash Tremont that sent a tingle up her spine. She usually kept civility and politeness between her and men, especially those she might be attracted to. She had secrets. From experience, she knew she couldn't share them. That was just the way it was.

But as Nash sat on the stool watching her ready his breakfast, she felt nervous and a bit excited. As she carried two rolls to the counter, along with two mugs of coffee, she asked, "Are you originally from Oklahoma or Mississippi?"

Nash's brows arched. "You didn't ask Dave Preston that when you called for a reference?"

"He told you I called?"

"He did. We're good friends."

Taking a seat next to Nash, careful their elbows didn't brush, she pulled the sugar bowl over to her mug of coffee. "I learned that from our conversation. He told me you'd been friends for years, that you often helped him out with construction projects around his house, that you were good with his kids and his dog. He gave you an A-plus rating."

Nash laughed. "Maybe Dave wasn't used to giving references. He wanted to make sure he didn't miss anything."

"He acted as a friend should. Anyway, your accent isn't pure Mississippi, is it?"

Again Nash gave her a short answer. "I was born and raised in Oklahoma, and if you put too much sugar in that coffee, you're going to crash later today."

She'd been too busy looking at Nash's thick brown hair, and studying the jut of his jaw. She hadn't been paying attention to how many teaspoons of sugar she'd put in her coffee. She'd have to drink it no matter how sweet it was. "No, I don't crash. I just eat more sugar or drink more caffeine."

"Let's see," Nash said with mock seriousness. "Didn't your website say something about serving healthy breakfasts and dinners?"

"That's for my guests who want *healthy*. I eat when I can and usually on the go, especially when I do Paint and Sip presentations."

"Paint and Sip?" He looked perplexed.

"It's a recent wine trend. Local wineries have me in for a Paint and Sip night. I teach their customers how to paint a painting in one night while they sip wine."

"What a great marketing tool," he said.

"It is, and it brings in extra money." She always needed to do that. Her life had been that way since she was a child.

"How about you?" Nash asked. "Are you from Austin?"

Should she tell him? Why not? After all, he wasn't from around here. "I grew up not so far away."

The cinnamon rolls were round and she took hers apart, licking the sugar glaze off her fingers as she did. When she turned toward Nash, he was studying her.

"What?"

"Do you always eat your cinnamon rolls that way?"

Noticing his was gone with two big bites, well, maybe three, she shrugged. "I prolong the experience. Besides...aren't sweets better if you can lick them off your fingers?"

Something glowed in Nash Tremont's eyes and she wished she hadn't said that. There was coiled energy in the man and plenty of sensual energy, too.

As she felt tongue-tied, not knowing what else to say, he drank most of the coffee in his mug. Leaning back a degree, he gave her a smile that didn't reach his eyes. "Your cinnamon rolls are delicious and the coffee is just what I needed. If you don't mind, I'll take a travel mug full of it along with me again."

"I don't mind. Would you like another cinnamon roll for on the road?"

"Yes, I would," he agreed.

"I'll wrap one for you. Will you be here for dinner tonight?"

There was no hesitation in Nash's voice. "No, I won't. I'll be having dinner out." He'd brought his travel mug with him and now he filled it from the urn in the dining area. "Will more guests be checking in?"

Cassie had hopped up from her stool and was wrapping a second roll. "Yes. Thank goodness there will be another couple today. Do you like to mingle when you go out of town or take vacations?"

"I don't take many vacations."

"A workaholic?"

"Something like that," he acknowledged.

Going back to the counter he picked up the roll she'd wrapped in foil. Then he gathered his Stetson from one of the hat racks on the wall and took out his keys. "Thanks again for breakfast. I'll see you sometime." Then, without another word, he was gone.

Cassie had noticed how he avoided personal questions and turned them around on her. She shrugged it off. Maybe Nash Tremont was just a very private man.

Nash gripped the steering wheel of his SUV tighter as he followed the car's GPS directions to the library. But even with that greater tactile stimulation of his hands, even though his thoughts should be perusing the dates of the archives he wanted to look up, he felt bothered by what had happened at the bed-and-breakfast. He shook his left hand, then he put it back on the wheel and shook his right. Still he could feel a tingle in his fingers from the warmth of touching Cassie Calloway. It was absolutely crazy.

He hadn't even looked at a woman with real interest since Sara. His bitterness over what had happened with her had leveled off into disappointment. The divorce rate among cops was well above the average. He'd told himself that over and over again. He'd told himself that his work was enough.

Suddenly his dashboard lit up. A female computer voice told him, "Mom is calling."

He reached to the dash and pressed a button on the digital screen. "Hi, Mom." He'd called her when he'd reached Austin so she wouldn't worry.

"I thought I'd give you a call before we both got involved in our days."

He checked the time on the dash. "This is early for you, isn't it?" It was only 8 a.m.

"I'm going into work early today, lots of new car policies to write up. Must be spring. Drivers like to spruce up their cars or buy a new one."

Nash smiled. His mother worked for an insurance company that wrote car and homeowner policies. She'd been working there for years and seemed to enjoy it.

"How do you like Austin?" she asked.

It seemed like an idle question but he knew she was fishing. "You didn't tell anybody I was coming here, did you?"

"Who would I tell?" she asked innocently.

"If anyone calls from my office in Biloxi, you tell them I went camping in the backwoods, okay? And if Ben Fortune phones again, stick with the story that you don't know where I am." Some of his half siblings had tried to get in touch by mail and phone, but he'd ignored their requests.

Nash heard his mom let out a sigh. "I still don't understand why you can't be honest about what you're doing at work."

"Because I'm not supposed to be doing it." He'd told

her this before when he'd explained why he was spending time in Austin.

"This is on your own time. Why would anybody care?"

"There's a hierarchy. The chief told me to drop this, so he'd be very unhappy if he knew I didn't."

"I get that. Are you sure you don't want to look up your father while you're there?"

"I'm sure."

"I told you before, he's not as terrible as the media makes him sound."

His mother had her memories, but Nash knew the facts. Gerald Robinson had supposedly walked away from the Fortune money and built himself up from scratch. But he'd had many indiscretions along his road to success. Most of them had made their way into the media. Nash still couldn't believe his mother wasn't bitter about what had happened to her. Gerald had been married when he had an affair with Marybeth Tremont, but she'd had no expectations going into the affair. He'd given her that old line about his wife being a gold digger and not understanding him. But a man who cheated was a man who cheated. However, Gerald's indiscretions were the reason Nash had so many half brothers and sisters he'd never met.

His mother's voice came through the speaker again. "Is what you're doing dangerous?"

"No, it's not dangerous. I'm just rounding up background information and this is the best place to do it. With the Robinsons living here, I can nose around, listen to gossip, maybe even get close to them without anybody knowing who I am."

"I want you to be careful," his mother warned him.

"I'm always careful."

He thought he heard her snort before she said, "You know Oklahoma isn't quite as far from Austin as Biloxi is. If you wrap up early what you're doing, you can fly home and visit."

He didn't get home as often as he thought he should. But there were memories there he didn't want to revisit. Still, his mother was right. If he did wrap this up quickly, he should fly to Oklahoma for a visit.

"Let me see what happens here, Mom. I took a month of vacation."

"You know, when I tell you to be careful this time, my advice isn't simply about being careful physically."

"What are you worried about?"

"I'm worried if you do run into a half brother or sister, or your father, you'll leave Austin, stay removed from people who *are* your family and have many regrets. But I'm also worried that if you somehow make contact, you'll get hurt."

"I won't get hurt. I don't have any expectations. This is an investigation about wrongdoing…and fraud, Mom. That's it."

"If you say so."

His mother often used that phrase when she didn't agree with him. He knew it and she knew it.

"Are you going to stop for breakfast instead of just drinking coffee?" she asked.

She also knew him too well. "I actually did have breakfast this morning. The bed-and-breakfast served cinnamon rolls."

"And? How were they?"

"Cassie gave me one to bring along for a snack." He said the words without thinking, and the picture of her unwinding her cinnamon roll and licking the icing from her fingers made him almost break out in a sweat.

"Cassie?"

Uh-oh. He should have been watching his tongue. This investigation really did have him rattled. "She owns the bed-and-breakfast."

"Is she old and gray?"

Again, as if a photo flashed in front of his eyes, he saw Cassie's pretty face, her long brown wavy hair, her chocolate-brown eyes. "She's probably about my age, but do not make anything of it."

"Didn't you say the bed-and-breakfast offers breakfast and dinner?"

"It does if anyone signs up for it."

"You're a growing boy. Take advantage of it."

What his mother was really saying was that he should sit down for meals, get to know people and not isolate himself. Isolation not only kept his job safe but his heart, too. You couldn't spill something you weren't supposed to when you weren't around anyone to spill it to.

"I know you," she went on. "You'll do what you want to do in spite of what I say. But I love you anyway. I've got to go now or I'll be late. You take care and stay out of trouble."

His mother still spoke to him as if he were sixteen. But they'd been through his lifetime together, watching out for each other. He loved her dearly. "You have a good day, Mom. I'll let you know if I can come for a visit."

His mother ended the call. When he thought about their conversation, he remembered her advice.

Should he have dinner with Cassie tonight?

## Chapter Two

Cassie was grateful when Trina and Joe Warner checked in. Sometimes guests didn't even bother to cancel their reservations when they weren't going to come, so she was never sure if a reservation would be kept. Not until her guests actually arrived.

Trina and Joe were in their early sixties, retired and on a road trip to visit family in Oklahoma. After check-in, they'd freshened up, then had come downstairs to join her as she cooked them dinner. Actually, she was cooking enough for four. It was possible that Nash might want to warm up something when he returned to the B&B.

Nash Tremont. She'd been thinking about him too much today...the way his brown hair dipped over his brow, the way his Stetson had set at just the right angle as he'd left this morning. What was it about the man that seemed to make her giddy?

The Warners had plenty to chat about and Cassie could easily see that many guests who stayed at a bed-and-breakfast enjoyed meeting people from different locales. She filled them in about Austin sites until dinner was ready. Tonight she'd cooked a beef-and-beans enchilada casserole along with cornbread biscuits and a salad.

She was pouring the Warners glasses of iced tea from an antique pitcher she'd found in a consignment shop when Nash came in. He frowned when he saw her and the couple at the table. Being the good hostess that she attempted to be, she was ready to acknowledge him when he raised his hand to her as if he wasn't going to stay, but rather go up to his room.

Her manners made her ask, "Are you sure you wouldn't like to join us? There's plenty. And I have chocolate cream pie for dessert."

The Warners waved at the casserole on the table. Joe was already scooping out a serving. "We watched her make it," he said. "Ground beef, chili powder, cumin, beans, chili peppers and sour cream. Tortillas in the bottom and the middle."

Nash's nose twitched as if it was catching the scent of dinner and it might intrigue him. He smiled at the couple, then Cassie, but Cassie thought it took an effort. She guessed he was going to refuse her offer of dinner.

However, he surprised her when he asked, "Did you say chocolate cream pie?"

Cassie laughed. "So the casserole won't do it but chocolate cream pie will?"

After a shrug, he gave her a boyish grin. "Like my

mama always says—I have a sweet tooth that just won't quit." He came over to the table and Cassie noticed again his no-nonsense stride, his confident posture, the twinkles she'd glimpsed in his eyes this morning. She made introductions. He took the chair at the side of the table where he could face the door.

Trina served herself a portion of the casserole and spooned a generous serving for Nash onto his plate. After he thanked her, he met Cassie's gaze. "It smells good. And I do like chilis."

After Cassie poured Nash a glass of iced tea, too, she took a seat next to Trina across from him. He'd taken off his Stetson and placed it on the sideboard. She didn't know if he knew how to ride, but she could easily imagine him on a horse. When she was a little girl, a school friend of hers lived on a ranch. Cassie escaped to Deborah's place as often as she could. Debbie had two parents who loved her, took care of her and cared about Cassie, too. She'd been grateful to have a motherly figure watching over her since her own mother hadn't been able to do it.

Silence reigned at the table as everyone dug into the portions on their plates or took a cornbread biscuit from the basket Cassie had lined with a napkin.

Joe slathered his biscuit with butter. "Delicious."

His wife nudged him. "You haven't even tasted it yet!"

"I can tell from its lightness." He took a bite. "Like I said—delicious."

Everyone at the table laughed.

"How long have you been married?" Nash asked.

"Forty years this summer," Trina answered.

Joe patted his wife's hand. "The best years of my life!"

Cassie swallowed hard. Was that kind of marriage even possible? She thought again about Debbie's parents. Yes, she supposed it was. She explained to Nash, "Joe and Trina stopped here on their way to Oklahoma. They're visiting family."

Nash's gaze met Cassie's and she knew why. He'd told her he was from Oklahoma. Maybe he didn't want her to bring it up. She, of course, wasn't going to spill his personal background.

"What part of Oklahoma?" Nash asked. "I was born and bred there."

"We're heading for Tulsa. Where did you live?"

"Oklahoma City. I was raised by my mom. She insists she did a good job. But I'm not sure how many people would agree with her."

Joe took another biscuit and chuckled. "If she's proud of you, that's all that matters."

As they ate, Nash asked leading questions of the Warners, and they delved into the subject of their children... and their grandchildren.

Cassie thought again that Nash knew how to deflect attention from himself. She noticed it because she knew how to do it, too. The people she'd come to know in Austin believed her parents were dead. She hadn't corrected them because she didn't want the truth to get out.

After coffee and chocolate cream pie, Cassie asked the Warners, "Will you be stepping out tonight?"

The husband and wife looked at each other and shook their heads. "No. We're going to enjoy our beautiful room and just watch some TV. Tomorrow, we'll go sightseeing to some of those places you mentioned."

Joe stood, patted his stomach, which protruded over his belt, and waited for his wife to stand, too. After good-nights all around, they crossed to the staircase and climbed the stairs.

"Nice couple," Nash said as Cassie started to clear the table.

It felt odd being alone with Nash…it seemed intimate in some way. That was silly. Yes, they were alone in her downstairs, but there was nothing intimate about it. Still, feeling self-conscious, she busied herself with clearing the table. To her surprise, Nash helped her and brought dirty dishes to the counter.

"You don't have to do that," she said. With him standing beside her, he seemed to take up all the space in the small kitchen.

"It's no bother. It's the least I can do after that good meal."

She decided to keep the conversation as light as she could. "A man raised with good manners is hard to find these days," she teased.

"Wow! That makes me wonder about the kind of men you date." With a brow arched, he leaned his hip against the counter, looking relaxed…and too sexy for words.

His comment was bait and she understood that. He was trying to find out something about her. "Date? I don't have time for dating," she explained, keeping her reason light and short.

"A busy life. I can certainly see *that*. I can't believe you run the B&B and still have time to take on art students…and volunteer somewhere. Let alone your winery nights."

Because of his comment, Cassie could tell he had

been thinking about what she'd told him. Why? "You have a good memory."

"Only when I'm interested."

He had to mean interested in the conversation, right? He wasn't even from Austin. He couldn't be interested in *her*.

Nash quickly opened the dishwasher and began loading the dishes inside. "I would help my mom with things around the house. I'm sure you did with your mom, too."

Cassie just nodded but didn't say anything else.

Nash gave her a sideways look.

Still, she kept silent. Too many memories of her taking care of the cooking and the dishes and everything else, while her mom drank herself into oblivion, played unbidden on her mental screen. Thoughts of her mother were frequent still. Her mother didn't want to see her or hear from her...not while she was in prison. Every day Cassie hoped that where her mother lived now, she might not have any choice but to find help and detox.

Her thoughts were cut off as Nash straightened and she realized how close they were standing to each other. She passed him a plate. His fingers brushed hers as he took it from her. There was heat...not only in her fingers. And when she looked up into his eyes, there seemed to be sparks there that ignited sparks in her. He was a guest. He'd be leaving at the end of April. She couldn't even think about sparks...and kissing—

*Kissing?* Where had *that* come from?

She turned away from him, picked up a dish towel and began wiping crumbs from the counter into her hand.

Nash asked lightly, "Anything else I can help with?" His deep voice seemed to affect her as much as his touch. But she wasn't a coward, so she turned to face him. "Nope. Nothing else."

Their gazes collided again for at least three heart-beats. Then he nodded and went to collect his hat that was still on the sideboard. He carried it with him to the stairway, but then he said to her, "Good night. Sleep well."

Before she could return the sentiment, he was up the stairs and gone. Had she imagined the chemistry between them?

Feeling as if she'd been caught in a whirlwind, she added detergent to the dishwasher and started it. She just needed a good night's sleep. That was all. She'd go to bed, close her eyes and forget all about Nash Tremont.

When Nash returned to the bed-and-breakfast the next day, it was almost lunchtime. He'd taken the morning off from doing research to drive around Austin to check out where the Fortunes' and Robinsons' influence could be seen. He'd also gotten a better handle on the city—the neighborhoods and the housing divisions. He had even driven around the college. Midmorning he'd found a leather goods shop and bought himself a pair of black dress boots. He'd also stopped at a men's store and purchased a sports jacket. That way, if he wanted to give Cassie the impression he was meeting a client, he'd fit the part better.

The part. He didn't know why it bothered him to play a part with Cassie, but it did.

The front door to the B&B was open and the screen door was allowing the spring air to flow in. As soon as Nash stepped inside, he heard a child's laughter. He liked kids. His old friend in Oklahoma—the one who had given Cassie a good reference—had three. He'd been to barbecues and Super Bowl parties with some of the guys at work. They had kids, too. Sometimes Nash liked the children even better than the adults.

Following the sound of childish chatter, as well as Cassie's voice, he crossed the dining area and passed the kitchen to the screened-in porch. There was an easel set up there with a chair in front of it. Cassie was sitting on a second chair beside a little girl who looked to be about eight. The girl's blond braids swung every time she turned toward Cassie.

Apparently hearing him approach the sliding glass door that was open today, Cassie spotted him peering through the screen. "Hi!" she said. "You're back."

Opening the screen and stepping inside the porch, he answered her. "Just for a little while. Then I'll be going out again. You're giving an art lesson?"

She motioned him to come farther inside.

He didn't move. "I don't want to interrupt."

"You're not," she assured him.

As he crossed to the area where Cassie and the child sat, the little girl turned around to face him. He noticed a child-sized cane propped against the wall. He raised questioning eyes to Cassie.

"Lydia, I want you to meet Nash. He's one of my guests here. Nash, this is Lydia."

"Hi, Lydia," he said easily. "Do you mind if I look at your painting?"

She gave a shy shrug and a smile, so he took that as a *yes*. Leaning down, he studied the picture of a Ferris wheel that was painted in bright colors and drawn with enough detail that he could see each seat. She'd painted people in the seats and she'd done a fairly good job of it, mostly drawing profiles. He wasn't sure he could do half as well.

"You have a terrific painting there. Did you ride on a Ferris wheel?" he asked.

This time Lydia grinned. "Mommy and Daddy took me to a carnival. I rode a pony, too."

"We're going to save horses for the next art lesson," Cassie confided. To Nash, she asked, "Have you eaten lunch?"

"Not yet."

"There are leftovers in the fridge."

"I'm going out again," he explained, ad-libbing.

"If you need a snack later, there's plenty. I didn't know if the Warners might be coming back for lunch and I wanted to provide something if they did." She frowned. "I had another cancellation."

With that declaration, Cassie looked and sounded worried.

Lydia had begun painting again, as if their conversation was of no consequence to her. He asked the little girl, "Do you mind if I sit and watch for a while?"

"I don't mind," she said. "I guess you wonder why I'm not in school today."

"The thought crossed my mind."

"My teachers had a meeting. Mommy had to work this morning. Cassie said she could give me a lesson, so Mommy's going to pick me up in a little while."

"You're lucky you could do this today."

"Yes, I am," Lydia agreed, bobbing her head and making her braids fly again.

Cassie suggested, "If you paint a fence around the Ferris wheel, it will ground it. Anybody looking at the painting will be able to tell the difference from the ground to the tippy top of the Ferris wheel."

Lydia nodded and went at it. "I'm going to mix two colors of brown for the fence."

Cassie squirted sienna and burnt umber on the palette. "See if you like those."

Fascinated by the process—and Cassie—Nash watched for the next half hour. Cassie was so patient with Lydia. Finally, he returned to the subject that seemed to have Cassie worried. He asked in a low voice, "Will it be a problem for you with another guest canceling?"

"I think I can make up the difference this month with the Paint and Sip party…if it's well attended. I have one coming up at the Mendoza Winery."

The winery was one of the Austin landmarks he'd noted. "I saw it today when I was driving around Austin."

He had driven around the Mendoza vineyard with its large acreage of grapevines. He'd discovered the winery had two offices—a small one at the edge of the vineyard and a larger corporate headquarters with its distribution center in Austin proper. Nash remembered he'd read somewhere that the winery had originally been named Hummingbird Ridge.

In spite of himself, he could imagine going to the tasting room with Cassie and sipping wine with her. He shook his head to erase the pictures from his mind. An attraction to her shouldn't even be an issue right now. He wasn't sitting that close to her because Lydia was between them. But he thought he could catch the scent of a flowery perfume. And Cassie's hair was so bright and shiny…and soft-looking. When she smiled, she had dimples. And there were freckles running across both of her cheeks. She was a tempting woman in so many ways. So many ways he was going to ignore.

Finally, Lydia was finished with her painting.

"Is she using acrylics?" Nash asked.

"They're so much easier for the children. As they become true artists, though, they can't mix them as well as they could oil paints. Some want to try water-colors, but using watercolors is its own art form—from the way you use the water to the texture of the paper."

"I can understand," Nash said, because he could. "More elements to deal with from the water spreading, the way the paper absorbs it, to the thinness of the brush."

The doorbell ringing suddenly interrupted their conversation. Lydia hopped up from her chair with her painting in hand. "I bet that's Mommy."

"I bet it is, too. Be careful with your painting."

Cassie opened the sliding screen door for Lydia. The little girl grabbed her cane and, as fast as she could, went to greet her mom.

"Why is she using a cane?" Nash whispered close to Cassie's ear. It *was* her shampoo he was smelling. And as his jaw brushed the side of her hair, he realized it was as soft as he imagined. Thoughts about kissing her were getting harder and harder to push away.

"She was in an accident riding her bike. She wasn't supposed to go onto a main street, but she did. A car sideswiped her. Fortunately, she was wearing a helmet and knee guards. That was three months ago. And she's just getting back on her feet. Her mom started bringing her to art lessons right after the accident. Lydia needed an outlet for all of her energy. Her mother had taken no-

tice of her drawings at school, and she thought it would
be a good idea. And it was. She's talented."

"It's bad enough when adults have to deal with dis-
abilities, but kids—" Nash shook his head.

As Cassie gazed into his eyes, he felt that connection
with her again. It was hard to believe he'd only known
her a few days, yet his pulse was beating fast.

Quickly, she turned away from him, took a few
steps back and said, "I have to say goodbye to Lydia's
mother."

In case Cassie had something private to say to Lydia's
mother or vice versa, Nash stayed on the porch, waiting for Cassie. When she returned there to clean up the
paints, Nash said, "Will you show me *your* paintings?"

She hesitated for a few moments. "I suppose I can.
The attic is my studio. It would have been too difficult
to make it into another bedroom for the B&B. But it *is*
the perfect place for a studio. Come on. I'll show you."

As Nash followed Cassie up the staircase, he wasn't
sure exactly *why* he wanted to see her paintings. Maybe
because he thought they'd give him a glimpse into who
she really was. Was she as sweet and caring as she
seemed? Or was it an act because she was the hostess
of the bed-and-breakfast? Hard to say. But he was an
investigator, so he was going to investigate.

Cassie ran up the stairs ahead of him. When she
reached the second floor, she waved down the hall and
pointed to the rope that hung from the ceiling. She
reached up and grabbed it and pulled down a staircase. The steps were narrow.

Nash commented, "This isn't exactly ideal working
conditions if you want to carry paintings up and down."

"Do you know any situation that's really ideal?"

Cassie asked as if she'd had a lot of experience dealing with curveballs life threw at her.

He knew exactly what she meant. People had expectations and what they envisioned rarely came to pass. At least, not without some adjustment.

Cassie wasn't as naive as he'd first thought she might be. It took years and life experience to know that nothing was perfect, that you couldn't wait around for it to *be* perfect. Just like his relationship with Sara. He hadn't realized until too late that it was never going to work... that in fact it was a lost cause.

After he'd climbed the stairs behind Cassie, Nash glanced around the attic. Light streamed in windows from both sides. Cassie had an easel set up with a drop cloth underneath much as she had downstairs on the porch. Only this easel was taller and wider, and it had a half-finished painting propped on it.

Before Nash studied that painting, he looked around at the others propped against the walls. The canvases were lined up, some overlapping. The colors were very much like the ones Cassie had chosen to use in the house. They were vibrant, with hot pinks and yellows and lime green, teal and even orange. And with those colors she'd captured her subjects beautifully—a hummingbird at a feeder, bluebonnets in a field with a child sitting with her back to the viewer, her blond hair blowing in the wind. Another one showcased an abstract cat, black and white against a sky-blue background. She'd also painted buildings that were a little more muted, a red barn and corral, a ramshackle house sitting in the woods, a blackbird sitting on a white fence. He could tell she was practicing styles, trying to find her own. Finally, his gaze fell to the canvas on the easel. This one was different from the others. Done mostly in pastels, it depicted an angel hovering over a child who was sitting on the grass reading a book. If it was up to Nash, he'd say that was her best work yet.

"How long did it take you to do these?" The creative process really did interest him.

"The past two years," she said. "I sell them when I can. Art shows are the best, but I often don't have time to give up a whole weekend for that."

"You're talented." It wasn't idle flattery. He meant it.

"Talent doesn't always pay the bills," she said, obviously being realistic about it. That was probably why she wanted to teach—for the consistent income.

Cassie was standing in front of the easel and he crossed to stand beside her. "I think that's the best one."

Her eyes widened in surprise. "Not the barn or the landscape outside of Austin?"

"Those are good," he conceded. "And if I had a den I'd probably hang them there. But aren't paintings supposed to evoke emotions?"

She pushed her hair away from her brow. "I'm surprised you know that."

"Because I'm a financial consultant?" he teased.

She shrugged. "Something like that. I mean, most people don't even know that that's why they choose a particular painting. I think art customers buy the paintings they do because that particular work resurrects a memory or a feeling they once had…or a feeling they want to have now."

Again, Nash was surprised at her insight.

"What?" she asked when she saw him studying her.

"You just surprise me, that's all."

They were standing very close now, facing each

other. He could easily reach out and touch one of the waves of her hair that flowed near her cheek. He was so tempted to lean in a bit to see what she would do. But he knew he was playing with fire. He knew he was being foolish, and she must have known it, too.

Suddenly she took a step back.

But he wouldn't let her escape just yet. "Are you sorry you brought me up here?"

"No, not sorry..." she trailed off, her voice a bit breathless.

He felt as if Cassie and her paintings had taken his breath away. "What then?"

In the afternoon light glowing through the window behind her, she looked vulnerable. "I don't often show my work to just anybody."

"You mean to a relative stranger?" he countered.

"Exactly."

A knowing came to him so swiftly that words came out of his mouth that he didn't expect. "After a few more days, I won't be a stranger, will I?"

"Maybe not," she murmured, then took another step back. "I have to make a grocery run and then prepare something for supper."

"And I have a meeting," he said, deciding if he was a financial consultant, he should meet with a client or two or three. After all, he now had boots to wear with a Western-cut jacket.

He motioned toward the stairs. "After you."

Once they were both on the second floor again and the stairs had been raised into the ceiling, he said, "So... I'll see you later. I have a few things I have to bring in from my SUV." He headed off down the hall, grateful he'd found a way to exit.

Because he'd almost done exactly what he knew he shouldn't. He'd almost kissed her.

Cassie was in the kitchen making a list of the groceries she'd need, trying not to think of her time with Nash in the attic. Just what had *that* been about? She'd felt such a pull toward him. He'd even seemed to understand her paintings. Unless that was an act...unless he was a player.

However, she didn't think so. She wasn't getting that vibe from him at all. Still, what did she know? It wasn't as if she had dated very much.

Almost finished with her list, she heard Nash's boots on the stairs. When he reached the first floor she glanced up and her heart beat in double time. He was wearing a Western-cut suit jacket, black dress jeans, white shirt and bolo tie. In his hands, he held his Stetson. He looked fantastic.

He turned toward her and smiled. "I thought you'd be out the door."

Because she'd run away from him so fast? She waved to the list on the counter. "I need to make sure I have everything written down that I need so I don't forget anything. Trips to the grocery store take too much time, and I don't want to be running there more than I have to."

"So you believe in efficiency? So do I."

She must have still been staring at him because he asked with a grin, "Do I have shaving cream on my nose?"

She felt herself blushing. "No. Of course not. What restaurant are you going to?"

She definitely thought he was meeting someone for

lunch. "I'm going to meet my client at his hotel and we'll go from there. Do you have any suggestions?"

"There's the Sundance Restaurant. Lots of business folk go there."

"I'll take that as a recommendation."

"Is there anything special you'd like me to pick up at the grocery store, maybe for snacks?"

"Corn chips and salsa," he responded with a wink.

"Mild or spicy?" she asked and then wondered if he thought that was a double entendre.

He must have because something sparked in his dark brown eyes. Something that made tingles dance on all her nerve endings.

"Definitely spicy," he answered.

"Got it." She definitely did. They were attracted to each other. Big-time.

He took his keys from his pocket and gave her a wave. "Have a good afternoon."

She said goodbye but wasn't sure he heard it because the door was already closing behind him.

She felt hot. How could a little conversation with a man make her feel hot? How could standing close to a man urge her to feel his kiss? How did looking at a man make her wish for so many things she couldn't have?

It was simple, really. A man like Nash wouldn't flirt with her at all if he knew her mother was in jail.

## Chapter Three

Nash sat in a chair at a computer in the library forgetting all sense of time and place. The text on the screen, as well as the notes he had made, caused a sinking sensation in his stomach. He actually felt sick. Research on Jerome Fortune or Gerald Robinson, however you wanted to look at it, was not a feel-good experience.

In a normal investigation, he could contact the Robinsons for more information. But because he was investigating Gerald's wife, he couldn't do that.

Nash thought about his mother again and her lack of bitterness against Gerald. She must have really loved the guy. She'd told Nash that Gerald was lonely and his wife was a witch. As far as Nash was concerned, it was that old "she doesn't understand me" line. But if Charlotte Robinson was guilty of the crimes Nash suspected she was guilty of, maybe she really had been a witch...and still was.

Putting his notes aside, he stopped reading about the Robinsons in order to focus on photos. Gerald and Charlotte were in the paper constantly at charity fund-raisers, community events, when a new illegitimate child made the news. Nash didn't want the spotlight turned on himself. He definitely didn't intend to make the news.

He studied his father's face, unsure of what he was looking for. Signs of recognition? Was he trying to see himself in his father's face? He certainly hoped he couldn't find his own. He'd rather think he inherited all of his mother's attributes and physical features. But there was that hint of stubbornness in Gerald's jaw that Nash knew he had to own up to also.

He continued to pore over photo after photo. More recent ones caught his attention. He found the Fortune name mentioned in conjunction with a Valentine's Day party at the Mendoza Winery. Cassie had mentioned that winery and the fact she'd be doing a Paint and Sip party there.

If she taught her Paint and Sip class there, he could tag along or stop in incognito. It would be the perfect opportunity to nose around. Certainly, someone at the winery would remember the Valentine's Day party and the people who had attended. He could just claim he was thinking about contacting the famous family to inquire if they needed his financial services. He had to keep his investigation moving forward. He didn't have that much time in Austin.

Wanting to ditch the suit he'd worn to his pretend meeting, he stuffed the small spiral-bound notebook with thoughts and facts about the Fortunes into an inside pocket. Then he closed down the computer. To his surprise, the afternoon had passed into evening. Immersed in his research, wondering how he could really get the goods on Charlotte, he'd lost track of time.

Rush-hour traffic was heavy as he headed back to the B&B. He found himself eager to see Cassie. She was like a bright star floating in and out of his mind, even as he tried to concentrate on grittier things like the Fortunes.

Fortunately, he found a parking space near the B&B. As he walked up the street, he thought again about the Paint and Sip party. The more he thought about going along with Cassie, the more he liked the idea. He was passing the house next door to the B&B when he realized someone was sitting on the porch in a caned rocking chair. The woman looked to be in her late sixties. She waved to him in a friendly greeting.

"Nice night," she called out. "But it's getting a bit chilly."

At the foot of the stairs to her porch, he stopped. "Yes, it is. Are you people-watching?" he asked with a smile.

"That's mostly what I do now," she said. "Especially in the evenings. I have a lot to watch with the B&B next door. I can see folks coming and going. I spotted you leaving earlier."

This woman must not have much to take up her time, and maybe not enough people in her life, Nash surmised. He went up the porch steps and extended his hand to her. "Nash Tremont," he said.

"I'm Renata Garcia."

"I'm enjoying the bed-and-breakfast. It's a nice atmosphere."

"Oh, yes, it is. Don't you just love the way Cassie painted those rooms? She has such a unique sense of style. Have you seen her paintings? She brought a few over after she moved in so I could see them. They're wonderful."

"She's very talented," Nash said noncommittally though he had really liked them. Apparently Cassie and this woman were friends.

"She is that, and she's such a lovely girl. She's helped me more than once when I wasn't feeling well. Some days my arthritis bothers me so much I can hardly get up and down out of the chair. But Cassie tells me to keep my cell phone close at hand and just call her if I need anything. In a way, I feel like a surrogate parent."

Nash knew he should get information about Cassie from Cassie herself, but he also realized he could learn facts from other people, too. "Aren't Cassie's parents around here?"

"It's such a shame, but Cassie's parents died in a car crash."

So Cassie had lost her parents. He felt for her. The compassion he'd seen in her was true. Apparently she knew what it was like to lose the people you loved.

He thought again about Sara and her refusal to marry him. She'd hurt his pride as well as broken his heart. Although he didn't intend to compare Sara and Cassie, he found himself doing it. Cassie seemed so bright and sparkling compared to Sara. Was it even fair to judge?

Cassie's neighbor broke into Nash's thoughts. "How long will you be staying at the Bluebonnet?"

"I'm not exactly sure," he told her. "More than a week and less than a month."

"I see. You know, you really should make a commitment. It would help Cassie figure out what bills she could pay and which ones she can't. She finagles her budget until it all works out. That's hard to do these days for me, too."

"I think we all have to adjust our budgets each month these days." He took off his sports jacket and laid it over his arm and then loosened his bolo tie. He couldn't wait to get into his T-shirt and jeans. "It was good to meet you, Renata."

"It was good meeting you, too. You tell Cassie I said hello."

"I'll be sure to do that."

As he descended the porch steps, he didn't know if he'd be seeing Cassie tonight. In some ways, it would be safer if he didn't. No temptation, no consequences. Maybe he'd change and go out again, grab some tacos and go over his notes. It would be a safe evening with nothing more on his mind than work.

The following day Cassie wished she could make a breakthrough with her eleven-year-old art student Danny. Art often could help children express themselves. She knew Danny could draw. That was one of the reasons his mother was paying for art lessons. But he wouldn't draw anything he really cared about.

The late afternoon was quiet on the porch as Cassie watched Danny paint the big sturdy tree, a realistic portrayal of one right outside the screened-in room. The only sound was the brush of Danny's strokes on the canvas and the sound of birds in the tree branches as they called to each other.

The almost-silence was the reason Cassie heard the front door open and then close. When she leaned back to peek through the rooms, she spotted Nash walking toward her. She hadn't seen him much for the last twenty-four hours. He hadn't eaten supper last night or breakfast this morning. He was dressed up again and he looked tired. Had he had meetings all day?

When he stopped at the door to the screened-in porch, Cassie motioned him inside. Maybe Danny would respond to another male.

"Danny, this is Nash. He's a guest at the bed-and-breakfast, and he understands paintings."

Danny gave her a quick glance and then turned back to his canvas.

"I really do," Nash said, obviously perceptive about what Cassie wanted him to do. "And Cassie's paintings are great. Have you seen any of them?"

Danny nodded but wouldn't turn and meet Nash's gaze. Nash lifted one eyebrow as if to ask Cassie what was going on. But she wouldn't talk about Danny with the boy there. Nash must have sensed that so he backed off, which was thoughtful of him.

He asked, "Is it okay if I make some coffee?"

She motioned to the sideboard in the dining area. "I brewed a pot about an hour ago. It should still be good. I made chocolate chip cookies, too. Danny had two before we started."

"What did you think of them?" Nash asked the boy.

"They were good," Danny answered, still keeping his eyes on the canvas.

But Nash didn't completely give up. "You know your tree is as good as any one of Cassie's."

Danny inclined his head as if he'd heard. He gave a little shrug, but he didn't respond. Nash's gaze locked with Cassie's, and he just pointed toward the dining room as if telling her he'd wait in there to talk with her.

A short time later, Danny's mother came in the door. Dorie Lindstrom always seemed to be in a rush. Now she came barreling toward the sunporch. Danny had his mom's blond hair and blue eyes, and when he saw her, he smiled. He always smiled around his mom.

As usual, she seemed to stop rushing when she was in the presence of her son. She stood behind him and stared at his painting. "That's a terrific tree. What are you going to put with it?"

"Maybe a playhouse on the grass," he said.

"You're good at painting buildings. I think that will fit well there, don't you think, Cassie?"

"Danny has an instinct for knowing what to fit together. I'm sure a playhouse will be just right."

Dorie handed Cassie a check. "Same time on Monday?"

"That works for me." As Danny rose to his feet, Cassie said, "I'll put your painting somewhere safe. It will be ready for you when you're ready for it." She placed her hand on his shoulder. "Good job."

He gave her a smile like he'd given his mom. Then the two of them left.

Cassie carefully propped the painting on one of the chairs, then collapsed the easel. By then Nash had come into the porch, coffee mug in hand. He'd removed his jacket and loosened his bolo tie. With the top button of his shirt opened, he looked too sexy for words. She swallowed hard and told herself again he was just a guest.

"So what's going on with your art student?" he asked. "Or can't you tell me?"

"Some things are confidential but it might help me to talk to you about it. I know you're not going to spread any gossip because you're not from here."

"That's right. No gossip passes my lips."

At the word *lips*, she stared at him...and them. That was a big mistake. She forced herself to concentrate on the subject they were talking about—Danny. "Danny's parents are going through a divorce."

"I see. Is he mad at his father? Is that why he wouldn't make eye contact with me? All males are taboo?"

How perceptive, Cassie thought. But she supposed Nash had learned to read his clients well. "That could be part of the reason. But even more than that, his father doesn't approve of Danny's interest in art. Danny's embarrassed about it himself because he's gotten teased at school. I'm trying to build his confidence along with teaching him about acclaimed male painters. I want him to know his talent is something to be proud of."

"You're right, it is. What kind of person is his father?"

"I haven't met him. He and his wife were separated before Danny started taking lessons. But he's a lawyer. From what Dorie says, I get the feeling he's narrow-minded in his thinking."

"And probably judgmental," Nash commented. "Narrow-minded people usually are."

"There are always two sides to every story, so I don't want to judge him without even meeting him. But from what Dorie has told me, both are true."

Nash leaned against the porch wall. "Do you know her well?"

"Not extremely well. She and I had a long conversation before I took Danny on. And we usually talk a little bit every time she picks him up. But today she must have been in an exceptional hurry. She seems to be a caring and attentive mom. She listens and he's completely relaxed when he's around her."

"And he probably wouldn't be that way with his dad," Nash guessed.

"Probably not. His dad wanted Danny to play football. That's not in the cards. I get the feeling that their differing views on raising children is one of the reasons the two of them broke up."

After another swallow of coffee, Nash said, "For what it's worth, I think you're doing the right thing building up his confidence. If he has confidence about his art, he'll have confidence in other areas."

Again, she was struck by his keen insight. She looked at him more closely. His hair was thick and a bit ruffled as if he'd run his fingers through it. He was a handsome man, that was for sure. "How did you get so wise?"

"The school of hard knocks."

She was thinking maybe Nash had had some counseling, but he'd just disabused her of that notion. Experience must have taught him everything he'd learned. She was eager to know what those experiences had been.

"Danny seems to be relaxed with you," Nash pointed out. "He wouldn't be able to concentrate on his painting if he wasn't. But then, I think anybody could be relaxed with you."

That compliment took Cassie by surprise. Truth be told, she wasn't used to receiving compliments from men. She'd dated back in Bryan before she'd decided to move her life to Austin. But once Cody Sinclair had found out her mother was in jail, he was out the door. Either his moral sensibilities had been offended or the idea of having a girlfriend whose mother was a felon was just too embarrassing or abhorrent. Cassie had known better than to get involved with anyone romantically after that if she didn't want a broken heart. Apparently romance just wasn't in the cards for her.

"How can you judge how relaxed people are with me?" she asked him. "You've only seen me with the Warners, Lydia and Danny."

"I had a talk with your neighbor yesterday when I came home. She was sitting on her porch and she waved and said hello."

"Mrs. Garcia is lonely," Cassie explained. "She's a widow."

"She said you spend time with her." His voice had gone gentle as if he appreciated that fact about her.

"I do. She's a lovely woman and has some great stories to tell. I think she's trying to keep her memories alive. She says when you reach a certain age, all of your memories tend to blur together. I enjoy spending time with her." Since her own mother wasn't in her life now—her mother's choosing, not hers—Renata Garcia helped fill a hole in her heart.

"She told me that you'd lost both your parents. I'm sorry to hear that."

Cassie was dumbfounded for a moment but maybe not entirely surprised that Renata had told Nash. Most of her neighbors and coworkers thought that was what had happened to her parents. The problem was—it was a lie. Somehow, making up a story for other people

hadn't seemed so bad. She'd done it to protect herself
and her mother and her business at the Bluebonnet.
She'd seen everyone's reaction to Carol Calloway's ar-
rest, trial and imprisonment. She'd learned it was better to propagate a myth and she'd had to do that to
start over.

But Cassie felt terrible about lying to Nash. Still,
hadn't her experience told her that was the best thing
to do?

She decided it would be better to lead the subject
away from herself. Since Nash *did* look tired, she asked,
"How was your day?"

"Long," he answered with half a smile.

"Did you meet with potential clients? Did you sign
any?"

Nash's brown eyes seemed to darken. His mouth
turned down as if he was chagrined at her question.

She hurried to say, "I didn't mean to pry."

After a moment he explained, "Sometimes I learn
information about my clients that I'd rather not know."

"I imagine a financial advisor's relationship with
clients is somewhat like a lawyer's."

"I suppose they could be compared," Nash said politely, maybe a little coolly as if he didn't intend to talk
about it anymore. He straightened, lifted his coffee mug
to his lips and drained it. "Good coffee," he said. "I'll
just set this in the sink."

"Will you be eating supper with us tonight?"

"No, I had a big lunch."

"There are sandwich fixings in the refrigerator if
you find you want something later. Tomorrow night
I'll be making a very early supper here. It's Paint and
Sip night at the Mendoza Winery. If you want to get to

know more about Austin, you could stop in. It's usually a friendly crowd."

"You've done this there before?"

"Two months ago. It went over really well, so we
planned another one."

"I'll definitely consider it," he told her. "You have
a good night."

Cassie followed him into the guest area and watched
him put the mug in the sink. Then he picked up his
jacket from the back of a chair and headed upstairs
without looking back.

Maybe she'd been all wrong about an attraction between them. Maybe only *she* was the one who felt the
attraction. Maybe she'd poked and prodded too much.
Whatever the reason, she felt a bit rebuffed. She'd just
keep her distance from Nash Tremont, and the attraction would go away on its own.

If Cassie had the opportunity and the funds, she'd
eat at La Viña, the Mendoza Winery's restaurant, as
often as she could. She liked the atmosphere there. The
interior had a lot of large windows that during the day
provided an extensive view of the vineyard. At night,
floodlights showed off the grounds. The ceiling was
oak-paneled and rounded to reflect the shape of the inside of a wine barrel.

The restaurant had been rearranged for the Paint
and Sip party. Easels were set up along two sides of
the restaurant. Patrons could pay the entire fee and actually paint a canvas with Cassie, or they could opt for
a lesser fee that would cover only hors d'oeuvres and
wine. That way friends who didn't want to paint could

come along with friends who did. There were always a lot of watchers.

Carlo Mendoza had greeted Cassie and made sure she had everything she needed. His fiancée, Schuyler, acted as a hostess of sorts. Already this evening, Cassie had taken her students through a step-by-step process. They could wander around and study her painting. They could listen in as she migrated from student to student, giving help where needed. Servers poured wine and served plates of hors d'oeuvres as patrons went to the tables to enjoy conversation, wine and everything from crab balls to mini tacos.

Cassie was helping one of her students, a woman who had been to her last Paint and Sip party here, when she glanced around the room and spotted Nash. He hadn't told her he was coming. Of course, he didn't have to. Was he interested in actually painting? Or did he just want to try the Mendoza wines?

When she and her student finished their conversation, she moved on and noticed Nash was talking to Carlo. They seemed to be having a detailed conversation. She kept her eye on him as she walked around the room. When he'd finished speaking with Carlo, he crossed to a server who was headed toward the kitchen. They had a conversation, too. She wandered what that was all about.

Nash was dressed in an Oxford shirt and black jeans rather than a business suit. Still, was he making contacts?

The next time Cassie looked up to see where Nash had gone, he'd disappeared. Apparently, he wasn't staying for the evening.

After the customers had finished their paintings, the

restaurant emptied quickly. She packed her car, then went to find Carlo.

He came from the kitchen and spotted her. "I have your check," he said.

He handed her her portion of the proceeds for the evening. It was a nice chunk of money and would pay many of the bills that had started to pile up.

"Thanks for letting me do this again," she told him.

"No problem. It's beneficial for you and for me. We draw tourists as well as residents. And all of them can spread the word about our restaurant and wines as well as your bed-and-breakfast. Win-win."

Carlo Mendoza was a handsome man. He was over six feet tall, with dark hair and dark eyes, and very white teeth against a tan complexion. He could have been an actor or a model. He was a charismatic guy and before he fell for Schuyler, the word around town was that he'd had trouble with commitment. But whenever he and Schuyler were together, everyone knew that wasn't the case anymore.

Carlo had always been friendly, and now she hoped he wouldn't mind a question. "I spotted you speaking to one of my guests from the bed-and-breakfast earlier."

"Who was that?"

"His name is Nash Tremont."

"Oh, yes. He told me he's a financial advisor and making connections with clients while he's in town. He did tell me he was staying with you."

"I'm accepting guests for extended stays now. He was the first to sign up for one."

Carlo had a twinkle in his eye when he asked, "Are you interested in this guest?"

"Oh, no," Cassie assured him quickly. "He's from

Mississippi and he'll be returning there. There wouldn't be any point in me being interested."

Carlo gave a chuckle. "That depends on how interested you are."

Cassie felt herself blushing, and she knew exactly what Carlo meant. She could have a fling if she wanted, but that wasn't in her DNA. She shook her head again. "I know Nash has meetings planned while he's here. I guess he was asking you for leads?"

"Yes, he was. Especially information about the Fortunes. He'd seen photos online that some of them were here for the Valentine's Day party."

"I see," Cassie said, but she didn't really. Then again, she figured if you're in a town that wasn't your own, and there were famous, wealthy families in that town, you'd try to contact them.

That thought kept playing in her head during her drive back to the Bluebonnet. From what she'd seen of Nash thus far, he had good public relations skills. She imagined he was successful at what he did.

She was carrying paints and canvases to the porch when the subject of her thoughts asked, "Can I help you with that?"

Nash didn't wait for her to answer but took the toolbox-like carrier filled with paints out of her hand. They went up the porch steps together and he let her precede him inside.

She propped her painting against the counter and he set her paints beside it. Glancing at the sitting area, she could see a hassock was pushed away from an armchair, and there was a laptop on it.

"You were working there tonight," she said, and she wasn't sure why.

"Yes, I was. Do you need help bringing more supplies in from your car?"

She wouldn't turn down help when it was offered. "Sure. There's a stack of palettes and another box of paints. Would you like a glass of iced tea? I'm sure I can find cookies to go with it."

"No cookies," he said with a smile. "I had hors d'oeuvres at the Paint and Sip. But the iced tea would be great."

After he brought in the rest of her supplies, he asked, "Where would you like these?"

"There's a storage closet down the hall next to my room. If you could just set them in there, I'll take care of them later."

After he did that, Nash came back to the kitchen. Cassie had placed two glasses of iced tea on the breakfast bar. He sat on one of the stools. "Tonight looked like a success. Did you feel it was?"

Again they were talking about *her*, and she wanted to know more about *him*. "My cut was enough to pay my mortgage this month, so I'm grateful."

He turned his glass around on the counter. "You worked hard tonight. You had lots of individual consultations. Is that the way it always works?"

"Pretty much. How did you like the wine?"

"It was excellent. I tasted a dry white, a dry red and a sangria."

"A glass of each?"

He shook his head. "No. I would have needed a designated driver if I had done that. Just a taste of each. I concentrated on the hors d'oeuvres."

When she laughed, their gazes met. She was seated beside him and their arms brushed. The hairs on his forearm tickled her skin. However, remembering how he'd rebuffed her, she didn't want to be distracted at this moment. "Did you get leads of possible clients from Carlo?"

"Possibly. You never know how cold calls will turn out."

"He said you were interested in the Fortunes."

"Among others," Nash said with a nod. "There are many upstanding families in Austin."

Although he was answering her questions, she had the feeling there was something he wasn't telling her. Maybe he sensed she was going to ask more questions because he slid off his stool and picked up his glass. "I'll just take this up to my room if you don't mind."

"I don't mind."

As if he were reluctant to leave, he said, "You look pretty tonight."

For these events, she dressed up more than usual. Tonight she'd worn a black pantsuit with an expensive label, though she'd found it at the thrift store.

"Thank you," she said.

She slid off her stool, too, and suddenly they were standing very close.

"Did *you* have any wine tonight?" he asked.

She shook her head. "I like to remain clearheaded, especially when I'm painting." The truth was she didn't drink, not after seeing what alcohol had done to her mother. Though sometime maybe she should taste the Mendoza wines, just for the experience.

"And even when you're not," Nash guessed.

"And even when I'm not," she confirmed.

He reached out and touched her cheek, and it seemed as if he wanted to say something but then thought better of it. Instead he moved away from her toward the stairs. "See you tomorrow."

"See you tomorrow," she murmured. She had a feeling Nash Tremont was holding secrets of his own, but she couldn't fault him for that, because she held secrets, too.

[faded text from previous page bleed-through, illegible]

## *Chapter Four*

When Nash sat at a computer in the library the following day, he took his list from his pocket. Now he had more specific names to look up. An investigator never knew where a line of information could lead. So Nash was going to read everything he could get his hands or eyes on.

Carlo had been upfront with him about who had attended the Valentine's Day party. People with cell phones had taken lots of photos and posted them to their social media pages. Therefore, Carlo considered the information public knowledge. Nash had explained he was a financial consultant staying at the Bluebonnet Bed-and-Breakfast, and because Carlo respected Cassie, he'd considered her a recommendation for Nash.

Nash didn't like the subterfuge but sometimes it was necessary. Sometimes he had to consider the greater good, which in this case meant nailing a thief. In his estimation, Charlotte Robinson, Gerald's wife, was definitely that. One thing he knew for sure was that she was deceptive.

After his mom had gotten pregnant with him, she'd tried to contact Gerald. But Charlotte had intercepted her messages. In fact, she'd intimidated Nash's mother by threatening her. She'd warned his mom to stay away from her husband or there would be consequences. For that threat alone, Nash wanted to nail her. He didn't know how his mother maintained her sweetness rather than bitterness, but somehow through all the years she had. He respected her for that.

The first name on his list was Ben Fortune and his wife, Ella. Searching specifically for them, he found photographs of the couple at charity events along with Ben's twin brother, Wes, and his wife, Vivian. Although she wasn't on his list, that had led him to Lucie Fortune Chesterfield Parker, a member of the Fortune family who was almost British royalty. He discovered quickly that Chase Parker, her husband, was part of an oil family but had chosen his own path and now owned a horse rescue farm.

Apparently, Lucie was heavily involved in work with the Fortune Foundation, helping younger kids right here in Austin. The articles about Chase and Lucie led him to her sister Amelia, her husband, Quinn, and their daughter, Clementine Rose. He also found references to Charles, their brother. He soon realized there was nothing underhanded about the English side of the Fortune family. He could delve further but on first glance, they seemed to be upright citizens.

Another name on Nash's list was Keaton Whitfield, who was Ben's half sibling. He was a renowned architect.

It wasn't long before Nash realized many of the Fortunes had seemed to find true love. His biological father certainly hadn't, though his mother still believed she had been in love with him and he with her. Love could delude a person. It could make a person blind. He should know. He'd been blind to Sara's doubts about being in a relationship with a cop. Looking back, he wondered how he had *not* seen the signs. Or maybe she simply hadn't been honest with herself. Maybe she hadn't wanted to rock the boat of a convenient relationship.

Research consumed Nash for the morning. He quit around lunchtime and headed back to the B&B.

When he arrived, he thought he heard Cassie out on the sunporch, so he headed that way. She looked a bit harried as she fussed with a tripod and her phone. He watched as she stood in front of it and checked her phone and frowned. She made the tripod higher and did it again. Still adjusting it, she checked her phone and shook her head.

She'd been so preoccupied with what she was doing that she hadn't heard him come in or seen him standing there. Leaning against the doorjamb, he crossed one booted foot over the other. "Having a problem?" he asked.

As she glanced up at him, her cheeks pinkened a bit. For some reason, she was dressed in a cute dress that had a red-and-white pattern and a full swingy skirt. He appreciated the shorter style. He knew he should turn around and walk away, not get involved in what she was doing. But she seemed to be having a hard time of it, and he found he couldn't just walk away.

"I'm trying to set up my phone to take a video," she explained.

His curiosity got the best of him. "Why do you need a video?"

Standing up straight to face him, she pushed her hair back over her brow. Drawn to her more than he ever wanted to be, he followed the motion of her hand, noticing the wave that swept along her cheek. He felt a lot hotter than he had when he'd come in.

With a sigh, she sat in the chair near the easel. "My dream is to someday hire someone to run the B&B. What I really want to do is teach. My goal is to be hired as an art teacher in a school district." She was quiet for a moment and he waited. Finally, she explained, "I went for two interviews in the past few weeks, and the principals of those schools told me they don't have positions now but they'll keep my résumé on file."

Stepping closer to her, he noted, "That still doesn't explain the video."

"Both principals hinted that getting hired these days requires *more* than a résumé. Many applicants turn in a DVD of themselves teaching a lesson. That way, the principal gets a taste of an applicant's teaching method and expertise. I want to try making a DVD, but I have to practice."

"So do you want to record a lesson to a general audience? Or do you want to film a lesson with one of your students?"

Her eyes widened at the thought.

"You'd have to have their permission, of course, and their parents' permission, but it seems to me that would be more riveting."

"*If* an art lesson could be riveting," she said dryly. "That's what you were thinking, weren't you?"

"You think you know what I'm thinking?" he teased. If she did, she'd be running for the hills.

Her cheeks grew rosier. "Not that I know what you're thinking exactly, but most people would be thinking that. Sometimes art is very internal. It's up to the teacher to bring out what's going on inside onto the paper or canvas. That isn't always easy to do. A lesson with a child could fail miserably."

"If it does, you just dump the video," he suggested.

"I don't know, Nash. It would be a lot safer just to teach to a general audience."

Now he frowned. "You don't seem like a woman who doesn't want to take risks. No risk, no gain. Isn't that the saying?"

"I thought the saying was no pain, no gain."

He laughed. "Those two are very different. But really, Cassie, the excitement of a child learning how to do something new could be riveting on a DVD. And it would be so much easier if you had somebody recording the video rather than you trying to set it up. I'd be happy to record for you, if you did it within the next couple of weeks. I can even put it on a DVD for you on my laptop."

She was already shaking her head. "I couldn't take advantage of you like that."

Leaving his relaxed stance behind, he walked over to her and stood right in front of her. "From what I've seen, and from what Mrs. Garcia told me, you're always doing things for others. I've got to wonder if anyone does things for you."

"I…uh…don't know what to say to that. Sure, people do things for me."

"Like?" he asked.

She thought for a few seconds. "At the grocery store the checkout boy often carries bags to my car for me when I have too many."

Nash gave her a look that obviously made her search her mind for something else. "Renata—Mrs. Garcia—often gives me embroidered handkerchiefs she finds in her drawers. She wants to pass them down and they're lovely. And the kids—the kids all give me smiles and joy."

"How about your friends?" Nash asked.

"I'm too busy to socialize much."

The investigator in Nash saw the red flag. Usually when someone didn't have friends, that meant they didn't want to get close to anybody. Either they didn't have self-confidence or self-worth…or they were hiding something. He had no idea what Cassie would possibly be hiding.

His reaction to Cassie always disconcerted him. He was so attracted to her he should hightail it away from Austin…or at least away from the B&B. However, instead of leaving, he reached out and touched her cheek. "You deserve to have nice things done for you. You wouldn't be taking advantage of me. I'd enjoy doing it. It would be a break from business."

Cassie seemed to think about it. She was staring at him with those beautiful chocolate eyes. All he had to do was slide his hand up her neck into her hair and bring her close. But he didn't do that. He took a step away.

She seemed to recognize that step for what it was. He was removing himself from temptation. She looked flustered, but she quickly recovered. "All right. I'll let you video me before you leave. But that means extra cinnamon rolls for you."

He laughed. "You've got a deal. Did you eat lunch yet?"

"No. I've been occupied trying to do this," she said with a frown.

"Do you have guests to take care of?"

"Only you," she joked. "The Warners are out for the day."

"Since you look so pretty all dressed up, how would you like to go out to lunch?"

His offer took her by surprise. "Oh, I don't know."

Although he knew he shouldn't—for so many reasons—he pushed. "I passed an outside café on my way back here. It looked nice. We could sit outside and enjoy the pretty day. I mean, really, how long has it been since you were out to lunch?"

"It has been a while. I usually just grab something in between errands or B&B business or art lessons."

"Then let's go. You can tell me again why you'd like to be a teacher rather than an artist."

A short time later, as Cassie and Nash walked down the street, she was totally aware of him. He was wearing his boots, jeans, a tan polo shirt, and of course, the black Stetson. Even in the polo shirt, she could see the muscles in his arms. Maybe financial consultants worked out. That would explain it. She didn't know what else would. Good genes?

Sometimes, the way he questioned her, he reminded her of a lawyer. But she supposed financial consultants had to ask questions, too. They had to get to know their clients, their needs and wants, their intentions for the future. So he was practiced at asking questions, she supposed. They must also practice not talking about themselves.

Now she looked over at him. "What did you really think about the Paint and Sip party?"

"What do you mean—what did I really think?"

"Does it serve a purpose, fill a need, or is it just a money-making scheme?"

He took a few seconds to think about it. But then he decided, "Everyone needs a job, Cassie, and they need to pay the bills. Using your talent to do that isn't a bad thing."

She'd never really had a moral compass in her parents, certainly not in her mother. She supposed she'd always looked toward her church and her priest for answers, and she found most of them there.

She could feel Nash studying her as they walked, the spring breeze blowing her dress against her legs.

"I'll tell you what I think of it," he said.

She braced herself for the worst.

"I think everyone needs a creative outlet. It could be writing in a journal. It could be building sandcastles. For you, it's painting. At the Paint and Sip, you shared that gift with everyone else. Do I think it's a little manufactured? Maybe. After all, don't some of your paintings take a week to do, not just one night?"

"Make that weeks, sometimes."

"Exactly. But what you're doing is teaching a technique. Beginners like immediate gratification. That's what you're giving them. And if they sip wine and enjoy themselves along the way, what's wrong with that?"

"I suppose nothing. But if I get a teaching position, I think that's one of the first things I'd drop. I'd want to keep volunteering at the art center and maybe give private lessons."

"You want to teach children to be true artists rather than teaching kids the techniques just to finish a painting."

"Yes. I want to teach them about techniques and the Masters, and the great museums."

"And I imagine you'll be a terrific teacher."

She didn't have to comment because they'd reached the outdoor café. Green-and-white-striped awnings covered the outside seating area. They migrated to a table that was near a wall and Nash pulled a chair out for her. She'd never had anybody do that before. As she sat and he pushed her in, she glanced over her shoulder. His face was very close to hers. In fact, her cheek brushed the rim of his hat.

"I'll get rid of this," he said, and went to hang his Stetson on one of the hat pegs tacked on the outside wall. She watched him as he ran his hand through his hair a few times.

After he sat across from her, he smiled. "The reason cowboys never take off their hats is that their hair's a mess underneath."

She broke into a genuine laugh. "So you're not a real cowboy?"

"I'm not even half a cowboy. I just enjoy boots, jeans and a good Stetson. You know, men wear them even in Oklahoma. In fact, as I was growing up, I thought ball caps and Stetsons were the only two kinds of hats there were for men."

"Are you serious or are you pulling my leg?"

"I'm very serious. Ever been to Oklahoma?"

She shook her head. "I've never been out of Texas."

He cocked his head and studied her again.

Breaking eye contact, she watched the passersby. Nash did, too. Their waiter came to take their order. Nash chose the roast beef panini with caramelized onions while she chose the turkey club sandwich.

"Order whatever you want," Nash said. "I'm paying."

"No, you're not," she protested. "We're going Dutch or we don't get lunch."

They stared at each other for a few seconds until the waiter looked at Cassie. "Would you like to order something else?"

"No, just the club and a glass of lemonade."

"Coming up shortly," the waiter said and went inside.

"You can be a tough cookie when you want to be," Nash admitted with some surprise.

"Not used to women who stand up for themselves?" she asked with a grin.

"Oh, you wound me! Of course I like women who stand up for themselves. I wouldn't want to be in a relationship with any other kind. Guessing what the other person is thinking doesn't make for good communication."

"You've had that problem?"

"Could be," Nash answered enigmatically.

He'd done it again. He'd shut down a perfectly good conversation. Silence dropped between them for a few minutes until Cassie bumped Nash's elbow. "See that man walking along the street?"

Nash looked the way Cassie's chin was pointed. She thought she saw a flicker of something in Nash's eyes but it was gone faster than she'd imagined it.

"Are you just showing me a representative Texas cowboy?" he asked.

"No." She kept her voice low. "That's Nate Fortune."

Nate definitely was eye candy for anybody looking his way. He was over six feet tall, with dark brown hair and brown eyes.

She noticed Nash studying Nate Fortune. His next words sounded as if he'd chosen them carefully. "I think the Fortune family has made every newspaper in big cities and every blog on the internet. Do you ever wonder what it would be like to be connected to a family like the Fortunes? Do they really have brotherly and sisterly relationships? Or is everything they do cutthroat, for business's sake?"

"They're a dynasty in themselves," Cassie responded. "I should hope among all those relatives there would be some strong connections. I would have loved to have a brother or sister. How about you? Do you have siblings?"

He hesitated a moment, then shook his head. "No, I don't."

"Were you lonely as a boy?"

Nash shrugged. She thought he was going to shut down this conversation, too. Instead, his gaze met hers and he answered her. "Some of the time I was lonely, but most of the time I was too busy to be lonely. I got jobs wherever I could find them to help my mom make ends meet."

Cassie wanted to tell him that she'd done that, too, but she didn't want to get into that subject, because he thought her parents were dead. If she never really told him her story, would she ever really get to know his?

A few hours later, Nash wasn't sure why he was calling his friend in Oklahoma. Maybe Cassie pointing out

Nate Fortune had unsettled him. He had to watch not only his words but his actions around her. Because of his research at the library, he'd recognized Nate Fortune. Nate had been one of the family pictured at the Valentine's Day party at the Mendoza Winery. Nash had an almost photographic memory, especially when it came to faces. That helped in his investigations.

He scrolled through his contacts and called Dave. He hoped his former partner was off shift. He and Dave Preston had gone to the Police Academy together and risen up through the ranks. When Cassie had asked him if he'd ever wanted a brother, he'd thought of Dave. His friend was the closest thing to a brother he'd ever get.

"Is this good news or bad news?" Dave asked when he answered.

"Maybe it's no news," Nash replied. "Maybe I just wanted to hear your voice. You know, a taste of home and all that."

"You haven't called Oklahoma home for a while now, even though your mom wants you to."

Nash sighed. "I know that. How's she doing? She's always cheery when I call her but I don't know if that's the truth."

"She misses you."

"She also misses the future I was planning on having, the one that would give her grandkids."

"You sound as if it's never going to happen."

Nash immediately thought of Cassie. But he answered his friend with, "Probably not."

Changing the subject, Dave asked, "So what have you found in your research?" Dave was the only one besides Nash's mother who knew what he was about here in Austin.

"Nothing yet that has led anywhere, but I'm still curious how these people live."

"'These people?' You mean your relatives?"

"They're *not* my relatives, Dave."

"You know what they say—blood is thicker than water."

Nash retorted, "And I say if you haven't known them as family all your life, they're not family."

Dave continued to disagree. "Open your mind a little, Nash. You might like one or two of them."

Nash thought about Chase Parker, who owned the horse rescue ranch, and his wife, Lucie, who was a Fortune. He remembered what he'd found about her helping kids. Was that all just PR? He also remembered her sister Amelia's husband was a rancher. But those were two of the female Fortunes. As far as the men went, he just didn't know.

"One thing I've learned, or I guess I've verified, is that Gerald Robinson was unethical, indiscriminate and generally someone I don't want to know."

"What if you came face-to-face with him?" Dave asked.

"It's not going to happen. That's not why I'm here."

"Are you planning on staying in Austin longer than a month?" Dave asked.

"Not unless I want to quit my job."

"With your résumé, I'm sure you could get a job in Austin if you wanted it. Think how much easier it would be to investigate the Fortunes."

"Okay, now you're mocking me. I'm going to end this call."

"I'm serious about the job, Nash. If you feel you have to be there, maybe a move wouldn't be a bad thing."

Nash thought about Cassie again. Her life was here. "I'm just taking it day by day. One leads to the next."

"And what's next?" Dave inquired.

"A drive around some of the Fortune addresses. I want to see how they live."

"How's that going to help you?"

"Call it curiosity. Maybe my eyes need a break from the computer. Besides, you know how stakeouts go. You never know what will turn up."

"No, you never know," Dave agreed. "Be careful, Nash. Nobody knows you're there but me and your mom."

"And the two of you need to stop worrying. The owner of the bed-and-breakfast would send out an alarm if I don't come back."

"She had a pretty voice."

Before Nash could stop himself, he said, "She *is* pretty."

Dave's silence met that remark, and Nash didn't intend to elaborate on it.

"I meant it when I said to be careful, Nash, and I'm not only talking about physically. You could end up in the middle of family you don't want to meet. They might not like another relative turning up. And as far as the pretty voice and the pretty face of the owner of the Bluebonnet Bed-and-Breakfast…"

"I've got to go, Dave. I'll check in again next week."

"I'm counting on it."

When Nash ended the call, he had to smile. Dave could be irritating at times, but Nash wouldn't want to go through life without him. His friend was right about one thing, though—he *did* need to be careful…with both the Fortunes and with Cassie.

## Chapter Five

It was 5 a.m. on Sunday when Nash awakened, not exactly sure why. Then he realized that he'd heard the pipes creaking. It was coming from the downstairs bathroom.

He guessed Cassie was taking a shower. No, he was not going to think about *that* too long. Punching his pillow and closing his eyes again, he wondered why she was getting up so early. She didn't serve breakfast until 8 a.m. He considered the idea that maybe she just wanted to get up and paint. Then why take a shower?

After another half hour of tossing and turning, he figured he might as well just get dressed and go downstairs and find out what Cassie was up to. Once on the first floor, his nose twitched. He smelled dough of some kind. Checking the kitchen, he didn't find Cassie but rather two huge ceramic bowls covered by towels.

He peeked under one of them. Yeast bread. It would probably take some time for it to rise.

Instinct made him go to the front door and look out. He spotted Cassie walking about half a block down the street. Not knowing what he intended to do, he decided to follow her. Maybe the investigator in him just needed something to investigate other than old photographs and news stories.

He hadn't tailed anyone for a long time, and he didn't know if he should be doing it now. But he was curious.

He didn't have to be curious for long. He was thirty yards behind Cassie when he saw her stop and then go up the steps of a church. Did he really want to follow her there? It would certainly bring back memories.

Once he reached the steps himself, he climbed them, then opened one of the wooden doors that led into the Church of the Good Shepherd.

In the narthex the doors were propped open, leading into the nave of the church. Straight ahead, hanging behind the altar, was a lifelike statue of the Good Shepherd. On the left in the rainbow light of a stained glass window was a statue of Mary and a rack of candles beneath her. In the sparsely populated church, he caught sight of Cassie about three rows back from the altar. Nash found himself slipping into one of the back pews, blessing himself, remembering his childhood.

The Mass was a ritual he hadn't been part of in a long time, but he found he still knew when to stand and sit and when to kneel. The homily was short, probably because this was such an early Mass and the priest knew everyone had somewhere to go.

At the end of the Mass, Nash wasn't sure whether to slip out so Cassie didn't know he'd ever been there, or to stay put and wait until she left. If she noticed him, well, then she noticed him.

It didn't take long for the church to empty. Nash spotted Cassie still sitting in her pew. He decided not to be secretive about this, at least. Walking up the side aisle, he slid into the pew with her.

She glanced at him and her eyes widened in surprise. She asked, "Were you here for Mass?"

"I was." He didn't feel a need to give an explanation.

"You're Catholic?"

"Lapsed," he said with a shrug. "My mother took me to church during my childhood, and I went to Catholic school until eighth grade. Then I went to a public high school."

If he was any reader of thoughts, he saw a myriad of expressions flit over Cassie's face. The main one—surprise he was telling her this.

"Why did you stop going?" she asked.

"You know how teenagers are," he said. "They question everything."

"I questioned," she empathized. "But—" She hesitated for a moment. "But when things in my life were tough, I gravitated back toward my faith."

"My mother wished I had done that."

"Why didn't you?"

He didn't see any harm in telling her. He wouldn't be revealing anything. "I had a father who let's just say wasn't the best guy. He left my mother high and dry. I never knew him. That didn't seem to bother me so much when I was a kid but when I was a teenager, when friends were going on fishing trips with their dads or camping or working on school projects together, anger set in. That anger just seemed to be at odds with faith."

"And now?"

"I guess I just got out of the habit of believing. Life and my job, especially, just seemed to take all my attention."

After they sat there awhile longer in silence, Cassie said, "I really have to get back or the bread dough I prepared will proof too much. But I'd like to light a candle first. You don't have to stay."

"I'll wait," he said, actually looking forward to walking her back to the bed-and-breakfast.

Cassie had worn a peasant blouse with three-quarter sleeves and a skirt that flowed to her calves. Her flats were soundless on the tile floor as she slipped by him out of the pew and walked up to light a candle. After kneeling at the statue for a minute or so—long enough to say a prayer, Nash guessed—she stood and walked back to the pew.

He rose to his feet and met her at the aisle. Together they walked out. The blues, yellows and reds from the stained glass windows flickered across Cassie's face as they walked down the aisle. Her hair swung against her neck and Nash was struck again by her vulnerability. Did she seem more vulnerable this morning because they were in church?

Cassie took a church bulletin from a stand by the door. Then he opened the outside door for her and they stepped into the sunlight and a beautiful Sunday morning in Austin.

They walked down the steps together, their arms brushing. That touch of skin on skin felt right, and Nash kept his thoughts from going further than that.

On the sidewalk once more, heading toward the bed-and-breakfast, Nash couldn't stop the question that echoed in his mind. She'd asked him some personal questions; now it was his turn. "Did you light a candle for your parents?"

Cassie seemed to take a deep breath before she answered. He guessed she still missed them. Instead of answering him, she simply nodded.

He remained silent as they passed a mixture of apartment houses and single-family dwellings, some in brick, some in stucco, some in stone.

"Do you have a busy day planned?" he finally asked her.

"I do. After making breakfast—we're having quiche and homemade bread if you're interested—I'm going to bake cookies and fruit breads to freeze. That way if I'm too busy during the week, I can pull them out. I'm also going to have guests checking in today. So there are rooms to get ready and freshen up as well as towels to put out. The Warners are leaving so I'll be cleaning their room. It will be a busy day."

"Do you have help?"

"Help? Such as a maid?" Cassie laughed. "There isn't any money in the budget to hire a maid. I'm it. Do you have a busy day planned?"

"Actually, I do," he said. "I'll be out most of the day." He didn't tell her he had a list of addresses where Fortunes lived. He was going to scope out their living arrangements and maybe get a glimpse of their lives.

When they reached the B&B, Cassie waved to Mrs. Garcia, who was out on her front porch. She was wearing a flowered dress and carrying her purse. Nash accompanied Cassie as they walked over to the widow's porch.

"Good morning," Mrs. Garcia said. "Were you two out for a stroll?"

"We were at church," Cassie said.

"That's where I'm headed now."

The day was already warming up and Nash remembered what Mrs. Garcia had said about her arthritis. "Why don't I drive you," he said to Mrs. Garcia.

"But aren't you going to eat breakfast?" the older woman asked.

"It won't be ready for about half an hour," Cassie said. "Maybe a little longer. I have to put the bread in to bake."

"If you make them into rolls, they won't take as long to bake," Mrs. Garcia said.

"That's a great idea," Cassie agreed. "And when you get home, I'll bring a couple over to you."

Mrs. Garcia beamed. "That would be lovely. And, young man, I think I'll take you up on your offer."

Nash went up Mrs. Garcia's steps and offered her his arm. This wasn't exactly the way he'd intended to spend his Sunday morning, but right now, it seemed like the best way to start the day.

After he drove Mrs. Garcia to church, he had breakfast with Cassie and the Warners. The couple was checking out after breakfast and he knew Cassie had a busy day, so he didn't linger.

What he did do caused feelings to roil inside of him. He drove past where several of the Fortunes lived. That took well into the afternoon. But then he went where he probably shouldn't have. He parked down the street from Gerald Robinson's estate. It had a stone wall surrounding it and an iron gate. According to what Nash had found about it online, the house looked like a Mediterranean castle. It was easy to see the Robinsons had an elevated lifestyle. So elevated that Charlotte never wanted to lose it. That had been one of the reasons she'd kept his mother from getting in touch with Gerald, or Jerome, or whatever anybody wanted to call him. The whole name change idea irked Nash. Supposedly Jerome wanted to change his name to build a life on his own. Really? He couldn't even keep his first name? None of it made sense to Nash.

During Nash's stakeout, no one came and went at the Robinson house. Nash felt the bitterness he had always pushed away rise up in his throat. He knew anger and bitterness weren't good for him, and he realized that maybe he was following this money trail of Charlotte's for revenge's sake. If he took her down, he took Gerald down.

Did he want to do that to his biological father? He'd told himself over and over again Gerald Robinson had been no more than a sperm donor. Yet his mother considered the man much more. She said she understood why he'd stayed with Charlotte. But did she really?

What if bringing Gerald and Charlotte down put a wedge between Nash and his mom? Would all of this have been worth it?

Cassie handed the Stengles their keys. They were an adorable couple on their honeymoon. They were from Kansas but they were taking a road trip to San Antonio, wandering here and there along the way. They were about her age, and she was happy to see two people who had found each other.

Cassie told them, "If you need anything, just call the front desk. My cell phone is also on the information sheet, so if you can't reach me at the desk, then call my cell. Will you be staying in for supper tonight?"

"Oh, no," they both said at the same time. "We're going out on the town," Tom Stengle told her. "We want to see everything we can see."

"You'll find a list of restaurants and attractions in your room near your phone."

Tom said, "I'll carry our bags upstairs." Cassie offered to help but he brushed her help away.

As Tom went up the stairs, his wife Annabelle leaned close to her. "We're going to spend some time in our room until dinner tonight. I hope there's a Do Not Disturb sign."

Cassie gave the newlywed a nod. "There certainly is."

Cassie had noticed Nash had come in while she was checking in the Stengles. He looked tired. Something about his expression bothered her. The lines around his eyes cut in deep. Maybe *troubled* was a better word than *tired*. He'd gone into the guest lounging area and drawn a cup of coffee. He was just sitting there on the couch now, broodingly staring into his mug.

She thought about their conversation at the church that morning and about his kindness to Renata. She didn't like to see anybody going through troubles.

The bed-and-breakfast was quiet now. The Stengles were in their room and she had a feeling they'd be there awhile. The other couple who had checked in had gone right out again. Cassie had finished everything she'd intended to do today. The way it looked, she might not even have to cook supper except for herself.

Crossing to the sitting area, she sank down on the couch beside Nash. "Rough day?" she asked.

He took a gulp of his coffee. "Rough enough."

"Anything you want to talk about? I hear talking relieves stress." She kept her voice light, hoping to get a feel for what was going on with him.

He just shook his head.

She realized she was prying and she had no right to do that. "As a financial adviser, I guess you have to be discreet. I shouldn't be asking any questions. I'm sorry."

But as she started to rise to her feet, Nash caught her hand. She felt his touch throughout her whole body. When she looked into his eyes, she didn't know what she saw. It looked remarkably like guilt. Why would Nash feel guilty?

"I'm going to trust my gut on this," he mumbled.

"Trust your gut?" She didn't understand at all.

"Can we go someplace more private?"

If any other man had asked her that, she'd refuse. But it was easy for her to see Nash's request had nothing to do with a line or romance.

She had a dilemma. She could offer to go out on the screened-in porch with him. That would be private. But even more private would be the sitting area in her room. She'd never asked a man into her room before.

"How are you at lighting fires?" she asked.

He looked perplexed.

"It's cool tonight and I have a fireplace in the sitting area in my suite. I never seem to stack everything right to get it started. We could light a fire and talk there. I might even be able to rustle up a cinnamon roll or two."

He studied her face for what seemed to be a very long time. Then he nodded. "I'm good at lighting fires."

She walked him down the hall into her suite, which was really just one big room with an en suite bath. But she had it divided into a small sitting area with a love seat and rocking chair at the fireplace, and a bedroom area with its single bed, nightstand and small dresser.

She pointed to the fireplace, where, on the hearth, kindling and a few logs lay in a basket.

He gave her a half smile. "You're making this easy."

"Matches are on the mantel," she told him as she left the room.

In the kitchen, as she took the cinnamon rolls from the tinfoil packet, she realized her hands were shaking. That was silly. Nash was just going to unburden himself. She shouldn't think anything of it, not anything at all. But as she carried the rolls and another cup of coffee for herself back to the sitting room, she knew she was going to get in deeper with Nash and wasn't sure about that at all.

Nash had a glow coming from the fireplace and he was sitting on the love seat with his mug of coffee. She settled next to him, setting the rolls on the small coffee table.

As he looked around her bedroom, he asked, "Is everything in your life in 3-D and color?"

She laughed. She liked bright colors and used them everywhere. There was a bright blue bedspread crisscrossed with violet and lime on her bed and matching curtains. They stood out against her lemon-yellow walls. A mobile with abstract colorful shapes hung above a file cabinet where she kept folders for each of her art students.

"Do you have something against color?" she joked.

"Not at all," he said with a shake of his head. "I'm just not sure how you sleep in here." Her love seat was also a shade of violet, and the armchair was lime green.

Cassie sat a little sideways and looked at him. "You don't really want to talk about the color of my room, do you?"

His brow furrowed. His eyes looked pained as he frowned. "No. I want to come clean with you."

Come clean? About what? She felt frightened for a few seconds, maybe even panicked. Then she remembered there was nothing to fear. She kept silent.

"I'm not in town as a financial consultant," he revealed, watching her carefully.

She must have made a little gasp.

He quickly went on, "I'm a cop on independent assignment."

A cop. Now she felt a bit of panic all over again. She remembered cops taking her mother away. She'd never forget it. "What does that mean?" she asked, totally taken aback. She didn't know how she felt about Nash being a member of law enforcement. After all, her mother was in prison…and he didn't know.

Nash set his mug on the coffee table. "I'm following up on a case that my boss didn't want me to pursue. I took vacation time to do it."

"Is the work dangerous?" she asked.

"No, it's not dangerous. It's mostly research. I'm not carrying a weapon if that's what you're worried about." When he turned to face her more directly, their knees were touching. "I'm supposed to be incognito. I guess you could say undercover. But I'm sorry I didn't tell you the truth up front."

The truth. Her life wasn't completely honest and she hated that. "You didn't know me. Why should you trust me? Besides, you didn't have to tell me now, either. You're entitled to your secrets. Everybody is."

"I suppose," he said begrudgingly.

Their knees were still touching and neither of them had moved away. The fabric of his jeans rubbed a bit against the cotton of her skirt.

"Why did you tell me now?" she asked softly.

"I'm not exactly sure," he admitted. "I don't trust people easily. That's an occupational hazard. But I do believe *you* can be trusted."

Cassie felt honored that he thought so. But she also felt guilty because she was keeping secrets from him. However, especially now that she knew he was a cop, she couldn't tell him about her mother.

"I don't trust easily, either," she confessed, but she didn't volunteer why.

Cassie was still trying to absorb everything Nash had said as they stared into the fire. Moments later, she turned to glance at his face. His jaw was set and his mouth was a thin line. She suspected there was a lot more to his story than what he'd told her.

"Is that all you want to tell me?" she asked.

"I should just shut up," he muttered.

"Why? I'm certainly not going to tell anybody anything. If you need to get it off your chest, feel free."

"Off my chest isn't off my mind. I'm personally involved in this."

"In the investigation?"

"Yes. And I'm sure that's part of the reason my boss wants me to drop it. We've had resolution in the main part of the case, but I stumbled on this other thread."

"What you're saying is hard for me to understand because I don't know the basics."

"The basics are—the suspect that I'm investigating is quite possibly my biological father's wife."

So many questions ran through Cassie's head, she didn't know what to ask first. "Do you *know* your biological father?"

"You mean 'know' like he lived around me or I lived around him?"

"Yes. Have you spent time with him?"

"Never." Nash's voice was firm and there was more in his tone that she was sure he didn't want her to hear.

"He left?" she asked.

"Oh, yes. He definitely left. He was married, but my mother loved him anyway. She thinks more highly of him than I do."

"Did you know him at all?"

"We've never had any contact, and that's a good way to keep it, especially now."

"He's in Austin?"

"Yes, he and his wife."

"You know, don't you, if you do get the goods on your biological father's wife, you might be ruining any chance you have of getting to know your dad."

Nash went rigid and snapped, "He's not my father." There was so much bitterness in Nash's voice that Cassie recoiled.

Nash saw it. "Cassie, I'm sorry. I don't talk about this. I never talk about it. And this is why. This man is not a good man. He's had other affairs. My mother tried to contact him about me, but his wife intercepted her. She threatened her and my mother isn't the type to push."

Cassie realized this was only the tip of the iceberg. The fact that he was both professionally and personally involved in this case had to be tearing him apart.

When Nash reached a hand out to her, she took his.

He shook his head. "I'm sorry I involved you."

"I'm not sorry." She wasn't. Something about Nash touched her deeply.

Reaching out, he stroked her cheek and then he pushed her hair behind her ear. "You are so sweet," he murmured, and then he leaned in.

Cassie didn't move away. Moments later his lips were on hers, creating a fire much more dangerous than the one that was snapping at logs in the fireplace. She knew this kiss could get her in big trouble, but she still responded to it, responded to him. Her fingers tightened on his shoulders and Nash brought her closer.

Suddenly, however, reality seemed to hit them both. As Cassie tore away, Nash leaned back, too, and rubbed his hand down over his face.

Then he gazed at her with questions in his eyes. "What was that?" he asked.

"I'm not sure," she answered.

Nash rose to his feet. "I'd better go, for both our sakes. Agreed?"

"Agreed," she said with determination, knowing that was best for both of them. But as Nash left her room and the fire still burned, she knew they weren't done with each other yet.

## Chapter Six

That night after dinner out, Nash went to his room. But he was restless. He didn't feel like staring at his laptop screen, either to work or to stream a movie. He couldn't forget about that kiss with Cassie. It had practically melted his boots.

He decided to search her out because maybe they should talk about it. He'd seen a lot of denial in his line of work, and it didn't solve anything. Sure, he could deny the kiss and Cassie could deny the kiss and they could walk around like it had never happened. But whenever they looked at each other, whenever they were around each other, it would be there.

First he went downstairs to find her. But she wasn't in the kitchen or the guest area, or out on the porch. Should he go back to the scene of the crime, so to speak?

But the door to her suite was closed and when he rapped, she didn't answer.

He called softly, "Cassie?"

Either she wasn't inside or she was ignoring him. Still, from what he knew about her so far, he didn't think she'd do that. There was one other place she could be. After he jogged up the stairs, he took time to notice what he'd been in too much of a hurry to see before. Down at the end of the hall the attic stairs were pulled down. She'd probably escaped for a while to paint. Should he bother her?

At least they'd have privacy up there to talk without him entering her suite. That might be good.

The stairs creaked as he climbed them, so she heard him coming. She had a white craft light positioned over her painting. When she looked over her shoulder and saw him, she didn't smile. Was she remembering their kiss?

Once again, he glanced around the room at all of the paintings. The landscapes were different from anybody else's he'd ever seen. They were bright and cheerful and would warm up any room. There were a few abstracts and he had to smile at the riot of colors. They reminded him of her house.

After she finished a stroke on the canvas, she dipped her brush into a jar and left it there. Before he asked about the kiss, he approached with a mundane question. "Relaxing?"

She rolled her shoulders and stretched her neck. "I'm trying to."

He didn't know if there was an underlying message in that response, but he reacted as if there was. "I suppose my being up here isn't helping that."

She turned on her stool to face him. She was wearing a bright blue Oxford shirt that came to her knees. The long sleeves were rolled up. He knew it was supposed to be a smock to protect her clothes from the paint, but she looked damn sexy.

Instead of getting to the subject he came up to discuss, he looked around at the paintings again. "Have you shown your work in any galleries?"

She stood and came over to him. "Not lately. I applied for the Art Alliance Showing at the Palmer Center this weekend, but I was turned down."

That astonished him. "Turned down? That doesn't seem possible."

He studied her face as she struggled to explain and be fair at the same time. "Artists from all over the country enter their work. I'm not sure how they decide exactly. As with most artistic work, opinions are subjective."

He waved his arm over the attic. "Do you have photos of all these?"

"Some of them."

"You should take photos of all of them and put an extensive portfolio together."

After she hesitated a few moments, she revealed, "A few years ago I won a contest. After the fact, one of the judges bought three of my paintings at the exorbitant prices that my agent suggested. I sold two more to an art patron from the gallery where the paintings were displayed. Those sales were enough for a down payment on the B&B. I never would have been able to get started without that. But since I've run the B&B, I cut ties with my agent. I haven't had time to promote my work or even set up a website. It's always which thing

on the to-do list takes priority, and this is never it because it's so hit-and-miss."

"You know that's the first time you've told me anything about your past." He couldn't help but wonder
about it. He'd shared his and hoped she'd open up with
him.

She didn't respond to his statement. Rather she
asked, "Why did you come up here, Nash?"

As he expected, she was forthright. "I thought maybe
we should talk about that kiss. It's going to be difficult
to ignore. I'll be here another three weeks and I didn't
want our interaction to be awkward."

Her eyes were studying him as if she were searching
for the truth. "It doesn't have to be awkward between
us. We just go on from here."

"And forget the sizzle we feel every time we're in the
same room?" he questioned with a raised brow.

"We have to," she reminded him. "You're going back
to Mississippi. What would be the point in…anything
happening?"

Just as he thought. She didn't indulge in flings. Neither did he. Nevertheless, a fling right now seemed just
the ticket to forget what he was doing. Just the ticket to
distract himself from the Fortunes. And to bring pleasure to them both.

They were standing close enough that he caught
Cassie's scent. It was flowery and drew him toward
her. He leaned a little closer and so did she.

But then he shook his head. "If we don't want that
kiss to happen again, I'd better go downstairs. You can
go back to relaxing and painting."

She didn't protest or ask him to stay, so he knew
she wanted him to go. After he crossed to the stairs, he

glanced over his shoulder at her. She was still watching him. She turned away first and he continued down to the second floor.

Once in his room, he went straight for his laptop. Pulling out the chair, he settled in at the small desk. This time he wasn't searching for the Fortune name. He went to a website he often used and typed in *Cassandra Calloway*. If she'd won a contest he might be able to find out something about it.

He did. But not much. Just her name and the information that she'd won first place in the Texas Winter Fest's Art Contest. The article said she was from Bryan. At least he knew something more now than he did before. And maybe, in the days to come, she'd open up to him and share more than a kiss.

Cassie had really tried hard not to remember that the Art Alliance Showing was at the Palmer Center this weekend. She didn't know if she wanted to see why her work was turned down or if everybody else's was so much better. The two couples who were staying at the B&B along with Nash had already eaten their breakfast and left. Cassie had seen Nash's SUV parked along the street, so either he had gotten up early and walked somewhere, or he didn't care about breakfast. He hadn't slept in any of the days he'd been here. But who knew? Today could be different.

He hadn't been around much this week. He hadn't sought her out. Was he sorry he'd confided in her? Did he regret the bond that had formed because he'd shared a secret? She had to stop thinking about him.

An hour later, she was slicing and dicing vegetables

for the evening meal. One of the new couples who had checked in this week had said they'd be here tonight.

When she heard the stair steps creak, she was surprised to see Nash. He wasn't dressed for a business meeting today. He wore blue jeans and his old brown boots along with a black Henley shirt. The Stetson was missing, though, which meant he wasn't going out.

"Not working today?" she asked as he came into the kitchen.

"Not today. Even investigators need a day off now and then. I had an idea, though. How's your day looking?"

"No new arrivals today. Dinner for a couple tonight. I should do some chores, but…"

"But?" he asked, his head cocked.

"What was your idea?" She didn't know if it included her or not, but the way he'd said it, it might.

"I thought you might want to go to the arts festival."

She frowned. "I was going to skip it this year."

"Because you weren't accepted to show?"

Too perceptive. He was just too perceptive. "That doesn't sound very good, does it? I should want to see other artists' work, right?"

"From the ads, it looks like the arts festival has more to offer than paintings."

"All right. Since I don't have a good excuse not to go—"

He gave her an offended look.

She laughed. "I think it sounds like fun to go with you. Just give me a couple of minutes to stow away the veggies and get ready."

A half hour later, they'd parked and were walking toward the Palmer Center. Nash had been quiet in the car and she'd wondered what he was thinking about. She'd left him to his thoughts as she considered hers. Had he asked her along today because he'd kissed her and maybe wanted to do it again? Just how did she feel about that? If she thought about it, she felt weak-kneed. All week her mind had skittered around the idea of kissing him again. Not only kissing. She wanted to be held in those strong arms.

As they walked into the Palmer Center, Cassie felt she had to make conversation. She said, "Art City Austin started out from a local street fair and progressed to this. This year they welcomed over a hundred individual artists from across the country, and there are twenty galleries from across Texas who are showcasing works."

"This place is something else," Nash commented, looking around. "The stone and tile, all the glass, the covered balcony on the second floor. It's really amazing."

"It's one of our Austin landmarks."

They turned down a hall that was decorated with paintings on the wall. Cassie turned to Nash and asked, "Why did you really want to come here today?"

He studied her for a few seconds as if he was gauging his reply. But then he said, "I'm tired of researching and going through public documents. There are so many and most of them don't have anything to do with my biological father's wife." He grimaced. Then he said, "It seems odd to be talking about it with you."

"Why?"

"Because I've kept what I'm doing under wraps for so long. I could be looking at public documents at home, but here in Austin, where the couple lives, I thought I could find out more."

"Like putting all the puzzle pieces together," she suggested.

"Exactly. And what better way to get away from the puzzle for a time than to go to an arts festival with a pretty girl."

She wrinkled her nose at him. "You don't have to resort to flattery."

Pure surprise registered on his handsome face. "Resort? You think I'm handing you a line?"

With a resigned shrug, she admitted, "The truth is, Nash, I really haven't dated, not for a very long time. So I'm not sure I'd know a line when someone was handing it to me."

He took her by the shoulders and looked deep into her eyes. "That wasn't a line, Cassie. I don't do lines. You are pretty and sexy and talented. End of discussion."

She blinked, but then she asked, "Is that your cop voice you're using?"

He laughed. "It usually works. Is it working on you?"

"No. If someone tells me the discussion ended, that just makes me want to continue it."

He shook his head. "You're one of those, huh?"

She laughed again. Then seriously she said, "I suppose you've run into people of all personalities, both male and female."

"I have. When I was a beat cop in Oklahoma, the work was rough,. We put in long hours, preventing domestic violence if we could, preventing shootings or getting in the middle of those shootings. But in spite of all that, I actually enjoy talking to ordinary people— for instance, a kid who is usually afraid of cops. Once he talked to me, then he wasn't afraid. I like the time I spent in schools, giving workshops on safety for kids."

"So why did you leave it?"

"I needed a new life."

To Cassie that sounded as if Nash's heart had been broken, but he didn't seem willing to talk to her about that. They hadn't known each other well enough or long enough, and this wasn't exactly the place to have that kind of discussion.

Still, she prodded a little. "So you went to Mississippi and—"

"And I became a detective. There was an opening in the white-collar crime unit, so I took it."

"And now?" she asked.

"I'm definitely not sure dealing with white-collar crime is what I want to do for the rest of my life. I investigate CEOs, money laundering possibilities, and then I call in the appropriate acronym."

"Acronym?"

"Government agency. Tax evasion is IRS, money laundering can be IRS along with FBI, drugs or guns can come under the ATF."

"Alcohol, tobacco and firearms."

He nodded.

"So usually you don't see something to its finish?"

"Sometimes. Maybe that's what bothers me most. Maybe that's why I want to see this to its finish."

"I can certainly understand that." She took hold of his arm. "But, Nash, this is personal for you, too. It could cause you damage even though you don't think so now."

He wrapped her arm around his and started walking. "Don't worry about me, Cassie. I'll handle whatever

comes my way. I've been taught to do that professionally, and I've learned to do it personally."

Cassie knew Nash believed what he was saying, but
she still had her doubts. How could he put his biological father's wife in jail and not have regrets?

But she wasn't going to ask any more questions because Nash was acting as if that discussion was over.
That was his way of dealing with questions he didn't
want to answer. Or maybe feelings that came up that
he didn't want to feel. Even though she didn't know
him well, she knew that. How was that even possible
in two weeks?

She glanced at his profile, the jut of his jaw, the
breadth of his shoulders. She wasn't sure. She just knew
she was mightily attracted to him as she'd never been
to another man.

They walked, paused and studied paintings. Cassie
tried not to compare anything to her own work, but that
was difficult not to do. "Some of these are so good,"
she murmured, studying a landscape of the Southwest
with its red rocks, almost turquoise sky, cactus and
many colors of earth.

"You've lost confidence, haven't you?" Nash noted.

"I don't know what you mean." She brushed off his
words as if they were too far-fetched to consider.

"You know exactly what I mean. You don't think
your work is as good as what's displayed here."

"How can I think anything else? They rejected my
work."

"Oh, Cassie. You know that saying? Beauty is in the
eye of the beholder?"

"Maybe."

They walked on, past booths from various galleries

that had displays. Cassie spotted Nash pocketing business cards from them. She didn't ask him why. Nash was an investigator. His job was to collect information, so maybe that was what he was doing. Who knew? She couldn't expect him to pour his heart out to her just because they'd shared a kiss...and a confidence.

She thought about their kiss again. Many more of those and they would know each other *very* well.

Pictures played in her mind that made her blush. She couldn't believe she was thinking about Nash in that way, imagining him without his T-shirt, fantasizing about running her fingers through his hair. She'd never had a crush on anybody, not even Cody Sinclair, who'd walked away because her mother had been deemed a criminal. This *wasn't* a crush on Nash, she scolded herself. This was just a woman's response to an attractive man. Completely natural.

When they'd walked around awhile longer, Nash said, "Have you looked at enough paintings?"

"Have you?" she returned.

He blew out a breath. "Another question doesn't answer a question."

"All right," Cassie said. "Tell me what you'd rather do instead of looking at paintings."

He narrowed his eyes at her. "You know, I think you could give a lawyer a run for his money."

She gave him a coy smile. "I have no idea what you mean."

He chuckled. "If you're ready to leave, why don't we stop at the tasting room at the Mendoza Winery? We can have a little fun, taste wine and bring a bottle back to the B&B. Do you have time for that?"

She'd like to thank Carlo again for arranging her

Paint and Sip social. Assuming he was there. She checked her watch. "I have time. I think that sounds like a great idea."

Although she didn't usually drink, tasting a few of Carlo's wines could be fun. She'd take a sip of each and that would be that.

Nash hung his arm around her shoulders and pulled her close. After he did, she could smell a hint of citrusy cologne and she liked it. She liked feeling his warmth.

Who was she kidding? She liked him.

Nash knew exactly why he'd asked Cassie to go to the tasting room with him. He wanted to spend more time with her away from the bed-and-breakfast. When she was there, it was as if she had a burden on her shoulders. Out and about she smiled more and laughed more. Maybe there was something about the bed-and-breakfast that reminded her of something else. Maybe if they spent more time together, she'd tell him.

This time at the tasting room they went in a different entrance than the one for the restaurant. The two of them faced a large rough-hewn wooden door.

Nash took hold of the brass handle and pulled the door open. It creaked and they stepped inside. There was a reception area with high vaulted ceilings with dark beams. Beyond that they could see a marble-topped tasting bar crowded with wine glasses and corked bottles. In the center of the room sat a wooden trestle table that must be used for the tastings.

A man in a black shirt and black pants stepped out of an office located down the hall to the right of the wine bar.

He smiled as he came toward them. "I'm Ricardo," he said. "Are you here for a tasting?"

"We are," Nash confirmed, his hand possessively resting in the small of Cassie's back. It seemed natural to touch her like that. She didn't shrug away so he supposed it was the right thing to do.

"Have a seat," Ricardo said.

"Is Carlo here?" Cassie asked.

Ricardo shook his head. "He's away for the day."

"Will you thank him again for me for hosting the Paint and Sip?"

"Surely, I will. Now tell me what kind of wine you prefer."

"Sweet," Cassie answered. "But I really only want a taste. I don't really drink often."

Nash gave her a surprised look. He leaned close and whispered in her ear, "If you don't drink, why did you want to come? Are you sure you want to stay?"

"I wanted to thank Carlo again. And I've never tried the Mendoza wines. A tasting is just that, a tasting. I'll have a sip or two of each one. We're good, Nash."

As he gazed into her eyes, he suspected they would be *very* good together. Had he hoped after a glass of wine or two she'd be receptive to his advances?

No. He'd already decided that shouldn't happen. That was why he'd stayed away from her this week.

Nash looked up at Ricardo. "I like dry."

"I'm sure I can satisfy both of your palates," Ricardo assured them with a wink. "Do you know anything about wines?" he asked.

"I know about types and some of the good years. But that's about it," Nash responded.

"That's more than most people know." Ricardo went

to the bar and chose two bottles. He brought them to the table with two wine glasses. "This is Sunny Days—a Chenin Blanc," he told Nash. "It's a dry white wine. It's not well-known by many consumers. For the lady, let's try Southwestern Comfort—a Muscat Blanc. It is also a white wine but a bit sweeter. It goes well with chocolate." Ricardo brought a plate of chocolate, a basket of crackers and dish of cheese to the table.

Nash swirled the wine around in his glass and then took a sip. He nodded to Ricardo that he liked it.

"Try yours," Ricardo directed Cassie. "Of course, you're going to have to try chocolate with it."

She swirled the wine in her glass as Nash had done and took a sip. The way she licked her lips afterward made Nash almost break out in a sweat.

"What do you think?" Nash asked.

She smiled. "I think my guests might enjoy having this on hand. Let me try it with the chocolate." She took one of the chocolates on the tray and bit into it. Her expression was so sensual Nash wanted to kiss her before she was even finished the bite.

"I'll take a bottle of this one," she said.

Ricardo laughed. "But you haven't tasted the red yet."

Next Ricardo brought out Desert Sunset for Cassie, which was a Syrah. He chose Rodeo Nights—a Cabernet Sauvignon—for Nash.

After Cassie sipped what was in her glass, she shook her head. "I prefer the first one."

"Do you want to try it again?" Ricardo asked.

"No, I don't need to."

He looked at Nash. "Anything else you'd like to taste?"

"No. I'll just finish up what I have here. I'll also take a bottle of the first one."

Ricardo looked from one of them to the other. "I'll go back to my office for a little while so you can relax and enjoy the rest of your wine and the snacks." He took his leave quickly.

Cassie exchanged a look with Nash. "I'm not sure what that was about."

"My guess is he thinks we want to be alone. That's not a bad idea, you know."

She took another piece of chocolate from the plate and popped it into her mouth. Then she brought her gaze back to his. "So we can enjoy the snacks?"

Nash leaned toward her, his lips not very far from hers. "Maybe I'd like to taste the wine you were drinking on your lips. Take a sip and we'll try it."

He didn't know if she'd do it. He'd practically ignored her all week trying to settle how she fit into his life... *if* she did. After today, he knew she did. If she did let him kiss her again, that meant she was open to more. Though more of what, he wasn't sure.

Cassie took a very small sip of wine and then turned back to him. He leaned toward her once again and met her lips, tasting the sweetness on her mouth. But the kiss itself was anything but sweet. He took her lips in a possessive kiss that quickly deepened, their tongues meeting, stroking, striving for more. He broke away before he couldn't stop something that shouldn't go on here.

He tried to treat it lightly. "It must be the wine. I feel dizzy."

But she wasn't smiling. "Nash, this isn't a good idea."

"The wine tasting, the kiss or being alone together?"

"Take your pick," she said sadly.

"Are you saying you don't want me to kiss you again?"

"No, I'm not saying that. I'm saying you *shouldn't* kiss me again."

"Because neither of us need those complications?"

She nodded.

"Maybe it doesn't have to be complicated. Maybe we can just enjoy being together."

"I don't know," she confessed.

"Can you tell me why you don't drink?"

"I'd rather not," she said.

He could easily see she didn't trust him. If she didn't trust, then she must have been betrayed by someone. There was a lot more to Cassie Calloway that he had to discover. Could he do it in another two weeks?

He was going to try.

## Chapter Seven

That evening Cassie cleaned up after dinner. Her guests had gone out for the evening and so had Nash. He hadn't come to supper. She thought about that afternoon and the tasting room at the winery. Yes, she still felt the effects of Nash's kiss when she thought about it, but her real focus was on the questions he'd asked. *If you don't drink, why did you want to come?*

She wished she could tell him her mother was in jail for vehicular homicide. She wished she could tell him her mother had been an alcoholic and that was why she herself didn't drink.

Cassie was wiping her hands on a kitchen towel when someone knocked at the front door. Cassie knew who it was immediately. Renata Garcia always knocked even though Cassie had told her over and over she didn't have to.

Cassie hurried to the door so the older woman didn't have to wait on the porch. She opened the door wide and Renata stood there, a smile on her face, a black shawl around her shoulders.

"Are you busy?" Renata asked.

"No, I'm not. The guests ate and left and I've finished cleaning up. Come on in. Can I get you something? A cup of tea? Iced tea?"

"No, I just came over for a little conversation."

In other words, Renata was lonely. That was one of the reasons Cassie was planning a birthday party for her next Sunday. Cassie had invited all of Renata's friends. After conversations with a few of them, she'd realized they wanted to help by bringing casseroles, so it was turning into a covered-dish social.

The older woman followed Cassie to the sitting area, where she seated herself in a comfortable armchair, letting the shawl drop back.

"You had a busy day today," Renata said.

Cassie knew her neighbor watched the comings and goings from her porch. "I did. Breakfast with guests and then I was out for a bit."

"With that nice Mr. Tremont."

Cassie had been hoping Renata hadn't seen that. "Yes, we went to the arts festival at the Palmer Center."

"I used to enjoy that," Renata said, looking a little sad.

"I wasn't allowed to take photos inside but I have some of the grounds. Would you like to see them?"

"Yes, I would."

For the next fifteen minutes or so, Cassie sat on the arm of Renata's chair showing her the photos on her phone.

"You and Mr. Tremont didn't come back until late afternoon."

Cassie moved back to the sofa. "We stopped at the Mendoza Winery for a bit. I brought back a bottle of wine for my guests."

"I see. Has he made any moves yet?" Renata asked.

"Renata," Cassie said with exasperation.

"Just wondering. He's very nice. You look good together."

Still remembering their kiss, Cassie felt the blush rising from her neck to her cheeks. "He'll be leaving soon. He lives in Mississippi."

"Tell me something, Cassie. What if you really liked this man? What if you more than liked him? And if not him, someone else. Would you think about moving?"

"No," she said immediately. "I can't leave Austin." And the reason? She wouldn't desert her mother. Even though her mother wouldn't see Cassie now, there might be a time when she would.

"Maybe I will take a cup of tea," Renata said, eyeing Cassie thoughtfully.

"Coming right up. I even have homemade oatmeal cookies to go with it."

"Wonderful," Renata said.

But right at this moment Cassie didn't think anything was wonderful. She had too many questions rolling around her head…and no answers.

On Monday, Cassie sat beside Danny on the porch. Their lesson wasn't going well because he seemed distracted. There was only one thing to do about that.

She put a hand on his shoulder and he looked up at

her. "You aren't pleased with anything you've painted so far, are you?"

He shook his head. Then he looked down at his shoes and wouldn't make eye contact again.

"Danny, there's nothing wrong with that. If you only knew how many paintings I've started and didn't finish."

That brought his gaze back up to hers. "I'm supposed to finish everything I start."

Cassie suspected that that was what Danny's father had decreed. Finishing for the sake of finishing when you didn't love what you were doing wasn't necessarily in your best interest or in the art's best interest. Cassie took the canvas of a landscape Danny had been working on off the easel.

When she looked into his eyes, she saw disappointment that she was giving up on him. But she wasn't.

Turning to the table where she kept extra supplies, she picked up a sketch pad. Without hesitating, she tore out one of the eleven by fourteen sheets and placed it against a piece of cardboard on the easel. Instead of paints, she picked up a carrier of colored pencils from the table and set it next to Danny. "I'd like you to draw something for me. Do you think you can do that?"

"Sure," he said, some of his confidence returning. The reason for that? She'd given him hope.

"Would you rather do it on the easel or over on the table?"

"I think I'd rather do it on the table."

"No problem." She made a place for him at the table and he brought over the paper. "I'd like you to draw what's on your mind. Don't think about it too much. Just draw it."

Danny took her at her word. He picked a few colored pencils from the carrier, set them on the table and then started. He drew quickly as if he didn't want to think too long about what he was drawing. His mind fed his fingers, and Cassie quickly saw the picture that emerged.

When Danny had finished, he laid down his pencil and sat back in his chair.

In the center of the picture, he'd drawn a fence. His mother was on one side of the fence and his father was on the other.

"Do you mind if I show this to your mom?"

His expression was worried. "I don't want her to get mad."

"I don't believe she'll get mad. I think she wants to know what you're thinking."

"Okay," Danny agreed reluctantly. "Can I try working on that landscape again?"

She positioned the canvas on the easel and let him go at it. Fifteen minutes later, she heard the door to the bed-and-breakfast open and then close. Before Dorie could come into the screened-in porch, Cassie smiled at Danny and picked up the picture he'd drawn. "Just keep on painting. I want to talk to your mom for a few minutes."

She stepped out from the porch and quickly went into the kitchen. There she placed Danny's picture on the counter.

Dorie crossed to her. "What do you have there?"

"Something I think you should see. Danny couldn't concentrate and I asked him to draw what was on his mind. This is what he drew."

Dorie's expression became so sad Cassie wanted to put her arm around her. The mom admitted, "I know his dad's leaving has been hard on him. I don't know how to make it easier." Her voice caught and Cassie could see tears in her eyes.

"The best thing to do is to keep Danny drawing and talking. When he seems troubled, ask him to draw what he's thinking about. He might be able to express his feelings that way rather than in words." Cassie knew how she'd kept everything inside all those years when she'd tried to hide the fact that her mom was drinking. Especially when her mom had gone to prison, painting had saved her.

She'd been so involved with her conversation with Dorie, she hadn't heard Nash come in. All of a sudden, he was standing there with them. She wondered how much he'd heard.

He pointed to the porch. "Is it okay if I say hello to Danny?"

Once again Cassie realized how well Nash handled people.

"Actually, it would be great if you could keep him occupied for a few minutes," Dorie said. "I have something to discuss with Cassie."

"No problem," Nash said with a smile.

As soon as Nash disappeared into the sunporch and started chatting with her son, Dorie assured Cassie, "I'll try to do what you suggest. Maybe I'll get him a set of watercolor pencils and he can begin experimenting with those."

"That's a great idea. When he finishes a drawing or a painting, ask him if he'd like to talk about it. Just take your cues from him. I was an introvert as a child and I spoke through my paintings. Not many people saw them but at least I was able to express my feelings that way."

Dorie looked nervous for a moment and twisted the handle of her purse. "You're so good for Danny and you've helped us so much. I have a favor to ask."

Cassie couldn't imagine what was coming. She just nodded for Dorie to go ahead.

"Do you mind if I list you as a contact for Danny at school in case of emergency? Some days I'm in meetings and can't have my phone turned on. His father usually has his turned off at the office, too."

After Cassie thought about the responsibility she'd be taking on, she said, "Sure. That would be fine. I can't imagine it would happen very often. Danny's a good student, isn't he?"

"He is. But in case he suddenly gets sick or has an accident on the playground, that would help. You'll have to stop at the school and have your picture taken and get an official ID."

"I can do that," Cassie assured her.

Dorie impulsively gave her a hug. "Thank you so much. With the divorce, I feel as if all my support has been kicked out from under me. Couples we were friends with suddenly don't want just a wife hanging around. And my friends have kind of drifted away because I don't have time for them. When I'm not at work, I'm with Danny and that's the way it has to be right now."

"True friends will understand that. They'll be waiting when you're ready for friendship again."

"I hope you're right. But I do feel as if I've made a new friend in you."

"You have." It had been years since Cassie had a close friend. She had a feeling Dorie could be one.

* * *

As Nash sat in the armchair in the sitting area after he'd chatted with Danny and the boy's mother had finished her conversation with Cassie, he thought again about an idea that had been plaguing him all day. He had his laptop on the hassock and he wasn't sure he should do what he wanted to do. As he thought about his kisses with Cassie, he tried to put them in perspective. Still, he didn't seem to have perspective right now. He just knew he felt closer to Cassie than he'd felt to anyone in a long time. All day he'd been thinking about telling her the truth concerning why he was in Austin. Yes, he'd told her the truth, sort of, but not the importance of who he was going after and not the burden of it.

He heard Cassie walk Danny and his mom to the door. He heard their chitchat as Cassie encouraged Danny to draw what he felt. He imagined she'd told Dorie to listen to her son, ask a few questions and see if he'd open up.

In his work, Nash had seen again and again how divorce impacted kids. He also knew firsthand what it was like to grow up without a dad, to miss that strong presence that could make a boy feel secure and encouraged. He'd had to do that for himself. Maybe that was one of the reasons he'd become a cop.

Cassie broke into his thoughts. She walked in carrying glasses of sweet tea.

She handed him the glass. "When you came in you looked as if you could use this."

"Maybe this and something stronger," he said, drinking in the sight of her.

Her eyes widened a bit as she sat across from him in

the corner of the sofa. After a few sips of iced tea, she set her glass on a coaster on the coffee table.

He took a few gulping swallows and set his down, too.

"Do you want to explain why you need something stronger?" she asked.

There was more caring in her voice than curiosity, and that was what decided it for him. "I have something to tell you."

From the look in her eyes, he could tell she knew this was something serious.

"Should I be worried about what you're going to tell me?" she wanted to know.

"Are there any guests still in the house?" He didn't want to be overheard.

Now she looked almost afraid. "No. Why? No one's coming after you, are they? You didn't bring a gun in, did you?"

"No and no." He sat forward on his chair. "I want to tell you who I'm investigating. I want to tell you who I really am."

"You did that, didn't you?" She looked confused now, but then she frowned. "Have you been lying to me again? You're not a detective, either?"

"Oh, I'm a detective," he hurried to assure her. "I didn't tell you the name of the family I'm investigating. I didn't tell you that that name is mine, too."

"This is about your biological father?"

"Yes. The family I'm investigating is the Fortunes."

Slowly she rose from the sofa and came over to sit on the hassock in front of him. "*The* Fortunes?"

Relief filled Nash at actually letting the information

out. "Yes. Jerome Fortune, also known as Gerald Robinson, is my biological father."

"Oh my gosh, Nash. Everyone in Austin knows who Gerald Robinson is. I mean, how many children he fathered has been plastered all over the media."

"Not all of them," Nash determined. "Amazing, isn't it? He couldn't have done better if he was a sperm donor, though I guess in a way he was."

Cassie still appeared astonished. "And this is the man your mother was in love with?"

Nash grimaced. "One and the same. I think part of her still loves him. She says he's gotten a bad rap, and I know she blames a lot of his misbehavior on his wife. But he's responsible for his actions. Every man is."

Cassie nodded slowly as if agreeing with him.

"I'm not after Gerald Robinson, per se," he explained.

"You said you found a thread when you were investigating that led to his wife. *She's* the one you're after, right?"

Apparently Cassie had listened well when he'd confided in her. "It depends. There's fraud involved. I'm trying to follow the money trail."

"You mean like bank transactions?"

"I did that back in Mississippi and I'm trying to make more connections now from here—bank transactions, buying and selling stock, deposits in her accounts and withdrawals, too. I made copies of all that. When I was in Mississippi working on the case, my investigation led me to a Charlene Pickett. I thought something about her looked familiar. Then it came to me. Charlene Pickett and Charlotte Robinson looked an awful lot alike. I believe they're the same person. Let me show you." He turned his laptop toward Cassie. He had a split screen with a photo of Charlene on one side, and Charlotte on the other.

"Those photos *do* look like the same woman—a younger version and an older version," Cassie agreed.

"A substantial amount of money disappeared from a major bank. I connected that to Charlene Pickett. If Charlene, now Charlotte, used that money to fund Gerald's rise to fame, he could be guilty, too."

Cassie looked him squarely in the eye. "If you're undercover, why are you telling me this?"

"I have to be undercover from the Fortunes, but I don't want to be undercover with you."

"Oh, Nash." Her voice held the same longing that he felt.

She was leaning toward him and he was leaning toward her. But they were both aware of that laptop between them. He had work to do and shouldn't be distracted. He'd hoped that by telling Cassie the truth, he would put an end to his distraction. But he could see immediately he'd just created more of a bond between them.

She was looking worried and she asked, "Is something wrong? You're putting an awful lot of trust in me. Why?"

Wasn't that a good question? For now, he'd give her a relevant answer. "Because I think you can handle it. You're not involved in the investigation. If I don't have to hide anything around you, then I can be myself. I can relax in between research jaunts, and maybe be able to think more clearly. I have to find incontrovertible evidence against Charlotte, not supposition."

"You have a hard road ahead of yourself. The Fortunes have power and influence. Gerald Robinson is rich. He can buy anything he wants, probably *anybody* he wants. Men like that don't get prosecuted. If they do, they get out of it, and the same would go for his wife."

Cassie sounded a bit bitter, which wasn't like her at all. "I suppose that's true some of the time, but I'm trying to prevent Charlotte Robinson from hurting anybody again."

"I suppose that's what being prosecuted for a crime is all about," Cassie murmured.

That thought seemed to energize her. She gently pushed his laptop off her lap and onto the hassock. Then she went back to the sofa, grabbed her glass of iced tea and took a few sips. He saw her hand was shaking a bit. Had he scared her?

Still sitting forward on his chair, he closed his laptop and then he asked, "Should I have kept this to myself?"

She instantly answered his question. "No, Nash. No. I'm glad you told me. Really, I am. I just…" She sighed. "I'm just not sure what it means for us."

"I'm not, either," he admitted. "But I didn't want half-truths to stand between us."

She nodded as if she understood. He so wanted to scoop her up from that couch and carry her up to his bedroom. But the way she'd moved away, she obviously wasn't ready for that. He didn't know if *he* was. So he remembered the other reason he wanted to talk to her. "I just didn't want to tell you my secrets," he said with a smile. "Are you busy? Is there something you need to be doing right now?"

"Not at the moment," she concluded, giving him a smile of her own.

"The light is still decent. Would you like me to

take photos of your paintings? Since we both have the time—" He left the sentence open-ended. He wasn't about to force her to spend time with him, though he really wanted to do this for her. "If you want to stay down here I could do it on my own."

"No, I'll come to the attic with you. I can pull out the ones that I think have the most merit."

"They *all* have merit. Have you worked any more on the one on the easel?"

"A little. But it's not finished yet."

"And you wouldn't want me to take a photo of your best painting before it's finished."

"Exactly."

"My camera's in my room. I can stop there on the way."

Cassie was nervous as she waited for Nash in the attic. She felt honored that he'd trusted her with the real story behind his visit to Austin. On the other hand, she was scared. He was a cop first and foremost. Her mother had committed a crime, whether it was unintended or not. Cassie couldn't imagine he'd ever understand what had happened or her feelings for her mother, or the fact that she still loved her even though her mother wouldn't communicate with her. Her mother thought she was protecting Cassie, and maybe she was. Maybe Cassie didn't want to know about the reality of prison and her mother's life there. But she'd been without a father most of her life. She didn't want to lose her mother, too.

How could Nash understand any of that when his feelings about right and wrong were so solid? She remembered all too well how Cody had ended their relationship after he'd found out about her mother. Why

should she take a chance on that kind of heartache
again?

She heard the steps creak as Nash climbed them.
When he appeared with his camera, she wondered if
she should rethink this whole thing.

But she didn't get a chance to do that because he
asked, "What do you want to start with?"

*Concentrate on your paintings*, she told herself.

"I'll just pick out a few," she said.

"Nonsense. We'll do them all, then you can decide
which ones you want in your portfolio."

That made sense, but it would take longer. They'd
be up here together for a while. Just the two of them.
She could handle it. She'd just make sure she stayed at
least three feet away from him at all times.

As she quickly thought about the best way to photograph her paintings, she suggested, "Let's do them
in batches—landscapes, then animal paintings, then
symbolic works."

"Sounds good."

His gaze locked to hers, and she decided maybe four
feet between them might be better than three.

Turning away from him, she went toward the corner where her landscapes were located. He, of course,
followed. She lifted first one, then the second, then the
third and positioned them against the wall. It didn't take
long for him to photograph each one.

He said, "I'll take two photos of each painting. That
way, if one isn't exactly the way you'd like it, you'll
have a choice."

Again, that sounded very reasonable.

Eventually they came to the last series of paintings.
She turned around the hummingbird and butterflies and

then the wildflowers. For these, instead of zooming in, he moved closer to each painting. As she turned the last one to reveal a gazebo with twinkle lights set against the backdrop of a full moon, he moved in again. They were only about a foot apart.

His voice was a bit husky when he told her, "I have a spare flash drive. I'll put together a file with the photos and you can have the drive. That way you can have them printed in whatever size you'd like."

He was watching her and she was watching him. The movement of his lips as he spoke was mesmerizing.

She cleared her throat. "I have a company that I send photos like that to. They do a good job."

"Terrific." He came even closer. Cassie was against the wall so she couldn't back up. She could scoot out around him, she supposed, but she didn't want to.

Nash was looking at her lips, his gaze intent and suddenly hungry. He moved and she anticipated his kiss. Instead, he bent to place the camera on the floor. She closed her eyes and let out the breath she was holding and that was when she felt it. The tingling sensation of his hand on her neck, sliding under her hair. Reflexively she turned her face up to his. As he came even closer, she could smell the lingering scent of aftershave. It was masculine and spicy, and she wondered if she opened her eyes what she would see in his. But the thought fled as she felt his breath on her lips.

Their other kisses had been fast and hot. She felt the heat now, too, but more than that, she felt Nash's sensuality meeting her own. After he kissed her cheek, he let his lips trail to her mouth. He was coaxing her into passion and she didn't need to be coaxed. She sighed and when she did, she could feel his tongue touch her lips. Although the kiss was slow, there was a rawness about it. When his lips finally took hers, she grabbed onto his shoulders and held on tight. Kissing Nash was all that mattered in the world.

She'd never felt such a disturbing desire to be one with someone, to be one with Nash. His arms were around her, and hers were around him. She slid her fingers into his hair and as the kiss went deeper, he groaned. They were both eager and hungry. She felt Nash's heat all around her, or maybe that was her own meeting his. Their tongues searched each other's mouths, and all Cassie thought about was both of them without clothes, in bed, doing what was coming so naturally to them. Maybe it was that picture that made her hesitate.

A small moan escaped her lips as she set her palms against his chest. When she opened her eyes, she thought he looked as dazed as she felt. She knew now that she was undoubtedly falling for him.

"You want to stop?" he asked in a gravelly voice.

"We have to." She knew she sounded a little desperate, but there it was. She wanted him, yet she knew she shouldn't want him.

Nash backed away. "That got more intense than I intended it to."

She simply nodded because she couldn't seem to find the words to speak.

"I think we're finished up here," he said with a wave at all the paintings.

"We are," she agreed.

He asked, "Do you want me to find another place to stay?"

She had to be honest with him. "No."

This time he nodded. "Are you coming downstairs?"

She took refuge in the talent she'd taken refuge in as a child. "No, I'm going to stay up here and paint awhile."

"Then I'll see you tomorrow," he said. "I'll give you the thumb drive then."

"Thank you, Nash. For everything." He'd made her feel like a woman again.

His smile was wry when he said, "No thanks necessary." Then he descended the steps onto the second floor.

Cassie had fully intended to paint, maybe to finish her work in progress. Instead she found herself reaching for her sketchbook and drawing the profile of Nash Fortune Tremont.

## *Chapter Eight*

Maybe because Nash was chasing after the Fortunes most of the day, he looked forward to getting glimpses of Cassie, to eat with her and her guests, even to help her clean up the dishes. Most of the time they didn't talk much, but there was a connection between them. He certainly couldn't understand it.

Tonight as they were clearing the table, Cassie said to him, "Soon I'm going to have start paying you for helping me."

"No chance of that," he responded. "It's good for me to wind down this way."

"Tonight I especially appreciate the help."

"Do you have an art class?"

"No. A Chalk in the Park event for kids."

He'd seen the sign Cassie had hung at the front desk, but he hadn't known exactly what it meant. But anything she promoted had to be good for children and families.

"What's that all about?" he said, very curious about the event.

She stacked plates and added silverware on top of those. "The volunteers from the art center put containers of those big sticks of colored chalk at intervals on the sidewalks in the park. There's a volunteer at each station. The kids draw what they like on the pavement."

"While the volunteers make sure everything's kosher with no disturbing graffiti," Nash guessed.

"Exactly." She carried the dishes into the kitchen. "I knew I wouldn't get there until later tonight so I'm not taking one of the stations. But I'm going to help with general monitoring, and if any of the kids need any assistance, I'll be there."

"That sounds like something I could use right now. A night in the park with kids and colored chalk."

"You're not having any luck with your research?" She sorted the silverware and placed it in the dishwasher.

"That depends on what you mean by luck. Maybe I'm finding out *too* much."

"Anything specific?" Cassie asked.

He joined her in the kitchen. "You want to get going. You don't need to talk about this now."

"We don't need to talk about it at all if you don't want to."

Cassie broke eye contact and moved away from him to load the dishwasher. He didn't want her to think he was shutting her out. This time he wasn't. He followed her and placed his hand on her arm.

Turning toward him, she assured him, "I really don't mean to pry. But if you need a listening ear, I'm here.

I don't have to worry about being late because no one expects me at a specific time."

Nash took a towel from the counter and folded it in half. "I wanted to see how some of the Fortunes live. Not all of them are rich, and don't want to be from what I read. And I really had no intention of doing this." He stopped.

"Something to do with your biological father?"

"Yes. I went to his estate and parked down the street from the gate. And it *is* an estate, not just a property."

"I don't understand the difference."

"It's surrounded by a stone wall and has an electronic iron gate and a long winding driveway. According to aerial shots I've seen online, it actually looks like a Mediterranean castle."

"Stone walls and iron gates mean he wants to keep people out...or his wife does."

Cassie's suspicions were very much like his own. "I guess it makes sense if he's rich. He can have any kind of house he wants...any type of security he thinks he needs."

"I'm not sure anyone needs a house like that," Cassie decided.

"My investigative training taught me a lot about fishing around the internet. I found other aerial shots that showed multiple wings, a pool and a whole lot of trees that hid pretty much everything else."

Cassie admitted, "I've read several articles written about Gerald Robinson."

"There have been many articles written about him. In one, there's a photograph of him in his library, where there are rows and rows of books, and even a rolling ladder."

After studying him carefully, she asked, "Do you resent it all?"

"You mean the butler and the Persian rugs? Those were mentioned in one of the articles, too. I don't know if *resent* is the right word. I think he's a despicable man who doesn't deserve any of it. And if I'm right about his wife, she certainly doesn't deserve it, either. But I imagine she's done everything in her power to keep it."

"You said you saw a photograph of him. Do you see yourself in him?" Cassie asked softly as if the question might irk him.

"I saw some resemblance. Fortunately, I take after my mother."

Taking off her apron, she perceptively suggested, "With a house like that, it sounds as if he might be afraid of the outside world."

"You mean paparazzi finding out all of his business? Maybe how many more illegitimate children he has?"

"Possibly that," Cassie confirmed. "But maybe it's his way of having a quieter life inside. You can read all the articles in the world about him, Nash, but that doesn't mean you're going to know him from them."

She was so right about that. "Thank you," he said.

"For what?"

"For letting me vent a little."

"I think about ninety percent of that venting is still inside you. But you're welcome if it helped."

"I think what would help more is the kids and the chalk in the park...and you."

She looked flustered. "Me?"

"You're a breath of fresh air in my life right now, Cassie. I appreciate that more than you know."

She looked a bit embarrassed, as if compliments

were foreign to her. He couldn't imagine why. She was a beautiful woman.

"I have to go get dressed," she said. "Jeans and a T-shirt will be a better outfit for kneeling on the pavement and getting covered with chalk. I'll meet you down here in ten minutes?"

"Ten minutes is good. I'll be waiting."

A half hour later Nash had parked his SUV in a public lot and he and Cassie walked to the park. It was a beautiful night.

"Are there lights in the park if this goes on for a while?"

"Oh, yes. There's a gazebo in the middle and that's all lit up. There are gas lights down each of the sidewalks leading to the gazebo."

"Do parents stick around?"

"Some do and some don't. It depends on how old the kids are, and how much freedom they have on their own."

"If I were a parent, I'd want to be there. Even with volunteers, I wouldn't want to leave my kids in anybody else's hands." When he glanced at Cassie, he saw that she was looking at him. "What?"

"I believe you've seen a side of life that I haven't."

"That's true. I've seen kids getting hooked on drugs too soon. I've seen men approach kids who shouldn't be anywhere near them. I've broken up domestic fights because adults can't act like adults. So I don't see the world as a safe place."

Cassie was frowning now and he didn't have a chance to ask her about that. As they entered the park, a boy about eight years old came running toward her.

"Cassie, Cassie. Come see my drawing. Micah says it's terrific."

"Micah Hanson is one of the volunteers," Cassie explained. "Okay, Rodney. Let's go find him."

Nash followed her but he examined the chalk drawings on the sidewalk along the way. Some of them were quite good. Many of them were funny and he had to smile.

At least he smiled until they reached the volunteer who was packing more chalk into a container to place on the sidewalk. The man, who looked to be in his late twenties or early thirties, was dressed in shorts, sneakers and a T-shirt. He had black hair and snapping brown eyes that now focused on Cassie.

"Cassie, hey! It's good to see you."

She went right over to him as if they were close friends. "Hey, Micah. How's it going tonight? Is everybody behaving?"

"Except the volunteers," he said with a roll of his eyes. "One of the dads came with liquor on his breath and I told him to go back home. His wife was with him and she stayed instead with their little boy."

"Good job," Cassie said.

Nash didn't like the looks Micah was giving Cassie. They were definitely interested looks, and he wondered how much the two of them worked together.

Rodney was pointing to his chalk drawing behind Micah. "Come look, Cassie."

"Give me one minute," she told the little boy. "Micah, this is Nash Tremont. He's staying at the B&B. He thought he'd enjoy this adventure, too."

Nash extended his hand and Micah took it. But it definitely wasn't going to be the beginning of a beautiful friendship. He suddenly wanted to put his arm around Cassie and tell Micah, *She's mine.* But that thought didn't even belong in his head. They weren't at that stage yet.

Yet?

What was he thinking? He may care for Cassie, but it could never work. His life was in Mississippi and hers was here.

"Excuse me, guys," she said. "Rodney needs me."

Leaving the two men alone, she knelt on the ground beside Rodney without giving a second thought to what she was wearing. In no time at all, two more children had joined her, a little boy and a little girl. Cassie was asking them questions and coaxing them to draw. They did…in as many colors as there were sticks of chalk in the bucket.

Micah said to Nash, "She's good with the kids. They love her."

"What's not to love?" Nash asked before he thought better of it.

Micah narrowed his eyes. "How long are you staying at the B&B?"

"Awhile."

"Are you from around here?" Micah asked.

Nash suspected the man was feeling out his competition. Nash wished he could say he *was* Micah's competition. "No. I'm from Biloxi."

"A long way from home," Micah commented, probably just to make conversation.

"Business," Nash said as if that explained it all.

"I see."

Nash thought Micah looked relieved.

Claiming his home turf, Micah commented, "I'd better help Cassie. I think she needs reinforcements. She'll soon have a whole herd of kids around her."

Nash supposed that was true and with Micah helping her—

She didn't need a clash between male egos or Nash watching her closely to see if her interactions with Micah were familiar or friendly.

Seeing a bench nearby, he crossed to it and sat. He had photos of documents on his phone. He could scroll through them for a while, at least.

He purposely did not pay attention to Cassie, Micah and the children.

It wasn't long before he heard laughter. In spite of himself, he looked toward the kids and Cassie. Apparently, each child was explaining what they had drawn. They were sitting in a circle with Micah and Cassie, and Micah's hand was on Cassie's shoulder.

Friendly or familiar?

Nash stayed where he was.

Darkness had almost descended when the kids finally dispersed as their parents came to fetch them. By the light of one of the lanterns along the path, Nash noticed Micah give Cassie a hand up. Then they hugged. From what he could tell, they didn't kiss. He supposed that was good news.

Minutes later Cassie sat beside Nash on the bench. She didn't speak for a few heartbeats. Finally, she asked, "Why didn't you come over and join in?"

"I thought three adults might be a crowd," he said tersely.

Putting her hand on the back of the bench, she turned toward him and studied him for a long moment. "Are you talking about me and Micah?"

Nash shrugged as if it didn't matter to him. Yet his words belied the shrug. "You two looked like something's going on."

"Yes, something's going on," she answered with some heat. Nash's heart seemed to drop to his knees, but then she continued. "We work at the community center together, and we're friends."

"The two of you seemed a little chummy for just friends."

That comment had Cassie rising to her feet. "Are you ready to go? I have to make sure all my guests are tucked in for the night."

"Including me?" he asked, in what was supposed to be a teasing voice.

"Including you." Her voice *wasn't* teasing in return.

Their drive back to the bed-and-breakfast was quiet. Letting out a resigned sigh, he gripped the steering wheel tighter. He knew Cassie was annoyed with him so there just didn't seem to be any point pushing conversation. However, he wasn't the type to let things go, or to just let them simmer. Once they were inside and he saw no one else was around, he stopped at the counter in the kitchen and so did she.

"I'm going to get a glass of iced tea," he said. "Can I pour you one?"

When she looked about to refuse, he pulled two glasses from a tray on the counter and went to the refrigerator for the tea. He poured two glasses before she could say no. Then he set one in front of her.

"Are you sure you and Micah are only friends?" he asked. "When I was talking to him, something about him told me there was more."

"Maybe on *his* side," Cassie explained. "He asked

me out once but I said no. As I told you, my life is too busy to date."

He'd questioned many suspects in his career, and he easily saw through that excuse. There had to be some reason she didn't want to date, and soon he'd ferret it out.

Before she could turn away from him, or go to her room, he placed his hands on her shoulders. "I'm sorry I didn't join in with the spirit of fun tonight. But I can tell you why. I didn't like the idea that you and Micah might be involved."

"You were jealous?" The surprise in her voice almost coaxed him to smile.

He took a deep breath. "I'm not going that far." When he noticed her lips turned up a little, he asked, "Do you like the idea of me being jealous?"

Her smile broadened a bit. "I'm not sure. I can tell you one thing. I've never kissed Micah."

As he brought her closer to him, she didn't pull away. "That's good to know. Because I'd like to be the only one who's kissing you, at least for now."

As soon as his lips touched hers, he knew he'd felt more than jealousy tonight. They generated heat whenever they were together, and it was a heat that wasn't strictly physical. That was what puzzled him most of all. He'd sworn he'd never get emotionally close to a woman again, but it had happened faster than he'd ever realized it could. He was still fighting the idea of caring too much. When he had Cassie in his arms, he didn't think at all.

As he came up for air, he rubbed his jaw against her cheek. He knew there was a bit of stubble from his five-o'clock shadow, and he'd wondered how she'd like the sensation. She seemed to like it because she brought her hand to his cheek and rubbed it along his chin.

"Your stubble is sexy," she whispered.

All he wanted to do was sweep her up into his arms and make love to her anywhere they could find a place to land. Yet he didn't want to push what was happening between them for lots of reasons. A short-term affair sounded great in theory. But in the long run, he didn't think Cassie was that kind of woman. And for him—

He hadn't had a serious relationship for so long he wasn't sure he knew how.

Sliding his hands into her hair, he leaned back. "I think the two of us are becoming more than friends. I also believe we should both think about that before we act on it." He lowered his arms. "And that's why I'm going to go up to my room."

She looked flustered but she quickly motioned to the glasses on the counter. "You didn't drink your tea."

He picked up his glass. "I'll take it with me, along with the memory of that kiss."

As he walked toward the stairs, he could feel her gaze on his back burning right through his shirt. He had to ignore the heat until he could think about the whole thing rationally.

But he had the feeling that *rational* and *Cassie* didn't belong in the same sentence.

Storms rolled through Austin after midnight. Cassie had just fallen asleep. It had taken her a while because she'd been thinking about Nash. Maybe it was the thunder that had awakened her. As soon as she opened her eyes, she saw the bright flash of lightning at the windows. A loud crack made it sound as if lightning had hit something close by.

Usually she checked the weather before she went to bed each night in order to give a forecast to her guests by morning. But tonight, she'd been distracted. She hadn't thought about the weather forecast.

The wind howled against the house as rain pelted the window. She hoped the electricity didn't go out. Each room was equipped with a battery-powered lantern tucked into the closet. That detail was listed on the page of conveniences that was in the binder by the telephone in each room. She also had flameless candles and lanterns downstairs in case guests wandered down there because they couldn't sleep. Still, she hoped the power would stay on.

Cassie was debating about making a cup of tea when the wind blew with a roaring gust. There was a streak of lightning and a second later a crack of thunder. Along with that, she heard a crash that sounded as if it came from the screened-in porch. She jumped out of bed and ran toward the porch. Switching on the overhead light, she covered her mouth with her hand.

A large tree limb had crashed into one of the screens and torn it. The wind blew her coral cotton nightgown against her legs. But she was almost unmindful of it as she tried to assess the damage. Not only had the screen been torn, but the giant limb had damaged the frame.

Suddenly Nash was standing there beside her, chest bare, hair tousled, a sleepy expression on his face. "I was going to ask what that noise was, but I see I don't have to."

Cassie's hair was being tossed all about and rain was blowing in.

Nash took hold of Cassie's arm and tugged her out of the porch. Then he slid shut the sliding glass door. "You're getting wet," he told her.

For the first time, she realized her wet nightgown clung to her. She should be embarrassed but she wasn't. She was too worried about another expense. "I have to figure out how to fix the porch on my own. I really can't afford a repair bill."

Nash took her hand and turned her to face him. "Cassie, it's not that bad. It's an easy fix."

"I suppose I can find a video on YouTube to tell me how. I'm just not sure what to do about the frame."

"I can fix it for you."

Now Cassie looked at Nash, really looked at him. His beard stubble, darker than it had been last night, was so sexy. Then there were his muscled broad shoulders, his strong arms, the brown chest hair that sprinkled his chest.

She swallowed hard. "I can't let you do that."

"Of course you can. I worked construction a couple of summers. I know how to do it. I promise. If you feel you have to help, you can paint the frame after I put it together. After a trip to the hardware store, a couple of hours ought to do it."

"I can't let you spend your time on this," she insisted.

They were standing practically nose to nose and she could feel his body heat. He could probably feel hers, too. Her nightgown wasn't much of a covering anymore as it clung to her breasts, to her waist, to her hips and legs. But to her amazement, Nash kept his gaze on her face.

"You have to learn how to accept help," he scolded.

"I know how to accept help," she said almost indignantly. "I just don't want to be beholden to anybody."

He cocked his head as if he was wondering why, and she was afraid he might ask the question. She knew better than to be indebted to anybody. She didn't want to owe them because she couldn't reciprocate.

She once had friends who she thought cared. She went to their houses and had supper with their families. Real families. They would watch movies and eat popcorn together. The problem was she'd never invited them to her house, or rather her mother's apartment. The main reason—her mother was usually drunk by the end of the day.

Her mother's disease had been a well-kept secret, at least from Cassie's friends. If their parents knew about it, they never mentioned it. Her mother was good about her drinking, if anything could be good about it. She took in sewing. She tried to do that or errands in the morning so she could bring in a little bit of money and keep the grocery clerk from seeing her swaying. The post office clerk wouldn't hear slurred words. But by early evening she was slurring, weaving and even blacking out. Cassie hadn't known whom to turn to for help. She'd thought about telling one of her teachers but what if that had gotten her mother into trouble? What if they had taken Cassie from her and put her in some strange house somewhere? At least her mother cared about her.

But because Cassie hadn't gotten her help, the inevitable had happened. The most horrific thing had happened. Her mother had run a red light, smashed into another driver and killed him. It was Cassie's fault she was in jail for vehicular homicide.

Nash gently swiped dampness from her cheek.

"Where did you go?" he asked. "Those looked like some heavy thoughts going through your head."

Her throat was tight and her chest felt so heavy. She couldn't return a light comment or shrug off the question. Not about this. Not right now. She remembered how after the accident all of her friends had ignored her, how she hadn't received any more invitations to their homes. Thank goodness she'd been twenty-one so nobody could place her anywhere she didn't want to be.

Her mind quickly swept over their conversation, and the present became more important than the past. Nash standing in front of her practically naked—well at least half of him was—was more important than any relationship she'd ever had with a man. She had to tell him something that was true.

"When I went to college, I had three part-time jobs. I'd received a scholarship but I still had to pay living expenses. There wasn't anybody to help me. I'm used to making my own way. I found out when people gave me something, they expected something back. Sometimes I couldn't give it."

"Are you talking about men?"

"Not just men. I learned to pay my own way, keep my own counsel and be my own person. So here's the deal. If you repair the porch, I'll comp you three nights."

"That sounds more than fair," he agreed. "We can go to a hardware store tomorrow and get supplies."

"There's an independent hardware store that I use. He always gives me good prices. He's fair, and I'd like to see his business keep on thriving."

"Independent stores are having a hard time of it these days."

She nodded. "They are."

Cassie could still hear the sound of rain beating against the house, though the lightning and thunder had died away. She was about to escape to her room when Nash said, "But I'm not thinking about small businesses right now. Are you?"

Standing here like this, so close to him, all she could think about was touching him.

"What are you thinking?" he asked her.

"That you look mighty good without a shirt."

The corners of his lips turned up. But in his eyes, she saw a smoldering passion that seemed to be all for her.

"And you look mighty good in that color," he said with a straight face.

Her voice was husky when she responded, "I'm sure your eyes are just on the color."

"I'm trying hard," Nash joked.

As Cassie had remembered past years with her mom, tension had strung her body. But now that tension faded away. Tonight, she was here with Nash. Maybe, just maybe, she shouldn't think so hard about what was right and what was wrong, what was proper and what wasn't. Nash leaned in and kissed her forehead. When he backed away, she found her hands going to his chest almost of their own accord.

Nash enclosed her hands in his. "Not a good idea if we're not going to spend the night together."

"But I…" Cassie began.

He cut in, "You're still not sure. If we sleep together, I want you to be very sure. I'm not one of those men who will repair your porch and expect something in return. Everything about us has to be no strings, Cassie."

"No strings," she repeated, knowing in some ways that was how she'd lived her life.

Releasing her hands, he ran his thumb over her lips. "One kiss would lead to another and another and another. When that happens, I want us both to be on the same page."

Slightly embarrassed, overwhelmed by the desire to have Nash kiss her, she said, "Good night, Nash." Then she turned and walked to her bedroom. She was pretty sure as she did, he wasn't just noticing the color of her nightgown.

## Chapter Nine

When Cassie awakened the next morning, she remembered changing her nightgown from last night. It had been damp and Nash had...

She was up at daybreak for a very good reason. She was sure the storm had left debris on the property and she needed to clean it up before the guests awakened. Breakfast would be an easy one this morning—omelets—so she could spend the next hour doing what she had to do.

After she showered and dressed, she went to the porch to examine it in the daylight. The sun was just streaking over the horizon, turning the sky fuchsia, orange and gold. It was in her eyes until she opened the sliding glass door and stepped onto the porch. There, to her surprise, Nash was already working. He had lugged the tree limb into the yard. He'd also stacked loose limbs and slight branches in a pile. Her backyard was cleaned up.

"I'll have to comp you another night," she said.

"Don't you dare." He shook his finger at her. "I needed physical labor since I can't work out like I usually do."

"At a gym?" she asked.

"I just do weights at my place. It's faster and easier. In my line of work, I don't punch a clock. I might be at my office overnight. That's a cop's life."

She supposed it was. "I bet your mother worries about you constantly."

"Not so much since I moved to Mississippi and have been investigating white-collar crimes. She tells me she sleeps much better at night." He shrugged. "Do you have a saw?" he asked.

"I do." She pointed to the rear of the yard. "See that shed? It has a padlock. The combination is eight-two-three, right, left, right."

"By the time I finish cutting up these limbs, it should be time for breakfast."

"Omelets this morning. What's your passion?" As soon as she said it, she knew she shouldn't have.

"I'll tell you about my passion another time when we're alone. As for omelets, I like peppers, onions and hot sauce."

"Coming right up," she said with a laugh. "If you can eat that first thing in the morning, you can eat anything anytime."

He wiggled his brows at her. "Including chocolate-covered strawberries at sunset."

Was he hinting that that was something they could do together? She could imagine the chocolate, the sweetness of the strawberries, feeding them to each other. Then she could imagine kissing Nash.

To avoid those thoughts, she said, "The hardware store opens at nine. Do you want to go this morning?"

"Meet you at nine if all your guests have finished with breakfast by then."

Her guests *had* finished by nine and she'd cleaned up. Including Nash, she had four guests right now—a couple and a young woman from Tennessee who was visiting relatives. She was hoping that by summer, reservations would pick up and all of her rooms would be filled.

Cassie was getting used to riding with Nash now in his SUV. She climbed in and fastened her seat belt. After he was inside, too, and had started the engine, she pointed to the GPS. "Does that really get you where you want to go?"

"Most of the time," he said with a smile. "Why? Doesn't your car have one?"

"No, I have an older car. People I run into and the parents of the kids I teach tell me I should have one. But I don't travel that much so it seems like an expense I don't need."

"That depends on how good you are at reading paper maps or downloading directions from the internet."

"I suppose if I ever take a long trip I'd think about it."

The hardware store was less than a mile away and they were there and parked in no time. Cassie led Nash inside. She waved to Phil Lebeau, who was the owner. Phil was stocking shelves with faucets and fixtures, so she didn't bother him.

Nash led her to the back of the store, where he found

the wood he needed for the frame. Then he pulled out a roll of screening.

"I can carry that," she said.

"Why don't you take the wood strips. They're lighter."

She frowned at him. "I'm stronger than I look."

He laughed. "Next time I'll let you carry whatever's heaviest."

Next time. She liked the idea of having a next time with Nash, but she knew she shouldn't get too attached to the thought.

"Do you have a good hammer?" he asked her.

"I do, and a set of screwdrivers and wrenches. I'm well prepared."

He dipped his Stetson to her. "I should have known."

After they had pieces of wood cut and brought everything up to the cash register, Phil came over to check them out.

After Cassie made introductions, Phil asked, "So you're not helping her paint more rooms odd colors of paint?"

"What do you mean *odd*?" Cassie asked with a smile.

"Lime green and that coral color aren't my cup of tea," Phil grumbled.

"Have you ever seen the house?" Nash asked.

Phil shook his head. "Never have."

"I don't know how, but it all works. Her colors, furnishings and that mural all just tie in well together."

"I suppose so or she wouldn't have any repeat business." Phil narrowed his eyes at Cassie. "You've never brought a beau along with you before." He gave her a wink.

"He's just a guest at the bed-and-breakfast," she explained once more.

"A guest is going to help you make repairs?"

In a confidential tone Nash said to Phil, "She's comping me a couple of nights."

"Oh, I see," Phil said with a knowing smile, and Cassie knew she turned a bright shade of pink.

Nash hooked his arm around her shoulders. "Cassie tells me she's good with a hammer. I might let her help me."

Phil laughed and bagged the smaller items they'd bought. "That house needed mostly cosmetic changes, and Cassie did them all herself. I've got to give her credit for that, no matter what color paint she used."

After they checked out and were in the car once more, Nash turned to Cassie. "Why haven't you ever taken a beau into the hardware store?"

"I didn't do that this time," she retorted.

"I think since we've kissed, I could be considered your beau. And we *did* have lunch together. That could have been considered a date."

"What did *you* consider it?" she asked softly.

"I consider our kisses very hot, and indicative of further exploration."

Cassie rolled her eyes. "That didn't answer my question."

"And you didn't answer mine."

"I did answer you before. I told you I'm too busy to even think about a relationship."

She could see Nash wasn't buying that, and she didn't want to lie. "All right," she said. "I had a relationship a few years ago, but it ended badly. I haven't wanted to take a chance since then."

"Did you break it off or did he?"

She was about to tell him that was a very personal question when she remembered what he'd told her about his family. "He broke it off," she said, still feeling humiliated by the idea and why it had happened. As soon as she'd told Cody her mother was in prison, he'd turned tail and run.

"He was a fool," Nash said.

Cassie appreciated the compliment but Nash didn't really know her. If he really knew her, he'd leave before his time at the B&B was up. She was sure of it.

Back at the B&B, Cassie helped Nash carry everything inside and out to the porch. Her guests were out and about, so noise wouldn't bother them.

Nash said, "I want to lay the boards out and mark them before I start. I had the pieces of wood cut according to the sizes I needed, but if for some reason we got it wrong, I want to know now."

Cassie could see Nash was as precise about this as he was with everything else. Cut-and-dried, black-and-white, practical and precise. He was a cop, after all.

Nash had been working about an hour and she'd been doing laundry, when the phone rang. Hurrying to the kitchen she picked up the cordless phone there. Caller ID said the call was from out of area. She often got calls like that for reservations.

"Hello," she said cheerfully. "This is the Bluebonnet Bed-and-Breakfast. May I help you?"

"I hope you can. My name is Marybeth Tremont. My son isn't answering his cell phone and he gave me this number in case I couldn't contact him on the cell."

Cassie introduced herself, then assured the woman.

"Nash is doing repair work for me, so he might have his phone turned off."

"Repair work? Did you have some of those storms that came up through Texas to Oklahoma last night?"

"We did. A large tree limb crashed through the screen on my porch."

"Oh my," Marybeth said. "We had a bit of hail but I didn't have any damage, thank goodness." She seemed to hesitate a moment before she asked, "So Nash is doing the repair work for you?"

"Your son is a man of many talents. But then, a police detective has to be, I suppose."

"So he told you about that, did he?"

"He did." Cassie wasn't going to go into exactly what Nash had told her because she wasn't sure how much his mother knew.

"His work comes before everything," Marybeth said with a sigh. "I certainly wish he could come home more. I miss him. I miss the days when he'd talk my ear off about sports and school and anything else that came into his head. He got quieter as he got older."

"Maybe that had something to do with his work, too," Cassie suggested.

"You're probably right." The woman hesitated a moment, then said, "I don't want to take up too much of your time. Would you give Nash the message to call me?"

For some reason Cassie had the feeling that Nash's mother was really missing him right now. "No need for that. I'll get him. Just hang on."

Cassie took the cordless phone out to the porch, where Nash was unrolling the screen. "It's your mom."

With an arched brow, Nash took the phone. Cassie

left him alone on the porch so he'd have some privacy. She was in the kitchen about ten minutes later when he brought the phone back inside.

"I did have my cell turned off," he said. "I didn't want an interruption while I was hammering and measuring."

Cassie wasn't sure how to broach the subject she wanted to discuss, so she started with an easy comment. "Your mother sounds very nice."

"Oh, she is. I've always told her she should have been a Southern belle. She always tries to be so tactful. Midwesterners are blunter."

Cassie laughed. "I think that has more to do with personality than the part of the country where you were born."

"Maybe so. Did she talk your ear off?"

"No, of course not. But I do think she misses you. Maybe you could take time to go home and visit her."

He was already shaking his head. "You don't understand my life. Work comes first."

Before Cassie could stifle the words, she said, "Work will always be there, but you won't have your mother forever."

Nash didn't respond to that, but his lips tightened and his jaw became a little firmer. "I just have to fit the screen and put the panel in place. I should be done in fifteen or twenty minutes."

"You can just leave the tools and remnants on the porch. I'll clean up after you're finished."

"I finish what I start," Nash said, then headed for the porch.

Cassie considered their conversation as she went

into the laundry room. She was folding sheets when Nash came by and stood in the doorway.

He asked, "Need help with that?"

She just gave a little shrug. He must have taken that for assent because he took hold of the two ends of the queen-size sheet and brought it up to meet hers. Their hands brushed. Cassie's gaze went to his, then she quickly looked away, folding the sheet again and again. She laid it in the wash basket.

"I thought about what you said," Nash told her, "and you're right. I should get home to visit Mom more."

He had her attention now.

"But there's a reason I left Oklahoma and there's a reason why I don't go back and visit more."

"And that is?" she prompted. She couldn't expect him to answer her, but she thought she'd try anyway. He took a few steps toward her.

"I grew up in a small town where everybody knows everybody."

"So did I," she admitted.

"So you understand how everyone knows everybody's business. If something happens in a family, it's like an announcement goes out to the whole town. If it's not in the small newspaper, it's on people's lips when they meet at the coffee shop or see each other at the family restaurant."

She wished she could take Nash's arm or his hand or give him a hug because he looked as if this was very hard for him to say.

He continued with, "People heard my mom had had an affair with a married man, an outsider. Those who knew her realized she did it for love. But others who didn't know her as well figured she was out to get something that she couldn't get in other ways."

"You mean they thought she was looking for a sugar daddy?"

"Yes. Exactly. Which *wasn't* the case. So I heard rumors when I was growing up. My mom told me the truth when I was six or seven, and she told it in stages. I probably became a cop because there was some authority in that, a *don't-you-mess-with-me* message."

*Because everyone is at least a little afraid of law enforcement?* Cassie wondered. She knew how afraid of law enforcement she'd been when they'd come to collect her mother.

"I had a girlfriend on and off during high school," Nash went on. "She didn't seem to care what anybody else thought of me. I liked that about her."

"I imagine she was pretty, too."

Nash sighed and answered, "Yes, she was. After high school, we kind of went our separate ways. I went to the police academy and she went off to college. She was earning a business degree so she could be her dad's office manager. He ran a carpet and tile home improvement store."

"And because it was a small town, you knew when she returned."

"I did. But we didn't reconnect again until a couple of years later. Her father was mugged on the way to the bank to make a deposit. I was sent to the scene."

"So you reconnected."

He nodded, but his lips tightened. A moment later he admitted, "We did. I went to work finding the kid who did it, and together we helped her dad overcome the effects of the mugging. I celebrated with her and her family the night the perp was caught. Right after that, she and I started dating again. When I turned twenty-six, we'd been dating for two years, and I had made assumptions during those two years. I expected we'd get engaged, be married and have a family. Something about turning twenty-six just clicked with me. I wanted something solid, not like what my mother had had. I had a job, though the hours could be crazy. I also had money in the bank from overtime and from security work."

"You were ready," Cassie acknowledged, thinking Nash must have always been mature for his age.

"I was ready and I thought she was, too. I bought a ring. When I gave it to her, I didn't see the happiness on her face that I expected to see."

From the lines etching deeper around Nash's eyes and mouth, Cassie could see the emotional toll his story was taking on him. But this time she didn't say anything, she just waited.

"The bottom line was that Sara didn't want to marry a cop. She didn't want to worry every time I left for a shift. She didn't want to settle down with me and not have a real life because of my crazy hours. It turns out during those hours, she was dating someone else in nearby Norman. He was a college professor."

"Oh, Nash, I'm so sorry."

He shook his head and waved his hand as if he didn't want her sympathy or pity. "I was a fool. I was blind. I hadn't read any of the signs. Because of that, I knew I wasn't husband material and realized I had to up my professional game. I decided to change my life. I moved to Mississippi and became an investigator for white-collar crimes."

"And you don't go back to Oklahoma because the memories are just too painful."

"And I don't want to go backward. I want to move forward."

"But aren't you going backward investigating your biological dad and his wife?"

"I don't see it that way."

"Then how do you see it?"

"I see it as trying to right a wrong. If Charlotte did what I think she did, she deserves jail time."

"What if your biological father was involved?"

"Then he does, too."

Cassie was dubious and shook her head. "I still think you'll regret it."

"I'll find out, won't I?"

Somehow she and Nash had stepped closer to each other. She caught the scent of his aftershave, sweat, the essence of everything male.

Nash gazed steadily at Cassie. "This conversation got way too serious," he decided. "I think we both need fun in our lives."

"And how do you suppose we find that fun?"

"I've been searching sites in Austin and I found what looks to be a great zoo. I think we should go."

That wasn't at all what Cassie had suspected he'd suggest, but maybe it was a good idea. "Tomorrow?" she asked.

"You're on."

When Cassie and Nash emerged from the zoo office and headed for the timber-lined gravel path, she told him, "This zoo is one of Austin's best-kept secrets. Wait until you see the tigers' play area."

"Play area?"

"Yep. You know how household cats have those condos and cat trees that go to the ceiling?"

"I'm not real familiar with the concept," Nash said with a grin.

"Maybe I could explain it better if I told you that it's like a kid's jungle gym. The tiger can go from one level to the other and play or sun himself. In fact, do you mind if we head toward the wolves, and bears, and tigers and lions?"

"You sound excited." He took her hand in his as they walked along the path.

"Oh, look! Look at the peacock." She pointed to the bird that walked not ten feet from them.

"They're not in cages," Nash said as if they should be.

"Aren't they beautiful?"

When he didn't answer, she turned to him and saw he was looking at her. His eyes dipped down, and she felt as if he was taking in every inch of her, from her sneakers to her lime green shorts, yellow blouse and colorful, beaded necklace.

"*You're* beautiful," he said, capturing her gaze again.

She might have given a little gasp, she wasn't sure.

"Why do you look so surprised?" he asked. "You *are* beautiful. Don't you know that?"

"I don't think of myself like that. I'm just like any other woman trying to make my way, make a living, follow my dreams."

"Well, it becomes you." He squeezed her hand a little tighter. This feeling she had whenever she was with Nash always took her by surprise. It was a giddiness that seemed to infuse her whole body.

They walked for a long while without speaking, stopping often, enjoying the antics of all the animals. Soon they were at the exhibit of hybrid wolves. The sign read *FRISKY—Husky Wolf Mix.* "One thing I like best about this zoo is that they rescue animals who've been neglected. Somebody probably found this guy as a cub. But as he grew they realized he's more wolf than husky. I'm glad he's found a home." Maybe she liked this zoo so much because she felt a kinship with the animals who'd been rescued. The difference was that she'd rescued herself.

"I like watching the animal population," Nash said as he observed the wolf. "It can give an insight into human behavior. Sometimes I think the animals have it right and the humans don't. In fact, sometimes, I *prefer* the animal population. My buddy Dave's dog is so good with his kids, and he's loyal."

"What kind of dog is he?"

"A yellow Lab. When I'm around him, I can forget about what I've seen on the job. I've seen things on the streets I never want to see again."

This time Cassie squeezed *his* hand. He let go and curled his arm around her waist. As they continued walking, Cassie felt closer to him than she'd ever felt to any human being. How was that even possible, she wondered, given that she hadn't known him that long.

*How close would you be if you told him the truth about your life?*

Unable to ignore that voice in her head, she thought about her mother in prison. Her mom had tried detoxing several times over the years, but she'd never been successful. She'd needed something to live for other than a drink to get through the next few hours. Cassie had never been able to help her. She hoped her mother had gotten help now.

Deciding to dip her toe into dangerous waters, Cassie suggested, "Maybe criminals are like these animals. They need to be rescued and rehabilitated."

Nash shot a quick glance at her. "The difference between animals and humans is that humans have intelligence. That's why if someone commits a crime, they need to suffer the consequences."

"But if we could rehabilitate instead of incarcerate—"

"There are cages here, Cassie, for a reason. The same reason there are jails for people. The truth is, states and counties don't have enough money, resources or volunteers to even think about rehabilitation instead of incarceration. Jail isn't a solution but at least it gets criminals off the streets."

Cassie pulled away from Nash, using the obvious excuse of wanting to get closer to the next enclosure. She had no doubt now that Nash would back away from her completely if he knew about her mother. She'd been entertaining a dream that she should have known was as elusive as smoke.

Swallowing the bitter disappointment, she walked from exhibit to exhibit, forcing herself to enjoy the day. She genuinely loved seeing the animals and the wonder on children's faces as they observed the creatures.

"Look at that little boy," she said, pointing to a child who walked up to the tiger enclosure beside them. "No matter how many tigers he sees in a book, it can never prepare him for the reality of the real thing." She pointed to a white Bengal tiger. "They're my favorite," she said. "They're endangered. It's such a shame."

"You care about everything, don't you?" Nash asked, studying her.

"I don't know what you mean."

"Most people go through life letting the majority of what they see and hear slide by them almost as if it didn't exist. But you're not like that, not about humans or animals. You're in the present most of the time and it's such a good thing."

Cassie had always had to live in the present because she'd never known what to expect next. She could come home one day to an empty apartment. She could come home the next with her mother drunk as a skunk. And then there was the odd night when her mom would be sober. Then she'd talk to Cassie like any mother would, asking if she wanted to invite friends over. That wasn't something Cassie could ever do because her mother was too volatile, too unpredictable, too enamored with a bottle of whiskey instead of her daughter. Maybe Cassie cared so much about everything because her mother had seemed to care about nothing. She wished she could say that to Nash, but of course, she couldn't.

"I guess I live in the present so I don't worry so much about the future, and I don't think about the past."

"It seems like I'm always thinking about the past or the future," Nash admitted. "Even when I'm chasing down a witness, I think about what his testimony will mean in the future. And as far as the past goes, I suppose I never realized how it affected me until you said I should see my mom more."

"I didn't mean to criticize."

"No, you were thinking about her. In a way, I was punishing my mom because of my memories of Sara. How stupid is that?"

Turning toward him, Cassie said fervently, "You're anything but stupid. Life is like this path we're walking on with twists and turns that we never expect. We make our way the best we can and hopefully we learn as we go. I guess that's the secret for being successful in life, learning as you go."

Cassie pointed to a magnificent male lion sleeping in the sun in the adjacent exhibit. At least she thought he was sleeping until he became aware of them, opened his eyes and yawned, exposing all of his huge sharp teeth. Then he stood, showing off the majestic creature he was.

"Now that guy has a confident attitude," Nash joked. "And probably a roar to match."

When Cassie laughed, Nash encircled her with his arm again. This time she didn't pull away. This time she was just going to enjoy the moment because that might be all she'd ever have with Nash.

## Chapter Ten

In the afternoon the following day, Nash established photo files with Cassie's paintings. As he thought about their trip to the zoo and everything they'd talked about, he decided he wanted to do something for her. They'd had fun together, enjoying all the animals. There were the animals you just looked at, but then there were some you could feed, like the goats and the llamas. They'd laughed a lot as they'd done that.

Beside his laptop on the desk in his room, he'd laid out the business cards he'd picked up at the arts festival. He'd pocketed about ten of them. He remembered what Cassie had said—that her paintings weren't good enough. That was a bunch of hogwash. He didn't know who the judges had been who had decided that, but he imagined everybody had different opinions. The same would be true for the gallery owners. Maybe, just maybe, she could score with one of them.

The first thing he did was compose a letter. He did it in his own name, acting as her agent. Then he attached the file. He made sure he wrote each letter individually so it had a personal touch. When he was finished, he sat back and felt as if he'd accomplished something.

As opposed to all his research on the Fortunes in the last three weeks?

He had to admit, all that work hadn't gotten him far. Maybe he would have to consider how he could speak to a Fortune incognito. But that would happen only as a last resort.

He decided to go downstairs for cookies and coffee. As he did, he heard the ringtone on Cassie's cell phone. He was familiar with the ding-dong ring now.

He heard her answer. As he went to the coffee urn and filled a mug, he recognized the strain in her voice. "Yes, that's right. His mother added me as a contact, and yes, I can pick him up."

Nash grabbed a napkin and stacked three oatmeal cookies on it. Anything Cassie baked was good and he had no doubt these would be, too. He listened to her phone conversation again.

"He was in a fight? That's not like Danny at all." She checked her watch. "I can be there in about twenty minutes." Again she listened for a few beats. "Yes, I'll stop at the desk and show my ID. He'll be in your office? I'll be there as soon as I can."

After she ended the call, she looked over at Nash. "Danny's mom asked me if she could add me as an emergency contact at Danny's school. Apparently, she has meetings when she has to turn her phone off, and

Danny's dad doesn't answer his cell phone when he's in court. When the school couldn't reach either of them, they called me. Danny got into a fight at school. They, of course, want to conference with his parents but they think it's best for Danny to leave the premises for now."

"You say this isn't like him?"

"Absolutely not. He's not the least bit aggressive and not even assertive enough. His mother brought him to me for lessons, hoping that his art could bring him out of his shell."

"Sometimes the quiet ones are keeping the most anger hidden."

"Maybe so, but I've got to get going."

"Is there anything I can do to help?"

"If any of the guests come back, just have them sign in that they're back. And could you answer the land-line if it rings? I don't want to miss a chance at a reservation."

"I can do that. I know you're in a hurry, but drive carefully."

She gazed at him with soft, brown eyes that seemed to wake up every part of him that had been frozen, or maybe asleep. That included his heart and soul.

"Thank you," she said as she took her purse from a drawer in the kitchen, dropped her phone into it and hurried out the door.

About an hour later, Cassie entered the bed-and-breakfast with Danny. Beside her, the boy was sullen, his eyes cast downward to the floor.

"Danny, go over there to the sitting area and get yourself some cookies. I'll bring a glass of milk over. I think we should talk, don't you?"

The boy shrugged his shoulders and went to the table where the jar of cookies stood.

Nash was in the kitchen when Cassie went for the milk. She kept her voice low when she said, "He wouldn't talk to me about it. He kept silent the whole ride back. The nurse put that bandage above his eye. The principal said it was a surface scratch."

"Do you think we should just leave him to himself until his mom or dad gets here?"

"I called his mother and left a voice message that he was here. I texted her, too."

"Do you know what happened?"

"Not really. I'd like Danny to tell me himself if he will."

"Do you want me to sit in?"

"I don't think it will hurt. If I can't get him to talk, maybe you can."

Cassie carried Danny's glass of milk to him. He'd picked up two cookies but they were sitting on the occasional table beside him. Cassie sat beside Nash on the sofa across from Danny, who had seated himself in an armchair. "I left a message for your mom that you're here. I didn't want her to worry."

"She worries a lot," Danny mumbled.

"I'll bet she doesn't usually worry about you when you're in school."

Then he gave another shrug.

"Do you want to tell me what happened?" Cassie asked.

"No," Danny said solemnly.

Nash sat forward a bit. "Danny, you know that explanation's not going to work with your mom. You could practice on us."

Danny looked at them and blurted, "I'm never painting again."

Cassie was shocked by that idea. "What do you mean you're not going to paint again? You have talent, Danny. I'd like to see you paint more, not less."

Nash had an understanding expression on his face. "Do you have a favorite sport?" he asked Danny.

"I like to watch basketball."

"I like to watch baseball. I dreamed about being a major leaguer someday."

"You were that good?" Danny asked.

Nash laughed. "Not at the beginning. I was never a major leaguer, not even close. But I did win a few games for my team."

"What position?" Danny asked.

"Pitcher, mostly. But the point is, when I first went out for Little League, I didn't know how to do much. I didn't have a dad. My mom tried to throw a baseball with me, but she wasn't very good."

Danny nodded as if he understood.

Cassie wondered where this story was going.

"Anyway," Nash continued, "I was terrible at practices, especially with batting. There were two older boys who kept making fun of me."

"What did you do?" Danny was listening intently now.

"I would have liked to have clocked them," Nash confessed. "But I got to know a police officer who often came to the school to talk with the kids. He told me the only way I could show up those boys was to get better. He offered to spend one night a week practicing with me."

"Did it work?" Danny wanted to know.

"It did. I soon started hitting balls instead of striking out, and my pitching arm got quite good. I guess what I'm trying to say is that fighting doesn't get the job done because nothing is resolved. There's always a way to settle a dispute without violence."

Cassie imagined Nash's story explained why he'd become a cop. But as a cop, he'd seen violence and that was why he had this philosophy.

Danny seemed to think about what Nash had said. "There's this one boy in art class who always makes fun of my drawings. I got really tired of it and pushed him. Then he hit me, and I hit him." He touched the bandage on his head.

"What are you going to do when you go back to school and have art class again?" Nash prodded.

"I don't want to go back to school. I want to drop art."

Now Cassie sat forward, too. "Danny, how would you feel if you could never paint again?"

"Terrible, but if people are just going to make fun of it…"

"Art is one of those things that you can't predict how people will react to," Cassie told him. "Look at me. I submitted my work for the arts festival and got turned down. Yes, it made me feel bad but I still want to paint, even if nobody else sees it. It helps me feel better."

"Painting and drawing help me feel better, too," Danny mumbled.

"Then why would you want to give it up?" Nash asked. "Because some dolt is jealous and knows you're better than he is?"

Danny's expression said that thought had never crossed his mind. "You really think that's the reason he picks on me?"

"I don't know for sure," Nash answered. "Your teacher might be able to shed light on that. I'm sure she's going to want a conference with your parents."

Danny's face fell.

"There *is* something else you could consider," Nash added. "Karate."

"I've only seen it in movies."

"Movies glamorize it a bit," Nash responded. "But there are maneuvers you can learn in karate that can help you deal with someone like a bully without actually hurting him."

"Really?" Danny asked.

Nash just nodded.

Suddenly the front door flew open and Danny's mom rushed in followed by a man Cassie had never met.

Dorie took one look at her son, saw the bandage on his head and hugged him. "Are you all right?"

"I'm fine, Mom, really I am," Danny assured her.

The man who had come in behind Dorie was frowning. "I'm Paul Lindstrom, Danny's father." He looked directly at Cassie. "I suppose you're the one who picked him up?"

Cassie squared her shoulders, not knowing exactly why. "I am."

"I'll be complaining to the school. You're a perfect stranger. I've never even met you before. What right do you have to pick up my son?"

"Paul, don't talk to Cassie that way," Dorie protested. "I put her name down as an emergency contact." She looked at Cassie apologetically. "I told him to meet me here if he wanted to be included in this discussion."

"Of course I'm going to be included in this discussion," Paul Lindstrom blustered. "My son was involved in a fight and got hurt."

"From what I understand, Mr. Lindstrom," Cassie said politely, "the other boy was hurt, too. He has a black eye."

Paul went to Danny and clapped him on the back. "Good going there. I didn't know you had it in you."

Cassie could have socked him, no matter what Nash said about nonviolence. Or maybe she just needed a few karate moves aimed at the right part of Danny's dad's body.

To Cassie's surprise, Danny stepped forward and faced his father. "Nash told me I don't need to hurt anyone. He said when words don't work, then karate moves might. I'd like to take karate along with art lessons."

"From what I understand, it's the art lessons that caused this whole problem. Somebody didn't like what you drew," his father reminded him.

"They were making fun of what I drew," Danny said, his eyes on his sneakers now.

"And what was that?" his father asked.

"A totem pole. They're real art objects, Dad. I saw a few of them online. But the boy I fought with said the Native Americans aren't real Americans and I said they were."

So this was about more than a drawing, Cassie thought. It always seemed to be.

Danny's father appeared not to know what to say to that. He cleared his throat, then asked, "And who's this Nash person you're talking about?"

Nash had been quiet up till now, just sitting back and observing. Since he'd been brought into the discussion, he stood and extended his hand to Danny's father. "I'm

Nash Tremont, a detective from Biloxi. I just happen to be staying here at the bed-and-breakfast. Danny and I have talked about his drawings before. He's very good. I imagine you're proud of him."

Cassie almost smiled. That certainly put Danny's father on the spot.

He blustered a bit and then declared, "Art lessons aren't going to lead him toward a career. He needs to find a hobby that will benefit his future."

"I won an art competition, and selling paintings enabled me to buy this bed-and-breakfast," Cassie told him proudly. "Danny could use his art in a million ways. It's up to him to find the best fit, or a counselor who understands his talents." She motioned toward the table at the side of the room. "Help yourself to a coffee and cookies. I want to show you something. I'll be right back."

She knew Nash could probably handle the conversation in the time it would take to pull Danny's folder out of her file cabinet. After she went to her room and did just that, she brought it back to the guest area. Paul was sitting on the sofa, munching on one of her cookies.

She sat next to him and handed him the folder. "Why don't you take a look at these? They're all pictures Danny has drawn. He's very talented."

After Paul paged through the folder, he sent a look to Nash that told Cassie he realized his son listened to him because he respected him.

"These are good," he confirmed. "He understands depth perception and shadowing. He's young for that."

"Since you understand that, maybe you had some art training?"

"I did as an undergraduate. I enjoyed it, but I realized

it really didn't fit into my curriculum since I wanted to become a lawyer."

"Maybe I like to draw because you did," Danny said, embracing Cassie's thoughts exactly.

"I suppose that's possible," Paul agreed. He rubbed his hand over his jaw. "I'm a corporate lawyer. I'm away on business so much that maybe I don't know what my son needs."

Dorie said in a soft voice, "If we talk to the principal together, maybe we'll get a better idea."

Danny's father nodded. "And we can talk about karate lessons if you're truly interested," he told his son.

"I am," Danny assured him.

Fifteen minutes later, the family left. After the door closed behind them, Nash asked, "Do you think they'll work it out?"

"Do you mean, will Danny's dad support his art? I don't know. I'd like to think people can change."

"They rarely do," Nash said, as if he knew that all too well.

"If Danny's dad can become interested in his son's art or even his karate training, then they'll have a common interest. That might be the first step to better communication."

"You *are* an optimist, aren't you?"

"I try to be. Is there a point to being negative instead of positive?"

Nash seemed to think about that. "Sometimes I'm flooded with the negative and I forget there's a positive. I'd like to think life can turn out well at the end, but when you're dealing with criminals and their habits, that's rarely true."

"Then we're back to whether anyone can change

or not. You know, you were really good with Danny. Maybe you should think about working with kids."

"When I was a beat cop, I did enjoy going to schools to talk about safety and the pitfalls of taking drugs."

"You talked to all ages of children?"

"Sure did, from bicycle safety with the first and second graders, up to the danger of drugs with the high school kids."

Cassie couldn't help herself from asking, "Do you want your own kids some day?"

"I thought about it when I believed I'd be engaged to Sara, but I guess I just put any thoughts about kids on hold since then. Do *you* want children?"

"I'd love to have children. But I'd have to meet the right man."

"Yes, I guess you would," Nash agreed, his gaze locking to hers.

When Cassie's cell phone dinged, the sound seemed to startle them both.

Nash asked, "Since no guests signed up for dinner tonight, are you interested in pancakes and bacon? I'm an expert chef at those."

Going to the counter to pick up her phone, Cassie nodded. "Pancakes would be great. After I get this, I'll help you."

She didn't recognize the number the caller ID showed—Senft Art Gallery. Why would an art gallery be calling her?

"Hello? This is Cassie Calloway at the Bluebonnet Bed-and-Breakfast."

"Miss Calloway, this is Mark Senft from the Senft Gallery. I'll get right to the point. I'd like to see your portfolio and meet you in person. Would that be possible tomorrow at 11 a.m.? That meeting would be in my office in Round Rock."

"How did you hear about my work?" she asked.

"I received an email with photo files from your agent."

"My agent," she repeated.

"Yes, Nash Tremont."

"I see," she said slowly, turning her gaze on Nash. "I forgot he was sending that out this week."

"So you've queried other galleries?"

"Yes," she said, not knowing whether that was true or not. She'd have to ask Nash.

"Have you made other appointments?" Senft asked.

"Not yet."

"Well, good. Can you meet with me tomorrow?"

"Yes, I can. Eleven, you say? Can you give me your address again?"

He did.

"I'll see you tomorrow at eleven."

After the requisite goodbyes, Cassie laid her cell phone on the counter and approached Nash. He'd just taken a frying pan from a lower cupboard.

"What did you do?" she asked.

"I was hoping I was doing something nice for you. Did it work out?"

"I don't know yet. I'm meeting Mr. Senft tomorrow. Did you query other galleries?"

"Yes, I did. About nine of them. So you might be getting other phone calls."

"Nash, you're wonderful." She couldn't help but throw her arms around his neck. After she did, they studied each other for a very long moment. In the next heartbeat, he was bending his head, holding her tight, kissing her with a fervor that made her want him in an elemental way.

As Cassie drowned in his kiss, she realized he kissed in layers—soft and coaxing first, then with some sweet taunting, and finally with a passion that not only took her breath away but shooed common sense into a corner of her mind where it wasn't yelling at her. But she knew better than to get involved with him. His body was hard and muscled and strong. With him holding her this tightly, she could tell. His chest was broad, his stomach was taut, his thighs as they pressed against her legs were solidly immovable.

This time, with this kiss, he didn't break away quickly and neither did she. It was as if they reveled in what they were doing. While his right hand held her close, his left brushed her back creating delicious shivers along her spine. Cassie wished the kiss could go on forever.

"You taste as delicious as your cinnamon rolls," he whispered on an indrawn breath. Then he was kissing her again.

She should have backed away. She should have told him to stop. But stopping didn't seem to be in her vocabulary at that moment. And the moment stretched and stretched and stretched. This was closer than she'd been to a man in years. And not just physically. She felt close to Nash emotionally. His kisses stirred up feelings and sensations that she'd long forgotten. She was totally caught up in Nash, not just the kiss. She reveled in the scent of him, in his male pheromones that seemed to unite with her female ones. Her hand caressed his neck as she pushed tighter against him. She heard the growl in his throat. Because he was aroused? Because he needed a woman? Because he needed *her*. She should be afraid of this much excitement…this much hunger. She should be afraid of making a fool of herself over a man who was going to leave. But she couldn't stop herself.

It was Nash who broke away. His eyes were stormy as he looked down at her and asked, "Was that kiss because I did a favor for you?"

It took her a minute to gather her thoughts and to remember where she was. It was difficult because she was still tingling from every sensation she'd felt while he kissed her.

"Of course not," she said. "Why would you think that?"

"Because you didn't pull away. I don't need thanks for what I did."

Feeling a little indignant and misunderstood, she took a step back. "If I wanted to thank you, I'd bake you more cinnamon rolls or chocolate chip cookies. Why did you kiss me?"

"Because that's all I've been thinking about since our last kiss."

She blinked at him. "Nash, this is crazy."

"Crazy it might be, but it's happening."

"What exactly is happening?"

He ran his hand through his hair. "I wish I knew. I just know I like being around you. I definitely like kissing you."

"Do you often kiss women when you go to a strange town?"

"No," Nash said, shaking his head. "Why would you think that after I told you about Sara?"

"Maybe *because* of Sara. Maybe you don't want any

attachment. Maybe kissing and sleeping with a woman is all you need. Or else you've convinced yourself that's all you need."

"So now you've turned into a psychologist?"

"No. I've turned into a woman who doesn't want to get hurt. You haven't answered my question."

"I shouldn't have to. But just for the sake of clarity, no, I don't sleep around, whether I'm at home or on the road. That's not me. I've dated since I've lived in Biloxi, but nothing ever came of it. So I just stopped."

"We're not exactly dating," she reminded him.

"Sure, we are. We went to lunch. We went to the zoo."

If this weren't so serious, she'd laugh. But it was serious because that kiss had made her realize she was in love with Nash Tremont, or fully on the way to it. Yet she couldn't really tell where he stood in all this.

"Tell me something, Nash. What if you find the information you're looking for? What if your month is up and you drive back to Biloxi? What if you think about kissing me while you're there? What happens next?"

"You're asking about a future I don't have a road map for. I can't tell you what's going to happen in a week or two or three. I don't have a crystal ball. Do you?"

His comment made her sound as if she was being totally illogical and completely unreasonable. But she wasn't. She always had to have a plan. Ever since she was a kid, when there was little food in the cupboard, there was a neighbor she could clean for, make some money and buy groceries. When her mother didn't show up at school for a conference, or anything else that was important to Cassie, she had a whole line of excuses in her mind why her mother couldn't be there. One or another would roll off her tongue as if it were the truth. If her mother didn't come home at night, Cassie would visit a friend, and those friends would ask her to stay over and spend the night. She wouldn't have to be in the apartment alone. But she couldn't say any of this to Nash.

Well, maybe she could say a little. "I had a lot of uncertainty in my life as a child, Nash. As I grew up, I wanted my life planned. I have part-time jobs so if I don't have enough guests in a month, I can still pay my mortgage. I like to know what meal I'm cooking tomorrow so I have the ingredients for it. I ask my guests if they have any allergies so I don't step into a crisis inadvertently. That's just me. So if I begin caring for you and you just leave, that's not okay for me."

"Cassie…" He reached out a hand to her, but she stepped back.

"I appreciate what you did for me, I really do. Right now I'm going to go up to the attic and pick out a few paintings to take along with me to my appointment tomorrow."

"Take the new one," he said.

"The new one isn't finished."

"That doesn't matter. It shows your talent."

"I'll think about it. You were going to make yourself pancakes. Go ahead and do that. The kitchen's yours. And tomorrow when I get back, I'll bake you cinnamon rolls as a real thank-you."

This time *she* was the one who left the room. *She* was the one who climbed the stairs. *She* was the one who turned her back on heartache.

## Chapter Eleven

Cassie was so excited when she returned from her appointment in Round Rock the following day. She parked her car in the gravel area behind the B&B, a wide smile still on her face. She'd been wearing it the whole way back from Round Rock. She was going to have an art show sometime this summer! Mr. Senft was going to call her with the date next week.

She wanted to tell Nash. She wanted to thank him again. But then she remembered how they'd left things last night. She hadn't seen him this morning. He hadn't even stopped for his usual mug of coffee. Either he'd left early or he'd been doing research in his room. She really had no right to know, either way. That made her sad.

She opened the back door of her car and pulled out the three paintings she'd taken along to show Mr. Senft.

She'd been up half the night finishing the angel, but she, of course, couldn't take that one along because it was still wet. She had taken a picture of it, though, with her phone. Nash might have been right about that, too. That was the painting that might have decided the gallery owner in her favor.

She was carrying the paintings up the back walk when she spotted Renata tending to the herb garden in her backyard. It was a raised bin so she didn't have to stoop over so far to reach it.

Renata waved to her. "Where have you been?" her neighbor asked her.

"Let me set these paintings inside the porch, then I'll come over and tell you." Cassie ran up the steps, deposited the paintings inside and then went back to Renata's yard. The smile was back on her face as she thought about her good news.

"You look happy," Renata said.

"I am *so* happy. My paintings are going to be shown in a gallery this summer."

"Which gallery would that be?"

"Mr. Senft, from Round Rock, has galleries in Austin, San Antonio and Dallas. He thinks he wants to set me up in the San Antonio gallery. He's going to let me know next week about that and a date."

Renata threw her arms around Cassie, making tears spring to Cassie's eyes. Her neighbor had become a mother figure in her life when she'd sorely needed one. "That's wonderful news, honey. I guess you took paintings along to show this Mr. Senft?"

"I did, along with a picture or two. Nash had already sent him photos of my work with a letter."

Renata leaned back. "Nash did?"

"Yes. He said he wanted to do something nice for me."

"That man cares about you. I can see it in his eyes."

Caring was one thing. Attraction was another. Maybe Renata had mistaken one for the other.

When Cassie didn't respond, Renata said, "You don't believe me, do you?"

"I like Nash, and I think he likes me. But we haven't known each other very long, and he's going to be leaving in another week or so."

Renata studied her. "Would you like him to stay?"

"He can't do that. He has a job in Biloxi."

"I see," Renata said with a twinkle in her eye. "You know, I have heard of these things called airplanes that fly back and forth, and cars that make trips comfortable."

Cassie laughed. "I understand. You get around."

"I not only get around, I'm old enough to have experience of the heart. My Luis and I, well, it was love at first sight."

"Where did you meet?"

"At the wedding of a friend. He knew the groom, and I knew the bride. We began talking over dinner, we danced, and that was it. We were married for forty-five years."

"I can't even imagine," Cassie said.

"When you're in love, when you have a life together, time passes by much too quickly. I only wish we'd had children. We took in two foster children."

"Where are they now?"

"The little girl, Olivia, was reunited with her mother after two years with us. Her mother got clean from drugs and every once in a while, I get a letter from her. Olivia has her own family now and lives in Kansas."

"And the other child?"

"Billy was a wanderer. He came to us when he was sixteen because he had nowhere else to go. He was all defiance and rebellion at first, but then Luis and he found some common ground. They both liked to fish. Billy stayed with us until he earned enough to buy his own car, and then he was gone. The last time I heard from him, he was running one of those shops along the beach in Venice, California. He usually calls me on Christmas."

Cassie imagined there was so much more about Renata she didn't know, but she did know one thing. Her birthday was tomorrow and Cassie was throwing a party. Renata deserved some caring, and Cassie wanted to make her feel special.

Renata patted Cassie's arm. "Someday you'll marry and have children, and then you'll have wonderful memories like I do." Cassie didn't know if that would ever be true, but she could hope.

Renata turned back to her herb bin. "Do you need any fresh herbs for your meals today?"

Cassie thought about the roast she was going to put in the oven. Three guests were staying for dinner tonight. Nash hadn't signed up, and she hadn't spoken to him so she didn't know if he'd be around. "I could use marjoram and thyme. I want to make a rub for the roast. Maybe parsley, too. I might make parsley buttered potatoes."

Renata had her snippers right at the bin. She said, "I'll clip some for you."

"Would you like some roast beef and potatoes and green beans tonight? I'll have plenty."

"Cassie, you're too good to me."

"Not possible."

"Hold out your hands," Renata said.

Cassie did as she was told.

Renata placed the stems of marjoram and thyme in Cassie's hands, then laid longer stems of parsley across those. "Don't drop them," she warned.

"I won't. I'll bring your meal over as soon as I serve my guests."

Renata's eyes grew suspiciously moist. She gave Cassie a hug. When Cassie left the protection of the older woman's arms to head for her own house, she missed them. She missed her mother, too, the mother she'd really never had.

Cassie went to bed that night with the scent of cinnamon rolls still pervading the bed-and-breakfast. She'd made them for Nash as a thank-you, and it was a point she wanted to emphasize. She'd left them on the desk wrapped in foil with Nash's name affixed to the package. Before she'd turned in tonight, they'd been gone, so she assumed he'd gotten them.

She tried not to think of Nash but rather concentrated on the show she was going to have this summer. She had paintings in her head that her fingers were itching to paint onto canvas. She thought about painting before bed, but it seemed more important to get a good night's sleep and start fresh in the morning. When she turned off the light, she expected to do just that.

However, she tossed and turned for about an hour, finally falling into a restless sleep. A dream began pleasantly enough. She was on a street lined with vibrant colored flowers and oil paintings in every style. But as she walked up the street, she suddenly felt as if someone were following her. She glanced over her shoulder but could only spot a shadow. As she walked faster, the shadow came after her faster.

She began jogging and the shadow seemed to jog, too. Next, she was running full out. The flowers disappeared. The paintings disappeared. Dilapidated row houses lined both sides of the street. She was streaking by them so fast she didn't know if she might have lived in one of them. Faster and faster she ran. There were no sidewalks here but she was running along the yellow line in the middle of the road.

Suddenly a car was speeding toward her but it wasn't on *its* side of the road. It was in the middle. It began weaving back and forth in wide swerves. She knew she should run back the way she'd come or run over to the side. But it was as if her feet were entrenched on that yellow line in the middle of the road. The car kept coming closer and her mother was driving. The car was going to hit her.

She was calling her mother's name. Screaming. Out of nowhere somebody grabbed her and pulled her out of the way just as the car reached her.

She woke up still screaming. Someone was rocking her in his arms, stroking her hair, murmuring, "Shush. You're all right."

She realized her hair was matted to her head. She was shaking, and she was in Nash's arms.

He held her protectively, stroking her cheek, brushing her hair out of her eyes. "You're fine," he said.

"You're safe." His strong baritone commanded her to believe it.

What she couldn't believe was that the dream had seemed so real. She grabbed onto Nash, still feeling a bit crazed. "A car was coming toward me. My—" She stopped. "It was going to hit me."

Nash was studying her, looking genuinely concerned. "Do you want to tell me what else was in the dream?"

She didn't want to talk about it. If she did, she could let something slip. She was sure the dream had something to do with her childhood and the fact that her mother was now in prison. But she couldn't say any of that to Nash.

She sat up straighter. "I'll be okay. Really, I will."

It was apparent that Nash didn't believe her. He just sat there holding her, and she let him because the strength of his arms felt so good around her.

"Dreams can be a way your mind settles problems. They bring fears to the surface so you can deal with them."

"You've had dream therapy?" she tried to joke.

"No, but I have had some training in PTSD, and a bit of psychology." Nash was still rocking her gently.

Cassie didn't want to delve into the psychology of her dream. She didn't want to talk about it at all. "Did you eat the cinnamon rolls?" she asked, hoping he'd drop the subject.

"I ate two and I have one left."

"You don't have to save it. I have some left for breakfast if you want them then."

"I'll keep that in mind."

The longer he held her, the more she could feel heat building between them. He was wearing a light T-shirt and soft lounge pants. She could not only see the muscles under his shirt, but she could feel them. She was so tired of fighting the attraction between them. In some ways, the dream had made her aware of how short life was. Maybe it was time she lived it instead of watching it pass her by.

She looked up at Nash, knowing what she felt was apparent in her eyes. She didn't know how to hide that kind of feeling. She didn't know how to hide the fact that she was falling in love with him.

"I want to kiss you, Cassie. In fact, I want to do more than kiss you. But I feel you're vulnerable right now, and I don't want to take advantage of you."

Nothing else Nash said could have made him more endearing to her. He was still trying to protect her, setting his needs aside.

"I'm not vulnerable. Since you've been here, a wall or two has fallen down. Why shouldn't I enjoy myself? Why shouldn't I enjoy *you*? It's silly to pretend we don't want each other when we do."

"You make it sound so reasonable." He ran his thumb over her bottom lip. She trembled and this time it wasn't because of the dream.

Nash's hand was a bit rough as he cupped her face. She took it and felt it, running her fingers over a callus or two. "You've done hard work."

"I told you I worked construction. Back when I was in high school I helped to build houses. So at times, in between investigations, I help to build houses for organizations like Homes for Families. I don't want to forget all those skills I learned."

When she still fingered his palm, he closed his eyes for a moment. She kissed one of the calluses and he let out a groan. "Cassie." Her name was a warning that she didn't intend to heed. She kissed his palm again.

"You shouldn't," he growled.

"Why not?"

"Because I might end up in this bed with you."

His words were so arousing she wasn't sure what to do next. But as she kept her gaze locked to his, his hands slid along her collarbone. She loved the feel of his skin on hers. Her heart raced and her stomach felt as if it were somersaulting. She didn't want to reach for him because she felt she'd been forward enough. What if he didn't want her? What if he didn't want to make love with her?

But she needn't have worried. He bent his head and murmured, "I came down to the kitchen for a glass of milk to have with that cinnamon roll, but I heard you screaming even through your door. It wasn't locked. Why don't you keep it locked?"

"Usually I do, but tonight I was distracted."

He bent his head closer to hers. "I'm distracted by *you*, morning, noon and night. But especially at night."

So he *did* want her. At first, she thought she was hearing the ticking of her clock on her bedside stand, but then she realized she was hearing her heart pounding and maybe his. When his kiss came, it drew her out of herself and into him. Before his kisses had seemed to have finesse. This one didn't. This one was abject hunger, on his part and on hers. She welcomed his tongue into her mouth. She couldn't seem to get close enough to him. Desire mixed with the exquisite feeling of being wanted. She kissed him back as if he didn't live in Biloxi, as if he weren't going to leave, as if he weren't involved in an investigation that could change his life in so many ways. She almost felt dizzy with the need he created in her.

He caressed her, his hands blazing a trail of heat through her nightgown, making her crazy with need. He dropped kisses onto her neck, nuzzled her nose and whispered, "Maybe we should take off your nightgown."

"It's about time you suggested it."

He laughed and took hold of the hem. It was up and over her head and on the floor in no time. "I don't know why women wear nightgowns," he said. "You should just go to bed nude."

"Do you?" she returned, amused.

"I do," he assured her.

She knew she'd keep with her the picture of Nash in his bed naked for all time. But soon she'd have an even better picture to remember. She pulled the drawstring at his waist.

"Tit for tat?" he asked.

"Something like that, unless you want to keep your clothes on."

"Not a chance," he said gruffly, proceeding to rid himself of his clothes.

Nash kissed her with renewed passion, but then suddenly broke away. "I hate to take the romance out of this, but I have to ask. Do you have any condoms?"

As her brain and her body settled from his kiss, the question suddenly resonated. She shook her head slowly back and forth. "No."

Nash's face fell, and his brows drew together. He seemed to move away from her a little. Before he could, she took hold of his hand and interlaced her fingers with his. "I'm on the pill, Nash." She knew he was going to wonder why when she said she didn't date. So she explained, "My doctor put me on it to help with my periods. I was having bad cramps." She saw the look on his face that said he wasn't used to discussing this, and she almost laughed. But she didn't. "I hope that doesn't come under the category of too much information, but I'm not going to get pregnant if that's what you're worried about."

He took her into his arms again. "Nothing's too much information when it's about *you*."

She didn't know if a man had ever said something so nice to her. She felt tears burning in her eyes.

As they lay there, skin against skin in her single bed, she could detect the scent of soap on Nash. He must have gotten a shower before he'd gone to bed. "You smell good," she said, nuzzling his chest.

"So do you," he murmured as he nipped at her shoulder. "You always seem to smell like cinnamon and vanilla."

"I don't know if that's good or bad," she said with a laugh.

"It's good, very good." Then Nash began to tell her in actions rather than in words.

His lips and tongue explored her all over with excruciating, sensual fervor. Cassie never expected she'd be capable of the passion that Nash drew from her. His every kiss and touch was exciting and brand-new. It all seemed so natural—his thumb teasing her nipple, his lips kissing her navel, his hands gently separating her thighs. In some ways Cassie wanted to prolong each kiss and each caress. In other ways, she wanted to hurry and find the satisfaction she knew Nash could give her.

She enjoyed exploring his male body—the definition, the strength, the tautness that she knew was due to tension because he was holding back. His next kiss was a claiming kiss, and she realized what it meant. They were both ready. As he rose above her, she gazed into his eyes, just trying to see the present because they might not have a future. Sadness about that didn't have a chance to take hold.

Nash urged her to raise her legs and she did. She wrapped them around his waist as he entered her slowly, teasing her with a fulfillment that they both wanted. Cassie felt the sensual excitement and pleasure that had eluded her all of her adult life as Nash thrust into her, withdrew and then thrust again. She knew with absolute certainty that tonight she was losing her heart to him completely. When her climax engulfed her, his engulfed him. Together they shouted each other's names. Together they found supreme pleasure. Not long after, Cassie fell asleep in Nash's arms, totally content to be exactly where she was.

Cassie awakened at daylight as she usually did. She could see the sunrise through the curtains at her window. Everything about last night came back, every memory, every pleasure, but she wasn't sure how to deal with it. She glanced over her shoulder at Nash, but didn't want to wake him. She'd simply slip out of bed, go to the kitchen and prepare a casserole for breakfast.

But as she moved only a few inches, Nash snagged her around her waist with his arm. "Going somewhere?" he asked into her ear.

She swallowed hard. "I was going to get breakfast ready."

He rubbed his chin against her shoulder. "Isn't it too early for breakfast?"

"Not if the egg has to soak into the bread, and I have to make bacon to top it with, and—" She was rambling but Nash stopped her.

"I get that you're rattled. I am, too. But don't you think we should talk about it?"

"Is there anything to talk about?"

"I guess not if you don't think there is."

He sounded...disappointed. She turned around to face him. "Last night was wonderful."

"Then why are you running off? Do you regret it?"

"I don't have any regrets," she assured him. She had no regrets because she knew she was already in love with Nash. But he was going to be leaving town soon. Could she coax him to stay?

"Then what's wrong?" he asked.

"Because you're leaving, this..." she motioned to the two of them in the bed. "Whatever this is has an expiration date."

"Only if we want it to," he said.

She was reminded of Renata's advice that there were planes and cars that could help a long-distance relationship.

However, distance wasn't the real problem for Cassie. She maybe could fly back and forth or drive back and forth to Biloxi, or maybe he could. No, the real problem was the truth that reared its ugly head between them. If they continued whatever was building between them, she'd have to tell him that her mother was in prison. Once she did that, he'd leave anyway. He had to. She knew what he thought about law and order. She knew he believed right and wrong was cut-and-dried, black-

and-white. To Cassie, her mom being in prison was all kinds of shades of gray.

"I really do have to start breakfast," she reminded him. "Can we talk again later?" That would give her time to think about it more.

He frowned. "We can talk later." He sat up on the edge of the bed, grabbed his pants and started putting them on.

"I'm throwing a birthday party for Renata tonight," she told him as she lay there. "A few neighbors are coming. I just want to make her feel special. I have a birthday cake to bake, too. Will you be around this evening?" She couldn't keep the hopefulness from her voice.

He turned to her and she saw that his frown had disappeared. "I wouldn't want to be anywhere else. What can I get her?"

"I got her a velvet throw for her sofa, though she insists she doesn't need anything. If you really want to get her something—"

"Tell me what you have in mind."

"I know she likes baskets. She has one that she uses to carry in vegetables from her garden. But hers is practically coming apart."

"All right. I passed one of those home stores. They should have baskets, shouldn't they?"

"They should."

"And I could fill it with things she needs—dish detergent, tissues, plastic wrap, that kind of thing."

"That's a wonderful idea!"

Cassie slipped her nightgown over her head and stood up. "So we'll talk tonight after the party?"

Rising to his feet, Nash plucked his shirt from the

floor. "We will." Then he gave her a kiss that told her he remembered everything about last night, too.

As he left her room, Cassie wondered if she'd have the courage tonight to tell him about her mother.

*Chapter Twelve*

Nash couldn't stop thinking about last night while he showered. Visions of making love to Cassie filled his mind and his heart. He hadn't felt anything near to this with Sara. What did that tell him?

That he was seeing something in Cassie that wasn't there? That he had healed from his relationship with Sara? That enough time had passed and romance now seemed a possibility?

Maybe all of the above.

He took his time dressing because today he simply didn't think he could keep his mind on research, records and the Robinson family.

He still had one of the cinnamon rolls Cassie had left him last night. Perfect. He took a bottle of water from the six-pack he'd brought to his room. Other than picking up Renata's present, he needed to hole up in here today and shut out the rest of the world. Maybe then he'd get some clarity on all of it.

Because after Mrs. Garcia's party, he and Cassie were going to have a talk. The problem was he had no idea what he was going to say.

Opening the bottle of water, he took a few swigs and settled at his desk. There he opened the foil that he'd re-wrapped around the lone cinnamon roll. Cassie's thank-you present. He sighed. In some ways, she was a tough nut to crack. He still didn't know that much about her, other than the fact that she came from Bryan. He wondered if the Austin library would have yearbooks from Bryan. Maybe he could learn something more about her from the yearbook.

He'd finished the last of the cinnamon roll and wiped his hands on a napkin when his cell phone buzzed.

It was early. Who could be calling him? Had his supervisor somehow learned what he was up to?

Only one way to find out. But when he checked the screen, he saw the caller had a blocked number. In the past he'd worked with confidential informants who had blocked numbers and burner phones. Back then it hadn't been that unusual. But now…

Needing a distraction, he decided to answer. "Tremont here."

"I understand you're looking for information on the Robinson family."

Nash didn't recognize the voice. And just who could know he was looking for information? He immediately distrusted whoever was calling. "What makes you think that?"

"I have connections," the male voice said. "But if you want the info I have, you have to meet with me."

"I suppose you have a meeting place picked out?"

"No, I don't. That's up to you."

That took Nash aback. Usually when someone like this anonymous source wanted to meet, they decided where the meeting was held.

Was he even going to this meeting? He was going nowhere fast enough on his own. Maybe this was the source he needed.

It was too early to meet at a bar, but Nash didn't want this meeting to wait. "There's a restaurant that serves great pancakes and strong coffee. How about meeting me at Dusty's Diner in an hour." He rattled off the address.

"That doesn't give me much time," the man said.

"Why do you need time if you're just going to give me information?"

"All right. I'll meet you in an hour at Dusty's Diner. I know what you look like."

"I'll be carrying," Nash said. His service weapon was locked in the glove compartment of his SUV, but maybe this was the time to take it out. After all, he knew many people in Austin had concealed handgun permits.

"Not necessary," the man on the other end of the line protested.

"We'll see about that. An hour. Don't be late." Nash ended the call.

He didn't know if he was doing the smart thing or a foolish thing, but he might as well get to Dusty's early and have eggs and coffee before his informant met him. He might not have the stomach for it afterward.

An hour later Nash had eaten eggs, toast and drunk two cups of coffee when a man in a suit walked through the door. Nash sat perfectly still in the rear booth. This guy looked out of place in the diner. Could he actually be Nash's informant? Nash felt the weight of his gun under his jacket. He knew from experience that you could never just go by looks.

The stranger walked toward him. The thing was, he looked familiar. Nash had checked out so many photos of the Fortunes and the Robinsons that he supposed he could have seen this man's picture somewhere.

The man stood at Nash's table and just stared at him. Then he extended his hand. "I'm Ben Fortune Robinson."

That surprised Nash.

The man didn't sit. He stood beside the table and said, "My family has connections all over Austin. There's no way you could inquire too deeply into the Robinsons without us finding out. Why didn't you just call one of us and meet with the family in person if you have questions? It would have been so much easier and it's what we've wanted all along."

"I'm not sure I want it easy," Nash said. "I didn't expect anything about this to be easy. The kind of information I'm looking for isn't the kind the family would want to give me." He kept a hard edge to his tone so Ben Robinson knew he was serious.

Ben turned to look out the window and motioned to someone, putting Nash on guard.

"Calling in reinforcements?" Nash asked.

"I don't need reinforcements, but *you* might."

At first Nash felt outnumbered when a man in a charcoal suit came through the diner's glass door, but he knew he could take both men down if he had to.

As the other stranger approached, Nash's glare must have been strong enough and hard enough that both of them understood what Nash was thinking. They both raised their hands at the same time and opened their suit jackets so Nash could see they had no weapons.

The newcomer extended his hand to Nash. "I'm Keaton Whitfield, one of Gerald Robinson's illegitimate children," he said in a slight English accent. "For some reason, this feels like a Grade B movie."

Nash relaxed a bit, studying the two men as they sat in the booth across from him.

The waitress came over, and Ben and Keaton ordered coffee. She brought it and then left again.

Ben looked Nash in the eye. "We know what you must think about Gerald Robinson leaving your mom high and dry."

So they had done their homework, Nash thought. Still he kept silent, letting them fill it.

"We're not bad people, no matter what you've heard about Gerald," Keaton added.

"Does Gerald know I'm in town?" Nash asked.

Ben shook his head. "No. While you were going about your investigation incognito, you obviously wanted to keep your distance. We didn't want to blindside you, but we want you to consider something. We *are* your half brothers."

Nash sighed. Of course they'd play *that* card. "You think that means anything?" he asked.

Ben frowned. "It could. What exactly do you want to know?"

"First of all, I want to keep my identity under wraps," Nash insisted.

"You don't want anyone to know you're a Fortune?" Keaton surmised.

"I'm *not* a Fortune," Nash protested adamantly. "I'm a Tremont."

Ben and Keaton exchanged a look. "We understand where you're coming from," Keaton said. "We've been there."

During the next fifteen minutes, Nash tried to determine if Ben and Keaton knew he was investigating Charlotte Robinson. They didn't seem to. So his secret was safe, though he didn't know for how long. At any time, these two men could tell Gerald he was in town, not to mention Charlotte. Charlotte was the Robinson he wanted to nail.

After about fifteen minutes of Nash asking questions, and Ben and Keaton answering, he realized these two men actually seemed like good guys. Could he deny getting to know his half brothers? Especially if they were on the up-and-up?

Nash addressed Keaton. "Lucie Fortune Chesterfield Parker connected you with Ben, didn't she? I saw that somewhere."

"She did," Keaton answered easily. "Lucie's a doll. We just happened to know each other in England. I designed a house for one of her mother's friends and Lucie and I ran into each other at a few parties. When Ben asked for an introduction to me, she didn't hesitate. She's like that."

Nash remembered reading that Ben Fortune Robinson had married a woman named Ella Thomas. He didn't know much about Keaton Whitfield.

Ben took a business card from the inside pocket of his suit jacket and passed it over to Nash. "I have the feeling you haven't asked us the questions you really want to ask. You're looking for something and we might be able to help you."

Keaton passed his card to Nash, too. "You can call either one of us at any time. We *do* want to help. We are related and the truth is, a detective in the family wouldn't be a bad thing." Keaton's eyes actually had some amusement in them.

Nash wished he could be amused. "I'll keep that in mind," he said, picking up the cards and inserting them into his jacket pocket.

Keaton laid some bills on the table. "Call us. If Gerald does happen to find out you're in town—and that won't happen through us—we'll let you know."

"I'm only going to be in town another week or so."

Ben said, "We're glad we met you. We hope you're glad you met us."

At that, both men exited the booth and left the restaurant.

Nash watched them go, not sure what to do next.

Cassie was putting the final touches of decorations on Renata's cake when Nash returned to the bed-and-breakfast late morning. He looked agitated, she thought. After a slight nod her way, he went to the coffee urn and poured himself a mug.

She was studying his face when he looked up at her and shook his head. "I probably don't need more caffeine in addition to everything else," he said, putting down the mug.

Finishing off the cake, she put it into the refrigerator, then she joined Nash.

"Is something wrong?"

He looked pensive for a moment before he said, "It's complicated." His expression became closed.

So conversation wasn't what he wanted right now. She murmured, "Sorry for prying again," and started walking down the hall to her room. But she didn't even get halfway there.

Nash strode after her, caught her arm and stopped her. "Cassie, this doesn't have anything to do with you and me. It has to do with the Fortunes and the Robinsons."

She looked him straight in the eyes. "Do you want to talk about it?"

After studying her a good long time, he nodded. She motioned toward her bedroom. Why not? It wasn't as if the bed was going to tempt them any more than it had before.

After they sat on the love seat together, Nash took off his Stetson and laid it on a nearby table. Then he rubbed his hands down over his face.

"Nash, what happened?"

"I got an anonymous call this morning. A man said he had information on the Robinsons for me, or the Fortunes. However you want to look at it. He wouldn't give me his name and he set up a meeting. I picked the place. I waited at Dusty's Diner."

She knew the spot where breakfasts were cheap.

"It turns out the man was Ben Fortune Robinson. Then he introduced Keaton Whitfield, too. Both of them are my half brothers."

Cassie knew a small gasp escaped her. "How did that go?"

"Ben said he called anonymously because he didn't

think I'd meet him if I knew who he was. He's probably right." Nash related the main parts of their conversation.

Cassie summed it up. "So you met two of your half brothers but you didn't tell them why you're really here."

He must have sensed disapproval in her tone because he turned away from her, studied the wall and said tersely, "I don't owe them or Gerald Robinson anything. If my biological father's wife is a criminal, she deserves to be arrested and brought to trial. I can't take a chance in telling either Ben or Keaton the truth. They could reveal it to Gerald or Charlotte. Both could try to wipe away any evidence."

Easily seeing his point, Cassie said, "Nash, I'm not judging you."

He turned to look at her once more, and she hoped the only thing on her face was the caring she felt for him. He must have seen that because he took her hand and rubbed his thumb against hers. Even that slight touch made Cassie want to be held in his arms again. But as he said, this wasn't about them.

She squeezed his hand so he knew she was sympathetic to what he'd said. But then she explained what she was thinking. "I'm just wondering if you realize how many bridges you'll be burning in pursuing Charlotte. What if you change your mind in a little while and you want to get to know your dad?"

"I won't want that," Nash insisted.

"If that's true, then why do you seem so upset?"

It took Nash long moments to answer. "Maybe because it's possible that Ben and Keaton are just caught up in this whole thing like I am, only in a different way. Besides that, I'm just angry that I'm going to have to approach this case from a different angle now. It's quite possible that either Ben or Keaton have a PI on me to keep up with what I'm doing while I'm here."

"An investigator on the investigator," she murmured.

"I don't know if they would do that, but they don't know me any more than I know them."

"You liked them, didn't you?"

"If my judgment wasn't clouded by how personally involved I am in this, I'd say they both seemed like upright guys. Everything about their backgrounds points in that direction, too. Another time in another place, we might even have been friends."

"It's all right if you feel something toward your half brothers…even toward your father. Can't you realize that?"

He blew out a long breath. "The only thing I'm realizing right now, is how much I'm beginning to care for *you*."

At that admission, Cassie wrapped her arms around him and hugged him. But that hug soon became much more as Nash bent his head and kissed her. Whereas they'd been talking about the Robinsons and the Fortunes and Nash had declared his upset had nothing to do with him and Cassie, the silent conversation between them suddenly changed. No longer was this about the Fortunes and the Robinsons. The kiss was about her and Nash—and *only* her and Nash.

His lips were hot and she returned their fire. His tongue was rough and she returned his need. Somehow he released passion she never knew she possessed. Somehow he was making her dream beyond the present. He cupped her face while he kissed her and every moment of that was sensual, too.

He broke away to insinuate his fingers underneath

the hem of her top. "I dreamed of doing this again," he said.

*Of doing this again,* she repeated in her mind. What was *this*? Did that mean he was falling for her the same way she was falling for him? Did it mean they were about to give more than their bodies to each other, but their trust, too? Could she really do that?

Fortunately, his actions made her forget everything else. He was lifting her top up and over her head, and she cooperated because she'd dreamed of making love to him again. That was how *she* thought of it.

It wasn't long before she was naked before him. The odd thing was, she didn't feel self-conscious. She felt proud that he was looking at her as if she were one of those cinnamon rolls he liked so much. His eyes devoured her and her anticipation grew. For some reason, she realized she had to be his equal. She couldn't just stand by and be a passive participant. Not in this.

Reaching out, she took hold of his belt buckle and unfastened it. A look of surprise crossed his face.

He asked, "Do you want help?"

"I've got it," she said confidently.

"Yes, you do," he agreed, and she felt as if he'd just told her she was the most beautiful woman in the world.

All was quiet in the house. She didn't even hear the creak of a floorboard or the tinkling of water from a spigot.

"I want to tell you something," she said, as she unzipped his fly.

"Something important?" he asked, his voice obviously strained.

"I don't know if it's important to you, but it is important to me. I've never had an orgasm before last night."

His eyes came open. Gruffly he took her hands in his and said, "That's it. I'm taking off the rest of my clothes."

She couldn't help but smile. "I don't mind doing it for you."

"If you do it for me, we're not going to have a reason to get into that bed."

A few minutes later, he was naked, too, and they were both in bed, tight against each other. He pushed her hair away from her face and let his fingers linger in it. "You know, last night was the first I've been in a single bed since I was a kid."

"How does it feel?" she asked, reaching for his chest, running her fingers lightly over his nipple.

He groaned. "Right now I feel like I've landed in my idea of heaven."

He kissed the soft spot behind her ear, kissed the pulse point at her throat and slowly made his way to her breasts. He raised his head to see her reaction and smiled. "Your cheeks are pink."

"That's because I'm hot all over."

He bent his head again and murmured, "The nice thing about a single bed is that it keeps you close."

He was making her crazy with need. She wanted to do the same to him. Reaching between them, she stroked his thigh. "How close do you want to get?"

"This close," he said, rubbing against her so she knew exactly how much he wanted her.

They kissed as if they couldn't get enough of each other. Maybe because they knew they had a time limit, maybe because the clock was ticking until the day he left for Biloxi. As she touched him more intimately, he kissed her harder. Suddenly Nash pulled her on top of him. She straddled his legs and looked down at him gazing up at her.

He said, "We'll have a little more freedom this way."

Freedom was a funny word. She felt free to be sensual with Nash, sexual in a way she hadn't been with anyone else ever before. Yet she didn't feel the freedom to tell him the truth about her life.

She stopped thinking about it when he said, "You set the pace. I want to make sure you have your second orgasm, and maybe even a third."

She was past ready to find satisfaction, and she imagined he was, too. Slowly she raised herself up and then took him in. He gripped her buttocks and groaned with pleasure. That was exactly what she wanted to hear. Soon each moment was all about giving and receiving, sharing and loving. She welcomed him deeper and the expression on his face told her he was experiencing what she was.

As they were both caught in a tornado that swirled them toward satisfaction, Cassie didn't want this moment to end. She trembled as each new sensation electrified her. She felt his hands, which were holding her waist, grip her tighter. The buildup of pleasurable tension suddenly unwound in glorious sensations that skittered through her nerve endings, making her weak. Then to her surprise Nash moved inside of her again and then again, and her second orgasm made her gasp. She collapsed on top of him and he wrapped his arms around her. His heart was beating fast against hers.

When she could finally breathe almost normally again, she told him, "That was incredible."

"I told you there'd be a number two," he said with a grin.

She'd never felt closer to another human being, and she didn't know how to tell him that.

After more time just holding each other, Nash reminded her, "We didn't have that conversation we were going to have."

"Maybe later?" she asked. "I have to start decorating for Renata's party."

"Having sex with you could make me forget all about a party."

*Having sex.* Those were the words he'd used to describe their lovemaking. Because he was afraid to say more? Was she?

"That conversation," she said. "It could be complicated. We need to know where we stand, Nash. We need to know what we're doing."

He frowned, but then he tipped her chin up to him and he kissed her. Afterward he asked, "Can't we just take one day at a time?"

Could they? Could she love him and then let him leave? Could she love him if he didn't love her?

But as he kissed her again, she knew she could because she was grateful for what they had right now. Still, a little voice in her head asked, *How will you feel when he leaves?*

She didn't have any answers and she knew she wasn't going to search for them now.

## Chapter Thirteen

Several neighbors brought casseroles and desserts to the party that evening. They were sitting in the lounge area when Nash arrived. He spotted Cassie at the counter placing candles on a sheet cake decorated in pink, white and lime green icing. As her gaze met his, it was as if the whole room lit up for him. Suddenly he realized the older women gathered in the sitting area, friends of Renata's, he supposed, were watching him with curiosity.

Renata, who was sitting in the wing chair in the place of honor, told everyone else loud enough for Nash to hear, "He's Cassie's guest, but he's sweet on her, too."

Cassie had heard and she glanced at Nash, probably to see if he minded that characterization.

He sent her a crooked grin. "What are you going to do?" he asked. "It's not something I can hide easily." Crossing to her at the counter, he ran his finger along the edge of the cake resulting in a glob of icing on the tip.

Cassie teasingly slapped his arm. "What are you doing?"

He wiggled his brows. "I'm just making sure the icing is five-star." He tasted some of it, then with a wink held his finger to her lips. After only a brief hesitation, she licked it. The sensuality of her tongue on his skin heated his blood like a flash fire.

He leaned close to her and murmured, "Maybe after everyone leaves tonight, we could share a piece of cake with icing."

She fanned herself with her hand. "It's hot in here, don't you think?"

He laughed. "I'll take that as a *yes*."

Turning away, Cassie picked up the pack of matches and lit the candles. She asked Nash, "Do you want to do the honors? I think Renata will appreciate it. She's sweet on you, too."

Without a comment, Nash carried the cake out to the guest of honor. Then he took out his cell phone and took a photo as everyone in the room sang "Happy Birthday" and Renata blew out the candles.

She was smiling broadly as she said, "Thank you so much for tonight. I feel special."

Cassie went over to the wing chair and crouched down beside her. "You *are* special." After she kissed Renata on the cheek, she stood and picked up the cake knife that she'd laid on the coffee table. "Now, who wants a piece of cake?"

There was a chorus of "I shouldn't, but I will."

Just as Cassie was flipping the first slice onto a dish, Nash's cell phone buzzed. The caller was Ben Fortune.

"I have to take this," he said to Cassie.

She nodded. "I'll be busy serving and they'll be busy eating. Go ahead. I'll save you a piece of cake."

Her face was upturned, her eyes were bright and her smile full of joy. Nash just wanted to kiss her. Not *just* kiss her. He'd have liked to take her back to her bedroom right now. But that would have to wait until the party was over.

He went to the farthest corner of the kitchen to take the call. "Tremont here."

"Nash, it's Ben."

It was still hard for him to think of Ben as his half brother. He wasn't sure if he wanted to or not.

"Still trying to make up your mind about us?" Ben asked.

"Something like that. How can I help you?"

"Keaton and I would like you to meet more of your Fortune half siblings. Maybe then you'll tell us the information you're looking for and maybe we can give it to you. What do you say?"

What would he be stepping into if he said yes? His cover was already blown. Was this the only way to get more information?

Since he'd met Keaton and Ben, he was wondering about the rest of his family and what they'd be like. Did he want to meet "family"?

Whatever the reason, he found himself answering, "All right. I'll meet more of them. But under one condition."

"What's that?" Ben inquired.

"I want to make it perfectly clear that I do *not* want to see or meet Gerald…at least not for now."

"I can make sure Gerald has nothing to do with this meeting. It may take me a little time to set it up, but I'll get back to you with the time and place."

"I'll be leaving in a week."

"I'll keep that in mind," Ben said. "You won't be sorry you're doing this."

But as Nash said goodbye and ended the call, he wasn't sure whether he'd be sorry or not. Did he still want to go after Charlotte? Maybe he would wait until after the meeting and then decide.

When Cassie awakened, she'd never felt happier. She was facing Nash, her arm around his waist, his arm around her. She'd slept tucked into his shoulder almost all night. *Almost* because they'd made love instead of talking after the party, then had made love again when they'd both awakened a few hours later. Cassie realized she should feel tired but she didn't. She felt energized and invigorated.

She must have made some tiny movement—she loved rubbing her thumb along Nash's skin—because his eyes opened and he studied her. "How long have you been awake?"

"Not long." With only a few inches between them, he didn't have to move much to kiss her. And once he was kissing her, they were entwined again, ready to start all over to climb the pleasure mountain they'd scaled more than once last night.

Cassie was totally unprepared for the sound of her phone ringing on the nightstand beside Nash.

On top of her, Nash looked down and asked, "Do you always get calls this early in the morning?"

"It's really not that early," she said, checking the clock beside her. "I should be starting breakfast. It's after seven."

Since her cordless landline phone was on Nash's side of the bed, he picked it up and in a professional voice said, "This is the Bluebonnet Bed-and-Breakfast. How can I help you?"

Cassie jabbed him in the ribs, but waited to see how he'd handle the call. If someone wanted to make a reservation, maybe he'd do a good job of it.

Soon she could see that the caller didn't want to make a reservation. Suddenly Nash was frowning and looking much too serious. He had a very stern look on his face when he passed her the phone. "She says she's your mother."

Her mother? Was this a joke? Cassie's mother hadn't wanted to speak to her or see her since she'd gone to jail. With trembling fingers Cassie took the phone in hand, staring at Nash, but thinking about her mom.

"Hello," she said tentatively.

"Cassie, it's your mom."

"I can't believe you finally called."

"I know, baby, and I only have a minute. I know I've been real stubborn about this, but there was a good reason. I've been getting counseling and I've finally gotten clean of my cravings. You know I was always good at tailoring and sewing. I'm studying fashion design. I just wanted you to know that."

Cassie swallowed hard and glanced at Nash again. His features were stoic.

Years ago her mom had made her clothes…when she

wasn't drunk. Was her mother really on the road to recovery? She asked, "Can I visit you?"

"Not yet. But I'll call you soon and give you another progress report. I promise. I want to make sure I'm strong and ready to be a proper mother when I get out."

If her mother wasn't drinking, maybe she'd keep her promise. "It's good to hear from you," Cassie assured her mom, her voice catching and tears coming to her eyes. "Call me whenever you want. Do you have my cell number?"

"I do. It's on my approved list of contacts. You take care of yourself, baby. I have to go."

Her mother clicked off and Cassie suddenly felt as lost as she had when her mother had gone to jail.

And now...now she had to face Nash.

Nash had gotten up and dressed. He sat on the bedroom chair, his gaze piercing as it targeted her. She imagined his expression was similar to when he questioned a witness in one of his investigations. She knew he wanted some sort of explanation. Just how was she going to explain this?

Instead of trying, she said, "It's complicated." He'd once told her that about *his* situation.

Apparently that wasn't enough for Nash and she hadn't expected it would be. But her response had bought her enough time to take a deep breath.

"That was your mother?" he asked.

How could she put all of her story into words? Moreover, how could she say she'd been afraid to tell him?

Nash's reaction to her silence wasn't patience. As if he wasn't willing to wait for her to find the right words, he asked, "What the hell is going on?" Anger was evident in his tone.

Feeling self-conscious, Cassie tugged the sheet up over her breasts. She didn't want to feel any more vulnerable before him right now. She felt too shaky, too exposed, too naked.

Finally, she raised her gaze to his and didn't flinch when his brown eyes locked to hers. "My mother is alive. She's living in Travis State Prison."

Nash looked as if someone had sucker punched him in the solar plexus. "Did I hear you right? Your mother is in prison?"

Cassie nodded, unable to explain further since her throat was tightening, her chest was seizing and tears were burning her eyes.

He stood. "You didn't think I'd want to know this?"

Before Cassie could find any more words, before she could even think about where she wanted to begin, Nash pulled his car keys from his pocket. "I have to go."

Her throat was so tight, her heart so panicked, that he'd left before she could pull herself together enough to get dressed. Not knowing what else to do, she dragged the sheet around her to the doorway of her room. But when she got there, she heard the bang of the front door. He was gone and she didn't know when she was going to see him again…if ever.

Cassie worried all day, not just about her own feelings or about her mother. She worried about Nash. She thought maybe he'd call or stop back in. But he didn't do either. At one point in the afternoon she couldn't stand the waiting. She took fresh towels into his room and saw that his laptop was still there along with a briefcase. He certainly wouldn't go back to Biloxi without them.

She checked in guests around four o'clock—a businessman and a cowgirl who was following the rodeo circuit. They both signed up for supper, so Cassie made a dinner any traveler would enjoy. As she planned it, she knew that if Nash came back for supper, he'd like what she made. She served the fried chicken and mashed potato dinner family style with cranberry-orange salad and a steamed veggie mix. Dessert was easy enough—chocolate cupcakes with chocolate icing.

But even cooking couldn't keep her mind off Nash. He wasn't back at the Bluebonnet by seven…or even by eleven. By one in the morning, Cassie was more than frazzled. She was panicked and sick at heart. She prayed that nothing had happened to him. She'd tried dialing his phone number over and over, but he wasn't answering. Her messages asking him to call seemed to become more desperate and she hated that about them.

She rose early the next morning and mixed a batch of cinnamon rolls. While the dough was rising, she found Nash's registration form in her file and called his friend's number.

Dave Preston answered with a laugh. "What's the matter, Nash? Did you lose your cell phone?"

Cassie was calling from the landline and she knew Dave Preston had seen the ID—Bluebonnet Bed-and-Breakfast.

"No, Mr. Preston, this is Cassie Calloway at the Bluebonnet."

"Something hasn't happened to Nash, has it?" Dave asked, obviously concerned.

"There hasn't been an accident or anything like that."

"That's a relief. But why are you calling? Further references?"

"No. But I'm worried about him. We had a…fight

of sorts and he didn't come back last night. I have no idea where he might be and I'm worried sick. I thought maybe if *you* tried to call him, he'd answer."

"I see," Dave said.

"I just need to know that he's okay. I need to talk to him, but if he doesn't want to talk to me, tell him I'll understand."

"I want to make sure *I* understand this," Dave responded. "Nash has become more than a guest at your bed-and-breakfast?"

"Yes, he has. We've become quite close over the last few weeks. But there's been a misunderstanding and I want to be able to explain to him why I...why I wasn't completely honest with him."

She heard Dave sigh. "Nash believes there's honesty and then there are lies. He calls it like he sees it."

She didn't need to be told that. "Can you see if you can get in touch with him?"

"I'll try. Do you have a number I can text you if I do reach him? I don't want to get in the middle of this, but you deserve to know if he's okay."

She rattled off her cell number, then added, "Thank you."

"No thanks necessary. I'll be in touch."

When Cassie replaced the handset on its base, she at least felt less alone. Dave Preston sounded as if he really cared for Nash. If that was the case, she'd just have to wait for his text.

When Nash's cell phone buzzed, he was just coming awake after lying atop the spread in a two-bit hotel for the night. He knew his phone couldn't have much battery left. His charger was still back at the B&B along with his laptop and the rest of his things. He was going to have to go collect them this morning whether he wanted to see Cassie or not.

Could she be trying to call again? Did he care if she was? His heart hurt just thinking about it.

Taking the phone off the nightstand, he saw Dave was calling him. "What's up?" he asked his friend.

"The bigger question is—are *you* still alive?" Dave asked with some sarcasm.

"Since I answered the call, I guess I am," Nash retorted.

"Well, that's good to know because now I have to text Cassie and tell her you're still kicking."

"Cassie? What do you have to do with Cassie?"

"Apparently she's worried about your hide. Apparently she dug out my number and called me. She asked me if I could find you because you weren't answering her calls. Is that true?"

Nash puffed up his pillow behind him and closed his eyes. "Yeah, it's true."

"Do you want to tell me why?"

"No, I don't."

"Do it anyway because now I'm in the middle of this."

"What did she tell you?"

"Not enough, and I'm tired of playing twenty questions. What's going on, Nash?"

"She lied to me."

There was a beat of silence before Dave asked, "What about?"

"I was under the impression her parents were dead. That's what her neighbor told me. But it turns out that's not true. Cassie just let me believe it because her mother's in prison."

"Whoa."

"That's all you have to say?"

"I have a lot more to say but you probably don't want to hear it."

Nash groaned. "I know that won't stop you."

"You're right. Just let me put a scenario in front of you. Just say, you fall in love with a detective."

Nash was about to cut in, but Dave stopped him. "Let me finish. You fall in love with a detective. You aren't one in this case. However, your father was locked up in jail for God knows what crime, and you were afraid you'd lose her if you told her."

Shifting restlessly on the bed, Nash was uncomfortable with Dave's example. "If I loved her, I'd have to eventually tell her."

"Yes, that's true. But how much time is enough time? And how deeply in love do you have to be before the person you love can handle the truth?"

Nash didn't have an answer to that. "My phone's ready to cut out. I don't have my charger."

"Isn't that such a good excuse not to listen to me? Think about what I said, Nash, and then go talk to Cassie. I know Sara hurt you. But don't use this as a barrier to keep from feeling again. I'll text Cassie that you're still alive."

The screen on Nash's phone went black. It matched his mood exactly. He had to go back to the B&B for his things, so he might as well talk to Cassie if she was there. If she wasn't, he'd be on his way back to Biloxi. After he returned to Mississippi, he'd give Ben Fortune a call. If a meeting was going to take place with other half siblings, he'd drive back here again for it. That just didn't seem as important as it had been. Neither did his investigation.

He didn't even want to think about that right now. His mind was buzzing with what he'd say to Cassie if he saw her.

A half hour later, he was climbing the steps to the B&B when a man and a woman came out. They were talking to each other. The man said, "That's the best breakfast I've had in a long time."

"Cassie certainly knows how to cook. I'm looking forward to tonight's meal. Are you going to be there?"

"I am. I'll catch you then."

The man and woman went their separate ways.

Yes, Cassie did know how to cook. He was trying to forget about that as well as her smile, the way her eyes lit up when she was excited and the sound of her laughter.

As soon as he walked into the B&B, he sensed Cassie's presence. She was cleaning up the kitchen.

He couldn't help but notice that she looked pale and there were blue half-moons under her eyes. Had she been up most of the night worrying about him? He felt guilty and, along with the love he knew he felt for her, he knew he never wanted to hurt her again. But what was she feeling right now?

When her gaze met his, he approached the counter. Because of all the emotion he was feeling, his voice was gruff when he asked, "Did Dave text you?"

"Yes, he did. Thank him for me, will you?"

Nash gave her a nod before saying, "I came to re-trieve my things."

Her eyes widened and glistened with sudden emotion. As she came from around the counter, he stepped back.

"You're being unfair," she accused.

Maybe he'd known that before he walked in the door. Still, he became defensive because she had lied to him. Because he hurt so badly thinking about going home, because he wanted to kiss her more than he wanted to breathe, he returned, "What kind of relationship could we have if you can't be honest with me?" He held his breath while he waited for her answer.

"Will you at least hear me out?" she pleaded.

She looked so doggone pretty in a hot-pink T-shirt and some sort of shorts that looked like a skirt. She was even in her bare feet.

He crossed his arms over his chest. "I'm listening."

She sat on one of the stools as if her legs were shaking and wouldn't hold her up anymore. She faced him. "When I moved here and bought the B&B, I told people my mom had died and so had my dad. That was easier than trying to explain the situation and having to endure looks of pity or horror. Even worse than those was the judgment that went along with knowing my mom was in prison. That relationship I told you about that the guy broke off? He did that when I explained my mother was in prison." She didn't give him a chance to speak, drawing a breath and accusing, "You kept secrets, too. Why are mine so much worse than yours?"

Secrets? Yes, he'd had secrets. But he'd told her all about them. Why couldn't she have told him? The question ate at him. He skirted the issue and asked, "What did your mother want?"

Tears came to Cassie's eyes now and one rolled

down her cheek. He felt his chest tighten and his fingers clench.

"My mother was and is an alcoholic. In my last year of college, she was driving drunk and hit another car. The man died. She was charged with vehicular homicide."

"What did you do?" Nash asked.

"I was on my own. My high school art teacher and I had stayed in touch. When she learned I had to move out of our rented apartment, she let me stay with her. Between my scholarship and jobs, I was able to make it. But my mom... When she went to prison, she didn't want to see me or talk to me. She told me it was better for me that way. So in a way, it was like my mom *had* died. When she called yesterday..." Cassie's voice broke. "That was the first I've talked to her in years."

Although Nash wanted to go to Cassie, he didn't. "That whole experience had to be awful for you." Silence lay between them until he asked, "Why did your mom call?"

"She couldn't talk long, but she told me she's been getting counseling and she's not having cravings."

"What about your dad?" he asked. "Is he really dead?"

"I have no idea if he's alive or dead. He left when I was a toddler, and my mom never heard from him again. That's when she started drinking."

As he thought about everything Dave had said to him, he imagined himself in Cassie's shoes. No communication with her mother and no dad. He understood the "no dad" part from personal experience. In his police work he'd seen families broken apart by alcoholism, and he could only imagine what Cassie had experienced. Did he want her to tell him? Would she?

"I'm going to go upstairs," he began.

"You're leaving?" She looked stricken.

"No. I'm going to get a shower while you make another pot of coffee. Then I'll be down and we can talk. Okay with you?"

She was crying openly now and she nodded.

Nash climbed the stairs, trying to figure out if following his heart was the foolish thing...or the smart thing to do.

When Cassie had received Dave's text that Nash was okay, she'd practically collapsed with relief. And now? She didn't know what was going to happen next. After they talked, Nash would probably leave. Maybe he just didn't want to leave on a sour note.

She'd just poured two mugs of coffee when Nash descended the stairs. He looked so good in a cream T-shirt and blue jeans. But she had to steel her heart against what he might say.

She couldn't read anything from his expression when he picked up both the mugs and nodded to the sofa. "Let's go over there and talk."

She followed him and sat on the sofa first. To her surprise, he sat right beside her...so close that their legs were touching.

He took both of her hands in his. "I *have* been unfair to you, Cassie. None of what happened to you was your fault. You had to cope with it as best you could. I think we both have some trust issues to work through. I've done a lot of thinking in the last twelve hours since Dave called me. He helped me look at your story differently. Can you forgive me for saying what I did...for leaving like that and not taking your calls?"

Obviously, Nash wanted the truth so she had to tell him the truth. "Yes, I can forgive you. But I have to ask—will you bolt again at the first sign of trouble between us?"

Gazing directly into her eyes now, he revealed, "No, I won't bolt. Because I realized last night that I love you. I fell hard and fast, though I couldn't admit it to myself, let alone you. That's why it hurt so bad when you didn't tell me about your parents. But I won't deny my feelings again, because they're too important. Love doesn't come around every day. I believe in vows and getting married in a church and swearing before God and everyone that we'll be committed to each other for a lifetime. Will you marry me?"

Cassie was shocked and surprised at Nash's question. Relief poured through her. She gazed at him with all the love she was feeling. "I promise I'll never keep anything from you again. Yes, I'll marry you. Would you want me to move to Biloxi? Do you want me to sell the B&B?"

He was shaking his head. "I don't want you to sell the B&B. You love it here. And Biloxi? Biloxi was just a stopping-over point for me. I'm going to look into jobs in Austin, either with the police force or with a private security company. But I do think we'll have to buy a double bed for your suite. We'll take our time. We'll get engaged. We'll really get to know each other."

"Will my mother be a stumbling block for you when she gets out of prison?"

"Your mom gave you the gift of life. You've turned out to be a wonderful person, so she can't be all bad, right? I know you think I see things in black-and-white, and that's why you couldn't tell me. But the truth is, since I met you, I see a whole spectrum of colors. We'll deal with your mom and anything else we have to deal with. I love you that much, Cassie."

Cassie took Nash's face between her hands. "I love you, Nash Tremont." Her voice was so joyous and her smile so radiant she knew Nash couldn't have a doubt about her feelings.

When he took her into his arms to kiss her, a kiss that spoke of love and forgiveness and promise, she knew she was exactly where she was supposed to be.

After they were both breathless from the kiss, he scooped her up in his arms to carry her to her bedroom. "Do you think you can get away for a few days?" he asked her.

"I suppose I can," she answered. "Reservations are spotty. I can easily block out a few days. Why?"

"Because I want to take you to Oklahoma to meet my mother."

Cassie had never been this happy, not in her entire life. She kissed Nash's neck and held on to him tighter. Then he carried her into her suite—their suite now—and closed the door.

## *Epilogue*

It was late morning a few days later when Cassie looked around her suite to see what she could do to make it suitable for her *and* Nash. She'd jotted down a few ideas and she was adding to those when she heard the front door to the B&B open and close…and the sound of boots.

Nash was back.

She stuck her head outside the doorway and called to him. "In here."

She couldn't tell anything from his expression as he met her in the doorway.

He saw the clipboard in her hands and raised his brows. "What are you doing?"

"I'm redecorating. But I can tell you that later. How did it go with your appointments this morning?"

"There's a good chance that I'll be part of the Austin PD. I'm set up for an interview tomorrow. Of course,

they'll have to do all the background paperwork. One
of their homicide detectives retired and they need somebody to fill the spot."

"Homicide?" Cassie asked.

"Does it scare you if I quit white-collar crimes and
become a homicide detective? I can probably find a job
in private security if it does. I sent a few résumés last
night to companies in Austin. We could see which job
pans out first."

Cassie knew what had happened in Nash's last
relationship…why he would do what *she* wanted, rather
than what *he* wanted. But that wasn't the way they were
going to live their lives.

She took his face between her hands and looked
straight into his eyes. "I want you to do the work that
will fulfill you and satisfy you. That's what matters to
me. If you're a homicide detective, I'll trust you to make
the right decisions to keep yourself safe. If you want
to work for private security, that's fine with me, too."

He gathered her into his arms and gave her a long,
deep kiss.

When she broke away, she told him, "Besides painting the room a color you'd like, I thought we could get
rid of the love seat and chair and put in a double bed.
We might still have room for the chair."

"A double bed, huh?" he asked with a sexy grin. I
don't think we'll need the chair as long as we have the
bed."

She laughed, stepped away and then became serious
again. "I have a question to ask you."

"Go ahead."

"My mother said she'd call again soon. When she does, I'm going to ask her if she'll let me visit her."

"All right," Nash said.

"I'd like to ask her to put your name on the visitors list, too. I want to tell her about *us* and I'd like you to meet her." Cassie studied Nash's face—the lines she was beginning to know so well, the jut sometimes of his stubborn jaw. Still, she couldn't tell exactly what he was thinking.

Not until he said, "I'd like to meet your mother… without judgment. Just face value. Then we'll go from there."

She threw her arms around him again. "Thank you!"

"I have a question for you, too."

"Ask," she said, ready to tell him anything he wanted to know.

Before she could realize what he was doing, he'd stepped away and he'd gotten down on one knee. Out of his pocket, he pulled a little black velvet box. When he opened it, she saw a beautiful antique ring of diamonds in white gold. She was speechless.

"I went to a jeweler who sells estate jewelry. I wanted something unique for you," Nash explained. "So I'm going to ask you again to make our engagement official. Will you marry me, Cassie Calloway, and spend the rest of your life with me? We can have a short engagement or a long engagement. But I want to know we're committed to each other."

"I'm committed to you," Cassie said seriously. "And, yes, I'll marry you…any time, any place…any how."

Nash took the ring from the box and slipped it onto her finger. Then he rose to his feet.

After he kissed her again, he murmured close to her ear, "I kind of like your single bed. Maybe we should use it as much as we can before we get the double." With his booted foot, he pushed the door closed, then scooped her up in his arms and carried her to the bed.

Cassie had no doubt that their trust would grow each day…just as would their commitment and their love.

* * * * *